# Praise for In Perfect Light

"[Sáenz's] attention to the rhythms and tones of language always evinces the care of a serious craftsman. Every sentence is carefully calibrated. His paragraphs have no wrinkles. [He] assembles an enormous cast of richly detailed characters." —*San Francisco Chronicle*

"Dignified . . . heart wrenching . . . Sáenz has plotted *In Perfect Light* impeccably." —*Texas Monthly*

"Sáenz's luminous prose shines." —*Houston Chronicle*

"A vivid story about a community of scarred, deeply human souls within a callous, indifferent America." —*Kirkus Reviews,* One of the Best Books of 2005

"Ben Sáenz's vivid imagination captures all that is beautiful, agonizing, and redemptive in the crossings we make through borders of geography and culture. . . . But it is in the interior journeys of the psyche and the soul that we must find salvation; Sáenz's brilliant prose penetrates to that core and he finds and exposes that truth." —Abraham Verghese, author of *My Own Country* and *The Tennis Partner*

"Only Benjamin Alire Sáenz . . . can capture, with his acrobatic skill of voice, character, and theme, the darkness, the hidden life of betrayal, and the nascent, eternal, always hopeful redemption to be found in the heat and dust of our misunderstood land." —Denise Chávez, American Book Award–winning author of *Face of an Angel* and *Loving Pedro Infante*

"Sáenz captures what we all do every day, really, to find peace for ourselves." —*Philadelphia Inquirer*

"Lyrical." —*Entertainment Weekly*

"A former priest and award-winning poet thoughtfully shares his meditations on multiculturalism and familial love—especially the struggle to survive its loss." —*Booklist*

"Visceral impact . . . this story is universal. Highly recommended." —*Library Journal*

# Also by Benjamin Alire Sáenz

**FICTION**
*Sammy and Juliana in Hollywood*
*The House of Forgetting*
*Carry Me Like Water*
*Flowers for the Broken*

**POETRY**
*Elegies in Blue*
*Dark and Perfect Angels*
*Calendar of Dust*

**CHILDREN'S BOOKS**
*A Gift from Papá Diego*
*Grandma Fina and her Wonderful Umbrellas*

# In Perfect Light

*A Novel*

# Benjamin Alire Sáenz

HARPER ● PERENNIAL

NEW YORK ● LONDON ● TORONTO ● SYDNEY ● NEW DELHI ● AUCKLAND

HARPER ● PERENNIAL

A hardcover edition was published in 2005 by Rayo,
an imprint of HarperCollins Publishers.

P.S.™ is a trademark of HarperCollins Publishers.

HarperCollins books may be purchased for educational, business,
or sales promotional use. For information, please e-mail
the Special Markets Department at SPsales@harpercollins.com.


FIRST HARPER PERENNIAL EDITION PUBLISHED 2008.

*Designed by Gretchen Achilles*

The Library of Congress has catalogued the hardcover edition as follows:
Sáenz, Benjamin Alire.
In perfect light : a novel / by Benjamin Alire Sáenz.—1st ed.
p. cm.
ISBN 978-0-06-077920-7
I. Title.
PS3569.A27I5 2005
811'.54—dc22                                    2004051317

ISBN 978-0-06-077921-4 (pbk.)

16  17  18   ID / RRD   10  9  8  7  6  5  4  3

*for Gabriela, who is like the sun*
*and for her mother, Patricia, who is the sun*

*What is the way to the place where the light is distributed,*
*or where the east wind is scattered upon the earth?*

—JOB 38:24

# Part One

*We reach for light, yet all we grasp is darkness.*

—ISAIAH 59:9

# Light and the Sadness of Dreams

Standing in the light, they look like salvation itself. Her son's hair, fine as strands of silk, his eyes as clear as water. Her husband's face is perfect as the flood of light. They are happy, at play, laughing, talking. The dream is always the same. Always, she is alone, apart, an exiled observer to their movements.

Always, she wakes when she hears them calling her name.

She lies in the darkness and steadies her breathing, trying to soothe herself. She can smell their clean sweat filling the air, sweet as summer rain. She runs her hand across the cool sheets—then waits for the beating of her heart to slow. She thinks of Mister. *Always, he was more yours than mine, Sam.* She thinks of their last visit, how they both left angry. She can still taste that anger in the back of her tongue, as if the words she had spoken were as solid as a piece of bitter fruit.

She sits up slowly and places her feet on the cool wood floors. She walks toward the French doors and opens them. She breathes in the desert air.

*Mister and me, Sam, we've lost our way.* Sam. So many years he'd been dead. And still she woke uttering his name. A part of her expected him to answer.

# Where They Found Him

*I would hurt you for the simplest of reasons.* That's what he said with his eyes. The streetlight and the empty city made him feel as if he were in a play. No one had come to watch him except for Dave. "Why'd you bail me out?" He kept his head bowed, his dark hair falling over his eyes.

"You called. I came."

"I shouldn't have called."

"I could throw you back, Andrés."

"What the fuck. Go ahead."

"Where'd you learn to be so fucking ungrateful?"

Andrés almost smiled. "Sorry, I'm fresh out of gratitude."

"Hating me is part of the whole deal—is that it?"

Dave was like everyone else. He wanted to be loved. He did want to be loved. Andrés almost laughed out loud. He closed his eyes, then opened them. His face was beginning to throb again, and he knew his bruises would be turning black and blue. A brown man turning blue. Like a chameleon. Ha, ha, fucking ha, God, tired, all he wanted to do was sleep, be in bed, dreaming of palo verdes in bloom, the yellow blossoms bursting in the blue sky like firecrackers. He wanted to dream soft hands rubbing his skin. He pictured himself melting beneath those hands, like butter or ice cream or anything else that wasn't human. He wanted to close his eyes and be somewhere else, *Toronto Madrid Paris.* He hated all this, his life, the days he lived, the nights he didn't sleep, arrests, police, questions being shot at him, phone calls to a lawyer he loved and hated and needed and hated and hated and God, and mostly he didn't want to feel this way, this thing, like the tick-tick of a bomb, like the click of a gun about to shoot a bullet. Like a chronic pain that was so much a part of his life that he almost didn't call it pain anymore. Maybe it was shame, this thing he felt. Partially, it must have been that. Sure. But it was other things, too. He knew that. And just then he hated himself for calling Dave at three-thirty in the morning. *Call anytime.* That's what he'd said. And so he'd called. And there he was, standing in front of him like some goddamned angel conjured up by a desperate prayer.

"I think we should get you to a doctor."

"Nothing open but ERs—"

"C'mon. Let's have you looked at."

"Nothing's broken." He didn't know why he'd said that. It wasn't true. He lit a cigarette.

"You could at least offer me one of those."

Andrés tossed him his pack of cigarettes. He watched Dave as he lit one. Manicured hands, no worker in them—but he had his own way of being a man. Not a worker, but another kind of man. He had something, Dave did. Sure. Anyone could see that.

Dave stared at him and shook his head. "God, you look awful. What'd they do to your beautiful face?" He said that so easily. *Beautiful face.* He could say that to a man or to a woman, and the man and the woman would look up in gratitude. Because he said it as if he was the first human being who'd ever noticed. Maybe that's why so many people trusted him, because he had something in his voice, because he was well-spoken and had learned to modulate his speech—just so—and somehow, with that calm and controlled voice, he managed to rearrange the chaos of the world in such a way as to make it appear as if there really were a plan. Yeah, the whole fucking world trusted him because he was nice to look at and because he was a gringo, and that still mattered despite what anybody said or wanted to believe, the whole fucking world.

Finally, he decided to look at Dave. Why not lift his head? "I wasn't as drunk as they said."

"You told the officer you'd kill him if he touched you."

He didn't remember that. Sometimes, when the rage set in, he couldn't remember. Like alcohol blackouts. He shook his head. But it could have been true. "I don't like people I don't know to touch me. So that makes me weird?"

"The officer said you were crying, that you couldn't stop crying." He stopped. Waited. As if his statement were a question.

"Yeah, I was crying." As if admitting it were nothing. Nothing at all. Easy as pie. Easy as biting into a Hershey's candy bar. Tears. They're like seeds in a watermelon. Good for spitting out. "And in public, too. Crying in public—now that's a fucking crime, isn't it?"

"It's reasonable for a cop to stop someone on an empty street at two o'clock in the morning, don't you think?"

"I may be the wrong person to ask. I'm no expert on being reasonable. Isn't that why I wound up in jail? Isn't that why I wound up calling you at three-thirty in the glorious fucking morning?—because I'm not reasonable."

"You couldn't stop crying." He had this look on his face, like he wanted to cry, too, cry because the whole thing made him as sad as anything. Dave wasn't reasonable, either. But that convincing look of empathy—it didn't go with his Italian suit.

"You look pretty well pressed for three-thirty in the morning."

"I was at a dinner party. A late one."

"Dinner party. Never been. Thank your fucking patron saint for cell phones."

"Yeah, where would I be without one?"

"At a dinner party. A late one."

They both laughed. Sometimes they did that.

"I was drunk. Didn't they tell you?" Andrés smiled.

"But not *that* drunk."

"No, not that drunk. But drunk. So maybe I'm just a drunk who was crying in my beer."

"Maybe. But you know something? I don't think you're a drunk."

"How do you figure?"

"I know you, don't I?"

"I'm not that kid anymore."

"I represented you in court, didn't I?"

"Ancient history, vato."

"I don't forget that easily."

"Memory. There's a beautiful thing." He didn't want to think back to that time. He didn't have the stomach for nostalgia. He didn't even re-member what he'd told him. About himself. About his predicaments. He sometimes told people different things. Not lies exactly—he left things out, sometimes. He let them fill the rest in. Like he was a coloring book.

"You're not a drunk, that's not your problem."

"Maybe you're wrong."

"I don't think so."

"You're a lawyer, not a fucking doctor." There was a hint of a smile on his face—as if he'd amused himself. He put out his cigarette.

"When you were in college—"

"I didn't go to fucking college."

The young man could see the surprise in Dave's face. It was there—then it was gone. "You speak like someone who went to college."

"Do I?"

"What are you, twenty-six?"

"You going somewhere with this?"

"I'm thirty-seven."

"We could be brothers."

"That's not where I was going. Still, there's a thought."

"Except you're a gringo."

"And you're a Mexican."

"With papers."

"Yeah, we could be brothers."

"Yeah. Sure. Get back to your party."

"It's over by now."

"What about your girlfriend?"

"She's over, too."

"Yeah?"

"She wants someone simpler. She wants someone to bring home the bacon and take her shopping. She wants someone to wear on her arm like a nice coat everyone will notice. She wants someone whose clients don't break into Spanish when they get mad. She wants someone who's the same every day. Me, I never know what I'm going to be like from one day to the next."

"Don't lie to yourself. You're as goddamned predictable as they come."

"So are you. We could be brothers."

"Fuck you, Dave."

"Fuck you, too, Andrés." He laughed. "You see, that's why she left me. I like to use that word too much. I'm not respectable."

"You want to be."

"No. I don't think so."

"Maybe you are too complicated." The young man laughed. It wasn't cruel, his laugh. But hard. Like cured cement. Exactly that hard.

Dave watched him laugh.

"So she doesn't fucking understand the words *pro bono,* huh?"

"Exactly. Why would I leave a bourgeois party to help a guy like you?"

"Bourgeois. There's a pretty word. A college word." The young man laughed. Something softer in his laugh this time. But not all the hardness had left, would never leave. "Well, I don't understand why you're here, either."

"Neither do I."

"So we're all on your girlfriend's side."

"Some people need to understand everything. They have to connect every damned dot—every damned, fucking one of them. Other people don't."

"Which kind are you?"

"Same kind you are."

"I don't think so." Andrés was so tired he was almost becoming soft. "Crawl back to her. The world's a cold place."

"Not here, buddy. This is El Paso, Texas. Our winters are hardly winters at all."

They looked at each other. Like they knew everything about each other. Like that. But what exactly did they know, these strangers who were so familiar and intimate? You fought a war with someone, and you knew them. But you only knew the part that was in the war, the part that knew how to fight. The other part, the pedestrian part that lived in the endless calmness of days, you didn't know that part.

"Andrés. You need some help. I mean it."

He didn't have to say it, could have thought it, could have thought anything he wanted. He had no right. He didn't have to fucking say it. "No, Dave, I don't need help. I need a ride home."

"You telling me the only thing you need in your fucking life is a cab?"

*Yeah, that's what I'm telling you.*

# Timing and Order in the Universe

It is five-thirty in the morning. Andrés Segovia is in his apartment in Sunset Heights, sleeping fitfully, his fists swinging in the air. Dave Duncan is listening to a woman's voice on his answering machine, *"Don't call me, Dave. Let's just let it be. . . ."*

As Grace Delgado is waking from her dream, fifty-eight passengers file out of a Greyhound bus at the downtown depot. Thirty of the passengers are just passing through. After a bathroom break and a breakfast burrito, they will reboard and continue on to Phoenix and L.A. Twenty-four of the passengers are greeted by at least one family member. The remaining four passengers—all of them men—have no friends or family to greet them. All four have been paroled to El Paso, though they have no previous connections to the city.

As terms of their release, all four men are required to meet with their respective parole officers at least twice a week. They are required to register themselves and their current addresses with the El Paso Police Department.

In the previous eight months, twenty such sex offenders have been released to the border area by parole boards across the country—though none of them had ever called El Paso their home. The men are not acquainted with one another. The fact that they are on the same bus is merely a coincidence.

At forty-one, William Hart is the youngest of them. He walks into the men's bathroom and shaves, refreshes himself by throwing water on his face. He reapplies some deodorant. He studies himself. Blue eyes, good teeth, nice smile. Still handsome and youthful in that wholesome kind of way that makes people trust him. A few wrinkles beginning to show, but nothing that concerns him. His only imperfection is the small scar above his lip. "Beautiful," he whispers. Prison didn't age him, gave him time to think and get in shape. An abundance of time was no reason to waste it.

He checks his luggage into a locker, then walks a few blocks south and crosses the Santa Fe Bridge into Juárez. There are no border guards to stop him. It is not the first time he has been to Juárez. He has good memories from previous visits. He still remembers that boy, that perfect boy, perfect as the morning light.

He smiles to himself.

By early afternoon, having found some release, he will cross back into El Paso. He will walk into the office of his parole officer and tell him he is ready to start a new life.

# Grace and Morning Mass

B reasts were odd and strange, when you stopped to think about them. Sam had loved to touch them, kiss them, smell them. Her son had nursed on them for nearly a year—they were useful then. Since she was a girl, she had noticed the way young men stared at women, stared at their breasts, became obsessed with them. She smiled to herself. *What do I need them for at fifty? And, anyway, I've been trying to lose some weight.* Isn't that what she'd told the doctor? He'd humored her by laughing at her joke. "Gallows humor," he'd said.

She knew her body. She didn't need a test result, didn't even need to feel bad to know that there was something wrong. It was like stepping outside and smelling the first cool wind of September, knowing that the season was changing, despite the fact that summer seemed like it might go on forever.

Even a tree knew when it was time to drop its leaves. Even a tree in El Paso.

It was odd—just then—that she should get the urge to have a cigarette. She swore she could smell a cigarette burning in the room. She took in a deep breath and smiled. She'd only smoked a few years, but she'd enjoyed the habit. She'd felt free and young and even sexy when she'd smoked. She'd never felt that way, sexy, like men might want her. Sam had always laughed. He'd showed her a mirror and said, *"God, Grace, don't you see? Can't you see what the whole world sees?"*

*"Why would I want to see what everyone else sees, Sam?"*

*"How can a woman who looks like you not understand?"*

"*Understand what?*"

"*You don't have an ounce of vanity in you, Grace. That's your problem.*"

"*I happen to think that the world would be a lot better off if we really looked at what people were instead of what they looked like.*"

"*Are you telling me you don't care what people look like?*"

"*I just happened to have married a very handsome man.*"

"*Oh?*"

"*You see, Sam? I'm as vain and shallow as everyone else.*"

She could almost hear him laughing. He always laughed. *You're too sincere, Grace, that's your real fault.* He'd been wrong about that. She was more cynical about the world, and more realistic about its corruption, than Sam could ever fathom. It was he who had been sincere.

What would happen if she drove to the store and bought a pack? What would happen? What was so wrong with that? She played the message on the machine over again, the doctor's voice, tentative. *Grace? Richard here. Listen, I have the results of your tests sitting here on my desk. Why don't you call me in the morning. Maybe you can come in. We'll talk.* He was trying to sound casual, matter of fact, *Oh this is nothing. Not to worry.* Most doctors were notoriously good liars—a disease they picked up in medical school. But not this one. As luck or fate would have it—though she believed in neither—her doctor went to morning mass every day. She'd seen him more than once, kneeling in the back, his head bowed in prayer. He almost looked like a boy just out of confession, bowing his head and uttering the prayers the priest had given him for his penance, *Oh my God, I am heartily sorry.* But he wasn't a boy, he was a forty-something-year-old doctor who was atoning for something he'd done in his past, repenting for sins committed in the name of success or pleasure or sheer selfishness, or he used daily mass as his one moment of quiet in an otherwise too-busy, too-loud, too-fragmented and chaotic day, or he was punishing himself for having a life, a good life, a very good life he just couldn't believe he deserved, a guilt that could not be unwritten by God himself. Of course, the possibility existed that he was the real thing, a person of faith, a true believer.

In any case, he was a good man, and if she were going to have a doctor at her side, it might as well be a doctor who wouldn't hide the truth. She didn't want or need the false comfort of doctors who made a virtue of sparing their patients' feelings—lying not only to their patients but to themselves because it was easier, the path of least resistance. She wouldn't let anyone play her that way because she was too smart and had grown up too poor and had fought an eternal war with idiots who mistook poverty for lack of ambition instead of for what it was—the accident of birth. She wouldn't let anyone play her that way because she was a beautiful woman who had learned not to rely on the shallow fact of her beauty, because she understood clearly that her beauty, like her poverty, was also nothing more than a mere accident of birth. She would not let anyone play her that way because she had worked too hard to be honest, honest not in the eyes of God, who had no eyes, not in the eyes of her friends and colleagues, not in the eyes of her son, Mister, not in the eyes of anyone but herself, the harshest, the severest of judges. She'd had too many clients, hundreds of them, clients who were too good at escaping everything with the lies they told themselves. Houdinis, most of them, with their lies. Magicians. But how could they not lie to themselves when that was all that they'd ever been taught? Did you chastise students for learning their lessons? But she, Grace Alarcon Delgado, had learned other lessons. She had lived her life trying to look straight at things, *straight at them* knowing that there would come a day when she would look at something so hard that it would look right back and break her. Well, wasn't she made of flesh and bone? Wasn't she made to break? Sure. Wasn't she a woman?

She took one last look at her breasts as she stood before the mirror. There was nothing wrong, to look at them. There was a certain beauty in the surface of things. She understood the seduction. She put her bra back on and buttoned up her blouse. *Well, if they have to cut*—and then suddenly she wondered what they did with all those cancerous breasts. Did they throw them away in some nearby surgical trashcan? Did they save them, freeze them, put them in some chemical to preserve them so that future medical students and doctors and surgeons could pull them off some shelf and study them as if they were library books? Would they check them out, take them home, keep them for a couple of days, then check them back in? And after they had served their purpose, were they burned along with all the other surgical materials? Shouldn't they be buried somewhere—all those breasts—buried deep on some piece of holy ground? Hadn't they been good once? Hadn't they given life to thousands, to millions? Even dogs were buried or disposed of with more ceremony and respect. *God, Grace, stop. Stop it.*

She closed her eyes. She imagined herself smoking a cigarette. She imagined taking in the smoke, then letting it out, all her anger dissipating in the afternoon light. She inhaled, exhaled, Sam lighting her cigarette, inhaled, exhaled, Sam's hand brushing against her breast, inhaled, exhaled. *There, there, Grace, all better.* She opened her eyes.

She had to hurry. She would be late for morning mass.

*Yesterday, you teased us. Do not tease the thirsty—give us rain.* After she prayed for rain to end the drought, she prayed for Mister, though she could feel her anger as she whispered his name. She prayed for Irma down the street who'd lost her boy. She prayed for her body, her breasts, her heart. *Make me bear whatever comes.* Sam had been good at *whatever comes.*

She closed her eyes, and when she opened them she found herself staring at the stained-glass window—Jesus walking on stormy waters. "I'm not like you, so give me arms to swim." She took a breath. "And Jesus, Jesus, bring us rain."

# The First Signs of a Storm

A ccording to the report, they found the sheets of papers in his shirt pocket—folded and neatly filed. According to the report, he'd fought like a demon to keep those sheets of neatly folded papers. According to the report, he'd spit and clawed and cussed and kicked. At one-thirty in the morning. On the southeast end of downtown. In an alley. Behind ¡Viva Villa! a bar on San Antonio Street. A bar not far from the courthouse. Not far from the county jail. Which was where he was taken. Which was where he was booked. For being drunk and disorderly. For resisting arrest. For spitting and clawing and cussing and kicking. All this, according to the report.

Grace had learned to be suspicious of reports, just as she knew others were suspicious of her own conclusions—also written out in that peculiar genre they called reports. She had decided long ago that reports existed to create the illusion of order. That was what made them readable. That was also what made them fiction.

She was doing it again. Questioning herself. Deconstructing her profession. Always, she did that when a new and difficult case made its way to her desk. And there it was, another one of those cases. Right there. On her desk. Out of habit, she beat her chest with mea culpas. That's how mass began, with mea culpas, *Lord have mercy, Christ have mercy.* Beat your chest, *Por mi culpa.* Embrace your limitations, *Por mi culpa.* Exorcise your paralysis. *Por mi gran culpa.* Take Communion, *Amen,* then go out to the world and do your job.

As she ran her hand over the sheets of paper, she tried to picture a young man trying to hold off four police officers with the sheer power of his rage. She ran the scene over in her head, the young man, drunk, sitting in an alley, reading his own writing in the dim light of the streets, and then suddenly, the lights of a police car shining on his face, the officers asking him questions *What are you doing there? What are you doing?* and him refusing to act like a deer about to be run down, refusing even to acknowledge their accusing presence *What's that you're reading?* and him folding the sheets of paper, slowly, carefully, and filing them back in the shirt pocket and them asking him again *What's that you have?* and him saying finally *The fucking Communist Manifesto,* and the now-angry cops insisting to see what he'd been reading, as if the act of reading were some kind of goddamned felony—and anyway he was sitting in an alleyway, drunk, and that was reason enough, and hadn't he defied them?

That man, that angry young man, he was lucky he hadn't been killed. The possibility existed that he'd wanted exactly that—to be shot and killed and finally fall silent and at peace because his days brought him anything but calm and he was so fucking tired of trying to make sense of a life that made no sense at all.

She made a mental note to herself, then shook her head as she stared at the man's handwriting. She didn't approve of the way the police and the judge had so easily placed his confiscated writings in the file they forwarded to her. When they took you, you were theirs, your clothes, your wallet, your belt, your cigarettes, the few dollars you carried in your front pocket, your keys, all you had—which was nothing anyway—it was all theirs now. That's what happened when they had you. And so the system had made her the inheritor of what had once belonged to someone else. The papers—his papers—now hers. An interesting progression. All legal and good, good for the young man who'd carried them, and good for the society that was protecting him, though it wasn't at all clear how he had harmed anyone except the policemen who had tried to take him by force. But it was all to the good, sure, now she could help him. And these pieces of paper, they would help her to help him. *Him* who needed help. So there they were—his words written on the sheets of paper, the creases still there. She kept running her hands over them, sheet by sheet, trying to smooth them out, her ironing hands as useless as the roots of a dead tree. You could never uncrease a piece of paper once it had been folded. Not ever.

She shook her head. Not a good business, this thing of having another man's writings in your hands. Not a good business at all. But like it or not, he was her client. So there was nothing left to do except to read the words that had not imagined her as an audience.

*Love is a storm that twists and mangles us. If you love—if you really love—if you have that kind of heart—then you know. (And if you don't, there is no explaining.) The storm comes from within. There is nothing you can do to prepare.*

Hardly the words of a criminal. Hardly the words of a lunatic, either. Except that lunatics often wrote well. They did. She'd seen it time and time again. Lunatics could write. They had that in common with pompous poets. On the second sheet of paper—though she had no idea if she were reading the pages in the correct order—she read and reread another passage on the same topic.

*Remember this: Nothing is as simple as a storm. Ask anyone. They will tell you—those who know about storms—to get out of its path. If you can. If you have time. They will tell you nothing can stop a storm. Save yourself. Run. But there is no running. Laugh at yourself for thinking of escape.*

*Remember this: Nothing can destroy a storm except itself. It must hurt and blow and wail till it dies. You will not be alive to clean up the debris. All the light will be gone.*

She was almost envious—not simply because of his obvious discipline, but because of the physical fact of his writing. Clean, legible, delicate. She was not used to seeing that kind of beauty in her line of work. *Damage*—now that was a word she was used to. That's what she was used to seeing. And she was used to describing that damage even if she did not believe that a damaged human being could be translated into words.

She looked at the handwriting again. This man, whoever he was, knew something about control, knew that control could kill, but also knew control could save a life. This man, he knew something about beauty.

• • •

On the third sheet of folded paper, he had continued writing on the same theme. But something had changed—not in the tone, but in the writing. Perhaps he had been drinking. Perhaps he had been tired. Perhaps he'd written the third page at a completely different time in a completely different place. The actual writing had begun to fall apart. He had stopped drawing one letter at a time. On the first two sheets of paper, the words seemed to matter as much as the message he was trying to convey. But, now, he let himself be drunk in the message. That kind of drunkenness had a different kind of beauty altogether.

> *I know a man and a woman. They had that kind of heart. A heart so pure it was nothing but storm. In the end, how could they have been anything else except misshapen and deformed and grotesque? Who would have guessed that they were beautiful? At least in the beginning. God, they were Beautiful. Their skin glowed in the light. I think their hearts glowed, too. Who would have guessed? But they were born with that kind of heart, so how could it have been otherwise?*
>
> *I hated watching them as they loved their way through life—though no one called it that. Not even the people who should have known better. They misnamed it other things. And goddamnit, it was all so obvious. Goddamnit! Goddamnit! Goddamnit! Why do people fucking do that? Why do they always overlook the obvious? All the fucking time!*
>
> *No one knew them.*
>
> *And even me who did know them. I—I hated being loved by them. But I couldn't run. I couldn't. It is useless to run from a storm. So I stayed. I know about storms as well as anyone.*
>
> *So what am I going to do with this mangled fucking heart? It isn't good for anything, not anymore. If my body was a computer screen, I would delete the file marked "heart."*

She couldn't help but wonder what had taken him there, to that alley behind that bar. She often wondered about her clients. She cared more for some of her cases. She was like a bad mother who played favorites. She was going to care about this one—that much she knew already. She always knew from the start. Not that caring changed anything. She had learned that what mattered most was not how much she cared, but how much the client cared. Some of them had been worn down to nothing long before they reached her office.

She almost didn't notice the phone was ringing. She always lost one of her other senses when her mind was engaged. Sometimes it was her sense of smell—but usually it was her hearing. She slowly reached for the phone. "Grace Delgado," she whispered, her greeting dry and distant.

"Grace, you busy?" Mister. He'd had a deep voice since he was a boy. He never called, but when he did, he called her at her office. Never called at home anymore—as if their relationship were purely business.

"Mister?"

"How are you, Grace?"

"The same."

"Are you with a client?"

"No."

"I saw you last week. I honked. You seemed distracted."

"I might have been."

"You were walking out of Dr. Garza's office. Is anything wrong?"

"No. Just a checkup."

"You sure?"

"For someone who never calls, why the sudden interest in your mother's health?"

"I'm trying to be civil, Grace."

"You're good at being civil."

"But not so good at being a good son."

"I didn't say that."

"You didn't have to."

"What is it, Mister?"

"Why don't we have a drink after work?"

She could almost see him biting his lip or pulling on his untamable hair. "Is there something you want to tell me?"

"Yes."

"You can tell me now."

"I'd like to see you."

Just then he sounded sincere. Like Sam. That was the thing about Mister—he was so much like his father. So why did she find it so difficult to love him? "Sounds serious."

"It is."

"Are you getting a divorce?"

"Sorry to disappoint you, Grace, but Liz and I are doing just fine." He took a breath.

She knew he wanted to scream.

"You always have to do this, don't you, Grace? You always have to go for the throat."

"I'm sorry. I apologize." She clutched the receiver tightly. She took a deep breath and looked out into the blinding midmorning light. "Where would you like to meet?"


She'd managed to make him angry in less than two minutes. Always, it was about the same subject. His wife. The first time she'd met Liz, it had been clear that she was capable of doing a great deal of damage. She'd concluded that her attraction to her son was a cheap attempt at inviting some kind of goodness into her life—as if goodness were something you could get secondhand. She and Grace had taken an instant dislike to each other. Liz had looked at her and accused: "You'll turn him against me, won't you, Grace?"

"No. He's not the kind of man who turns against the people he loves."

"Does that mean he won't turn against you either, Grace?"

"That's exactly what that means."

She'd been wrong, of course. Mister had turned against her. But that had begun long before Liz had entered the picture—so it wasn't fair to blame her. Liz was just salt on the wound. She had understood nothing about the man she'd married. Nothing that mattered, anyway. Six months. Just six months. And she'd run off with another man. Mister had shown up at Grace's door, drunk and sobbing. "How could she have done this? How, Grace? Look at me, Grace. Look at me."

A few months later, he'd taken Liz back in.

*"She just had the jitters, Grace. You know, she was scared."*

*"Scared of what?"*

"*Of being married, of being loved.*"

"*Oh, I see, so she goes off with another man.*"

"*Forgive her, Grace.*"

"*I can't.*"

"*You mean, you won't.*"

"*She wrecked your car. She totaled it. While she was with another man, Mister.*"

"*What's a car compared to a fucking heart, Grace?*"

She resented thinking about Liz, about Mister, about what was wrong with them. When she thought of them, they took over the room. She shoved them away, then turned back to the file she'd been reading. Other people's problems had always been more interesting to her than her own. She noticed the name on the file. Andrés. Andrés Segovia. She smiled at the irony and half wondered what his parents had been thinking when they named him.

She reread what Andrés had written. She couldn't help herself. Much as it bothered her to have these pages in her possession, these words said more about the author than the rest of the file, where he was referred to mostly by the word *suspect*. Files had too many rules and limitations. A police report regarding the arrest. The judge's mandate to see a counselor, the terms and conditions. It was all there. A name, Andrés Segovia. An age, twenty-six. All these things were clear enough. But what about the face? The look in his eyes? The movement of his hands? The stubborn or quivering lips? Those things said more. They always did.

She put the file down.

Andrés Segovia. Andrés who'd been found on the streets, yelling and cursing and howling like an alley cat or a dog with rabies. He'd scratched and kicked and even tried to bite. Not like a person. Like an animal. That's what the police report said. She half smiled. Policemen weren't writers. But sometimes they tried. *Like an animal.* As if people weren't animals.

She tried to put a face on him. His eyes would betray the chaos of his heart, the riots that were exploding everywhere inside him. His eyes would be so black that they would shine blue in the sun. That's what she decided about Andrés. Andrés, who wrote words as if they were portraits. Andrés, who knew about storms.

# Lost Files

Programming and installing. Cleaning out viruses, restoring lost files. The getting to the root of a problem. There was always a source, always a solution. Computers were systematic, had a built-in logic with wires and chips that corresponded to specific functions. They were programmed, and they carried out the functions for which they were created. You could count on it. When something went wrong, you could fix it.

Not people. People were wired to hell. He wanted to growl like a rabid mastiff when he heard someone say, "The body is a machine." What asshole thought of that? Screwed up and angry and wanting love, fucking desperate to get it and not knowing how to get it, and willing to do anything just to get a taste of it. Or worse, striking out because you couldn't get it—all that love you wanted. The body was *not* a machine. Machines and computers, he could deal with. There was always a solution for the problem.

What was the solution for him?

"What happened to your face?"

He hated Al. Always interrupting him, always asking him questions. "Nothing."

"You get in a fight?"

If he didn't answer, maybe Al would just go away.

"Does it hurt?"

"What?"

"The bruises? Do they hurt?"

"Actually, they feel good." Andrés stared straight into his eyes until Al looked away. He smiled, then laughed nervously. Then walked away.

Andrés shook his head. He should've stayed away from work for a couple more days. But his bruises would last longer than a couple of days, and he couldn't afford to stay away from work, even though he knew there'd be questions from people like Al. So what did it matter? He did his job. And did it well. He did it very well.

He could still smell Al's cologne as he sat and read his e-mail. He wondered about guys who wore so much cologne. The world was full of them. As if they were trying to hide what they smelled like. As if there was something terrible in their smell, something mean and rotting inside them. His father had worn something sweet on his skin every day of his life—even when he worked out in the yard. His brother, too. Lots of it. You could smell him when he walked into the room. And keep on smelling him when he left.

"Armando, you've used up all my goddamned cologne. Your mother gave that to me for my birthday. Armando!"

Armando kept his eyes on the television set.

"Dad's talking to you, Mando."

"I didn't hear anything."

"He's shaving. In the bathroom. Shaving and yelling at you. Can't you hear?"

"I didn't hear a thing."

"I think Dad likes to yell from the bathroom."

"Dad likes to yell from every room in the house."

"You make him mad."

"Doesn't take much."

"Armando! ¿Me estas oyendo?"

"He's just gonna keep yelling until you go and talk to him."

"I don't hear anything."

"The whole neighborhood can hear."

"You've got to learn to ignore some things in life, Andy."

"Don't call me Andy. You can't go around ignoring dads, Mando."

"What do you know? What are you, ten?"

"Ten and a half."

"You don't know shit."

"You think you know everything, don't you? Don't you? Just because you're gonna be eighteen next month."

"I know more than you, you little shit."

"Mando, I'm talking to you. Get your ass over here!"

"He's mad. You used up all his aftershave last week. And this week, you've used up all his cologne. Why do you like that stuff, anyway?"

"Girls like it, Junior."

"I don't think so."

"Like you really know what rukas like."

"Like I really care."

"Maybe you're just a little homo."

"Shut up, you asshole. And just wait till Dad finds out about that shirt you stole from his closet."

"What shirt?"

"I saw you. It's one of Dad's favorite shirts—like he's not gonna know it's missing. Like he's not gonna know who took it."

"You tell, and I'll kick your ass."

"So what? Go ahead. I don't care."

"Mando!"

"I'm coming! Just wait—I'm coming!" Mando got up from the couch, and muttered to himself. "If he fuckin' doesn't want me to use his cologne, why doesn't he put it in a place where I can't find it?"

Andrés picked himself off the living room carpet. "I hate cologne. I swear I'll never wear it. I'm not. I'm not." He heard Mando and his father yelling at each other. Their arguments were getting worse. Every day, something new to yell about. He walked out the front door. He saw his older sister and her boyfriend leaning on the car in the driveway. He walked up to them. He smelled the air. Yup, someone was wearing cologne.

"Andrés, you're weird. Why are you sniffing like a dog?"

"I was just investigating, Yolanda."

"Investigating what?"

"Nada. Never mind."

He saw his little sister riding her bicycle up and down on the sidewalk. He walked up to her and kissed her, his favorite thing to do. She laughed. "You're silly, Andy!"

"Yes, I am. But tell me something, Ileana. Do you like guys who wear cologne? You know, do you like the way they smell?"

"Like Daddy and Mando?"

"Yeah, like Daddy and Mando."

"They smell pretty, don't you think so, Andy?"

"Yes, they do. They smell very pretty."

# Grace

She was nervous—about seeing her own son. She wondered what he had to say to her. Serious, he said. And what should she say to him? It had all been so much easier when Sam had been around. He'd always been the buffer between them. And they'd both adored him. Maybe they fought over him in their hearts. And when he died, that fighting in their hearts spilled over into their lips. And they had words. And over the years, she and Mister, well, over the years it had just gotten worse. Maybe they just were painful reminders to each other. They preferred to look away. Because it hurt too much.

He would ask how she was. That's how he would begin. She would say, "Fine." And she *was* fine, wasn't she? And if she wasn't fine, what could she or Mister or anybody do about it?

He was at a table for two. In the corner. Waiting. Always a few minutes early. Just like Sam. He waved, a smile washing over his face, and for an instant, nothing between them was wrong. She smiled back. He started to get up, but she motioned for him to stay seated. By then she was pulling out the chair and seating herself across from her son. "You look fine, Mister. You look just fine."

"So do you, Grace."

They looked at each other, then looked away, then looked at each other again.

"How's Liz?" She tried to sound sincere.

"She's fine. It's nice of you to ask, Grace."

"I'm feeling nice." She smiled.

Mister nodded. "Are you sure you're feeling okay?"

"Of course I am."

"You were walking out of an oncologist's office when I saw you."

"My doctor happens to be an oncologist. He also happens to be a very fine internist."

"Yes. I remember."

They both nodded.

Mister caught a waiter's eye and waved him over. "Would you like a drink?"

"I'll take a scotch on the rocks."

"Chivas. I remember."

A Chivas for Grace. A beer for Mister. They sat quietly as the waiter walked away. "Grace," he said softly, "Liz and I are going to adopt a baby."

Grace nodded.

"We can't have any."

"I'm sorry."

"Don't be. It's not the end of the world."

"So you're adopting."

"I got a call from this lawyer I know at the Child Advocacy Center, and well, this kid, they found him in a trailer house. He was naked and soiled and soaked in his own urine and sweating and roasting to death. It must've been 110 in there. Hell, the police had to open all the windows, couldn't stand the stench of urine and rotting food. God, Grace. They were looking for his mother—drugs, well, you know the story, drugged out, makes her money dancing in clubs, leaves the kid at home. Jesus Christ, Grace—" He stopped. "Anyway, we had a home study done about six or seven months ago, and we've kind of been waiting, and this seems—well, Grace, this boy, Liz and I want him."

"He may have a lot of problems, Mister."

"It'll all work out."

"You can't just order a kid and say everything is going to be fine. The world isn't a waitress asking to take your order."

"Oh, I thought she was. I thought she chewed gum and was always about to serve me apple pie—and looked a little like you."

"Don't mock me, Mister."

"I won't mock you, Grace, if you don't mock me. We're not kids. We know what we're doing."

"Do you, Mister?"

"We want this boy."

"You haven't met him yet, have you?"

"I'm twenty-eight years old, Grace. I want to be a father. Liz wants to be a mother. There something wrong with that?"

"This boy may have a lot of problems, Mister."

"I know that, Grace."

"And does Liz?"

"Don't start with Liz."

Grace clamped down on her jaw, then relaxed her face. Her poker face was useless in Mister's presence. The waiter placed her drink in front of her. She reached for it. She took a sip and then another. Why was all of this so hard? "What if you can't save him, Mister?"

"What if we can? What if Liz and I take the chance? What if we take a child into our home and try to love him?"

"What if you fail?"

"So we shouldn't do it—because we might fail?" He took a swallow from his beer. He tried to smile. "Sometimes I really want a cigarette."

Grace nodded. "Me, too." She put her finger in her scotch and stirred it. "Mister, you can't fix everyone who's broken."

"Well, Grace, you're the expert. You've spent a whole career trying to fix people who were broken. You're a fixer, Grace. That's what you do."

"I'll let you in on a little secret, Mister, I didn't always succeed. And I never brought them home with me."

"Now, that's a lie, Grace. You brought a helluva lot of clients home with you. I could see them written all over your face in the evenings. You brought them all home."

"Is that why you're mad at me?"

"I don't know. Maybe that's part of it."

He was so like Sam. So willing to let other people see him, touch him, examine him. That's why people hurt him. Not that he seemed to care. A part of her wanted to reach over and hold him. Another part of her wanted to get up and walk out of the room. They sat for a while, each of them sipping on their drinks. A scotch, a beer, the quiet.

"I'm going to visit him tomorrow night."

"What's his name."

"Vicente Jesús."

"It's a good name."

"Yes, it is." He bit his lip. "You can go with me if you like."

She was surprised by his question. "What?"

"I'm inviting you to go with me to see the boy who's very probably going to become your grandson."

She took another sip from her scotch. She understood the depth of his gesture, was moved by it. "Liz won't mind?"

"She doesn't hate you, Grace." He smiled.

God, he looked so much like Sam. So much like her Sam.

"Liz is out of town this week. Her father died."

"Oh, I'm sorry. Is Liz—is she all right?"

"She never knew him."

"That's sad."

"Yes. It's a common enough experience—children not knowing their parents."

Grace nodded.

"You'll come with me, then, Grace. To meet Vicente?"

# Night

The night brings its own kind of memory and revenge. The lucky ones sleep through the chaos. But tonight, Grace is not among the fortunate. No sleep for Grace, who is thinking of the color of death. Is it white? Is it black? Is it warm or is it cold? Is it a coffin in a cemetery, or is it a door? She puts the questions to Sam—though Sam does not answer. She stores so many of his words in her head that she feels as if she has become nothing more than a book he has written. "You have to die at the right time. That's the secret." He'd died at thirty-eight. Just after dawn. How did you know it was the right time? Many died too late. Why overstay your welcome?

She tries to think of something more soothing. She gets up from the bed and walks into the backyard. She takes a breath. She thinks of Mister. She tells herself she will try to love him. But she does love him. Not that love made anything easy. This is how Grace will spend her night. Thinking and asking and thinking.

Andrés, too, is wide awake. He lights a cigarette. He is thinking of another kind of death. Being held prisoner by his claustrophobic past, that is the worst kind of death—the kind of death that doesn't let you touch or breathe, that makes your heart feel as if it's a stone. "I died before I died." He'd read that somewhere. He knows exactly what it means. He thinks of a bicycle. He thinks of a ring. He thinks of a little girl who'd called him Andy. He thinks of a man who was a woman. He thinks of a mother holding his face between her palms, the only paradise he's ever known. Tonight, sleep will not be among his visitors.

Mister is doing what he always does when he can't sleep. He picks up a book and thumbs through it. He finds a passage, then reads it. Then rereads it. Then rereads it aloud, *Vine a este mundo con ojos/ y me voy sin ellos*. I don't know what this means. Tonight, he can't translate. He puts the book down, then looks up at the ceiling as if it were the sky. He thinks of Abraham sacrificing Isaac at an altar in the middle of the desert. He was a boy when Sam read the story to him. "You wouldn't kill me, Sam, would you?" Sam had held him in his arms. "Eres mi vida," he whispered. "Even if God told you to kill me, Sam?" "Even if God told me. Even then. Someday, Mister, you'll understand the story." At twenty-eight, he did not understand the story. Just as he did not understand why the story had entered his head. On nights like these, there is no logic to the visitors who make their way into his house. They come, they enter, they have their say. He reaches for Liz, then realizes she is gone tonight. He picks up the phone. He needs to hear her voice.

William Hart has found an apartment near a park. He is lying in bed, drinking a scotch, thinking of that boy, that beautiful boy he'd met so many years ago in Juárez. Maybe that's why he'd gone back there—to look for him. But of course that beautiful boy was a man now. That was the problem with boys. They grew up to be men. He had no interest in men.

*Repent from the evil!* his pastor yelled—then laid his soft, uncallused hands on him. He pretended to be slain in the Spirit of the Lord Jesus. He fell backward, his arms raised, *Praise the everlasting God!* But it was all still there, his incurable, impossible addiction. That's what his uncle had told him, when he was a boy. *This is impossible and beautiful.* If it would only go away.

Dave tosses and turns. He hadn't dreamed that accident in years. Now the dream has returned. Tonight, he does not want to sleep. And so he does what he always does when he doesn't want to sleep. He calls a woman. This one is named Cassandra. *Hello and what are you doing, did I wake you up and would you like some company*. Mostly they said yes, the women he knew. Tonight, it is *No, no, hell no, and tomorrow we need to talk*. Cassandra cares nothing for his aversion to sleep.

# Some Day We'll All Be Happy

It wasn't the wisest thing to do—go out to a bar just because you couldn't sleep. Bars were trouble, bars were places where bad things could happen, where fights could break out, where angry men drank too much and got even angrier—and God help you if you happened to get in the way. Bars were places where you could get talked into following a woman home, a woman you did not know, a woman who could steal your money. A woman who could hurt you in ways you hadn't yet imagined. Bars. But what was a lousy Jim Beam on the rocks? Just a drink to relax, to loosen up, let go of all the tightness in his shoulders, let go of the thoughts in his head that kept spinning around like clothes in a dryer that were trapped forever, spinning and spinning. A drink to get him out of his small apartment, with its bad plumbing and dull beige paint that covered the olive lead paint underneath. A drink to make him feel a part of something bigger than this room, this neighborhood, this goddamned city that was suffocating him. God, he couldn't fucking breathe. Just a drink. One lousy fucking Jim Beam on the rocks in a dark bar full of dark men and their dark women.

He laughed at the name of the place, El Ven Y Verme. He couldn't imagine gringos coming up with a name for a bar that would match its irony and humor, gringos who thought they had a corner on the market on irony and humor and anything else that spoke of intelligence and that word *civilized* that they liked to throw around like a pair of dice at a gambling table in Vegas. He couldn't imagine seeing a flashing neon light in English that read, "The Come and See Me." He laughed. Sure. He liked the name. Maybe one day he would buy the joint. Sure.

He liked that he could sit at the bar, and people would leave him alone. Sometimes there was a fight, but mostly it was just a place where guys came in and had a drink. A girlfriend or a wife here and there, but the place wasn't nice, not nice—that was part of what he liked about it. No forced conversations. He'd come here off and on since he was eighteen. That old bartender, Mr. Anaya, he was dead now, but he'd liked him, never asked for his ID, served him, didn't ask any questions, made just enough small talk to be friendly, had a picture of his wife and two girls where everyone could see. He remembered now—he'd been killed. In a car wreck. Just like his parents. He'd come here one night just to have a drink, and some regular had given him the news about Mr. Anaya. He'd pitched in ten bucks for a nice funeral wreath.

For no reason at all, he pictured the accident, a car running a red light, Mr. Anaya's body tearing in half like a piece of paper. Goddamnit, why was everyone so in love with cars, insured them, washed them, souped them up, Mexicans especially, hell, the barrio loved cars, made them feel American. Yeah, that was it. Yeah, yeah, get a piece of America anyway you can get it.

"So what do you think of the new car?"

"I like it, Dad."

Mando looked at Andrés and spit. "It sucks. How come you can't ever get a new car, Dad?"

"It is a new car, Mando." Andrés leaned into his father.

"It's not fucking new—it's a used-up Chevy someone traded in for something new. All we ever get is fucking leftovers."

"That's enough, Mando."

Andrés put his head down and moved away from his father. They were going to fight again. Last time, it had been a fistfight, both of them winding up with bloody lips. He could see Mando's hand tightening into a fist. "Don't, don't please don't." He hadn't meant to cry.

Mando walked away, maybe because of his tears. He could feel his father's fingers combing his hair.

"You want to take a ride in our new car, mi'jito?"

He nodded.

"Maybe we'll stop off at the Dairy Queen."

"¿Que dices? What's the word?"

Andrés looked up at the bartender. He was much younger than Mr. Anaya had been. He nodded. "Nada, nada. Wild Turkey on the rocks."

The bartender nodded as he put down the glass he'd been drying. Andrés watched him as he poured. A little extra. That was another thing he liked about this bar—not like those places on the West Side that poured you exactly a shot. Exactly a shot and no more. You wanted more—hell, you'd have to pay more. Those places understood money and exactitude and profit margins—but they didn't understand a damned thing about why people came to a bar. He stared at the drink in front of him. He took a swallow, not even a swallow, just a sip, just a drop, and held it on his tongue. He swished it around, then nodded, then lit a cigarette. He heard the sound of coins dropping in the old jukebox, a couple of clicks as if the old machine was struggling just to hold on—and then the song, *that* song, he hadn't heard it in such a long time, had only heard it in his house, an old record his mother loved to play as she cleaned house, *Blue, blue, my love* . . . He took a drag from his cigarette, then downed his drink. He caught the bartender with a glance and pointed at his empty glass.

Just as a fresh drink appeared in front of him, he heard a voice beside him. "Aren't you Andrés? Andrés Segovia?"

Andrés found himself staring at a vaguely familiar face. That was the thing about sitting in bars—you ran into people who looked familiar, and then all the malicious dogs you kept chained up suddenly tore themselves free, baring their teeth. "Yeah. That would be me. Andrés."

"I'm Pepe. Remember? Pepe Tellez. I was a friend of your father's."

He looked at the man for a second. "Yeah, yeah, I remember." He *did* remember. He lived a few blocks down. He and his father were always talking, drinking beers, hanging out. He looked older, looked as if things hadn't gone so well for him—hell, if they had gone well for him, he wouldn't be sitting here at the Ven Y Verme on a Wednesday night.

"God, you look like your Dad. De veras que si."

Andrés nodded. What was he supposed to say to that?

"Hey, listen, let me pay for your drink."

God, he hated this. Having a drink with your dead father's drinking buddy. "Yeah, why not."

Pepe pulled up a seat next to him and set down the bottled beer he was drinking on the bar. "Irma and I always wondered what happened to you kids. Well, we heard about your brother. It's too bad, I mean, I know he and your dad never got on, but you know, it's just too goddamned sad."

Andrés nodded. What could he do but sit there and listen to the guy? He'd nod and listen and hope to God he'd shut up sooner than later. "Yeah, it's sad."

"So you doin' all right?"

"Yeah. I'm a computer guy at the university."

"Hey, well, hell, that's fuckin' great."

"Yeah, I guess it is."

"So you landed on your feet."

"Yeah, guess I did."

"So how come you're hanging out in a place like this—good-lookin' kid with a steady job and money in his pocket without a girl?"

"Couldn't sleep. I like this place."

"Reminds you of the old neighborhood, huh? You know, if you were born raza, then, hell, you'll live and die raza, ¿a poco no?" Andrés could see that Pepe's hands were shaking as he lit a cigarette.

"Yeah, raza. You know, I guess I just come in here because I like the name."

"Yeah, me gusta el nombre tambien. Pinchi raza. Nos lleva al cabrón. I think they should put a blinking neon light that says, 'Gringos welcome, gringos welcome.' " He laughed his ass off at his own joke. And then he stopped laughing and shook his head. Andrés knew he was half gone. "You know, Irma left me."

"Irma?"

"My wife."

"Sorry."

"Yeah, well, too fucking bad. Pinchi vieja. Said she was sick and tired of my shit. She left me for some gringo. Can you believe that shit?

A fucking gringo. They met at Big 8. He was looking for authentic Mexican bread. The cabrón was looking for bolillos. My wife should have told him that he *was* one. Instead, she hooks up with him. Me dejo solo. She said I could take the house and shove it up my ass. You know, I picked her up from . . ."

He hated this. But as long as he kept the conversation on his sorry-ass-pinchi-raza-my-wife-left-me-for-a-gringo life, he could put up with it. So long as he didn't ask any more questions about Andrés' family.

"Screw 'em all. Hell, oyeme, just fucking listen to me. You don't want to hear nothing about mi pinchi vida. Listen, how are your sisters? How are they doing?"

The guy didn't know. How could he know? He looked at his drink, lit another cigarette. "They live in Kansas."

"Kansas?"

"Yeah." He finished his drink. "Yeah, fucking Kansas." He didn't bother shaking Pepe's hand, didn't bother thanking him for the drink as he walked out the door.

"Take good care of your little sister."

"I will, Mom."

"You always do." She took his face and held it between her palms. "You're the sweetest kid in the world, you know that? Where'd you come from?"

"From you, Mom."

She smiled—then laughed. She shook her head. "It gets to you, doesn't it—their fighting."

"No, it's okay."

"You can tell me the truth."

"I guess so. It's no big deal, Mom."

"I'm sorry. I'll make them stop."

"They'll never stop, Mom."

"Maybe for me, they will."

He nodded. "Okay, Mom. So, where you going?"

"To a dance. That's the one thing your father and I have in common—we love to dance."

"Mando likes to dance, too."

"Yeah, well, Mando likes a lot of things. He goes out, doesn't he?—when we leave."

"Mom, I can't—"

"It's okay, I know."

"Yolanda goes out, too, doesn't she?"

"Mom, why are you asking me? Mom, I can't—"

"I know. I know. What am I gonna do with them?"

"It's okay, Mom. Ileana and I are fine. We're pals."

"I know. There's you and Ileana—and there's Mando and Yolanda. It's like having two different families."

"Mom, you worry too much."

She leaned down and kissed him on the cheek. "Some day we'll all be happy. I promise you. And there won't be any more fighting."

He didn't want to think about that night. He was tired of it. The whole thing. Pepe Tellez, and all the fucking dogs were set free. Growling in his ear. Ready to tear his flesh apart. And then the anger lifted, just as suddenly as it had appeared. Storms in the desert were like that. They came on you. Beat down, down on you until you thought that the storm would last forever—and then just as you were about to lose your last crumb of hope, the storm left. And he was left alive and humiliated for overreacting to the drama that was no more than a small play, with him in the lead—miscast. Humiliated. And something worse was left in the aftermath. That thing in his heart that made him want to cry. Because he was relieved that he had survived the storm—but sad, because if he had not survived, then it would all be over. And *over* meant *rest*. And, God, it would be good to rest.

He sat in his car, trying to think of something else. Anything. Maybe he'd go home and get on the Net—that helped sometimes. It did. Maybe he'd just go to sleep—if sleep would come. Sometimes it did, sometimes it didn't. He thought of the counselor's name, the one he had an appointment to see. Tomorrow he would see her. He couldn't remember her name. He took out his wallet, opened the door so he could see the name and the address on the card that Dave had given him. He stared at the name, whispered it, "Grace Delgado." He tried to picture what she would look like, what she would talk like, but all he could see was his mother, *Some day we'll all*—he put the card back in his wallet. He was about to shut the door when he saw her standing there.

She smiled at him. Pretty. But it was dark. Lots of things looked pretty in the dark. "¿Quieres irte conmigo?"

He shook his head.

"I speak English," she said.

He nodded.

"You like me?"

He shrugged.

"You don't like to talk? Maybe you want to do something else— something better than talking."

He shook his head.

"It'll be okay," she whispered. "I can make you feel good."

"No," he said, more to himself than to her. "No, you can't."

He looked at her for a moment, then slammed the door and turned on the ignition. He shoved the car into gear and pressed down on the gas pedal. He didn't bother to look back at her as he drove away. He already knew her. She was just like him. Spending time with her would be like being alone. Only it would hurt more.

God, it would never go away, this anger, this rage that was like the ceaseless movement of the spring winds through the desert, this knot in his guts, this splinter in his heart that shot a pain through him that eventually found its way into his lungs, then out of his mouth and into the open air, the sound making the whole world turn away from him. It would never go away, never, never, and there would never be any peace. What was that? Peace? And even his slumber would be crowded with this, this thing, this anger that was handed to him like a fucking precious heirloom. Maybe he had it all wrong, maybe he wasn't a victim at all, not at all, because he had decided that this was the only thing that would ever be truly his, and so he clung to it, would cling to it forever. He tried humming. Sometimes humming helped. And then he heard his mother's voice. He turned on the radio, but her voice was still there, in the car. In his head. Sometimes, when she visited, she stayed all night.

# Why He Hated Them

Not that he wanted to go. Not that he had a choice. He'd gone to them before for this reason and that reason, for things that happened, for good reasons probably—even he knew that. In his moments of calm, he knew the intentions were good. But Mando's intentions had been good, too, and everything in his life seemed to be nothing more than an illegible and tragic footnote to his older brother's good intentions.

Interventions—that's what they called them. If he didn't come through, there was the matter of a suspended sentence hanging over his head. He'd escaped jail once. A crack through the door. Dave managed to get him through that crack. To the light on the other side. And for what? Here he was again, so maybe not a damn thing had changed. Well, this time he was a man and not a boy. As if adulthood was a simple matter of age. *Plead guilty, get a suspended sentence, and get yourself some help.* Dave and his goddamned ideas. He was like a farmer plowing fields. Nothing was going to stop him from the planting season. And was Dave wrong, to take charge of someone else's life like that? Court mandated counseling. How did that help? They could all feel good about their intervention.

The failure would all be his. And the counselor, what did she have to lose? And Dave? And the judge?

He wondered what she would be like. She would dress in a way that would ensure you didn't notice what she was wearing, the lady with MSW behind her name. The trained professional with the neat office who kept the pictures of her family in the desk drawer, kept her nice family far away from people like him.

He always thought about what the next counselor would be like. Mostly they were women. Sometimes men. Sometimes. But mostly, the ones he'd gone to were women. They were mostly nice. Sometimes a little severe, but that was only in the beginning—to show him they weren't weak just because they were women. They were all good girls, all nice and decent and caring in predictable ways. Always decent. Always predictable. Some of them from bad families, and by some miracle they had escaped. But no escape was ever complete, and so, as if some severe priest had given them a lifelong penance, they wandered to and fro on the earth fixing things, picking up stray dogs and cats and fixing them, fixing damaged people, fixing grotesque and shattered families that were as bent and unfixable as theirs had been. They were up to every challenge, fixing and fixing, trying to get at something that had gone wrong with their own screwed-up lives. He could always tell when they were wounded. They couldn't hide—not from him.

Others were just ordinary and normal, nothing special, but someone had told them they were good with people, and they had believed it, and having no other calling, they had decided to do something useful in the world—counseling screwed-up people made them feel as if their miserable lives were worth something. He had decided a long time ago that no one with a good mind would make a living talking to people like him. Who could respect that? The worst ones were the ones that had found Jesus. They wanted you to see the light—even if they never said it. Didn't matter that they never spoke the name of Jesus. It was there, in the shallow little prayers they hung on a wall where you could see it, along with their framed degrees. They wanted you to walk in the light, walk hand in hand with Jesus. Then it would be all right.

The one he was going to, her name was, he'd forgotten. Grace. Grace Delgado—that was it. A Mexican name, and she was probably a Catholic, and for the most part he didn't mind Catholics. They mostly left their crosses at home. He could picture her. In her late forties or early fifties—something like that. They were always that age. Probably she'd have a nice voice. Probably she knew how to keep calm. Probably nothing would shock her. Shit, they heard enough stuff, all kinds of crap. He wasn't stupid or arrogant enough to believe he was telling them something new. Hell, what had happened to him had happened to a million other kids. In China and Mexico and Chile and fucking London and Belfast. Who could be shocked? He'd talked to lots of women with nice voices who went to church and had sex with their tax-paying husbands on Saturday mornings and who had become immune, had become incapable of being shocked, had trained themselves to listen as if everything he was saying was normal or neutral when they knew it was all too fucking much. They nodded in all the right places. Sure. And when they spoke to him, there was something in their voices that made him feel as if he was a disobedient dog who'd had a bad owner. *Not your fault. Here, let me get your chain.*

He would hate her. He would talk to her. He would answer her questions. She would take notes. Sometimes they took notes on a piece of paper. Sometimes they took notes in their heads. But they always took notes. They were mothers, most of them, and like all mothers, they had good memories, learned the habits of their children, the things they did and didn't do—though they didn't talk about that. Their children. Not ever. But he knew. They felt sorry for him, because of the things that had happened. Because he was an orphan. Because they were sentimental, and they mistook their goddamned sentimentality for care. But who could blame them? If he had been them, he would've fucking wept at the mere sight of a man like him.

He would talk to her. He knew that. He would tell her about his life. Some of it, anyway. He would have to decide how much to tell. But he knew this—the more they knew about him, the more they pitied him. That's why he hated them.

# What's a Boy? What's a Son?

He'd been thinking of the boy. Vicente Jesús. The boy that might be *his*. But he would never be his, that boy he was already in love with. And anyway, boys weren't belongings—boys weren't something you owned. He remembered the harshest words Grace had spoken against his wife. "She thinks she owns you. Tell her you're not a car or a pair of jeans." Boys and girls and men and women and husbands and wives and sons and daughters, they weren't something you owned.

He drove through the streets of downtown, through the streets of Segundo Barrio, catching glimpses of a mural here and there. He loved this part of the city. He headed south on Campbell, then headed down the César Chávez Border Freeway. Grace would hate the fact that he was driving around and thinking about things. "Don't think and drive. You're going to die in an accident—and all because you were thinking about something. What if you kill someone? What will you do then?" Grace was great at worst-case scenarios.

*Grace, I want to be a father. You disapprove. I can tell. You disapprove of so many things, Grace.* She was always there, in his head. *And Grace, you're wrong about Liz.*

He stopped at a gas station. He felt the slap of the hot air as he stepped out of his truck. *This is the kind of light that makes people sad and tired.* That's what the old priest had said, the one that used to come over for dinner when Sam was alive. The priest was long dead, but there was something of his death in the punishing light of the afternoon.

On certain days, the sun was in no mood for mercy.

# The World Comes to an End
# (in One Apocalyptic Moment)

Grace took out Andrés Segovia's file for the third time that afternoon. She had questions. She'd written them down on a piece of scrap paper and stuck them in the file. *Who hurt you? When did it happen? How many times? Where? Tell me. Why do you hate yourself? Where do you keep the hurt?* There was no art to this, coming up with these questions. But she would never ask them. They were too direct and unsubtle and disarming. And too unearned. Unearned questions deserved no answers. Everything had to be earned.

She kept the questions in the file. A compass for the journey.

She tried to think of more practical questions. Not real questions. Not important questions, not questions that needed answering, but questions that were like doorways. They could walk through them. Questions that would let him know she was listening, that would let him know she wasn't a lawyer deposing a client. The trick was not to sound too prepared—as if you could be too prepared to listen to young women and men as they stumbled to articulate their sufferings. Maybe, if she worked hard enough—if she could make him work hard enough—maybe he would answer the questions. And he would let it out and listen to his own words. That would be a start. If he listened to the sound of his own breaking voice, if he could hear the rage and the hurt. But what if he already knew? The possibility existed he already knew everything about himself, and knowing everything brought him no closer to a cure. And what constituted a cure? What was healing for a damaged human being? Who needed help and who didn't? And anyway, was there really a cure for the truly hurt? People could be totaled, just like cars.

Maybe there was just management. More painless days than painful ones. Sometimes that was the supreme victory. Some, she sent to doctors and psychiatrists who were competent to deal with their maladies, doctors and psychiatrists who decided they needed meds—and for some, it worked. For a few years, anyway. But for a lifetime? Who knew? But hadn't she seen it happen before? People healed. Cripples who learned to walk. Hadn't she been a witness to recoveries? Somehow, miraculously, they forced themselves, told themselves they were going to live. They wrote themselves new lives. Fictions, perhaps, but what did it matter? They had kept the chaos at bay. They had managed to stop cursing the darkness. They'd lit a torch.

Others stopped swimming, their arms and legs limp in the dark waters. And they drowned.

*Andrés Segovia, tell me what happened that night?* That was a good first question.

The resemblance to Mister was uncanny. They could have passed for brothers. He almost took her breath away. Not that she showed him what she felt. She'd always had the kind of face that hid her emotions. She offered a handshake, natural, friendly, at ease. Andrés hesitated for an instant, then smiled back at her as they shook hands. He sat down on the chair across from her desk.

"We can sit here," she said, "the safety of this large desk between us—or we can sit over there." She pointed to the opposite side of the room, which was arranged like a living room. A small couch, a coffee table with a stack of books on it, two comfortable chairs.

"This is good," he said. He looked around the room.

She noticed a pack of cigarettes in his shirt pocket. "You're either looking for an escape route, or you're searching for an ashtray?"

"Both, I think." He looked straight at her. "This wasn't my idea, to be here." He started reaching for a cigarette, then stopped himself. "You let people smoke in your office?"

"Depends."

"On what?"

"Some people claim they can't really talk to me without a cigarette."

"And you believe them?"

"What I believe isn't always important."

"But you let them smoke?"

"You want an ashtray?"

"No." He leaned back on his chair. "I had to take off from work. Now I have to work tonight. To make up for lost time. I don't like that. My boss doesn't like it either."

"I can change the time of your appointments. That won't be a problem."

"Good," he said. "I still don't want to be here."

"But you came."

"You saw my file?"

"Of course."

"The judge thinks I need to learn to manage my anger before I get into deeper trouble. He said I'm a good candidate for Huntsville, if I'm not careful. And my lawyer, he thinks I need help."

"And what do you think?"

"I think the judge—never mind the judge. Fuck him. And my lawyer, he needs a project. So I'm the project. He thinks I need saving."

"And do you need saving?"

"Everyone needs saving. Isn't that why people go to church?" He laughed. "My lawyer's full of crap. I bet he called you."

"As a matter of fact, he did."

"He wants you to check in with him every time I come in, doesn't he?"

"He just wanted me to know that he thought you were—" She paused, weighed her words for an instant. "He cares about you."

"That's nice."

"Yes, it is. It's very nice."

"So he just wants to make sure you're on board to save me, too. Maybe I should go find one of those churches and let myself be slain in the holy spirit. Let Jesus come into my heart."

She couldn't help but laugh. Not a loud or boisterous laugh. Not like that. "That's funny."

He tried to hide his smile. "So you don't think Jesus saves?"

"I don't believe in cheap shortcuts." She chastised herself—not for what she said, but for the way she said it. Too much edge in her voice. Not that he seemed to mind.

"Counseling doesn't help, you know? I've tried it. I've talked to you people before. I've talked and talked and fucking talked. I've even played the game of refusing to fucking talk. I've answered questions and refused to answer questions—and sometimes it even felt good. For about a second. And nothing's ever changed." He reached into his pocket and took out a cigarette. He played with it. "Look, these are my choices. I either come to talk to you every week until you write a nice report and say, Look, Judge, this guy can walk the streets again. I either do that, or I go to jail. Hell, I'm probably going to wind up there, anyway. Maybe I should fucking save us both the time." He got up from where he was sitting, nodded at her. "Look, I'm sorry."

"Why don't you have a cigarette?"

She'd thought of chasing him down, pleading with him, convincing him that he was worth it. That's what Dave had told her on the phone, "Look, Grace, this guy, he's worth it. Do what you can. I'm counting on you." Wasn't that her job, to convince them all that they were worth the trouble? But she wasn't a pleader, and it didn't work that way. She wasn't a jilted girlfriend, and he wasn't a little boy. He was a man, articulate, and whatever it was that he had in him, she couldn't pin him to the floor and yank it out of him, any more than he would be slain in the spirit and be saved by Jesus.

What a waste.

She would have to call his probation officer. She would have to tell him that he wasn't interested in counseling. This was the part she hated. She picked up the phone, then stared at it. She looked up, her door open. He was standing there. He was looking at her. He lit his cigarette. She took out an ashtray from her desk and slid it across the desk.

"You can't help me."

"Probably not."

He sat back down on the chair. "Were you going to call Dave?"

"I don't know who I was going to call."

"You know him, don't you?"

"Yes."

"How? How do you know him?"

"I think you should ask him about that." His cigarette looked good. He nodded. "So what do you want to know?"

"What happened that night? The night you were arrested?"

"I went out."

"Went out?"

"I was at home. At my apartment. I was writing something."

"Writing?"

"I write sometimes."

"What do you write? Stories? Poetry?"

"Poetry?" He smiled. Not a smile, a sneer. "Nothing like that. I just write things. Things I'm thinking."

"Does it help?"

"Sort of. Like having a cigarette when you need one."

"So you were writing, and you decided to go out."

"Something like that. I got restless. And I went to this place I like to go to. El Ven Y Verme."

Grace smiled. "I like the name. Makes me want to go there."

"You wouldn't like it. It's a dump. So I was there, and I got to thinking. Sometimes too much beer makes me think about things."

"Like what?"

"Things that make me sad. And I'd brought along the stuff that I was writing. And I took out what I'd written, and I wrote some more—right there in the bar. And this guy starts hassling me, asking me what I was writing, was I writing a letter to my girlfriend or maybe I didn't like girls and was I writing to my boyfriend, and I wanted to punch his goddamned lights out. So I just left. I don't know what time it was. I just wanted to be alone. So I just walked. I don't even know where I was, but I sat down under a streetlight and I just started reading what I had written, and then these cops come along. And they treat me like I'm some kind of goddamned animal—like I'm some kind of wild dog on the loose—that's how they treat you. And I wasn't going to let them treat me like that. I wasn't. So I wind up in jail."

"What happened between you and the cops?"

"I don't know. I don't remember."

"Were you drunk?"

"No. Maybe a little drunk. But not very."

Grace took out a file. "Would you like to see a copy of the police report?" She handed it to him.

He read it slowly. "I don't—I don't remember any of this. I don't remember acting that way."

"Is there any truth there?"

"I didn't say they were lying. I just said I didn't remember."

"What happens—when you get mad?"

He pushed the file back toward Grace.

"You don't think I know that I hurt people?"

Grace pushed the file aside. "Tell me something about yourself. Something important."

"Is this a game?"

"No. Not a game exactly. Let's call them ground rules. You come and see me twice a week, and—"

"Twice a week?"

"Then later, maybe just once a week. Every time you come and see me, you tell me something important about yourself. Something absolutely necessary."

"I don't like that rule." He put out his cigarette. He wanted to light another. He stopped himself. He looked at her. She was beautiful. And young. Like a girl, but a girl who had always been a woman. He hadn't expected that. She was old enough to be his mother. And still she was beautiful. "I don't have a family," he said.

"How did that happen?"

He took out a cigarette. He held it tight. "I was ten years old. I was ten that summer. It's hard, sometimes, to remember. I remember my dad had bought me a bike that day. It was Saturday. It was a nice day. Not too hot. Dry. Like today. I hate Saturdays. He was a funny guy, my dad. Unreliable. A party guy, I think. That's how I remember him. He'd gotten me a bike because my dog had died. I loved that dog. And he'd died. I found the dog, dead, in the backyard. He'd gotten mad at me because I started crying. But I didn't care if he was mad. It was *my* dog, and my dog was dead, and I wanted to cry—so I did. My mom helped me bury him. She said a prayer, and I put a cross in the ground. And I think, later, my dad felt bad. Because I'd lost my dog and because he'd gotten mad at me. So I think that's why he'd gotten me a bike . . ."

• • •

"A bike! You got me a bike!"

"Sure I did. It's summer. What kind of summer would it be without a bike?"

The boy looked at his bike. Then looked at his dad. He wanted to kiss him, but he'd told him that the days for kissing dads were over. He didn't understand that. But those were the rules. "Can I ride it?"

"Go. Go on!" And so he'd ridden his bike up and down the streets. Up and down, showing everyone his new bike. God, a bike! His heart was bursting, God, he could ride all summer. He rode all afternoon—until it was almost dark. When he got home, his mother was at the door.

"I was starting to get worried."

"You don't have to worry, Mom. You don't. Not about me." He looked into her hazel eyes. She wasn't happy. He knew that. Maybe she'd had another fight with his father. Or maybe his father had been fighting with Mando again. Sometimes she got in the middle of it. Sometimes she succeeded in making them stop. Sometimes they refused to stop and cursed her. Both of them. She'd been crying. He could tell. "Can we go to the movies tonight, Mom?" She liked the movies.

"Not tonight, mi'jo. Your father and I are going to a wedding dance." That's why she was all dressed up.

"Oh. Where's Dad?"

"He went to put gas in the car."

He nodded. "Will you come home late?"

"Not too late. But Yolanda will be here."

"And Mando?"

"He's gone out."

"Oh." He knew what that meant. It meant he'd left as soon as his father had gone out to gas up the car. He'd come back when he felt like it. It wasn't a new story. And Yolanda, she would stay until they left—and then her boyfriend would come, and then they would leave for a while, and he would be the only one left to stay and take care of Ileana. But she was good, and she went to sleep early anyway, and the house was peaceful and he could watch anything he wanted on the television—sometimes there was an old scary movie. Sometimes he'd just read a book. He liked the quiet of reading. "And Yolie?"

"She's putting nail polish on Ileana's nails." She winked at him. "I made tacos for dinner. They're in the oven." She always made tacos on Saturdays.

He heard the horn of his father's car. He turned around and waved. He'd shaved his mustache, and he looked like a different man. He looked like he was really nice. He yelled at him from the front of the house. "How was your bike?"

"It's great, Dad. God, it's so great."

He nodded as he lit a cigarette. "Vamonos, vieja. Ya vamos tarde."

"Let me just run in and get the present."

He walked up to the car and studied his father's face. "You shaved."

"Yeah, what d'ya think, mi'jo."

"I like it. Does Mom like it?"

"That's why I did it—to make her happy."

He nodded. "That's good, Dad."

His mother came out, holding a gift wrapped in silver with a white bow and wedding bells. She kissed him on the cheek. "Love you," she whispered.

"Love you more."

"No. It's me who loves you more."

"No. Me."

They both laughed. It was a game they always played. She rubbed his hair and walked around to get into the car.

"You treat him like a baby." That's what his father said when she got into the car.

"He's the only man in this house who knows anything about love."

He stood there watching them. His father shook his head. "Be a man," he said. His mother looked past his father and blew him a kiss. "Bye." His father threw his cigarette out the window and drove away.


"Am I boring you?"

"No."

"Maybe I'm making the story longer than it needs to be."

Grace smiled at him. "Your hour isn't up yet. Besides, you're just repeating a memory. That's different than telling a story."

"Well, it's a sad memory."

"If it was a happy one, you wouldn't be repeating it. You might not even be sitting here telling it."

"I told this story to Dave once. A long time ago. I don't know why. He cried. Dave is funny that way—he cries. I don't understand him. Are you going to cry?"

"No. I don't think so."

"I watched them drive away. I went around the block one more time—even though the sun was setting and it was hard for drivers on the street to see me in that kind of light. Mom had told me about that—she called it a dangerous light. It's beautiful to look at, but it blinds people, she said, that kind of light. It's not good to be out in it. That's what she said." He lit the cigarette he'd been holding. He blew the smoke out through his nose. Grace watched him. She realized for an instant how seductive a man with a cigarette could be. The right man, anyway. "But I went out. I hopped on my bike and went out in that light, anyway. . . ."

When he came back from his bike ride, he went into the house and opened the oven. There were plenty of tacos on a cookie sheet. He counted them. Twelve tacos. Ileana only ate one. That meant he could eat five or six. But really, four was all he could ever eat. Maybe tonight he could eat five. He was hungry from all the riding around he'd done. He took out a plate and served himself. He poured on some of his mother's salsa. He liked it hot, the way she did. They were the only two people in the house who could stand that kind of heat. He added some extra grated cheese she'd left in the refrigerator. He walked into the living room and turned on the television. He sat on the floor and bit into his first taco. It was gone in three bites. He could hear his sisters in the other room. They were good together. Yolie was okay most of the time, but her boyfriend was trouble. As soon as the adults disappeared, he was always kissing her. She always wound up pushing him away. He would get mad. It scared Andrés. He hoped he wasn't coming over tonight. He wasn't supposed to come over when his mom and dad were gone. But he came over, anyway. Yolie always called him when they went out.

God, but the tacos were good. One was gone. And then another. And then another. He devoured a fourth. He knew he wouldn't be able to finish a fifth. No way. He walked back into the kitchen and looked for something to drink. There were Cokes. Not that he liked Coke. But Mando and Yolie liked it. Cream soda, that's what he liked. But his mom never bought any. He grabbed a Coke and walked out the door, into the front yard. He didn't feel like watching television. He was full, and as he looked at his bike, he was happy. He touched it, and kept touching it, and finally he decided to take it around to the backyard. Where it would be safe. And then, for no reason at all, he thought it would be nice to try a cigarette. He liked them. Once in a while, he snuck one out of his father's pocket. That's what he wanted to do tonight. Smoke a cigarette. He walked into the house. Yolie and Ileana were eating tacos in front of the television set.

"Is your boyfriend coming over tonight?"

"I don't know. He wasn't home when I called." She sounded mad. Or maybe just bored. She got that way. She was always bored. He wondered, when he got to be sixteen, if he would be bored, too.

He walked into his parents' bedroom and looked through his dad's things. He found a nearly empty pack of cigarettes in the shirt he'd been wearing. He took one out, smelled it. Breathed it in. He liked the smell. Maybe because it reminded him of his father. He wasn't so bad, his dad. He just got mad about too many things. Mando was like that, too. Mad about everything.

He took the pack of cigarettes and some matches and went out into the front yard. He sat on the front porch in the chair his father always sat in after dinner. He would sit in the chair and smoke. And sometimes have a beer—or, if it was a Friday night or a Sunday afternoon, he would sit here and smoke and have a bourbon. He would always pour the bourbon for his father.

He was about to light the cigarette when he noticed a car stopping in front of his house. It was a police car. Oh, shit, he thought, Mando's gone and done it now. He's gone and done something bad. And Dad's gonna kill him.

Two policemen got out of the car. They walked up to the front porch. "The Segovias live here?" one of them asked.

"Yeah."

"Santiago and Lilia Segovia?"

"Yeah. That's my mom and dad."

"Is there anybody at home?"

"My older sister. And my little sister, too. My older brother, he's out."

"How old is your sister, son?"

"Sixteen."

"Sixteen." He nodded. "What's your name, son?"

"Andrés."

Why was he asking his name?

"You want to tell your sister to come out here?"

"Why? What's happened? Is it Mando? Is Mando in trouble? Did something happen to Mando?"

"No, son, this isn't about your brother."

"What?"

"Go and get your sister."

He knew something was wrong. It was bad. He knew that by the way the policeman was talking to him. Serious. And he was trying to be so nice. It was bad. He walked inside and told his sister the police wanted to talk to her.

"Policeman?"

"Yes. Policeman."

"You better not be lying." She walked outside. She looked at her brother, then at the policeman. The light of the front porch was dim, and everything seemed far away.

"Are you the oldest?" one of them asked.

"Well, no. My brother Mando. But he's out. I don't know when he'll come back. Sometimes he stays out pretty late."

"Do you have any relatives you could call?"

"We don't have any relatives that live in town," she said. "We have two aunts and one uncle—but they live in California. We don't really know them."

"What about your grandma and grandpa?"

"They died. We never knew them."

He nodded.

The two policemen looked at each other.

• • •

" . . . I remember that part. I remember how they kept looking at us, then looking at each other. Finally, one of them said, 'Do your parents have any friends? Good friends?'

" 'Yeah. The Garcias.' I can't remember if I said that or if my sister said that.

" 'Where do they live?' 'Two blocks down,' I said. I think it was me who said it. They walked over to the Garcias, the two policemen, and they came back a little while later. Mrs. Garcia was crying, and she hugged us. And I knew. I knew they were dead. I don't remember who actually told us. I don't remember if that's when they explained that there had been an accident. That my father had run a red light and crashed into another car. I don't remember if that's when I heard the whole story. Maybe I didn't get all that until later. I just remember Ileana's howl. I didn't cry. Later, I remember crying—but not then." He'd finished his cigarette. "I don't have a family. That's an important thing you should know about me. My mom and dad were the first to go."

Grace nodded. "Are you okay?"

"No, I'm not. Isn't that why I'm here?"

# The World Is Born
# (in One Apocalyptic Moment)

Mister smiled at his mother as he stood at the door. He was perfect when he smiled. Young and optimistic and undamaged. She wondered, for an instant, how she could have thought that her son and Andrés Segovia looked alike. Maybe it had been the light.

Grace smiled back at him. As if he came by every day. As if nothing was wrong between them. Her dog, Mississippi, fourteen years old and legs beginning to go unsteady, looked up from where she was sitting and barked.

"Love you, too, Missah." He walked over to the dog and kissed her. "You think I look okay?"

"She's going blind. And I'd lose the tie. Looks like you're trying too hard, Mister. Who wears a tie to meet a three-year-old boy?"

"A lawyer."

"Where did I put the three years while you were in law school?"

He started to take off his tie. "You're a million laughs, Grace."

"Relax."

"Okay," he whispered.

"Just then you looked like your father."

"I miss him."

Grace nodded.

"We never talk about him."

"Do we need to?"

"Maybe I do." He took a deep breath, then another, then pushed the hair out of his eyes, something he did when he was nervous. "God, Grace, I'm a wreck. What if he doesn't like me? What if I don't pass the test?"

"This isn't a college exam, Mister. If he doesn't like you or if things aren't right, well, then, it wasn't meant to be."

"Grace, since when did you start believing in fate?"

"Day before yesterday, when I was crossing Stanton Street."

"You really are a million laughs today."

"You used to laugh when I'd say things like that."

"Did I?"

They looked at each other. *We won't fight. Not today.* "Listen, Mister, do you think this child will save you? Is that why you're doing this, because somewhere deep down you feel you need to be rescued from your life?"

"I don't need rescuing, Grace."

"I hope not, Mister. Salvation is too heavy a load for a child to carry."

The Rubios lived in the middle of a working-class neighborhood near Ascarate Park. Some of the houses were neat and well kept; some of the houses were run down and showed all the signs of careless owners who were either as worn out as the houses they lived in or too wrapped up in other pursuits. "Drugs," Grace said, "and alcohol—look what it does to us." She shook her head—and then, typically, tired of her own lectures, she changed the subject. "What do you know about the Rubios?"

"Not much. They have three grown kids, and they've adopted two other children, one is in his teens, the other is nine or so. Linda tells me they're good people. Humble. Love kids, can't stand to see them hurt. They'd adopt Vicente except they feel they're just getting too old."

Grace nodded as she stretched out to see the street sign. "It's the next street over." She knew these streets, this neighborhood, she remembered all the details, white and pink oleanders in every other yard, shirtless middle-aged men watering their front lawns, a beer in one hand, a watering hose in the other, Sam riding a bike, twelve and talkative and happy as a Saturday morning. Happy Sammy. *"You like my bike?"*

"Looks like an ordinary bike."

"It's not ordinary."

"What's so special about it?"

"I'm riding it."

"Conceited boy. I don't like conceited boys."

"Hey! Hey! Don't go. Where you going?"

"Home. And you better not follow me on your ordinary bike."

"If I told you you were pretty, would you stay?"

"You're conceited and you're a liar."

"I'm not a liar."

"Yes, you are. I don't think it's funny or nice to make fun of people. Everyone knows I'm not pretty. Everyone."

"Everyone thinks you're beautiful."

"Please, stop it, Sammy."

"I won't."

"I'm as ordinary as your bike."

"No, you're not."

"I don't like to be teased. I don't like it. And I don't like you, Sammy. I don't."

"Are you sure?"

"Of course I'm sure."

"When I grow up, I'm going to find you, Grace. And I'm going to kiss you. And you're going to kiss me back. And you're going to whisper my name—except I'll be a man and you won't call me Sammy, you'll call me Sam. You'll see. We'll kiss."

"Grace?"

"What?"

"Are you okay?"

"Your father and I grew up in this neighborhood."

"I know."

"He used to speed down the streets on his bike and tell all the girls they were pretty."

"Did he ever tell you?"

"It was a long time ago. No me acuerdo. There—is that the address?"

Mister parked in front of the house, but kept the car running. "Just one more thing, Grace. Something I forgot to mention."

"What?"

"Vicente. He's blind."


Mr. Rubio was a quiet man with a friendly smile. Fifty-eight, thin, a careful way about him. He opened the door as if their coming was both something unexpected and something completely familiar. Ordinary as their lives that were as ordinary as a thousand other Mexican families in this city full of ordinary families that were ordinary and not ordinary at all. He led them to the kitchen, where Mrs. Rubio sat looking over someone's homework. "I don't understand this," she said. "How can the children understand? How can anyone? Yo no se. Soy muy burra."

Mr. Rubio shook his head. "We weren't meant for school, vieja. Y no eres burra."

Mrs. Rubio nodded, slightly amused by her husband's endearment. Vieja. Neither she nor Mr. Rubio seemed to be at all self-conscious about letting people see them as they were. Perhaps it came with having social workers dropping in on them unexpectedly. Perhaps it came with the trappings and the freedoms of their class—they did not expect or privilege the god of privacy. *Let them come in. Let them see us.* She stuck her hand out. Grace reached back, and as their hands met, she uttered her name. "Grace Delgado."

"Esperanza Rubio."

They smiled at each other as if already they were on the same side against an ill-defined enemy. Mrs. Rubio turned her attention to Mister.

Mister smiled awkwardly, then reached out to shake her hand. "Mister Delgado."

"Entonces eres un joven muy formal?"

"No, no. My first name's Mister."

"Your name is Mister?"

"Yes." He smiled at his mother. "Blame her."

She smiled—then laughed. She enjoyed the joke. "I like it," she said. She stared at him again, then looked at Grace. "He's a beautiful son. Muy alto."

Grace nodded.

Mrs. Rubio didn't say anything else. She'd made up her mind about him. She looked at her husband, who took the signal. Like a handoff in a football game.

"He doesn't speak, your Vicente. Sometimes he points. At first we thought, pobrecito, ciego y tartamudo. But we knew he could hear, reacts to everything. Loves to touch, and he's not afraid to explore. The doctor says there's nothing wrong with his hearing and that he's very intelligent, and that there's no reason at all why he shouldn't be talking—except that maybe he hasn't been—" He looked at his wife. "¿Como dijo?"

"He said maybe Vicente hadn't been stimulated enough."

They both nodded as if they were pondering the meaning of that word, *stimulate*. Mr. Rubio studied Mister's face for a minute. "Tengo un hijo. As tall as you. Older. And your wife?"

"Her father died. She went to his funeral."

Mister Rubio made the sign of the cross and nodded. "She wants this boy?"

"We both want him."

Grace watched the expression on his face, then looked over at Mr. Rubio. He was a man who liked to nod and ask uncomplicated questions. His nods were more a conversation with himself than a means to communicate assent to whomever he happened to be talking to. He seemed satisfied enough with Mister, though he didn't seem like a man who was demanding and difficult to please. "If you lead Vicente into a room, he'll smell the air. He knows about chairs and tables, and he knows to keep away from hot stoves. I think he's burned himself before. He has a scar on one of his palms. Not a big scar—but a scar, ¿sabes? He likes baths. He knows how to wash himself. Lo dejó solo por muchas horas al pobrecito—so he's used to being alone with nothing to do. But I think he writes stories in his head."

Mrs. Rubio shook her head, "It's you who writes stories in your head."

"We all do," he said, "¿A poco no?"

He winked. And Mister had a sudden urge to hug this man who behaved as if he wanted to become everyone's grandfather. He patted Mister on the hand. "Mi'jo, you have to listen at night. Sometimes he sleep walks and he runs into things and he cries—so you have to make sure there's nothing in the house that can hurt him. Sometimes he wakes up crying in the night. He won't let Esperanza comfort him. Only me. He'll let me hold him until he feels better, then he pushes me away. Sometimes I think he wants to kiss me, but he won't. He likes to eat. But he only eats a little. He likes orange juice mixed with Coca-Cola. He likes chocolate and tacos and burritos and hamburgers—but he doesn't like French fries. He'll smell everything. And he likes to study people. He listens to their voices. Esperanza's training him to use the bathroom."

"Ya mero," Mrs. Rubio said, "Ya mero aprende. He's very smart, and he'd know by now if his mother had taught him. But she did teach him how to brush his teeth." She shrugged. "No entiendo."

"Dios la perdone. We don't know what she's been through, Esperanza."

"I don't forgive people who treat children as if they were no better than dogs." Her eyes were hard as stone for an instant.

Mr. Rubio shook his head. He looked like he was having another conversation with himself. "No sabemos," he whispered. "And anyway, her son isn't ordinary." He looked at Mister and ran his hand over the young man's hair, as if to comb it.

"My hair can't be tamed," Mister said.

The old man smiled. "Are you patient?"

"Yes."

"I think Vicente is going to need a lot," Mrs. Rubio said.

Mister nodded.

"He's watching TV with the kids. Not that he's very interested in that thing. Maybe because all he can do is listen to it. I don't know what he gets out of it, but he sits there. I think he likes the company—you know, after being alone so much." He shrugged, then stepped away, disappearing down the hall.

Mister looked at Mrs. Rubio. "Does he know—I mean, does—?"

"He doesn't know anything. Or he knows everything. Solo Dios sabe. Sometimes I think this child is very old. He hates the social worker. When he doesn't like someone, he wants them to know it. And if he likes someone, I think he gets afraid. I think. I don't know. Really, I don't know. He's not ordinary."

Mr. Rubio walked back into the kitchen, three-year-old Vicente Jesús in his arms. He put the boy down and placed his small hand on the kitchen table, so the boy would know exactly where he was. Mister studied him as his small hands searched the table. He had black eyes that were a smoky gray with clouds in them. He had thick black hair, dark skin, and dimples. "This is Mister," Mr. Rubio said. "And sitting right next to him is Mrs. Delgado. She's Mister's mother."

Vicente turned to Mr. Rubio and put his hand on his face. He nodded, then turned in Mister's direction, as if he could sense his presence. As if he knew exactly where he was sitting. He remained expressionless, and again he turned toward Mr. Rubio. "It's okay. You want to meet Mister?" The boy did not assent with a nod. But he did not reject the offer with a shake of his head, either. Mister moved closer to the boy, then bent his knees until he was eye level with him. He stuck out his hand. "Hi," he whispered. The boy awkwardly reached, gently slapping at Mister's arm. He took Mister's hand and began turning it over in his own small hand—almost as if he were sighted and looking for a promised toy that was hidden there. After he had examined Mister's hand thoroughly, he dropped it. His searching hands reached for Mister, first touching him in the chest, and then slowly, his hands moved over his neck toward his face. He felt his chin, his jawline, his ears, his lips, his nose, his eyes and cheeks and eyebrows and forehead. It was impossible to tell who was more fascinated by the experience—Mister or the boy. And after feeling the entire surface of Mister's face, the boy smiled and held Mister's face between his small hands.

And then he laughed. His laughter filled the kitchen, then the house. The entire world, it seemed, was filled with this boy's laugh. And then he let go of Mister's face, patted his right cheek—and kissed him.

"Bendito sea Dios," Mrs. Rubio whispered.

Grace saw it happen in an instant. It passed between them so quickly. Just like that—in one apocalyptic moment—simple and beautiful. A birth. But also a kind of death. Like lightning in a storm. In one flash of light, the whole desert was lit, and you could see the universe. That's what she had seen—the universe in the hands of a child feeling the face of a man. The Rubios had known it, too. It was so clear—and yet nearly impossible to comprehend. She reran the image in her mind, the boy touching Mister's face, the look in her son's eyes as the boy laughed—

and kissed him. She had seen that look in Mister's eyes a hundred times, a thousand times. When he'd looked at his father, that is the look he'd worn. And there it was again, that love, confronting her, asking her to be a part of it. She'd grown so hard the past few years, as if all the softness inside her had been worn away.

"What are you thinking, Grace?"

She was glad it was night and that Mister had his eyes on the road, glad he couldn't see the expression on her face.

"He's really very beautiful," she whispered.

"That's not what you were thinking."

"The Rubios are good people."

Mister nodded and kept driving. He didn't say anything for a long time. Finally, he glanced over at Grace. "That wasn't what you were thinking."

"The neighborhood. We used to call it 'Dizzy Land'."

"Dizzy Land?"

"On certain days, the wind would blow the smell of the sewage treatment plant right into the neighborhood. It was a joke."

"Getting nostalgic, Grace?"

"I'm too mean for that."

"You're not mean, Grace. Just a little hard, sometimes."

"I lied. Earlier. Your father told me I was pretty. I told him I was as ordinary as the bike he was riding. I told him he was a conceited boy. I told him to stop teasing me."

"And what did he say?"

"He said when he grew up, he was going to find me. And he was going to kiss me. And he said I was going to kiss him back."

"And is that the way it happened?"

"A day before my twentieth birthday, he walks up to me on the campus of the university. He looked at me and said, 'Grace? Is that you?' I hadn't seen him in five or six years. His family had moved out of the neighborhood. But I knew him. God, I'd have known him anywhere. Really, your father—" She stopped talking.

They were quiet again. Mister turned on the radio, Frankie Valli's falsetto voice melting into the voices of the Four Seasons. He imagined his mother and father, young, kissing on the campus of the university. He had seen their wedding picture. They were beautiful, both of them.

To have been that beautiful—if only for a blessed second. "Is that when he kissed you?"

"Yes."

"And you kissed him back."

"Yes. In one apocalyptic moment, I kissed him. It was like I had died."

He parked the car in his mother's driveway. Neither of them made a move. He wanted to ask her more questions, but decided against it. Grace was private. She always backed away when she started talking about herself. Sam had always said it was because she was shy. But Sam always made excuses for her. "So do you think I'll get to keep Vicente?"

"The mother's relinquishing her parental rights. You've had a home study done. You have a good lawyer. The Rubios like you—"

"Actually, I think they liked you, Grace. They only liked me because I was your son."

"That's not true."

"Yes, it is. That's okay, Grace. Being your son has made this process a whole lot easier."

"When they did your home study, how many interviews?"

"Three or four."

"When they interviewed you, and interviewed you again, and then interviewed you one more time, was I there?"

"Hell yes, you were there, Grace. The first thing out of everyone's mouth was, You're Grace Delgado's son, aren't you? That's all anyone needed to know."

"That's not true."

"Okay, it's not true."

"You don't think they'd have approved you and Liz as potential adoptive parents if I wasn't your mother?"

"Being your son didn't hurt."

"There's a little edge in your voice when you say that."

"Is there?"

"What exactly is so bad about being Grace Delgado's son?"

"Everyone thinks you're perfect."

"I'm good at what I do."

"I'm sure you are."

"Mister, I'm not responsible for what other people think—about me or you or anyone else. And why do you always have to pick a fight with me?"

"I pick fights, Grace? Me?"

"We used to get along just fine."

"We got along when I agreed with you. When I went along with what you wanted. We always got along Grace, so long as I did things your way. Which is why you can't forgive me for staying with Liz."

"She left with another man, Mister."

"And I forgave her, Grace."

"Well, I don't."

"It's not yours to forgive. And you know who you don't forgive, Grace? Me. Because I didn't do what you would've done. Well, I'm not you. And I don't do things the way you do them. That's what you don't forgive." He took a deep breath. "Are we going to sit here and fight all night, or are you going to ask me in?"

"No, Mister, I don't think I will ask you in."

# The Order of Things
# in the Universe

William Hart is surfing the Internet. You can see things you dream of doing. You can do everything but touch—and it's the touch that matters most. He is bored with virtual boys. He thinks of the preacher and wonders what his life would be like if his faith had been real—but his faith had been as virtual as the images he is staring at in the computer. Virtual faith. The Lord had not found him worthy.

He turns off his computer. He tells himself he will go out and have a glass of wine. That is what normal people do. He has envied normal people all his life. Tonight he will pretend to be one of them. He looks at his watch. It is just after five-thirty. He changes into a nicely pressed shirt. He likes to be neat when he goes out. As he walks out the door, Grace Delgado is talking to her doctor. He is looking at her files and shaking his head. "I'm sorry, Grace, I'm very sorry."

Mister is driving home. He is repeating the word *father* over and over again. He parks the truck and sits for a minute. He thinks of Grace and Sam and wonders what their lives would be like if Sam had not died. He tosses his cell phone from one hand to the other. He calls Liz. When he hears her voice, he whispers, "I love you, I love you, I love you."

There is no reason in the world why William Hart decides to pick this particular bar when there are ten or fifteen others in the same area. He randomly selects *this* bar. This one.

# Andrés Segovia.
# What a Beautiful Name

He never went to bars after work. Just El Ven Y Verme on nights he couldn't sleep. Happy hours after work never did anything for him—young people who looked more or less like him who were looking for relief from their jobs or from their lives. He had stopped looking for relief. But there he was, sitting at a bar, having a beer after work. Without even knowing why he was there, except that talking to Grace had kicked up some dust. So he didn't want to be alone. Being alone would lead to thinking. And thinking would lead to being sad. So here he was, sitting and drinking a beer, just like everyone else. Looking for relief.

As luck would have it, Al walked through the door. Al, his annoyingly friendly colleague. He was good for two things—small talk and working on computers. He sat right next to him. Of course he did. Shit.

"Well, well, if it isn't Andrés Segovia."

Andrés grinned, but said nothing.

"Do you play the guitar?"

"I've heard that joke."

"You have a girlfriend?"

"Do you?"

"You live alone?"

"Do you?"

"You like to party?"

"Do you?"

"Yes, I like to party. Yes, I live alone. And my girlfriend dumped me."

"Because you talk too much."

"This is going well." Al smiled, then laughed.

"Yeah, this is fun."

Al looked at him. "C'mon, lighten up. Let someone in."

"The house I live in is pretty crowded. No more room." Andrés finished his beer, then set the glass on the bar. "Gotta go."

"But I just got here."

"That's why I gotta go."

"C'mon. Have another."

"I don't want another. Look, Al, me and you—look, if I have another, will you promise not to fucking interview me? Can you do that?"

"I can do that."

"No, you can't. Al."

"Yes, I can. I promise—"

Just as he heard the word *can,* his eyes got caught in the face of the man who was sitting on the other side of Al. Caught, as if he'd just swallowed a fishhook. For an instant, there was no motion in the room, no breathing, no air, no sound. He knew that face, that stranger sitting next to Al, someone from the past who was almost, *almost* forgotten, those gray eyes, the scar on his thin lips, the neatly pressed shirt, the milk white skin.

"Are you okay?" He could hear Al's voice and wanted to pretend that his easy voice was the only thing in the room, but he found himself pointing at the man. "I know you."

Al looked at him, then turned to the man Andrés was pointing at.

"I fucking know you."

"I've never seen you before."

"I was twelve." There was a dryness in his throat, as if he was swallowing sand, and he knew his voice had been reduced to a whisper. His voice always changed in that way when a storm came. Sand everywhere. "I was twelve."

"I don't know what you're talking about."

"You do. Yes, you do."

"I'm sorry, but—I'm very sorry." The man shrugged and turned away. He stared into his drink.

It was him, that voice, a voice that pretended kindness, that pretended sincerity, that pretended a polite and gentle manner. *I won't hurt you. I like you. Don't you know how much I like you? Can't you see?*

"You know me."

"I'm sorry."

"You know me."

The man looked up at him, and they stared at each other, and though the man wanted to look away, he didn't, something in the young man's eyes forcing him to look. "You're mistaken. I don't know you," he whispered again, but there was nothing convincing about the way he uttered his words.

"Yes, you fucking do!" God, sometimes it was like heaven to yell. So good to clear the sand that was clogging his throat, preventing him from breathing. *Andrés Segovia. That's a beautiful name. You're named after an artist. A guitarist from Spain. Did you know that? Just come over here and sit next to me. See? Now that doesn't hurt now, does it?* "Yes, you fucking do!" He didn't feel himself leap toward the man, shoving Al to the floor, didn't feel a thing. He didn't even feel the pain in his own fists. But God, God, it was good to feel his fists pounding his face, pounding his ribs, pounding and pounding, trying to find a way, just the right spot to break through toward the freedom he'd always wanted to have, a real kind of freedom, not the kind that was just a nice word. Everything was glowing and perfect, as if the sun were setting in the room or as if he were right in the middle of a rainbow, everything bright and haloed, no shadows anywhere. God, he could live in this light forever.

"Stop, Andrés, stop! Stop!" Someone was yelling, but the voice was distant. He felt himself being pulled away from the man, but even then, it was like someone else was being pulled away, like someone else was fighting the man whose name he'd never learned, the man who *you're a beautiful boy, don't you know that?* "Andrés, stop it, fucking stop it!" He could hear a voice coming closer, Al, yes, that was him, closer now, yelling in his ear, pulling him away, but it was all so strange and none of it seemed real at all. All he could see was the man *That wasn't so bad, was it?* the man just lying there, and he wanted to hit him again and again, but he felt hands all over him and they didn't let him move, and he watched as the man slowly picked himself up, his lip and nose bleeding, and already his face was starting to swell, and they looked at each other for what seemed a long time *That wasn't so bad, was it?* Maybe the sun had set. Maybe the rainbow had lifted—because the light was gone.

# Irony and Touch

She'd always appreciated irony. So now she smiled—ironically, of course—as she thought about Richard Garza. An internist. An oncologist. He'd been young when she'd first gone to him. She'd liked that his last name was Garza. She'd liked that he spoke English as if he'd majored in it. She'd liked his face, his eyes, his warm, steady hands. She'd liked that he spoke Spanish as if he'd been raised in Mexico. She'd liked that he had olive skin and dark eyes and a Mayan nose. She'd liked that he asked questions and looked at you and didn't pretend to know everything. She'd liked that he faxed her information about health issues that affected her. She'd liked the way he touched her when it was necessary that she be touched. A good doctor. An internist. An oncologist.

Mister had insisted he wasn't the right man for the job—as if Mister knew.

"He's not a woman's doctor, Grace. Don't you need a woman's doctor?"

"A gynecologist?"

"Yeah, that."

"If I need a gynecologist, then I'm sure he'll send me to one. Besides, when I get cancer, I won't have to change doctors." She'd said that—laughing—years ago. And now, as she let that memory linger, she laughed again. She'd always appreciated irony.

The receptionist smiled at her, holding a question, but not asking it. Grace signed in her name on the sheet. The waiting room was mostly empty—too late, everyone had gone home. She thought of pouring herself a cup of coffee, despite the fact that she'd already had too much of it for one day. Coffee. Her love for it had rubbed off on Mister. When he'd opened up his coffee shop, she hadn't approved. "It's your fault, Grace. Where the hell do you think I got the idea?" She took a deep breath, took in the smell of some kind of antiseptic cleaner and coffee. Not particularly good coffee, she could tell. But it was a doctor's office, not Starbucks. She'd skip the coffee.

She sat down in the almost empty waiting room and looked at her watch. She thumbed through the stack of magazines. *People, Newsweek, Business Week.* Why couldn't doctors order magazines like the *Nation* or *Mother Jones* or *El Andar*? She put the magazines aside. There was no reason to care about them.

She studied her watch. She was early for her 5:30 appointment. She was always early. Too afraid of being late—that's what Sam had always said, "If you're late once in a while, nothing bad will happen."

"*Nothing good will happen, either, Sam. What's so great about keeping people waiting?*"

"*Important people keep other people waiting all the time.*"

"*Important people are rude.*"

"*Important people are busy.*"

"*Well, I never want to be that busy.*"

He'd kissed her. That's what he'd always done when he was losing an argument.

She'd been thinking about him lately. Could almost smell him. Too much. Too much of Sam. But it was better to think about him than think about the news Richard Garza was about to give her. She concentrated—turned her thoughts toward Mister. And then, as she whispered his name, she remembered that afternoon when he'd come home and confessed he'd gotten an F in English. He was in the eighth grade. He'd gone to his room and sat for what seemed like hours. When he came out, he said, "This is a list of books I need to read." He'd looked at her and said, "Take me to the library." And he'd read them all. And never stopped reading after that. Years later he'd confessed, "*I was getting back at you.*"

"*For what?*"

"*You loved books. So I decided to fight you.*"

"*What made you decide to stop fighting me?*"

*He'd smiled at her.* "*I figured out I'd never win.*"

Maybe he'd gotten tired of never winning. Maybe he'd gotten tired of trying to please her. *Anyway, Grace, you can't be pleased.* Isn't that what he'd accused her of? And he was more right than wrong. She'd wanted to tell him that he pleased her more than he could imagine, but that's not what she'd said to him. What had she said? She couldn't remember now.

"Grace Delgado." She looked up at the woman who called her name. She walked down the hallway into Dr. Garza's office, and for an instant she wanted to turn back. She took a deep breath. *No one can run from a storm.* She smiled back at Dr. Garza's nurse.

"How are you Grace?"

"Fine, Flora. Fine."

"How's your son?"

It comforted her, this small talk. "Oh, he's the same." She knew the routine. She got on the scale as she talked.

"I love his coffee shop."

"He works hard." She watched Flora's hands as she pushed the weights of the scale.

"Work, Grace, it saves us and it kills us." She wrote down her weight on the form. "You've lost a little weight."

"A little."

"Gain it back, damnit. You're making the rest of us look bad."

Grace laughed. She looked at the scale before she got off. Five pounds. Without even trying. Women her age didn't lose weight without trying.

As she got off the scale, she caught sight of Richard Garza. "Grace? Como estas?"

His Spanish comforted her even more than the ritual of small talk. "Encatanda de ver nacida."

He smiled. "That's nice. Didn't know you were so poetic."

She shook her head. "Something I read in a novel."

She followed him into his small office. Neither of them said a word as they settled in. He took out her file, flipped it open. She knew he was studying the files more out of nervousness than anything else. He looked at her, smiled, then quickly looked back at the files. He'd keep his head in those files all evening if she'd let him. "No matter how hard you stare at those damn things, the results won't change."

He put the file down. "Grace, I wish I had better news."

"Just don't lie to me." She had the urge to laugh. "Not that you're any good at it. Bet your wife wins all your arguments."

He bit the side of his mouth, then nodded.

She could see there were tears in his eyes. She thought more of him for their presence. Sam, he'd have cried, too.

"I wish there was—Grace, it's not the end. I think we should—"

She placed her finger on her lips, stopping him in mid-sentence. "Richard. Let's save the talk for another day."

"Grace—" She saw his lips moving, but she didn't hear a thing. She wished Sam were in the room so he could hold her.

# How Everything Comes Back

Sitting. In a car. Like a stone. Everything about his body heavy. He could sink into the earth. As he stared into his hands, he understood that they were throbbing as if they had become his heart. He rubbed them as if to rub out the tightness, but the rubbing made the hurt even worse, and so he stopped. Ice. That was what he needed, to soak his fists in ice and freeze the pain. That was the answer to this simple problem. But how did you freeze a heart, the days and weeks and months that made a life? How the hell did you freeze that?

He looked around, confused, trying to remember how he came to be in that car. He looked at the driver. Al, yes, he had been with Al in a bar, and there had been a man, yes, the man. And he'd remembered him, remembered how that man had lied to him years ago, and how the smell of him just came up through his nostrils and settled in his throat and how he'd wanted to take a bath because just smelling him made him feel dirty and—for the longest second—how he'd wanted to jump in an ocean, scrub himself raw until all of his skin was gone so he could grow a new outer shell, a shell *that man* hadn't touched, and he hated how everything came back to him in an instant almost as if it wasn't a memory at all but a moment in time he was condemned to live and relive, a scene in his life he'd have to step into over and over again until he got his lines right, but he would always get it wrong—and just then *he was in the scene again,* a boy again, young and inexperienced and stupid and inarticulate and how the man was making him do things he didn't even have a name for because he was twelve, *twelve,* and what did twelve-year-old boys know, and then he stepped out of the scene and looked at the man and he felt nothing but the purest kind of rage, an anger so distilled that it was as clear and sparkling as champagne and he knew that what the man had done to him, that man, that man who was sitting there, *there, right there*—what he'd done to him had started something inside him because something started to break then—and there he was—sitting right in front of him—and it wasn't fucking fair that he was sitting there all nice and neat and put together like some gentleman out of a maga-zine, like some reproduction of a suave movie star, wasn't fucking fair when he, he, Andrés Segovia, was all broken into pieces and he knew that he had this one chance to do something, to say something, to try, to try, to act, to not be passive because he wasn't twelve anymore and for the longest time he hadn't had a say in how he got to live his life, and it wasn't even a conscious decision, no, it wasn't like that, it wasn't as if he had decided *I will hurt this man, I will hurt him* but God, it had felt good to say *I hate your fucking guts for what you did to me, I hate, I hate,* God, it was good to say that even if he was saying it with his fists, but even then, he knew that it was his fists that were in control and not him, not his mind, not his heart, and maybe it wasn't possible for a guy like him to be led by his heart because something was broken, so god-damned broken that nothing could fix it, not all the saints in all the churches in Mexico, not the Virgin herself, not his mother if she came back to life, nothing, nothing in the large, ugly, violent, fucking world, nothing in its past or in its future could fix what was broken.

He looked at his fists and opened his hands and he felt his hands so tight that he couldn't really open them, not really.

"You could've killed him."

He looked in Al's direction.

"Yeah," he whispered.

"Why did—" Al didn't finish his question, already knowing that Andrés didn't have an answer, and knowing, too, that his disapproval did not matter in the least. "You're lucky he didn't call the cops."

"Yeah. Lucky."

"He could've called them, you know?"

"Yeah."

"Except he knew something, didn't he?"

Andrés shrugged. He didn't want to talk about this, not with Al, not with anybody. "Look, doesn't matter."

"Maybe not. But you could've killed that guy."

"Maybe I should've."

"Yeah, well. What did he do to you?"

"It's a long story."

"Yeah, well, it must've been something really bad. No cops, that's what he kept saying. No cops. There he was, all beat up to hell, and all he kept saying was *don't call the cops.* So you must have something on him that's really bad."

Al nodded and kept nodding, and then they were both quiet for a long time. Al seemed to be just driving, not really going anywhere. Andrés didn't care. He just sat. He wanted to sleep. That's what he wanted to do.

Finally Al whispered something, and Andrés looked over at him.

"Where do you live?"

"Sunset Heights. On Prospect."

Al nodded, then drove. It wasn't far.

Andrés nodded off. Couldn't have been long, though he felt he had been sleeping for hours. He opened his eyes and found they were on his street. He pointed. "Over there." Al slowed down, then stopped in front of the run-down apartments. "Nice place," he said, then laughed. Not a convincing laugh.

"Yeah," Andrés whispered. "I'm tired." He reached for the door, but found he couldn't turn the handle. He winced.

"Here. Wait." Al got out of the car and opened the door for him.

Andrés got out, and for an instant he felt like an old man. "You treat your dates really good," he said, then laughed. He didn't notice if Al laughed or not. And then he couldn't stop laughing, but he knew, really, that he was crying. And then he didn't want to stop, so he just let himself cry, and he didn't give a damn about anything. Not anything.

"Can you get in all right?" He heard Al's voice, but he couldn't speak, he just couldn't. He didn't remember if Al had helped him into his apartment. He didn't remember if it was Al who'd placed his fists in a bowl of ice. He had a fragment of Al inside him, of Al whispering something to him. Maybe it didn't happen. Did it matter how he got there?

The pain in his fists, maybe that was the only thing that was real. Him, sitting there in his chair in his small apartment, his fists stuck in the ice. He looked around the room, then pushed himself onto the bed, and he was so tired, but he couldn't sleep, so he forced himself to get up and he forced himself to find the bottle of bourbon that he almost dropped because he couldn't really hold it very well because his hands were so numb, but he managed to swallow some of that liquor that soothed him like a lullaby, and he liked how it burned, and he drank some more, and then he felt better, sure, better, so he stumbled to his bed and fell on it.

Before he went out, he swore he smelled his brother, Mando. And maybe he heard him, too. He wasn't calling for him, not for him. He was calling his sister, searching for her, but it was useless because she was lost forever. And then, all of a sudden, his father was saying something to him, and his mother, too, and he could feel and smell his father's hot to-bacco breath on his neck as he rode a bicycle through a lost city. He was dreaming them—all of them—but even in his dreams he was pushing them all away, pushing them toward a place so dark that not even the angel of God would bother to search the face of it to find them.

# Studying the Light

Mister woke thinking of his mother. Of his father. Of Vicente. Of Liz. Why did people think they could be alone? Everyone you loved or hated or touched or who made you tremble or bruised you—they were always there, ready to enter and take over the room. It didn't matter at all if you opened the door or not. They came rushing in. They knew the way, knew how to make themselves at home. His entire house was crowded when he woke. It was like waking up in the middle of a cocktail party, all the guests staring at you—waiting for you to say something intelligent, something interesting, something they didn't know.

He pictured Sam holding Vicente. He pictured himself standing next to Grace, both of them watching Sam and Vicente. He pictured himself and Liz holding Vicente, and then Grace standing next to them—and then Grace disappearing. It occurred to him that the problem with Grace had almost nothing to do with him—or with Liz, for that matter. Grace was looking for Sam. She'd been doing that ever since he died. And she'd never find him again. And despite her iron will, and her refusal to fall into a permanent state of self-pity, she had become nothing more than Sam's widow. Sam's widow, who spent her free time trying to fix people who were so broken they were beyond fixing. But she was trying. So why couldn't he just give her a break? "For the same reason she can't give Liz a break." The sound of his own voice startled him. The anger in it. Where had that come from, he who had been the happiest of boys?

He walked into the kitchen and stared at the light in the room. Always staring at the light. He'd learned that from Grace and Sam. Sometimes, when he was a boy, they would all study the light in the room. Sam would sketch something, and he would watch, trying to see what Sam saw, trying to understand what he was learning, wanting to be the light, wanting to be the pencil Sam was holding.

They would all three sit in the light.

All morning.

Not saying a word.

Because you didn't need words when you were sitting in the light. Things weren't that simple anymore. Not even empty rooms filled with light. Because rooms were always full, full of memories and voices and people who were either dead or impossible to love.

# Good Things, Bad Things,
# Good Things

Mister?"

"Yeah."

"It's hard to hear you. Is it your cell?"

"The place is packed. Just a second. I'm walking toward the office." Mister looked at Sara and pointed at the cash register. He spun his finger in the air, his signal for "Take over." He walked past the morning coffee crowd and made his way down the hall, cell phone in hand. "Keep talking, I'm heading toward my office."

"I just wanted to go over a few things with you."

He took the keys out of his pocket and opened the door to his office as he talked. "Few things?" He pushed the door open. "Good things, Linda?" He switched on the light and shut the door.

"Hard things—but good. They're good things, Mister."

He sat down at his mostly clean desk. Bad things, good things, bad things, good things. But good things. Hard things, good things, bad things. "Okay, I can talk in peace, now. Busy day." He tried to keep calm. There was news. About the boy. Good things, good things—

"Mister? Mister? Are you there?"

"Oh, sorry. I must've zoned out for a second. Something gone wrong?"

"No. Nothing's gone wrong. I was talking to the Rubios, and they thought maybe you could bring Vicente home with you for a visit."

"A visit?"

"You know, just a small visit, so he can get to know you and Liz. Is she back yet?"

"No. Day after tomorrow."

"We'll wait till she gets back."

"Good." He stared at the blank wall in front of him. Why was it blank? "I'm a little scared here, Linda."

"That's normal."

"Liz isn't scared."

"Women are stronger."

He liked the sound of her laughter over the phone. "Like I needed you to tell me that."

"He might be scared, too," she said.

"But he might not be."

"No, he might not be, Mister."

"Still, it's a good idea that he come over and check out his new home."

"The Rubios think so?"

"Yes, and they're right. As soon as Liz gets back, we'll arrange it."

He felt his heart beating. Just like when he came back from a four-mile run. Like that. But there was something in her voice. Something else. Sure there was.

"Mister?"

"I'm here."

"You okay?"

"I'm fine. But you wanted to talk to me about something else."

"Yes."

"What?"

Linda was choosing her words, he could tell. She was careful around judges and clients. Probably careful with her husband, too. "She wants to meet you."

For an instant, Mister felt off balance. And then he suddenly understood who *she* was.

"Mister?"

"What about Liz?"

"She doesn't want to meet Liz."

"Why not?"

"She said she wanted to meet the father. That's all she said."

*Father,* he thought. "When?"

"You don't sound too sure. You don't have to meet her, you know. She's relinquished her parental rights."

"She did it. She really did it?"

"Yeah. This morning. The ink's not even dry yet."

God, his heart could be loud sometimes, loud as if it had its own will, its own logic, its own voice. "Really?" He could feel his voice cracking.

"Yes, really. He's not hers anymore."

"It's not that simple, is it, Linda?"

"No, it isn't. But legally—" She stopped as if she was composing her next line in her head. Never rash. Too much rashness in the world. He liked her. "He's free to be adopted. That's all I'm saying."

"Free to be adopted," he repeated. A sad kind of freedom. Or maybe not sad at all. Or maybe not a freedom. Or—

"Listen, Mister?"

"What?"

"Are you sure you're okay?"

"I'm fine."

"Look, you're not required to meet her. A lot of people would counsel against it."

"What would you counsel, Linda?"

"There isn't a right answer here."

"There probably is a right answer. We just don't know what it is."

"I like you, Mister."

"I like you, too, Linda." For an instant he wished he smoked. As if a cigarette was capable of aiding the situation. In old movies, cigarettes always helped. Helped to keep men from screaming—kept them from becoming violent, kept them silent and serene and self-composed.

"Mister, you've left me again."

"Sorry. When would she like to meet?"

"Soon as possible. I think she just wants to put all this behind her. And I think, if you decided to meet her, it would help. Her, I mean. But let me just say this, okay, let me—look, frankly I'm more worried about you and Vicente. Her life—look, I don't mean to be crass, but it's not your job to worry about her. Are you getting this? Mister? Are you there?"

"I'm here. I'm just stewing. I can be a pretty good stewer." He could be. He got that from Grace.

"I know."

He felt his heart still racing. He pictured him and Liz walking down the street. He pictured Vicente walking next to them, reaching out. His heart was quieting. He was holding Vicente's hand. It was morning. They were in a park, and he was studying the look on Liz's face as she kissed their son. In the light.


Yes, that's what he'd said. Yes. He'd see her. So he'd know what she was like, what she talked like, what she looked like, so he could look into her eyes and maybe see her son, the one she was giving away. Maybe she would be holding something in her voice, a clue that would tell him why she was letting go of this boy, this son of hers, this beautiful boy. She was letting him go. It was like letting go of the sky. But it was more complicated than that. Somewhere along the line something had gotten broken, something in the way the world handled her had damaged her heart or her mind or her body. That's the way it happened—the breaking world was careless and cruel, and it took bodies and molded them in its own image, bodies and hearts and minds all shattered and the million shards were scattered everywhere on the globe, and this woman and her son, hell, they were just the smallest piece of the picture. And it couldn't be fixed. That's why she was giving him away. Some people, they were broken, broken all to hell—and they still kept their kids, kept them and fed them and twisted them and bent them and made them into grotesques, little images of themselves. She was putting a stop to it. Wasn't that the right thing to do? Wasn't it? *It stops here. The whole damn thing stops here.* There was something good in her. That's why she was letting go of the sky.

# The Angel of God

Mister is standing at a window, watching Vicente's birth mother disappear down the street.

William Hart is waking up—dizzy—his head spinning like a top. He tries to remember where he is. Yes, in an apartment, yes, a new apartment, and yes, he remembers now, he'd gone out for a drink, and that man had attacked him, hit him and hit him, but there was something familiar—and somehow he'd driven home, though he can't remember—and yes, he's remembering cleaning himself up, a loose tooth, blood on his cut lip, the taste of it mixing with the scotch he was drinking to dull the pain. Yes, he remembers now.

The light is disappearing from the room. *I have to get the light back in the room. Yes, that is what I have to do.* He stumbles to the mirror and sees his face, swollen and ashen. He feels a throbbing in his head, then feels his knees buckle under him. He struggles to stand, but the pain owns him now. He crawls to the door, manages to turn the knob. He pulls himself out into the hallway *have to scream for help* but he has lost his voice. He lies there, the world spinning—then it slows—then it stops. Everything is so calm. He can hear his own breathing. He looks toward heaven and thinks he sees a boy. *That boy, that beautiful boy. That Angel. He's come for me. The angel of God has come for me at last.*

The darkness is gone. He smiles at the light hovering over him. *Pray for us, Oh Holy Mother of God, that we may be made worthy of the promises of Christ.* Everything is so clear. The light has been looking for him all his life. Finally, it has found him.

# What's a Mother?

A neutral setting, safe, nice office, small, three comfortable chairs that looked like they belonged in someone's living room, chairs that said, *Sit, sit, this is home,* but it wasn't, wasn't home at all. A small conference table with expensive wooden chairs around it, the tables and chairs shining in the light of the room as if they were posing, beckoning an artist to paint their fleeting perfection in a still life. Things. Things were more perfect than people. Even the Diego Rivera reproduction was perfect—an original to the casual observer who'd never heard of the artist. Real. Sure.

He stared at his trembling hands. He sat on the chair, then got up and paced the room, then sat back down. He'd come early. Because he was nervous, because he didn't want to keep anyone waiting, because he hated to be late. For an instant, he hated Grace for teaching him there was virtue in being prompt. So un-Mexican. *What are we, gringos, Grace?*

He looked toward the door as it opened and smiled at Linda.

"You look nervous."

"Yes," he whispered.

"Don't be."

He smiled at her. Nervous.

"She's in the waiting room. She said she'd like to talk to you alone. I think—"

"I'll be all right."

She smiled back at him as she left the room. He took a breath. He ran his fingers through his hair, combing himself. His hair was always out of place, like he hadn't combed it after his shower, like he'd been up all night, like there was a fire burning inside and his hair was nothing but flames, a sure sign that he was about to self-immolate. God, he'd never even learned to comb his own hair. How in the hell did he think he could manage a three-year-old boy? A three-year-old boy who didn't talk. A three-year-old boy who—She walked into the room. She sat down on one of the comfortable chairs, one of the chairs that said *sit*. She pulled out a cigarette from her purse, looked for an ashtray, saw one on a small table next to a vase of fake daisies permanently in bloom. She walked across the small room, took the ashtray, and set it down on the conference table. She lit her cigarette, Marlboro Lights, same brand he'd smoked once. She kept looking at him, saying nothing, studying him. Just like he was studying her. She took another drag from her cigarette, then blew the smoke out slowly through her nose. "Want one?"

He shook his head, then decided to sit at the table. Across from her.

"You ever smoke?"

"Yeah."

"I don't trust ex-smokers."

"How come?"

"They're superior. They look at smokers and think, *Dumbass, don't you know that shit will kill you? Don't you care enough to quit? Aren't you strong enough? Smart enough?* No, I don't trust ex-smokers. They're like fucking prostitutes who've found God. You know, people who find God, they like to shove him down other people's throats. God's worst enemies, if you want to know what I fucking think." She looked at him. It was his turn. To say something.

"It wasn't that hard for me to quit. I never made a good addict."

He couldn't tell if she was sneering at him or if she laughed because she thought it was an interesting thing to say. Not that what he said was interesting or charming or intelligent.

She stared at her polished nails. "I spend more time making sure my nails are perfect than I spend on my kid."

Mister didn't say anything. He just looked at her.

"You don't like me."

"I don't know you."

"You think you do."

"No, I don't."

"I'm a dancer. Course, you know that, don't you?"

"You don't look like a dancer."

"You think I don't look like a dancer because I'm wearing a nice dress and I'm all made up? I could be a secretary. I could be a CPA. I could be a lawyer. I could be a professor. To look at me, I could be any one of those things, couldn't I?"

"Yes."

"No, I fucking couldn't. You should see me with my clothes off as I dance on a stage for a man who imagines that all I want is to feel him inside me. I make him believe that. Not that it's all that hard. Most men want to fucking believe every woman wants a piece of him."

"Not all men."

"That's right. I forgot. You're better than those men. Most of them still smoke."

"I'm not better. I just have a different idea of having a good time."

She laughed. He didn't wonder any more what the laugh meant. "So what do you do for kicks—mow the lawn?"

He looked at her. She was beautiful. Perfect. Except she was angry and callous and her voice, which might have been as beautiful as her face, was petulant and angry and shrill and it made her seem almost grotesque. Maybe it had to be that way. Maybe she'd had to fight for everything, so the fight in her was permanent—like a scar or an immutable tattoo. Mister looked at her and tried to smile. No harm in that, no harm in rolling with the punches. "Well, mowing the lawn—that's a pretty good time. Some days, I get high on the fumes of freshly cut grass."

"That kind of humor doesn't appeal to me."

Mister nodded. "Can I ask you a question?"

"Ask away."

"Why did you want to meet me?"

"What? You want me to be nicer? Did you want me to love you? To fall on my knees? To thank you endlessly?"

"I didn't want anything. I came because you asked."

"Don't do things for people just because they want you to. You can get into some real trouble by doing shit like that." She touched the bottom of her lip. "I just wanted to see what you were like." She studied him, not caring that the way she was looking at him made him uncomfortable. "What's it like to be looked at like that?" She smiled. "Does it feel good?"

"Great," Mister whispered. This is not what he wanted.

"You're just the kind of guy I thought you'd be." She put out her cigarette.

"What kind of guy is that?"

"Soft. Decent." She got up to leave. "Educated Mexican who looks and acts more American than most gringos. And you speak Spanish."

"Sure."

"And you're married to a gringa, aren't you?"

"Yeah."

"Well, that makes us even, I guess. Vicente's father's a gringo, too. Makes it all nice and neat." She took out another cigarette. "Bet you out-gringo the gringos. And I bet you speak a good Spanish, not that fucking in-between crap the rest of us speak."

Mister said nothing. She was throwing stones. Why not? He kept his mouth shut.

She looked him over, from top to bottom. "He'll be fine. That's all I wanted to know." She looked at him. "Look, whatever your name is—"

"My name's—"

"Skip it. I never ask my clients' names. And I never kiss them on the lips. I don't believe in pretending to be intimate. The only thing you need to know about me is that I shouldn't be a mother. I knew that before anybody ever told me. You think I need the moral police to tell me that? You think I need a judge? You think I need a caseworker who doesn't know his head from his ass?" She lit another cigarette. She looked at the chair, then decided to stand. It was better. To stand. She was leaving, anyway. "It's not hard to give him up," she whispered. "I'll just screw him up. I don't need anyone to fucking tell me that." She turned toward the door.

"You know what decent is?" Mister hadn't planned on talking—but sometimes his own words took him by surprise.

She turned around and stared at him. She ignored his question, like she hadn't heard it, like she'd only heard a sound and was turning around to see what it was, maybe a rat in the room or a cockroach or a moth flinging itself against a lightbulb. She looked right past him, never said a word. But she looked at him like she wanted to remember. Was that it? It was as if she wanted to put her anger away, if only for one damned, irrepeatable, blessed second. She was beautiful and perfect in that one second. "He talks," she said.

"What?"

"He talks. When he wants to."

Mister nodded his head. "Thanks."

"For what?"

She reached for the doorknob.

"Do you know what decent is?"

"A woman like me doesn't know anything about decent." This time, she didn't bother to face him.

"Decent is letting go a son because you love him."

"Don't break my heart," she said. Almost soft, but the rage coming back into her voice when she said *heart*—like a wave that is about to crest and crash against the shore. "Don't break my fucking heart."

He could still smell her as he sat in the office. Nothing cheap about her perfume, nothing cheap about the way she dressed or the way she talked. She had her own kind of unmistakable grace. Somewhere along the line, something really bad. Really bad. Maybe she'd already figured out her own end and was powerless to change the way the story ended. She'd die of the drugs she took, in an empty room, in an empty house, the stench of wanting men all around her. She would die of a liver disease from too much booze, her eyes yellow, her teeth rotting, her skin gray as a winter sky. She would die of something a man gave her. Or she would die of a bullet piercing her heart, a man shooting her for reasons that were inane and banal and insipid and predictable. Or maybe she'd catch herself one day, and shake herself awake and say, *enough*. She would put on her clothes in the middle of a show, kick some dirty middle-aged man right in the teeth as she walked off the stage, and she would just stop, stop dancing, stop doing the drugs, stop with the whole damn thing, reform herself, live the straight and narrow life in a humble, ordered house. Maybe she would marry. A man who would know and understand what she was. Maybe she would have another child—one day another child—and she would be a mother, a good mother, a mother who loved and cared and nursed and fed and clothed and sang lullabies. Or maybe she would simply live alone, in mourning, and wake up every day screaming Vicente's name. She would go to bed each night, exhausted, whispering his name. The scar of his memory killing her. Slowly. Every day.

Mister shook his head. He walked to the window and looked down at the street. He could see her walking away on the sidewalk. She could have been a secretary. She could have been a CPA. She could have been a lawyer. For an instant she seemed to be nothing more than light.

And then she just disappeared.

He felt a hand on his back. He turned and smiled at Linda. "It was okay," he whispered. He looked away from her and looked out at the day, the sidewalk hot with the heat of the desert sun. He saw himself, a boy. Barefoot. Walking on the sidewalk. That's what he'd done on summer days when he was a boy—he'd walk out of his house barefoot, and see how far he could walk before he could no longer stand the heat of the cement. Once it had been so hot that he'd gotten blisters on the bottoms of his feet. Grace had rubbed ointment on them and lectured him. He'd kissed her—and kissed her and kissed her. Kisses had come so easily to him. When he was nine.

"What are you looking for out there?"

"History."

"What?"

"Nothing." He smiled and turned away from the window.

# Dead, You Say?

William Hart is moaning on the hallway floor of his apartment, his eyes fluttering. The frightened neighbor calls 911. When a detective comes, he shakes his head as he looks down at the body. "Looks like someone beat the holy hell out of this guy. Mother of God. I'd say this guy bled to death—of internal injuries. I've seen this kind of thing before. Poor bastard should've gone for help."

The detective begins to look. He likes to look. That's what makes him good at what he does. In Hart's apartment there is a new computer, the boxes still in the room. He finds a napkin in the man's shirt pockets, from a bar. The Tap. He discovers his ID and the business card of a parole officer whose name he recognizes. He gives the parole officer a call, "You know this guy, this William Hart?"

"Registered sex offender, just moved into town."

"What's he into?"

"Little boys."

"Why'd they let him out?"

"Can't keep 'em in forever. Has an appointment this afternoon."

"He won't be keeping it."

The detective drives to the Tap. He talks to the bartender. The bartender says, Yes, some guy, he starts beating the holy shit out of this other guy—took four guys to pull him off. But the other guy, the one who's beat up all to hell, he kept on saying, No cops, no cops. Beat up all to shit, dead, you say? Holy fuck. And no, he'd never seen the guy, but he was talking to another guy—Al Mendoza—a regular. He works with computers at the university. Yeah, sure, next time I'll call the cops.

# Grace at Work

Grace sat—nearly motionless—at her desk. The light streaming in through her large window was the same light that was streaming in through the waiting room where Mister was pacing back and forth. Four blocks from each other, but each of them alone. For the moment. But it was Grace who was calmer and more focused. It was Grace who had the capacity to let go of her preoccupations and turn her attention to the things that calmed her. The light—that could always calm her. After forty-nine years of living in the desert, she had become an aficionado of light and how it reshaped the surfaces of her environment—how it fell on the desert floor, how it hit the rooms in her house, how her garden glowed at certain moments of the day, how it softened her office. That had been the very reason why she'd chosen this space for her work. She had wanted something that faced the morning. She had passed up a bigger office because it faced west, and she'd decided to spare herself the punishing light of the afternoon. Unforgiving, that light.

Just as Mister looked into the face of that woman who was as angry as she was beautiful, the name *Andrés Segovia* entered Grace's thoughts. Her first two appointments had canceled, had left her with some unexpected time on her hands. Unwelcome, this extra, unexpected time. So she willed herself to think of Andrés Segovia—think of him and spare herself from thinking of her breasts, which looked like they were fine and healthy but weren't, spare herself from thinking of her body, the decay, the final test that was coming. She spared herself of thinking of useless radiation and treatments and medications, and she spared herself of thinking about Richard Garza, the way he'd kissed her hand, and what she'd seen in his eyes in that endless second of recognition. She spared herself from recalling the bitter tears that fell like a summer storm as she walked back to her car. Hadn't the tears stopped? Hadn't the trembling ceased? Hadn't she known that she wouldn't cry again, not ever again, because that's not how she was going to spend her final months or years or however long it was that she had left? Hadn't she decided right then that whatever was coming, she would take it and hold it and not be afraid, and make no room in her house for self-pity? So wasn't the worst over now? Hadn't it hit like a hurricane, like one of those storms Andrés Segovia had written about—hadn't it hit and left her standing? And what was her death, anyway, after Sam's?

She thumbed through the two files on her desk. She shook her head at her morning cancellations. That was a way of putting it. Cancellations. One of them was back in juvenile hall for attempted rape. *Women take things from me they do, you don't know what they've taken. What? What do they take? Tell me.* The other was in the hospital, car wreck, drunk driving and *No, no I don't have an alcohol problem—I swear I don't.* Women problems, alcohol problems, symptoms of diseases that were as deeply embedded and alive as the cancer in her breasts. If they could only get at something in themselves to hold onto. Didn't they all have some kind of safety belt to protect them from all their wrecks? If only they could reach that place. *If only* was a place, a desert where her clients were condemned to wander like La Llorona wandering the river, looking for her drowned children.

Six months' worth of counseling, and nothing to show for it. Her fault, mama's fault, whose fault, daddy's fault, their fault, personal responsibility, yeah their fault. *Their fault.* Wasn't it? Wasn't it that heartbreakingly simple? Too bad they weren't corporations—then they could legally be people without having to be responsible for the havoc they caused. A shame that they were just flesh-and-blood people. Too damned bad. Damnit! These two were smart, both of them. She shook her head and put their files back in their place. In case they ever came back. She made a mental note to go see the girl in the hospital. But not to accuse. She'd had enough of that.

# Andrés Was Crying

All Mendoza had to tell them. Not that he liked to squeal. Even on a guy like Andrés Segovia, who was permanently pissed off at the world. When they came up to him, the two detectives, he knew why they were there. He had a bad feeling. He hated this shit. So they asked. And he gave them Andrés Segovia's name. He answered all their questions. "And you took him home? What did he say?"

"Nothing, he said nothing."

"Nothing?"

"He was crying."

"Crying?"

"Yeah, crying. That man hurt him."

"Yeah? How?"

"I don't know."

"Then how do you know?"

"I just do. Andrés was crying. He's not the kind of guy who does that sort of thing."

"Kills people with his fists, or cries?"

"He doesn't do any of those things."

"Well, a few nights ago, he did both."

# Timing and Order in the Universe

At two-forty-five in the afternoon, Grace is listening to a boy talking about his father. *He hates me. He says I'm only doing this to get back at him. I told him being gay was a helluva way to get back at your father. I told him if I wanted to get back at him, I'd have sold his golf clubs.* He smiles. The other kids in the group laugh. *He loves his golf clubs more than he loves me.*

Andrés Segovia is sitting in a room—two detectives are asking him questions. *Why'd you kill him, son? What did he do to you? When did you meet him? Tell us. We could book you. We have enough evidence. A whole shitload of people saw you beat that man with your fists. And he's dead. We got a coroner's report that points the finger at you, son. We could take it to the DA right now. Right now.* Andrés Segovia looks up at them. *So what's stopping you?*

Dave is in court. The jury is in. The head juror says *guilty.* He utters the word with respect. His client bows his head and whispers, *bastards.* In his heart, Dave knows his client is guilty. He is wealthy and has paid him top dollar. Top dollar, and today they've lost. Guilty. He whispers to his client that they will appeal. And anyway, he thinks, they will suspend the sentence—or most of it. White-collar crime. No one was killed. It was only a few bucks that were stolen. Only money.

Mister is talking to Liz on the phone. "She hated me, Liz." *She's just angry, Mister. Maybe she has a right to be.*

"When do we stop being angry, Liz?"

# Dave? Grace?

H er afternoon was relatively easy. Some paperwork, some reports, a phone call from a lawyer that informed her that another
one of her clients would not be returning. *Back in jail. Sorry.*
But would she like to have lunch? No thanks. *I eat lunch with the birds
at San Jacinto Plaza.* She actually told him that. She hated men who
mixed business with pleasure. Especially the ones who were married.
Call your wife.

She had one last session with a client who was moving to Chicago.
And she had a two-hour session with eight gay and lesbian high school
students. She'd never cared for group sessions—but these kids, she liked
them. They were smart and wonderful and a lot less damaged than most
of the people she saw. Survivors, all of them. She let them talk. That's
mostly what they needed. She asked questions. No crisis among them
this week. A discussion of who was worse, ignorant teachers or homo-
phobic bullies. "Those are our choices?" one of them asked. They all
laughed. Not a hard afternoon. She was grateful for that.

At five-thirty, she wrote out an informal report on her first session
with Andrés. He was self-possessed and well spoken. He was clearly the
man who'd written the words on those creased pages she had in her possession. It was also clear to her that he was the man who'd held four
policemen at bay.

She looked around the room. It still smelled slightly of smoke, despite the fact that she'd opened her window and lit a cinnamon candle.
Not that she cared all that much.

There was a knock at the door. Before she could say, *come in,* the door opened. She found herself staring at the smiling man in the doorway. It had been a long time since she'd seen that smile. She remembered the first time she laid eyes on him. No smiles, not back then.

"Dave? What are you doing here?" She got up from her chair and offered him a friendly, if formal hug. He kissed her on the cheek. Too much cologne. She preferred cigarette smoke.

"How are you, Grace?"

"You didn't really come here to ask me how I am."

"No. But that doesn't mean the question was insincere."

"I suppose not."

"God, Grace. You're still the same."

"Older."

"Probably tougher."

"Probably. Life does that. You haven't changed much, either. Well, your wardrobe's changed."

"Why does everyone pay so much attention to what I wear?"

"Because you want them to."

"You know, you should've gone all the way and become an analyst."

"I'm fine where I am."

He shook his head. "How come you never remarried, Grace?"

"How do you know I didn't?"

"Did you?"

He was wearing that familiar grin. "I didn't want to remarry."

"You're really very beautiful."

She ignored his compliment. "What about you? What are you, in your mid-to-late thirties?"

"So?"

"You're really very beautiful."

"You're mocking me."

"You had it coming."

He laughed. "Women keep breaking up with me."

"For no reason, I suppose."

"You sound like my mother."

"How is she?"

"Never better—since my father died."

"That's a mean thing to say."

"Yes. But it's also true."

"You came here about Andrés, didn't you?"

"You don't change, do you, Grace? Always getting to the heart of the matter."

"You should know better than to show up at my doorstep and expect me to discuss a client."

"Grace—"

"What?"

"He's been arrested."

"What?"

"They say he killed a man. With his fists."

"I don't—" She stopped in the middle of her sentence. "You think he did it?"

"It doesn't matter what I think."

"It does matter. It always does."

"I think there are extenuating circumstances. That matters, too."

"So you're taking his case?"

"Absolutely."

"I suppose you came to tell me he won't be seeing me again."

"Of course he will."

"From jail."

"I can work that out. He needs to see you, Grace. He needs to see someone."

She nodded. "But I don't work for you, Dave. I work for him."

"Meaning?"

"What he says stays in this room."

"If he tells the story once, it hurts less the second time."

"You think that if he tells me what happened, then he'll tell you, too."

"Something like that."

"I hope you're right."

"You'll keep seeing him, then?"

"I'll wait to hear from you."

She looked at him. There was an urgency in his voice. She nodded, remembering. How old had he been when he'd come to her office? Hard and lost and still a boy. No, a man who had not yet learned to be a man.

"Are you all right?"

"Yes, I'm fine."

"You don't seem fine."

"Don't I?"

"I think I can tell."

"You haven't seen me in years."

"He's important to you, isn't he?"

"Yes."

"Why?"

"It's a long story, Grace."

"Listening to long stories is what I do for a living." The faint smell of cigarettes kept nagging at her senses. And then suddenly the odor of stale cigarettes gave way to the smell of gardenias and agave. Gardenias and sage and agave. How very strange.

"Grace?"

She looked at him. His eyes seemed to be holding a question. Such a handsome man in that particular white-boy-all-American-no-one-can-hurt-me kind of way. Except that he had been hurt. But he was fine now. More or less. And she was overcome with a strong sense of affection for him. But he seemed so far in that instant.

"Grace?"

Everything was fading, all the lights in the room going out. And the sun, too. It was all so odd, as if the whole world had stepped out, run away from her—left her. Alone. In the dark. God. Everything was as black as Andrés Segovia's eyes.

"Grace? Grace?" She heard a voice. It was Dave. The boy who had been sent to her by his desperate mother, *will you see our boy? Will you talk to him?* Dave, who had refused to speak to her for sessions and sessions until one day he did nothing but cry, for hours. And she'd held him all that time, and she remembered how her blouse had been soaked in his tears. Dave. She stared in the direction of the voice. Dave?

"Grace? Are you all right?"

She reached out her hand in the darkness.

# The Light

Mister surveyed the room. Another sleepless night. He rose from the bed and walked into the kitchen in the dark. He poured himself a glass of water. He put the glass to his lips and drank. He thought of rain. He thought of his father, how he told him that they were children of a God who died bleeding and crying out for water. Tonight, he felt as thirsty as his father's God.

He walked into Vicente's room. Newly painted. Yellow and orange. Liz had painted it—just in case. "A happy room," she said. So many unhappy rooms in the world. So many unhappy boys. "The child who lives here is going to be very happy." Liz was so certain. That was their job now, to make a boy happy. That's what Sam had done for him—make him happy. And Grace, too. *Grace, I don't want to fight anymore.*

He pressed his face to the wall and breathed in the smell. Vicente would be able to smell the fresh paint. He would take him in his arms and describe the room, and find a way to translate the morning light and how it made the room look like it was a candle burning in a dark room. *Vicente, this is the room where we reinvent ourselves.*

He sat there. In the darkness. He tried to picture his father, what he had looked like, the color of his eyes. He tried to picture Vicente. He tried to understand what it meant to see.

In the morning, he woke and found he was lying on the floor, the light flooding the room. He smiled. Liz was coming home today. He would make love to her. They would bring Vicente home for his first visit. God, the light in the room was beautiful.

# The Dark

They take you to a room in the downtown station. They ask you questions. You decide you do not want to answer them. They ask you if you want a lawyer, and you tell them you do not want a lawyer—but you do not want to answer questions, either. They play the game. You know what role you have been assigned. Finally, you get tired of them. You say only, "Do what you have to do." And so they say they have enough to charge you with. You nod. They are angry because you will not sign anything. You will not say anything. It will be better if you sign a confession—that is what they say. But you know it is not your job to sign anything, no, not your job to help them.

They lead you to a small room and search you. They pat you down, look in your shoes, make you take off your belt. They put handcuffs on you. An officer walks you outside, his hand on your shoulder. Another officer accompanies him—he has your file with him.

They run into a fellow officer, and you are there on the sidewalk, in handcuffs, and you hang your head, and you tell yourself that no one is looking at you. You tell yourself you are invisible, and you keep your head bowed. You do not look up, not for any reason. You think they will talk forever—they are laughing and joking and making small talk— and finally, they haul you into the jail. You are relieved you are no longer on public display. And again, you are searched. They make you take off your belt and your shoes, again. It does not matter that they have done this already. They do it again. And then they put you in a holding cell. It is not too busy, so you do not have to wait in the holding cell for hours, and you are glad you do not have to wait there for very long because there is a drunk man in the cell and he is shouting out his life story, shouting it out to anyone who will listen *My father was the biggest bastard since Hitler.* . . . And they call your name and lead you out of the holding cell and they photograph you, and the photograph goes directly into a computer. And then they fingerprint you on a new machine. Like your picture, your fingerprints go directly into the computer. So, now everything about you is in the computer. And you will be in that computer until the day you die.

And then, like magic, a bracelet with your photograph appears out of a printer hooked up to the computer, and the officer puts it on your wrist, and they lead you to a counter where they will classify you. They ask you questions—they want to know if you are violent or gay or if you have a disease or if you are crazy. You say you are not gay and that you have no diseases and that you are not crazy—but you also tell them that you feel like hurting them. And then you smile. But they do not smile back. And then they take you to a woman dressed in dark blue who gives you a TB test. You do not have to wait in line for a long time. She smiles at you, and you wonder why. And you smile back at her—and you wonder why.

And after that, they take you to another counter. A large young black man with a smile as large as his hands gives you a basket full of things for your new life: an orange jumper, a blanket, a towel, cheap canvas tennis shoes, a cheap toothbrush, a bar of soap, toilet paper. As he turns the basket over to you, he points to a place—a special cell—and you are forced to take a shower. And you feel dirty as you shower, and you shiver as you dry yourself because you are cold and you feel more naked than you have ever felt—and then you put on your new clothes. And they take away everything you walked in with—your wallet, your watch, your belt, your jeans, your shirt, your shoes, the receipt and the quarters you had in your pockets.

And you belong to them.

*"I'll get you out of here as soon as you're arraigned."*
*"I did it, Dave."*
*"It's not that simple. You didn't mean it."*

*"How do you know?"*

It was strange that Dave was more concerned than he was. Maybe he'd care tomorrow. Maybe he'd never care about anything again. He was glad he didn't have a cellmate. Tomorrow, they would move him in with other men—but not tonight. Tonight he was alone, and he was glad. Maybe, when he got to prison, he'd beat on someone, anyone who needed beating, anyone. And they'd put him in solitary. And he'd work to stay there. So he wouldn't ever have to see another human being.

He looked around his cell. It was odd, that the room was so familiar. Dark and not really dirty. But not clean. How could a place like this be clean when it was filled with men like him? He thought of Mando. This is what he'd seen. Maybe this was even the same cell. So here he was, following in his brother's footsteps. This was their fate. This is where they belonged. Here—in an exile they had more than earned.

He thought of the courtyard in Juárez, and that house they'd lived in. It wasn't so very different than this place. He whispered the word *emancipation*. He knew the word from somewhere in his past, but he was too tired and too numb to search his memory. And, anyway, it was a word that had no meaning.

In the morning, there wouldn't be any sun in this room. *I'll get you out, I promise. I promise, Andrés.*

"It's all right, Dave. Some people prefer the dark. Don't you know that by now?"

# Part Two

*Let the stars of night be dark;*
*We will hope for light, but have none,*
*May we never see the eyelids of the morning.*

—JOB 3:9

# Normalcy and Apocalypse

The sun flickers. Like a flame hit by a sudden gust of wind. Like the lights of a bomb shelter during an air raid. Even the sun flickers. That's what she kept telling herself. A gust, a bomb, a small explosion. Then the disruption passed—everything calm again. Everything returning to normalcy. Except that she felt herself trembling. Except she knew that this was the beginning. It was her body that had flickered.

Had it begun this way for Sam? There were so many things he never told her in the end. Maybe that's the way it was with people who entered the liminal space between living and dying. When you stepped into that space, you stopped telling people things. You started letting go of the need for words the same way you began to let go your need for food, your need for water, your need for anything associated with the strange and capricious hungers of the body. Perhaps, when you began edging toward death, you began to fill yourself with silence.

She had sifted through all these theories when Sam was dying. She had clung to them when she should've been clinging to Sam. Hadn't that been her sin? She'd lost her nerve, had told herself it didn't matter, all those wordless hours that hovered over them like vultures over a carcass. But it had always mattered. That she'd let him suffer alone. Because she didn't want to know, because it hurt too much, and hurt even more pretending it didn't hurt at all. Because she hadn't really believed he was mortal, her Sam. She had expected him to find a way to live, just like he'd found a way to fix everything in their house, the plumbing, the electricity, the foundation, the drawer that was always sticking. Oh, God, she had, she'd expected him to live. And so she'd waited in dumb silence. But now she had another chance. She wouldn't make the same mistake. God damn her if she made the same mistake again with Mister. But how could she find a way to pull him close when she'd pushed him away without even knowing she was doing it? *You're more interested in being right than in being kind—that's your problem, Grace.* He'd tossed the accusation at her like he was lobbing a hand grenade. She steadied herself against the desk. The momentary darkness lifting. See how easy it is to stop yourself from trembling. She didn't even know she'd whispered Mister's name.

"I think I should call a doctor."

"I'm all right, Dave. I'm fine now."

"Are you?"

"Of course."

"What happened?"

"I'm just tired."

"I don't think so."

"You don't have a medical degree, Dave."

*You're a lawyer, not a fucking doctor.* He smiled to himself. First Andrés. Now Grace. Maybe he was more predictable than he thought. He bit his lip. "Grace—"

"I just came back from a visit to the doctor. I know exactly what is and what is not wrong with me."

"Well, now you sound like the Grace I know and love."

"I had no idea you had so much affection for me."

"I had a crush on you from the very beginning."

"You were a boy."

"I was twenty-one."

"And looked sixteen. And stop looking at me like that."

"Like what?"

"With that grave look of concern. It's a little too earnest."

"Earnest?"

"I thought lawyers were supposed to be a little more calculating. A little more callous."

"Oh, I can be callous. And according to the women I date, I can be calculating as hell."

"That's reassuring."

"Did anybody ever tell you that you were very pushy?"

"The word *very* is so unnecessary, Dave." Her hands had stopped trembling. She felt strong again. "I'm fine. There's that look again. You must be very good at eliciting sympathy from juries."

"It's all for a good cause." He was studying her. "Mister? Isn't that your son?"

"Yes. Why do you ask."

"You whispered his name."

"Did I? He must be on my mind."

"Would you like to have dinner? I mean, if you're well enough?"

"How about a drink?"

"You think that's a good idea?"

"I think it's an excellent idea. Then you can tell me about how you've managed to become such a successful lawyer and be such a dismal failure with women."

"I find the word *dismal* as unnecessary as you find the word *very*. This isn't going to be a counseling session, is it, Grace?"

"No. I've done all I can do on that count."

"I'm functional."

"That was my great accomplishment with you?"

"You can't take all the blame, Grace." He could be shy. She could see that shyness in his smile. She'd seen that side of him—such a long time ago.

"You're studying me, Grace. What are you discovering?"

"A man who works too hard. It's making you old."

"It's not the work. Gringos don't age well—didn't anybody ever tell you that?"

She almost laughed. "That rumor was started by other gringos."

"To what purpose?"

"To elicit sympathy."

He laughed softly. "I like you, Grace."

"You are, aren't you?"

"What?"

"Sincere. You are. You take the world home with you every night."

"Not the world."

"Maybe just Andrés Segovia."

"It's complicated, Grace."

"Would I need a law degree to understand the whole situation?"

"Well, no, not a law degree."

"Explain it to me, then, this complicated thing. I'm relatively intelligent."

"Relatively?"

"I thought by now you understood I didn't like the word *very.*"

He really did like her. He couldn't help himself. He wanted to ask her how many men had fallen in love with her. But she wasn't the kind of woman who let you ask that question.

"I want you to keep seeing him."

"He's in jail."

"He'll be out. Of course, right now, he doesn't want to see me. He doesn't want to see anyone. But I'll get him out one way or another."

"You sound so sure."

"I know the system."

"They'll let him out with that temper?"

"They can't keep you in jail for having a temper."

"He got into a fight with four policemen—went at them, resisted arrest, was intoxicated—"

"Why do you think I got him out so easily? The cops beat the crap out of him. The charges were dropped altogether."

"Does Andrés know that?"

"I haven't gotten around to telling him."

"Why not?"

"If he knew the charges had been dropped, then maybe he'd stop seeing you."

"So the state isn't going to reimburse me?" She smiled.

He smiled back. "Nope."

They stayed that way for a moment.

"You see—my man Andrés had no record."

"But I thought—"

"He was a juvenile. And he was cleared of all charges."

"Was it murder?"

"*He didn't kill anyone, Grace.*" His face turned to stone in an instant, then turned back to flesh. "He doesn't have a record."

"None that they can use against him in a court of law. Isn't that what you mean?"

"I can get him out on a PR bond, Grace—and I'm going to."

"That simple, huh?"

"Nothing is that simple. Getting him out on bail until his trial is the easy part." He studied Grace's face. "You think he belongs in jail?"

"I don't know."

"Well, I know. They won't set a trial date for him for another six to nine months. Maybe longer. That's too long for him. He doesn't deserve that."

He was upset. She could see that. "Maybe letting him out isn't the best thing."

"The best thing, Grace?" He reached for a cigarette, then put it in his mouth.

"Grace, it's not too late for him. He's got something, Grace, this kid."

She nodded. "Yes, I think he has. But—"

"No buts."

"Why do you care so much?"

"Because, like Andrés, I've got something, too." He broke into a smile, then laughed. The cigarette falling out of his mouth. He laughed. "You want to know a secret?"

"That's what I do for a living—listen to everyone's secrets."

He picked his cigarette off the floor. "Remember that accident?"

"How could I forget?"

"The people I killed—"

"You'd think at this point, you'd stop talking about that car accident as if you'd killed them with a gun. You want to play the dictionary game?"

"The one where you push the dictionary across the table and have me read—"

"The word is *accident*."

"Grace, that couple—they were Andrés Segovia's parents."

# Grace and Morning Mass

The world could be as small as it was cruel. She wondered at God sometimes, his schemes, his plans, his plots, his sense of order. Maybe he was just like the Bible—beautiful and overwritten and redundant and badly in need of editing.

Andrés Segovia and Dave Duncan. It made so much sense, now. Not that anything made any sense.

She walked outside in her bare feet and searched her garden. The century plant would bloom this year. It hadn't bloomed since Mister was a boy. The green stalk was reaching out to the morning sky. She shut her eyes. She vaguely remembered her dream and wondered if it had come to her last night. Perhaps it had. She couldn't tell—a sure sign that the dream was too familiar.

She took a deep breath and tried to clear her head of everything that was in it—Andrés and Dave, her work, the lingering smell of cigarettes on her skin.

At morning mass, she prayed for Mister. It wasn't fair to put him off. She would have to tell him about her conversation with her doctor. She wondered if it would be easier to tell him if they got along better. Not that getting along had anything to do with the measure of his love. She knew that Mister loved her, knew he would do anything for her—*if she asked*. That was the problem; she had always hated to ask. Would telling him that she had cancer sound too much like she was begging for affection?

She tried to picture his face as she told him. He was, in the end, a good man. Every ounce Sam's son. He would object to her early exit. He would demand to know why she was already waving the white flag of surrender so soon after the first shot had been fired. *Already you are counting yourself among the dead. Already you are casting yourself into the bin of history. How can you let death take you so easily? Even the roots of a dying tree cling to the soil that it loves.* That is what he would say.

He would object to the way she had decided to handle the whole matter. He would demand that she go to another doctor, and assure her that the other doctor would expose the ineptitude of the first. He would debate and object and look for loopholes. He would argue with her—and for once, the argument would be a beautiful thing.

He would shout at the unfairness and randomness of this whole scenario. He would say that they were in this fight together. He would say that together they could defeat anything. Cancer was a puny, unworthy enemy. They were sure to conquer it. He would urge and cajole and beg her to roll up her sleeves, *Get in the ring Grace, fight, damnit!* He would volunteer to be her manager, her trainer, her anything she needed him to be. And they would be close again, mother and son—closer than they had ever been.

But how would she phrase it? There had to be an aesthetic to this. She would tell him over a glass of wine. *Your mother is dying.* Or she would invite him and Liz to dinner—finally she would have them both over to her house. And over dessert and a cup of coffee, she would tell them. Delicately. Matter-of-factly. Flippantly. Serenely, like a nun taking final vows. *I'm going to buy the farm. I'm going on a long cruise over the river Styx. I'm going to see Sam. I'm leaving the country and I'm packing light. And really, the air's gotten so bad that I've decided I simply don't want to breathe anymore. I'm going to see Sam. God is honking out front. Look, Mister, I have cancer. I'm going to see Sam. I'm walking into the light. I'm going to see Sam. I'm going to see Sam. I'm going to see Sam.* No matter what she said, it would sound horrible and trite and sad and self-pitying and theatrical and sincere and moving and melodramatic and manipulative all at the same time. Sam had been right. Words were a great poverty when confronted with the pleasures and the limitations of the body. A touch said more. A look. But she knew her son better than to communicate the news with a look—though she had no doubt she was capable of communicating just about anything without the use of words. But hadn't she and Sam taught Mister that words were salvific? Hadn't they used that exact phrase? It was too late to tell him that they had been mistaken. He had learned his lessons well, their Mister.

*I thank you for this son of mine, whom I know and do not know.* She looked up at Jesus. She stared at the flames of the sacred heart. *My heart is hard. Can you make it tender?*

# Do You Love Me, Mister?

As Mister waited for the light to turn green, he noticed his mother's car parked on the street. She was attending morning mass. She'd taken up the habit when Sam died. It was as if he'd handed her some kind of torch. Grace carried it without complaint, but he knew that the ritual of morning mass was a duty for her in a way that it had never been for Sam. He smiled to himself. He pictured Grace sitting in one of the pews at the cathedral, the light shining through the stained-glass windows and falling on her, half hidden in the shadows of the morning light. He held her image for an instant, then tore himself away from his mental photograph at the sound of a car honking at him from behind. He stepped on the gas, then looked at his watch.

He'd get to the airport just in time.

When their eyes met, Mister laughed, then reached for her. It was such a natural thing to do, reach for her, hold her, smell her. They held on to each other, tight, as if they'd lost each other, then found each other again.

"You should've let me go with you," he whispered.

"Believe me, you didn't want to be there, Mister."

They both shrugged, then took each other by the hand. "My mother will never change," she said.

"Don't feel so bad. Grace will never change either."

"It's not the same, Mister. Grace may be difficult, but she's not crazy and she's not a bad person. Not really. But my mom, hell she's crazy *and* bad *and* difficult. And, Mister, *she's just plain mean.*" She shook her head. "God, it's good to be home."


Liz pushed her empty plate away. "God, you're a good cook."

"Sam and Grace—they taught me."

Liz nodded, kissed Mister on the cheek, then refilled her glass of wine. "Honey, why do you insist on fighting a civil war with your mother?"

"It's pretty bloodless as wars go."

"Then why don't you stop?"

"You knew why, Liz. You know damn well why."

"The she-doesn't-like-my-wife reason. That reason? I'm tired of being used as an excuse for what's wrong between you and Grace."

Mister emptied what was left of the bottle of wine into his glass. "What are you talking about? Has she ever been nice to you?"

"As a matter of fact, she *is* nice to me, when we happen to run into each other. She's always nice, and she's decent enough to make conversation. She tries, Mister."

"That's because she's not the kind of person to make a scene. She's civil to people—so what?"

"You know, Mister, I should've let you come to Dad's funeral. I should've let you see my mother in action. Maybe you'd get some perspective on—"

"I can't believe this. Has she ever had us over to her house, Liz?"

"Have we ever invited her to *our* house, Mister?"

"She knows she's welcome any time."

"You're more like Grace than you think."

"I'm not the bad guy here, Liz."

"What makes you so sure it's Grace that's the bad guy?"

"Since when are you a member of her fan club?"

"You took me back, Mister, without any questions."

He nodded, then smirked, then kissed her. "That was my prerogative."

"I told Grace to go fuck herself—did I ever tell you that?"

"No. But—"

"But what?"

"She was standing up for you. You, Mister. *Her son.* And I told her to go fuck herself. I had a few choice words for you, too, as I recall."

"Things are different, now, Liz. And believe me, if Grace was around, we'd have problems again."

"I don't believe that. I don't think you believe it, either. You know what I think? I think it's easier for you to keep Grace mostly out of your life. I think it's easier for you to tell yourself how difficult she is." Liz looked away from him. "You wished that she had died instead of Sam. You don't know what to do with that, do you?"

"What?"

"I think we should try being a family, Mister."

"I can't believe you said that."

"It's true, isn't it?"

"What happened when you were with your family, Liz? What happened?" He shook his head and gulped down his glass of wine.

"You always drink too fast when you get mad."

"Do I?" He got up, picked another bottle of wine, pretended to read the label, and opened it. He poured himself a glass and stared at it. "Liz, remember when you left me?"

"Yes."

He took his eyes off the glass of wine and looked at Liz. "She made it very clear to me what she felt about you."

"You know something, Mister, that woman Grace didn't like me very much. And that's exactly how I wanted it. I wanted her to hate me. I made sure she'd hate me."

"And now you've just fucking changed your mind."

"It's not that simple."

"Okay, let's just all be friends again. Just snap your fingers and say, Grace, just kidding, c'mon over."

"Stop it, Mister."

"I'm sorry," he whispered. He poured down his glass of wine. "You're right, I do drink fast when I get mad." He stared at the empty glass. "Grace has a long memory."

"Apparently, we do, too, Mister."

"I don't want to fight."

"We're not going to fight. Look, Mister, my family—my family is screwed up beyond repair. I mean it. It breaks my fucking heart to say it. You haven't a clue, Mister. And that's just it. I see that Grace is crazy about you. I can't believe you don't see that. It's what scared me about her—that I could see how much she loved you. God, that scared me, Mister. Scared me to hell and back again."

"What makes you think we can just become an instant family?"

"I didn't say that. I just think we should try."

"It's not going to work."

"Do you love me, Mister?"

"Of course I love you."

"We'll be bringing Vicente home with us soon. We'll have a son. It won't be easy. He'll have a lot of special needs. And wouldn't it be lovely to have Grace around him?"

"What is this fantasy you're having, Liz?"

"Do you love Grace?"

Mister bit his lip, then turned away.

"Mister?"

"Of course I love her."

"I think we should have her over to dinner. If you don't call her, then I will."

# Timing and Order in the Universe

Had she had the time to glance at the morning paper before she walked out the door, Grace would have found herself staring at a picture of a smiling eight-year-old girl who is showing off a new dress. Purple. With ruffles. She has dark skin and a small flat nose. She is obviously a descendant of the Mayans. She is also an obviously happy child. Perhaps the photograph is just a fiction, a predictable construct. Nothing original about the image of innocence in the smile of a child. But the image does its work.

The girl—according to the story—was taken from a grocery store the previous evening. Her mother had been picking out fresh apples at the Food Basket on the corner of Kerby and Mesa. When the woman turned around, an apple in hand, her daughter was gone. According to the story, a videotape revealed a man taking the girl by the hand. The camera watched passively as they disappeared out the door.

The authorities speak of hope. But she is already dead and lying in an alley. The man who took and molested and strangled her is lying in bed. He is sleeping peacefully. In a few days, the police will arrest him. He will confess. The public will be spared the details.

The girl will not be found until the late afternoon. But this morning, hope lives in the heart of a mother.

Grace has no knowledge of this. Nor does Andrés Segovia.

This sad and disgusting and familiar story of a missing girl has saved Andrés from appearing in the newspaper. The television stations, having gotten wind of a strange tale of a man who died in a hallway of an apartment complex, were already considering leading off the broadcast with the story. The bartender had already been taped by two of the three major stations. "This guy just starts beating on him," the bartender explains, his hands waving in the air for emphasis. But the story was quickly abandoned in the rush to post pictures of a little girl on the screen. Today, the girl's story is the only story in the city.

Andrés will be spared.

Dave shoves aside the headlines in the newspaper in disgust and turns his attention to Andrés Segovia's case. In the afternoon, he will be taken before a magistrate. A cattle call, no doubt. He will ask that his client be allowed to post bail. The DA will argue that his client is dangerous, that he is a flight risk. He will argue that the police found his client at work. The DA will argue that the only reason Andrés did not run was because he did not know the man he had beaten at a bar was dead. "Exactly," he will say, "because the man walked away—and according to witnesses and the police report, the man himself begged that the police not be called." He goes over his presentation in his head. There is work to be done. He will be ready. He will leave nothing to chance. He is a good lawyer—a very good lawyer. He knows the system. He is not ashamed of what he does. Today he will use his knowledge to help free a man from jail. He believes Grace will help save him. He wants to believe this. He tells himself, As long as he keeps going to see Grace. Then repeats it. As long as he keeps going to see Grace.

Mister opens the newspaper and shakes with anger. He does not know the girl. But he cannot help himself. He does not understand why a man would do this. He tells himself that his anger is useless—but anger has its own logic, has little to do with utilitarian philosophies. He puts the newspaper down, and when Liz takes the newspaper in her hands, he tells her softly, "Don't." He takes her hand and leads her to the shower. They undress each other, wash each other, kiss each other. For a moment, they are clean. But they cannot stand under the shower forever.

Mister will think of Vicente all day long. *When he comes to us, I will not let anything happen to him. I will not.*

Andrés, dressed in the bright orange jumper befitting a man of his status, is trying not to hope. Hope has never brought him anything but despair. He thinks of the man. His name was William Hart. He had a name. He is not sorry for what he did. Was William Hart sorry for what *he* did? To him? To a hundred other boys? Was he sorry? He could tell them that he did not mean to kill him. This may be a true statement. It may also be a false one.

He does not want to see Dave. Dave's eyes are always full of hope. He wants to hate him—because he is a lawyer, because he is a gringo, because the world is his fucking playground. Because, again, he has power over his life. May God damn him and his life and his hope and his power. *When I see him today, I will show him my ugly heart. I'm not fucking sorry.*

# What's a Mother?

Grace clenched her fists around the steering wheel, then loosened them. She repeated the motion several times. Gripped it—then let it go. Gripped it—then let it go. "Come to dinner, Grace." Just when she was about to have them over, they beat her to it. Hell, it wasn't a contest. And would she tell them? Would she mention the word *cancer*?

When I was nursing him, he'd look up at me, his dark eyes filled with gratitude. Even as an infant, he had a grateful heart.

He learned to say *gracias* and my name on the same day—when he was two. For weeks everything was "Gracias" and "Grace."

When he was three, he'd wake each day at dawn and sneak into our room. He'd climb the rocking chair and watch us sleep. When we would stir, he'd laugh, climb down from that old chair, and jump into our bed.

I thought Sam's heart would break from all that morning joy.

When bad dreams came, he'd wake up screaming. Sam and I would rush into the room. We'd kiss him back to sleep.

When he was eight, I thought we'd lost him. Wandering the neighborhood, looking for his best friend's dog. Sam and I spent hours walking up and down the streets, until we found him. "We can't find the dog!" he wailed. We didn't have the heart to lecture him. Sam woke each hour that night. To make sure he was safe.

The doctor says that there's a chance—that I should fight. I don't mind dying. I don't know why. I am a mystery to myself. I wonder. Should I fight? And if I lose?

I pray, in death, a mother's heart forgets the son she loved.

Memory is the cruelest of God's gifts.

After a few times around the block, she parked the car, got out, and walked up to the front door. She rang the doorbell, and felt the beating of her heart. Like a wave about to crash into the rocky shoreline.

Mister opened the door and stood there, smiling. Nervous, she could tell, but happy. He looked so young and unscarred, and she wanted him always to look like that. She had the urge to reach over and touch him, this man, this beautiful man who was her son. He had her eyes. And Sam's face. And Sam's smirk. "Hi, Grace," he said as if the words were the first lines of a poem.

She reached over and kissed him on the cheek.

They smiled at each other.

"That was very sweet, Grace."

"It was, wasn't it?" she said. And then they laughed. And then he led her into his house.

The house was neat. Rows of books on one wall, a painting on the other, wood floors that shone. "Nothing's out of place," she said. "Except for me."

"That's not true, Grace." She looked up and found herself staring at Liz. She wasn't the wild-haired girl she'd remembered. She was wearing a deep blue sundress and makeup. She was much prettier than she'd remembered. Of course, she hadn't seen her in over a year—and that had been outside a movie theater in the dark. Grace smiled.

"What will you have to drink, Grace?"

"I want to say scotch. But I'll settle for a glass of red wine."

"Why settle? On the rocks or neat?"

"On the rocks."

Mister watched his wife and his mother. They both seemed to be in such perfect control. He was the only one in the room who didn't know what the hell to do or say. He watched Liz leave the room, then heard the sound of ice on glass.

"Who does the cleaning, you or Liz?"

"We both do."

"That's nice. Sam was always something of a slob."

"Yes, I remember. I must take after you in that category."

"Or maybe I just pushed you too hard."

Mister nodded. "Well, I came out just the way you and Sam raised me."

"You're not a stalk of corn." She sat down on the rocker she'd given him as a gift when he'd first moved out of the house.

"I'm a Sam-Grace hybrid. An All-American, left-of-center bilingual Mexican who's addicted to coffee, work—and to reading poetry in Spanish."

"You sound schizophrenic."

"He is, Grace. He really is."

They both watched Liz as she walked into the room, carrying a small tray with three drinks and a small bowl full of salted peanuts. She lowered the tray and let Grace take her drink, then turned to Mister, who took his glass of wine. She set the tray down, took her drink, then placed the peanuts in the middle of the table. Her movements were steady and sure, a woman completely at home in her own skin.

Grace took a sip from her scotch and nodded. She noticed Mister was watching her. She looked at him. "Still watching people, huh?"

Liz nodded.

Mister shrugged. "I used to watch you when I was a kid. You'd be sitting at the table or in the yard, and you'd be lost in thought. And I knew you were thinking about one of the people who'd come to you. They were written all over you. Sometimes I felt like our house was inhabited by all the people you were counseling. You know, I was a greedy little kid. I was a sponge for affection."

"I never thought of you as being that needy, Mister."

"I kept my own counsel."

"You still do." Liz's comment wasn't so much an accusation as a statement of fact. Mister said something to her, and she laughed. And she said something else. Only Grace didn't hear them—or didn't really care what they'd said. She only knew that she'd stayed away too long, and she felt stupid and silly, and as she took a sip of scotch she thought it was all very good, the scotch and Mister and Liz and her. It had all been a big joke, the kind that took a long time to tell, the kind that went on and on forever, and when you got to the punch line, the joke was all on you. All this time she'd thought they were strangers—but they weren't. She wanted to break out laughing. She looked at Liz. *Isn't she pretty? Isn't she?*

She could hear them in the kitchen, knew that they were tasting his red sauce, deciding what it needed. But it would be perfect. Good cook, her son. She heard the pop of a cork. She noticed a piece of folk art hanging on the wall. It was a painting on clay, the figures almost childlike. God's torso broke through the clouds in the sky. He was the center of all light as he held a small globe in his hand. The earth, his toy. And in the garden, the usual suspects, a serpent wrapped around a tree, smiling in that particularly sinister way that serpents in the garden always smiled. A bitten apple littered the otherwise pristine lawn. Adam and Eve were walking away from the garden, both of them covering themselves with a cloth. Eve wore her requisite and predictable look of guilt, and there was a look of pain and stunned disbelief on Adam's face.

Grace was mesmerized by the drama. It dawned on her that death was a kind of exile. Exile from your body, from your home, from the garden you had maintained for a lifetime.

Mister walked into the room and saw his mother studying his new piece. "You like it?"

She nodded. "It's very good. The serpent's always in the shadows."

"Yes, he is. Serpents are sneaky. They're—Grace?"

"What?"

"You're smelling something?"

"Yes, I am. Fresh paint."

"Oh, I've been painting Vicente's room."

"You really are going to make me a grandmother."

"Yes. He's beautiful, isn't he, Grace?"

"He is, Mister. He's very beautiful."

"I'm happy, Grace."

Grace nodded. He *was* happy, and he *was* more graceful and at home with himself in that instant than she had ever remembered. And she didn't feel sick. And she didn't feel like dying. And she wondered if she had enough fight to send the cancer away.

# What About the Sky?

Dave sat there—calmly—in the stale and dark and suffocating booth of the county jail. Andrés didn't smile, didn't wave, looked at him, then looked at the ceiling, then studied the booth, then looked back at Dave. Dave waved, then picked up the phone. Andrés sat down on the chair—slowly—then picked up his phone. "I didn't call you."

"You've been sitting in here for three nights."

"Just three nights?"

"You've turned me away four times."

"Just four times?"

"You like it in here?"

"Sure."

"Don't be an asshole."

"Maybe I am one. Maybe I've always been one."

"I'm getting you out."

"Maybe I don't want out."

"You have five thousand dollars?"

"What kind of question is that?"

"Do you?"

"I was saving for a new car."

"New car will have to wait. Get yourself a bicycle."

*Bicycle? Done that. Been there.* He pounded the table lightly. "They'll let me out for five grand?"

"Bail bondsman takes care of the rest."

"What do I have to do?"

"Put up ten percent. Sign a document. Show up twice a week to see your bondsman."

"For how long?"

"Until the trial."

"How long?"

"Nine months—maybe longer."

"Speedy trial, huh?"

"That's as speedy as it gets."

"So they'd let me out?"

"The law says that bail ought not to be an instrument of oppression."

"That's the sweetest thing I've ever heard."

"You don't fool me, Andrés. You're not as hard as you make out."

"Sure, Dave." God, he wanted a cigarette. He could have one—if he got out. That was the only way to get a cigarette.

"I'll get you out."

"Garcia's fired me by now."

"There are other jobs."

"Sure. What do I put in the blank that says, *Have you ever been arrested?*"

"Why don't you go back to school?"

"Oh, there's a thought. And how the fuck am I going to live? How the fuck am I going to make the rent? Jail is rent-free, Dave."

"What about the sky, Andrés? This is the most fucking sunless place I've ever been in."

"I get sun time. Every day."

"Yeah, for a whole hour. They cut your days into hours, here."

"How do you cut your days, Dave?"

"I like my prison better than yours."

"Who wouldn't?"

"I'm not about to let you stay in here." Dave looked at his watch. "Look, I have a hearing. I've arranged for you to see Grace this afternoon."

"What?"

# Order and Timing in the Universe

Mister has spent the day hiking in the desert. He has been hiking for more than five hours. He has brought plenty of water and a hat and the right clothes. He has hiked through the desert many times and has learned to respect the sun and the landscape. As he walks, he is thinking of Grace. He remembers how she used to watch him when he was a boy. That is how he knew she loved him. Often, when she looked at him, he felt as though he was the most startling and beautiful creature in the world. He understood her looks to be the way she touched. The thought suddenly occurs to him that she'd looked a little thin, and much more vulnerable than she had ever appeared. He keeps running her image over in his mind. Something is wrong. He cannot let go of that thought. Something is wrong with Grace.

He is glad to be spending the morning in the desert. He loves the sand, the plants that fight each day to live. He loves the light.

Grace is sitting in a jury room in the courthouse. A judge has lent her the room for the afternoon—to have a session with Andrés. As she sits in the small room, she smiles at the thought of Dave. He has managed to put the session together. She knows it was not an easy thing to accomplish. She admires people who do not understand the word *no*. She looks at her watch, then gets up from where she is sitting and looks out the window. She has a perfect view of Juárez and the pale blue summer sky. She cannot remember a time when she did not feel small in the presence of the sky.

Rosemary Hart Benson buried her brother today in Lafayette,

Louisiana. The funeral was small: herself and her husband, two frail aunts, and her next-door neighbor. He'd had no friends. The priest kept the mass simple and short. Her eulogy was two sentences long: "He was a sinner in need of salvation. Let us pray that God is even more generous than the most generous of us can dare imagine." She did not call her children. She did not want them to attend her brother's funeral. Though she did not fully understand how her brother came to be killed in El Paso, Texas, she did not doubt that he had a hand in his own murder. She does not hate him—but neither does she forgive him for his crimes. She has always been aware of his proclivities, and when her twin sons were born, she never allowed him near them. Once, when they were nine, he showed up and offered to take them to an afternoon movie. "Of course," she said. "We'll all go." She was relieved when he moved to Texas.

She is in her kitchen, recounting all these memories. She is cooking a small dinner for her aunts. She feels numb and relieved. She does not understand why life is like this. She breaks down and sobs. Her husband finds her in the kitchen and holds her.

Dave is sitting in his office. He is thinking of William Hart. He decides he will send an investigator to talk to his sister in Louisiana. Or perhaps he will call her himself. He knows William Hart was a sick man. He is looking at his criminal record. The whole thing turns his stomach. He decides, yet again, that in his profession, he must take the low road to morality. I will put the victim on trial. *That is what I'll do. What I have to do.*

Andrés is walking down a tunnel. The tunnel leads from the basement of the jail into the courthouse. As he walks down the tunnel, he feels the shackles on his ankles. They have spared him the handcuffs. "We just don't want you to run, that's all." The officer smiles. Not a bad sort. He is doing his job. He walks down the tunnel, and it seems to go deeper and deeper into the earth as he walks. Maybe he is walking toward hell.

# There Might Have Been Thunder

I don't remember very much about the funeral. But I could conjure some details. I could write the scene and make the whole story sound convincing as hell. I could. Sure. Why not? It was windy and threatening to rain. There might have been thunder. And I was wearing a white shirt."

"A white shirt?" Grace's voice was casually challenging. Not really impatient. Just a hint of *This isn't necessary*. Just a hint of *Let's not waste time*.

"But I *was* wearing a white shirt."

"Okay."

He liked that little hint of challenge in her voice. He had decided he liked her. Still, he had to test her. An easy test. He wanted her to pass. Because she was beautiful. Because there was lightning in her eyes. Because he was tired of being careful, and tired of his dreams and tired of everything about his life. And maybe there was still a chance for him. That's what Dave told him. *There's still a chance, buddy, so don't fuck it up.* And there she was, sitting in front of him, in this jury room in the county courthouse, a jailer just outside the room. Dave had gone to a lot of trouble.

*"Why skip a session?"*

*"Because I killed someone, Dave."*

*"Grace will see you—there's an empty jury room a judge has lent us. She'll see you."*

*"I don't want to talk about what happened."*

*"Then don't. Talk about something else. Something else. Start from the beginning"*

*"From the fucking beginning?"*

There she was—unafraid. Completely in charge—as if this were her office. She *was* different. When the jailer told her he had to be in the room, she had not argued with him. She had merely looked at him with an authority that made him shrink. "No," she said. "That won't be necessary." He did not even bother to argue with her. None of the others had looked like her or acted like her—or talked like her. Not the foster mothers, not the social workers, not the counselors who always wanted him to talk. Not that she tried to be different, and not that she tried to be beautiful. That was the thing. She didn't paint her nails, and her makeup was barely visible, and there was only a hint of perfume. "Well, it wasn't threatening to rain. But it *was* windy. My dad liked white shirts." That was the truth. And he *had* probably worn a white shirt at the funeral. Certainly Mando had worn one. *That,* he *did* remember.

"Is it important, that your dad liked white shirts?"

"No. Probably not. My mother bought them for him. No, it's not important. It's just something I remember."

"What else do you remember?"

"My sisters took turns crying. I could hear them. I think that's all I really heard, the sounds of their tears. They stayed in their room. They didn't want to come out. They howled like one of those winds that won't quit, those winds that make you afraid. But I thought that maybe it wasn't such a bad thing, because they were washing themselves. They were trying to get rid of the hurt. That's what I thought—but still, I just couldn't stand it. All day. And in the night, too. I couldn't stand it, all that crying. I couldn't. And Mando couldn't stand it, either. He would go into their room, talk to them, talk and talk. And listening to his voice, they would stop. But when he would leave the room, they would start again. And Mando, he would stomp out the door, hells and damns and fucks on his lips. . . ."

• • •

Santo Niño de Atocha Catholic Church was full. Mostly families from the neighborhood. Women dressed in black or gray. Women he knew because they'd been to visit his mother in their house. Women they'd seen every Sunday in the same church. Women who looked like they'd been crying, and he wondered about their tears because, really, they were strangers. And little girls, clean and dressed up in dark blue dresses. Little girls who had been instructed not to giggle, who had been lectured that this was a sad and sober and serious business. Little boys wearing pressed shirts and wearing looks of curiosity. Andrés could see that. He wondered what kind of look he had on his own face as he studied the whole scene.

He recognized some of the men—the pallbearers, an uncle he didn't know, his dad's friends from the neighborhood or from work or from the garage where he and his friends liked to go to have a beer and get away from the chores that were waiting for them at home. His dad had referred to them as his compas. Compa Johnny and compa Joe, who was a real compa because he was Andrés's godfather, and compa Chepo and compa Lazaro. And compa Henry. He knew them. They'd spent hours and hours in his front yard and backyard, smoking and drinking beer and laughing and making jokes about their wives or about their bosses. He recognized them. Today, they weren't making jokes.

He was sitting next to Mrs. Fernandez, his mother's best friend. They were always talking on the phone. "We went to school together." That was his mother's explanation for their friendship. "Since first grade." She was a nice lady, Mrs. Fernandez. Pretty—though not as pretty as his mother had been. But she had the kindest voice in the world. And she never seemed to be in a bad mood. She didn't have any children of her own. The other women in the neighborhood whispered about that, the tragedy of it, as if she wasn't as good as the other women, the women who'd been able to have children. Women who had children, they were real. More real than Mrs. Fernandez.

She'd always been good to them, Mrs. Fernandez. Even before the accident. But since that night, she'd practically moved in with them. Taking care of things, funeral arrangements, making sure they had everything they needed, feeding them. She was good to Ileana. Yolie didn't like her. But Yolie could be hard on people. She could be just like Mando.

Mrs. Fernandez would take them in. Maybe she would love them. That's what Andrés was thinking. He got mad at himself. He was only thinking of himself. He was supposed to be thinking of his mom and dad. He was supposed to be praying that they would find their way to heaven. That's what his friend, Nico, had told him, that when you died, some kind of angel put you in front of these roads. And you had to choose. And you had to take one of those roads and hope that it was the one that would lead to heaven. And if you had been good, then the angel gave you a light so you could see better, so you could choose wisely, so he shut his eyes and prayed for his mom and dad. He knew that an angel would give his mother a light, because she'd been good. And she would share the light with his father. Because that's the way she was.

He was praying so hard that he was shaking. He felt Mrs. Fernandez's hand on his shoulder as he knelt. He shut his eyes. Finally, he opened them. He didn't want to cry in front of anyone. Mando said it was okay if he cried. "But don't let them see," he said. "Don't let anyone see." So every day he would take a ride on his bike and cry as he rode around the neighborhood. He couldn't even see where he was going, didn't care either. He just rode and cried and rode and cried. He'd done that every day since that night. He would fall asleep, his legs aching almost as much as his heart.

He felt Ileana taking his hand and leaning into him. "They're in heaven, right, Andy?"

He didn't want to tell her what he'd heard about the roads. And the long walk his parents were taking right now. It would scare her, and she didn't need to know about the angel who gave people lights, either. "Yes. They're in heaven."

Yolie didn't say anything. She didn't cling to him like Ileana—but Yolie was older. She was dressed in black, and he'd heard someone whisper "Ya se hizo mujer," so maybe Yolie *was* a woman, now. And if Yolie was a woman, then Mando was a man. And only he and Ileana were still kids. Only he and Ileana needed taking care of. Maybe that was it. Maybe if he had been older, he would have been mad, too. Mad like Yolie and Mando. But he wasn't. He was sad. And he was scared. And Ileana, too. But not Yolie. Maybe, when you were older, you got scared and sad in a different way. He knew that Yolie cried at night, when everyone was gone. Just like him and Ileana. But in the daytime, she was mostly mad.

Yolie knelt in front of their dad's casket first, to look at him for the last time. Andrés, too. He knelt next to Yolie. Ileana didn't kneel. She wanted to see, so she just stood and leaned into her brother and peeked inside the casket. He could feel his little sister's clean breath. "Andy, does it hurt to be dead?"

"No," he whispered. "It doesn't hurt anymore."

She nodded. He could tell Yolie was crying. Soft. She made the sign of the cross—then she reached toward her father. At first, Andrés didn't know what she was doing. And then he understood. She was trying to take off his wedding ring. She wasn't afraid. To take it. At first it seemed like she would break his finger—but then it just slid off. She handed it to him. "Here."

Andrés just stared at the ring his older sister had thrust into his hand.

"Maybe you should give it to Mando."

"No. He wouldn't care about it. We'll give him all of Dad's shirts. He likes them." She sounded so sure. Like she knew exactly what to do. Like she'd thought about all these things. Not like she was lost. Not like that. She rose and kissed her father on the forehead, then made the sign of the cross again. It seemed like she knew everything. It was true, what people were saying. She was a woman. She walked slowly to her mother's casket. Andrés and Ileana made the sign of the cross and followed her.

This was too hard for Andrés—to kneel in front of his dead mother. He didn't want to cry. But he did. And Ileana cried, too. And Yolie put her arm around him. "You were her favorite," she said. "She loved you."

"I wasn't. I wasn't," Andrés said softly. He didn't like the accusation. He wanted to ask her why she was saying those awful things.

"It's okay. It doesn't matter anymore."

"She loved everyone."

"Yes. All of us. She loved all of us. But you were her favorite."

She reached for her mother's wedding band and slipped it off. She clutched it in her hand. Andrés could tell she was about to cry. But Yolie wrapped her hand tight around her mother's ring, and refused to cry. They knelt there, the three of them, for a long time. And then, all of a sudden, Mando was beside them. He smelled of cologne and cigarettes. "Let's all say a prayer," he said. He seemed different. He was like Yolie. Not lost. A man. Andrés could tell. And he'd been crying. Even though he was wearing sunglasses, Andrés could tell by the sound of his voice that he'd been crying. Maybe that was okay, to be a man and to cry. Especially if your mother and father were dead. Mando took Yolie's hand, and then she took Andrés's hand, and Andrés took Ileana's hand, and they all clung to each other and whispered: "Hail Mary full of grace, the Lord is with thee, blessed art thou . . ." Their mother's favorite prayer. And when they finished they made the sign of the cross, and Yolie and Mando started to walk back to their seats.

But Andrés refused to move. He just stayed there and began howling like a hurt dog. He didn't have any control, now, over his body, over the awful sounds that were coming out of him. And he felt Mando's arms around him, and his arms were soft and kind and good. Mando had never placed his arms around him, not like that, not ever. And he kissed him on the top of his head and he said, "You have to be strong, now, Andrés. You have to be." And Andrés stopped crying. And nodded his head.

And when they lowered his mother and father into the ground, he didn't cry.

The house was full of people all afternoon. All the Compas and their wives and their kids, the whole neighborhood. Mando smoked cigarettes in the backyard with all the men. And they let him have a beer, just one—but it wasn't the first time he'd ever had a beer, Andrés knew that. Maybe the men knew it, too, but they knew the women were watching, and so they let him have only one.

The women had filled the house with food: borracho beans and beans cooked in ham hocks, and refried beans and calabasitas con chile y queso and enchiladas and brisket and bolillos and tortillas and tamales and chile colorado con carne and tacos and chiles rellenos and more than a few buckets of Kentucky Fried Chicken and homemade potato salad and macaroni salad with jalapeños and cilantro. And everyone just made themselves at home, and Mrs. Fernandez oversaw everything in the kitchen and Yolie helped her and Ileana ate and ate because she was hungry—but after she finished eating, she fell asleep. She looked so little. And Mando carried her into the bedroom she shared with Yolie, and it suddenly occurred to Andrés that they had no money, and how were they going to pay for the house? But he shook his head and prayed for his mother and father's journey, the one they were taking that very minute, and so he went into his room and prayed. He prayed in Spanish, too, just to make sure. And when he finished praying, he took out his bike and went for a ride—but he told Mrs. Fernandez so she wouldn't worry, because the day before, when he'd gone out, he'd forgotten to tell her and she had all the neighbors looking for him. "Just half an hour," she said.

He didn't have a watch, but he nodded. Half an hour. So he rode around for a long time. Maybe it was an hour, he didn't know. He thought of his mother and father and he wanted to remember them, and never forget, so he just pictured them, and tried to paste that picture to the walls he had in his mind. So he'd never forget.

And then he went back home with his tired legs and his tired heart and his tired mind, tired from trying to picture his parents. So he wouldn't forget. When he walked back inside his house, people were beginning to leave, and they all hugged him as they left, and the women put their hands on his face and told him he was a beautiful boy and they said it in English and in Spanish, que muchacho tan bonito. And by the end of it all, he was tired of being touched and talked to and he just wanted to sleep.

And finally, when it got dark, all the people had gone home—except the uncle he didn't know very well and whom his mother didn't like—him and Mr. and Mrs. Fernandez. They were the only ones left. Mrs. Fernandez was cleaning up the kitchen and putting the leftover food away and Mando and Mr. Fernandez were cleaning up the backyard and Yolie was holding Ileana and sitting on the couch and they were both more asleep than awake—and Andrés just watched them.

And then his uncle said it was time for him to go. And so he gave them all a halfhearted hug, and then Andrés knew why his mother hadn't liked him. He didn't care. Not about any of them.

Mr. and Mrs. Fernandez told them they could stay the night with them, so they wouldn't have to be alone.

"No," Mando said, "Maybe, tonight, it's a good thing for us to be alone. Just for tonight. We'll be okay."

Mr. Fernandez nodded. Mrs. Fernandez was less quick to nod, but she did. She nodded. "I'll be back in the morning," she said.

"Okay," Mando nodded. "That's good." He seemed to know what to say. What to do. He seemed almost as old as they were. Mrs. Fernandez hugged them all, kissed them, told them to rest. "Duerman con los santos de tata Dios." He would rather send the santos to walk with their parents.

Mando went out the front door with Mr. and Mrs. Fernandez. He walked them to their car, just like his mother and father would have done. They were talking about something, but he didn't know what. Part of him wanted to know. Another part didn't care. He was tired. And he didn't care about anything.

When Mando came back inside, he lit a cigarette. He nudged Yolie and told her to wake up. She sat up and looked around the room. "Did everyone leave?"

"Yeah."

She looked at Mando. "Give me a cigarette."

"I don't want you smoking."

"I already smoke. Mom knew. She said she couldn't do anything about it, but she wasn't going to let me smoke in the house. Anyway, I have some in my drawer."

Mando handed her one. She lit it. She knew what she was doing. "You're all going to live with the Fernandezes."

"What about you?"

"Compa Johnny has a garage. He's going to hire me. He says he'll start me out minimum wage—but once I learn about cars, he'll pay me more. He has a small apartment above his garage. He says I can live there for as long as I want. He says he doesn't use it for anything, and his wife would be glad because she thinks he just has that place so he can cheat on her."

"Can't we live there, too?"

"It's too small. And besides, they won't let me keep you."

"Can't you come live with the Fernandezes, too? With us?"

"No. I'm eighteen. I'm an adult. I'm emancipated."

Andrés knew that word. Had heard it in school. It had something to do with the slaves. When they were freed. Andrés would hear that word many more times in his life, and he would come to know that the word had many meanings.

"I don't know what that means," Yolie said.

"It means no one's going to take me in, because I'm a man."

"Well, I'm a woman."

"The law says you're not a woman until you're eighteen."

"Fuck the law. Why can't we all live here? Don't we inherit this house or something?"

"Mom and Dad rented it."

"What? But they bought it."

"Yeah, but Dad hadn't finished paying on it. Remember when he wasn't working for about eight months? Remember?"

"Yeah."

"Well, he had to sell the house, because he had debts to pay. And he couldn't afford to buy a new one. And since the guy Dad sold it to was going to use the house as a rental, he let Dad rent the house. Even let him live here for free until Dad finally found another job."

"In other words, we inherit shit."

"Well, Mom had some money in the bank. Not much. Eighteen hundred dollars."

"That's a lot."

"Yolie, that's nothing. Trust me."

"Can't we just pay rent to the guy?"

"The law won't let us, Yolie. If you go with the Fernandezes, then we stay together. That's what we need to do. Stay together. Isn't that right?"

"Who writes these fucking laws?" That's the way Yolie had been since the accident. Always using that word.

"Yolie, look. It's just for a while. I have a plan." He looked at her. Andrés knew that the look meant something. The look meant they were going to talk later, and he would tell her what he meant by having a plan. The look meant that they weren't going to say anything else about the plan in front of him and Ileana.

Yolie shrugged. "Bueno pues. But that lady's gonna have a lot of rules."

"Mom had rules, too. No boys in the house when no one was home. A rule you broke all the time. No smoking in the house. Take your turn washing dishes. Clean your room. Do your homework. Mom had rules. Mostly, you stuck to them. You can stick to them now."

"I don't care about school."

"Just keep going for now, ¿entiendes? Trust me."

"Mrs. Fernandez is nice," Andrés said.

Yolie nodded. "Yeah, she's nice. You'll be her favorite."

Andrés looked down. It made him sad, to hear her talk that way. But she kissed him. "I'm sorry," she said. "I can be mean. I'm sorry, Andy. I'm just kidding."

He was glad. That she said she was sorry.

"Will you visit us, Mando? Will you?" Ileana climbed into Mando's lap. "You have to promise."

"I promise," he said. And then he kissed her. Mando was good with Ileana. Sure. Why not? She was gentle and pretty and soft and easy to love.

Things weren't so bad at the Fernandezes'. He didn't miss the shouting. But he missed his father. He missed his mother. But he did get to keep his bike, and Mr. Fernandez let him ride it around in the neighborhood, and he even bought him a watch so he would know when he was supposed to come back home. He had his own room, and he didn't have to share it with Mando, but he missed Mando. He didn't know why, because they'd never gotten along, but he missed him. Missed the smell of his cologne. Mr. Fernandez didn't wear cologne.

Sometimes Ileana cried. Sometimes she would sneak into Andrés's bedroom and say, "Andy, will you hold me?" and Andrés would let her fall asleep in his arms. But Yolie. Yolie never cried again. She didn't fight with Mrs. Fernandez, but she wasn't warm. She did what she was supposed to do. Sometimes she would sneak out at night. And Andrés wondered if the Fernandezes knew. He never saw Yolie and Mrs. Fernandez fight. Not ever. But sometimes he saw this look on Yolie's face. Like she was a prisoner. Like she wanted to be eighteen. Like she wanted to be emancipated.

Mando would visit on Fridays and Sundays. And they seemed like they were almost a family. And Andrés didn't think that things had turned out so bad. Not really bad. But when he thought that, he felt ugly and awful and bad. Because his mom and dad were dead. And he didn't think he should be thinking things like, Things didn't turn out so bad. He was being selfish. God didn't like selfish people. But his mother hadn't been selfish, and she was dead.

Compa Johnny threw a party for Mando when he graduated from high school. Mr. and Mrs. Fernandez took them all to Sears, and they all got to choose a gift for Mando. Yolie picked a beautiful shirt because Mando loved beautiful shirts. Andrés picked a toolbox with Mr. Fernandez's help. Ileana picked a nice pen. And then they went to a restaurant to eat. It was a happy day. Shopping for Mando and going to a restaurant to eat. Even Yolie seemed happy that day.

Yolie almost cried when they called Mando's name. And Mrs. Fernandez *did* cry. And she said their mother and father would be proud. And Andrés, he was happy. Because his brother graduated, and that was a good thing. Everyone said so. And someday he would graduate, too. And maybe go to college. He'd always wanted to do that. Once his father had taken him to the university. And he'd liked it there. And he'd liked all the books in the library. The biggest library he'd ever seen.

Afterward, at the party at compa Johnny's house, he saw Yolie and Mando whispering about something. He had never seen Yolie so happy. He was glad. That she was so happy. He wanted to be as happy as her. As happy as Mando.

". . . A week later. Maybe two weeks. I don't remember. It was a Saturday. The Fernandezes always went to buy groceries and do other errands on Saturdays. Sometimes we went with them. That Saturday, Yolie told them Mando was coming over, and that he was going to take us to Chico's Tacos. So the Fernandezes went off to the grocery store and to do their Saturday errands. . . ."

He was watching her, even as he told her his story. Watching her. Making sure she was listening.

• • •

And Mando *did* come for them. Yolie had already packed all her things. Ileana's things, too. Mando brought in a suitcase and packed all Andrés' things, everything that would fit. "Where are we going?" Andrés asked. He was scared. He wanted to stay. He wanted to tell Mando to leave without him. "We're safe here, Mando."

"They're not your mom and dad," Mando said. "We're going to be together, now. Mom and Dad would've wanted that." He must have read Andrés' mind, because he hugged him. That was the second time he'd ever hugged him. "Yolie and I are going to take care of you." He wanted to believe Mando, but he didn't. And he thought maybe Mando knew he didn't believe him. And that scared him even more.

"What about my bike?" Andrés asked.

"You'll have to leave it here." There wasn't any patience in Mando's voice. He was in a hurry.

"No. Dad gave me that bike." Andrés got out of the car and walked toward the garage.

"We don't have room for it, Andy."

"We'll make room."

"*Get the hell over here, Andy!* We can't take it."

"*I won't go without my bike.*"

Mando got out of the car. He grabbed Andrés by his arms. "I'll come back for it."

"You promise?"

"Yes."

"I don't believe you."

"I promise, Andy. I promise." He was whispering now. Mando was a good whisperer. That's why girls liked him so much.


". . . I got in the car. I remember looking toward the garage. I think I was saying good-bye to my bike. I don't know. I was just a kid. I don't know where Mando got the car. I guess he bought it. I mean, he worked in a garage. Maybe he got a good deal on it. Maybe he stole it. I don't know. I don't even remember what kind of car it was." He stopped. "Oh, yes, I do. It was an old car. A Chevy Impala. Something like that. It was blue. Like a pale blue sky."

He looked at Grace. She was nodding her head. He took out a cigarette and lit it. "It's not that hard to tell you all this, you know?"

"Does it get old?"

"No."

"Does it feel new?"

"It's the only pair of shoes I have."

"That's an interesting way to put it. You read a lot?"

"I used to."

"What happened?"

"I gave it up."

"Why?"

"I only liked sad books. They only made me sadder."

"Why didn't you read happy books?"

"Happy books? They bored me. They struck me as being a little too easy."

"So you gave up reading."

"Yes. That's when I decided to take up beating on cops." He smiled.

Grace laughed. "I shouldn't laugh. That's not funny."

"No. Nothing I do is funny. Especially not this story I'm telling."

"Does the story ever change?"

"The ending sure as hell doesn't."

# Grace at Morning Mass

She was early for mass. The church was warm.

She made the sign of the cross and thought of Mister and Liz. She smiled at their banter. They had laughed and talked and—cancer had not entered the conversation. All three of them had been so hungry to talk. Liz spoke of her father and his death. She spoke of a mother she clearly did not love. She came to this city to find herself. And found herself in Mister. Grace nodded as she sat in the pew. *I know now why she ran from my Mister. Love can frighten. I wanted to run from Sam when he first loved me. And almost did.*

She looked at Jesus, his arms outstretched, his familiar heart on fire. *I saw the room they've fixed for Vicente. Remember how Sam and I would linger in the room we both fixed up for Mister? Before he came to us? Sam would pace that room and wear a look. Now Mister wears that look. He wants the child more than she does. This is her gift to him. That's love, to give a gift like that.*

*She will give him this gift.*

*She is not the woman she was.*

*She has learned how to love. I can see that.*

*I wasn't cold. I wasn't. I could've been warmer.*

*The words I'm sorry did not appear in the conversation, though it was what we ate for dinner.*

*When I left, he held me tight and called me Mom, my son, my Mister. He hadn't called me Mom since he was four.*

*I saw that she was watching us, this woman, Liz. There was no envy in her eyes.*

*Perhaps this is a temporary truce.*

*Make it permanent, then, you, God, who are all-knowing, all-seeing, all-powerful. God, with a burning heart, make the truce into a peace that lasts.*

# Shirts and Things That Matter

Mister gets in his truck after his six-hour hike in the desert. He is tired from the walking and the thinking and the hoping and the arguing with demons. He is spent from the heat of the sun. But he likes this tiredness, and he knows that tonight his sleep will be deep and rich.

He turns the engine over and feels the heat of the air conditioner. He sits in the hot truck, the door open, sweat pouring down his face. Slowly, the air conditioner starts to do its work. He loves the way the coolness feels on his damp skin. He's decided to buy Vicente a new shirt. A token. He wants to give him something. Anything will do—he's settled on a shirt.

He drives to a department store and walks into the children's clothing section. He looks at the shirts for little boys. He eyes the shirts, to see if they are Vicente's size. The size fours seem like they will fit him perfectly. There are so many shirts. So many, many shirts. He himself does not spend much money on clothing. He has what he needs. He prefers to buy art and books. He prefers to buy things for Liz.

As he studies the small shirts, he smiles at the thought that he, too, had once been this size. He remembers his father letting him pick out his own clothes. Grace had never let him do that. Sometimes she would come home and announce, "I've bought you this shirt," or "Mister, I've bought you this pair of pants." She would hand the article of clothing to him, and he would smile. He would thank her and kiss her. He lived with her choices, even when he didn't like what she'd chosen. She had been thinking of him—that was what had mattered. When had things between them grown more complicated?

He suddenly feels Vicente's hands on his face, and he shudders at the thought. The awesome beauty and burden of it. He feels the material of the shirts with his fingers. That was the only way Vicente would come to know the shirt, through the feel of it. He would buy the shirt that had the kindest feel to it. He feels shirt after shirt. He finally finds a shirt that is soft and giving. He takes it from the rack and studies it. He takes out his cell and calls Liz. He smiles when he hears her voice. "How was your hike?"

"Good. Great. Guess where I am?"

"Tell me."

"I'm buying a shirt."

"A shirt?"

"Yeah. For our son." He laughs. "I'm crazy about you."

# Still Life of Beauty

I know a man. He works as a janitor. He told me he used to work at the county jail. He said there was a room on the second floor where they hang all the handcuffs and shackles. He said each handcuff and shackle has a number, and when they all hang together on the wall—at rest in a kind of still life of justice—it is a beautiful thing. That's how he put, "a still life of justice. . . . A beautiful thing." I try and picture the wall where all the handcuffs and shackles hang. I try and picture looking at this scene every day. I try and picture me saying, "This is a beautiful thing."

I am sitting in the county jail. I have no complaint. I refuse to say I don't belong here. I know where I belong. A jail is as good a place to live as any. I am learning what it means to despair. We should at least know the meanings of the words that pass our lips.

I am on the sixth floor. Four floors below me, there is that room with the shackles. Right now it is night. They turn off the lights at ten. I don't know how long I've been lying here. Hours maybe. I am thinking of the room, how no one is there—how it is a still life of justice in the darkness, and no one is in the room to admire the cuffs and the shackles. I wonder what it's like to be a keeper of the gates, a keeper of the keys, a keeper of the shackles. It does no good to think about these things, but I think them anyway.

I think sometimes that it doesn't really matter where I live. Because, really, where I really live is in my head. My home is my head. Not in this room where there is a man sleeping below me, on the bottom bunk. His name is Henry. He is from Alabama, and his eyes are charcoal gray. Two days ago he killed the woman he once loved. Six feet across from us, on the top bunk, a guy named Freddy is snoring. "Anyone wake me because I'm snoring I'll kick his ass like it's a goddamned soccer ball." Below him, Angel is thinking something. He watches. He doesn't know a word of English. He looks at me like he wants to say something. I look back at him so that he will understand it is better to say nothing.

Our cell block is full tonight. Four cells, four men each. Each cell opens into our living room. That's what one of the men called it. "Our fucking living room." Another guy just laughed. "It's a nicer place than the pigsty I grew up in."

I don't live in this room. I don't live in this jail. Dave says I'll be out tomorrow. Where will I go then? Where will I live? Dave will have a plan. The living, that's what they do. They plan.

# Conversations
# (Because We Live in Our Heads)

You want me to leave you alone, Andrés? I don't believe you. There are things you know that I will never know. There are things you've seen that I will never see. You've been used, abused, raped, and pushed around. Your pain's become the only light you know. You want to punish yourself. You think your life has to be a tragedy. I know that goddamned song—I've hummed more than a few bars of that tune myself. You tell yourself you've killed a man. You tell yourself you deserve to pay. *Leave me the fuck alone, Dave.*

You tell yourself you hate me. Why not? Rich gringo rides in on his well-bred, paid-for, expensive white horse and saves poor Mexican boy. I'd hate me, too. I'm everything you never got to be. Deep down you know you're smarter. I know that, too. The accidents of birth—I wind up rich, and you wind up with what? We wind up living in the same neighborhoods we were raised in. You spit on all of this.

I'd like, someday, for you to call me friend. I mean to earn that office. Grace, she taught me that. Whatever office that we hold, we'd damn well better earn it.

*We can't applaud what he did.* That's how the DA put it. So who's applauding? This isn't a play. Andrés is not a vigilante. He wasn't trying to prove a point. He wasn't making public policy. He went crazy. Did you ever think about what made him crazy? Prosecutors make me fuckin' nuts. They want the same ending to every story—crime and punishment. They spin such easy plots.

I spoke to Al Mendoza. *Andrés just went off on this guy. I've thought and thought about it. Andrés isn't a bad guy. He's not. Whatever this guy, Hart, did to him, it was bad. That's what I think.*

And Mr. Hart, you could have saved yourself. You could've called the cops. No cops, you kept repeating, no cops. So what's the deal? You could've saved yourself. You could've driven to a hospital. You could've gone to a doctor. You went to college. LSU. And then to Yale. There was alcohol in your system. You went home, got drunk. Scotch, the bottle half empty in your new apartment. And then you died. Some would say that you committed suicide. You could be alive today. You hurt Andrés. I'll find out how. You bet your dead ass I will.

# Still Life of Freedom

They called his name. Segovia, Andrés. They looked at his wrists, studied his number and the miniature photo on his bracelet, looked at him, nodded. They opened the door, then motioned for him to follow. The correctional officer offered a token of recognition— "So someone sprung you." Andrés accepted the token by nodding.

As they waited for the elevator, he stood behind the stripe on the floor. He stared at the number six on the elevator doors. No shackles today. No handcuffs. He was leaving. No need for that kind of insurance. When the elevator door opened, a new arrival stepped out, shackled and cuffed and a look on his face that said, If I could break out, I'd fucking kill you. Andrés did not look away from the man's sneer.

On the second floor, he stood in a short line at the same place where he'd picked up his blanket and orange jumper. The friendly black man who looked like he could break any man in half smiled and handed him a basket with his clothes and personal belongings. "Good luck," he said. Andrés nodded back. Sure. Luck. Yeah.

They led him down the hall. There was a counter with a clerk who was busy looking over some paperwork. "You can change in there," he said, pointing at the stalls. The doors were cut at the top and the bottom. The only things the doors hid were the midsection of his body. Jails weren't meant for delicate men who needed privacy. He took the basket filled with his clothes and personal stuff into one of the stalls. He stepped out of his orange jumper and put on his own clothes quickly. It was good. To wear his own shirt. His own pair of pants. His own socks. His own pair of shoes. He took in his own smell as he put on his shirt.

At the counter, they cut his bracelet off, signed him out.

A man his own age led him to the front doors. They did not speak.

Dave was there. Waiting. He smiled, then handed him a pair of sunglasses. "You'll need these," he said. "You look a little thin."

"I haven't been hungry."

He pushed the door open, the blinding sun slapping his face. Even with the pair of sunglasses Dave had given him, he could hardly see. He stood for a moment and looked around, letting his eyes adjust.

"I'll take you to breakfast," Dave said. He pointed as they walked down the sidewalk. "I'm parked on Campbell."

"And then what?"

"I'll take you back home."

"How am I going to pay the fucking rent? I'm sure Garcia's fired me by now."

"I've paid your rent."

"I don't like that."

"I want to help."

"I don't like being charity case number seventy-nine."

"Seventy-nine? My list doesn't go up that high." He shook his head. "Did the thought ever occur to you that I might care about you? People are allowed to care about each other."

"You don't know me well enough to care about me."

"Let me clue you in on something, Andrés. Just because you hate yourself doesn't mean that I have to hate you."

"Fuck you, Dave."

"Go to school. Registration starts in two weeks. By the time May rolls around, you'll have two semesters under your belt. Trial should start just about that time." Dave pointed at his car. "I'm parked over there." He smiled. "Look, I'm happy to pay your rent until we come to trial. You don't even have to fucking thank me."

"Good. I'm not the grateful type." As he stood in front of Dave's car, he took off his sunglasses. He closed his eyes and let the sun hit him in the face. He took a deep breath as he stood in the morning heat, his face looking upward, his face shining in the rays of the sun. He felt the tears rolling down his face.

Dave was good enough to say nothing.

# Timing and Order in the Universe

ndrés Segovia is looking up at the morning sky. Tears are streaming from his eyes. He wants to live in this sun all the days of his life. He is suddenly afraid of spending years and years in prison. Perhaps he deserves to be punished. But in this one second of clarity, he wants to become that old word he heard long ago. Emancipated. He is thinking that he will never be worthy of that word.

Father Enrique Fuentes, pastor of San Ignacio Catholic Church, is blessing the casket of an eight-year-old girl named Angela Gonzalez. He is sad for his church and for his people. These people have nothing. And after today, they have even less. The people who live here, most of them live for better days.

The church is filled to capacity. All the news stations have a reporter present. Angela will be headlines for yet another day. Politicians have sprinkled themselves among the congregation—two county commissioners, three members of the city council, two judges who are running for reelection.

Among those present is Mister Delgado. He could not keep himself away. Liz had lectured him the night before about attending a stranger's funerals. "It's not a zoo, Mister. It's not a show."

"I know, Liz." But he is there. His presence is sincere. After mass, he will stop in and visit Vicente. He will hold him tight, then go back to work.

# Maybe Everything
# Would Be All Right

W here are we going?"
"To our new house."
Ileana squealed. One of those squeals only a five-year-old could manage. One of those infectious squeals that made everyone who heard it happy. "A house! A house!"

Everyone in the car laughed. "Can we go for a picnic, Mando?" she jumped up from the back seat and threw her arms around Mando's neck as he drove.

Andrés smiled. Maybe everything would be all right. Mando looked handsome in a nice shirt. He was different. He remembered that his dad was always yelling at Mando and telling him he was too fucking irresponsible and that he'd never amount to anything. But maybe his father had been wrong. He seemed responsible now, and old, like a father—because that's what he was, now, their father. And maybe he'd saved lots of money. Maybe they would all be happy. And maybe his mother and father were happy, too, because they'd found their way to heaven—because of his mother's light. The light the angel gave her.

"Does Mrs. Fernandez know you came to take us to our new house?"

"Yes. I told her." Andrés knew his brother was lying. Sometimes you couldn't tell if he was lying or not. But sometimes you could.

"Why weren't they there to say good-bye, Mando? Don't they like us? I thought they liked us." Andrés thought Ileana always asked the right questions.

"Of course they do. They just had some important business."

"Will they come to visit us in our new house?"

"Yeah," Mando said, lighting a cigarette.

Ileana looked at Andrés and laughed. "He's just like Dad, isn't he, Andy?"

Andrés nodded. "Sure," he said, "like Dad."

Yolie lit a cigarette, too. She turned on the radio. She and Mando started singing along with the song. They were happy, emancipated. So this had been their plan. He knew they had been planning this since the night of his parent's funeral. Planning and planning. And so they were happy, because their plan was working. Yolie turned around and smiled at Ileana and at Andrés. She saw the look on Andrés's face. The apprehension. "Are you worried about your bike?"

*What's going to happen? What's going to happen to us?*

" 'Everything's gonna be just fine, Andy.' That's what Yolie said. And then she added, 'You look like you could use a cigarette,' 'No thanks,' I said. 'Mom wouldn't like it.' She laughed, and then she looked at me. And then she said, 'Don't ever tell me what Mom would or would not like—not ever again.' She was hard as stone. And I hated her. I think I still hate her. Though in between then and now, I loved her. I would have done anything for her. And I did. I did everything she asked." Andrés played with the cigarette he was holding. He put it back in his pack. "Have you ever smoked?"

"Yes. Sure. I used to smoke."

"You don't sound sorry."

"I'm not sorry. I smoked. I liked it. I quit." It wasn't necessary to tell him she was currently backsliding.

"How long did you smoke?"

"Three or four years—I can't remember exactly. Maybe a little more."

"I started smoking when I was thirteen." He looked at his cigarettes. "My oldest friends." He laughed. "How'd you quit?"

"They weren't good for me. It's a sort of self-hatred, isn't it?"

"I never looked at it that way. It's a way of coping."

"It's a way of not coping. Name one problem a cigarette's ever solved."

"Maybe they've stopped some men from killing someone."

"I don't think so. I think a lot of men smoke a cigarette after they've killed someone. Probably smoked one right before."

"Okay. So maybe it's just an addiction."

"So why don't you quit?"

"Because I'll explode."

"Maybe you'll explode anyway."

"Of course, you fucking know I have exploded, don't you?"

She didn't smile, didn't frown. "I guess I do," she said. Calm as a breeze.

"Are you afraid of me?" He knew she wasn't.

"No."

"Why not?"

"When we're afraid of someone, that means we think they might hurt us. You won't hurt me."

"How do you know?"

"You're not a saint, Andrés. But you're not the devil, either. You won't hurt me."

"You know, huh?"

"Yes."

"What if I do—hurt you, I mean?"

"I'll scream."

They both smiled. He was ashamed of himself for the silly game he was playing. He took a cigarette out of the pack and lit it.

He looked beautiful with a cigarette in his mouth. It was an aesthetic Grace had always appreciated. She looked at her blank pad. She wouldn't write. Not today. He'd told her he didn't mind if she took notes, but he wasn't telling the truth. He minded like hell. "Did you ever see the Fernandezes again?"

"No."

"Did they ever try and find you?"

"I don't know. Yes, I think they did." He paused to search through the clutter in his mind. Sometimes he felt his mind was like a room filled with a stack of newspapers, and his whole life was there—but he never knew where to find the information he needed. "Yes," he said finally, "they tried to find us. I found that out later. I don't remember when exactly."

"Have you ever looked for them?"

"Once I went to their house. They weren't home. I sat there for a while, outside the house."

"When was this?"

"Oh, ten years ago. I was sixteen. I was going to be placed in a foster home at the time."

"Why didn't you go back?"

"After what we'd done?"

"You didn't do anything, Andrés."

"I didn't run away from Mando or Yolie, did I?"

"You were ten when they took you."

"And I knew what we were doing was wrong."

"So it's your fault, then?"

"I didn't say that. I just said I couldn't go back to the Fernandezes after the way we'd played them."

"So you never saw them again, either of them?"

"Mrs. Fernandez—she went to my trial. Every day, she was there."

"Trial? I don't see anything in your files about a trial."

"There wouldn't be a record of that. I was a minor. I was tried in juvenile court. And I was acquitted. Or maybe not acquitted, but found not guilty. Or maybe the charges were dropped. I don't remember."

"You don't remember?"

"I didn't care what happened. Dave cared. All I knew was that somehow he got me off."

"Maybe Dave got you off because you were innocent."

"I don't think so."

"So the only reason you were let off was because you had a good lawyer?"

"Something like that."

She nodded, then looked at him. She wanted him to know he might be wrong. She'd decided that Andrés Segovia was incapable of believing he had any virtues. "I think your lawyer had something to work with— if you want to know what I think."

"You don't even know what I did."

"No. I don't." She decided now wasn't the time for this particular conversation. Not today. "Did you ever talk to Mrs. Fernandez ever again?"

"No."

"Why?"

"I was too ashamed."

"Is she still alive?"

"Yes."

"How do you know?"

"I went to Mr. Fernandez's funeral."

"When did he die?"

"Six months ago."

"How did you find out?"

"I read it in the obituary section."

"Do you normally read the obituaries?"

"No. People your age, they read them."

She smiled. In acknowledgment of his joke.

He smiled back. He looked like a summer morning when he smiled, exactly like a summer morning. She was certain no one had ever told him that. "So how'd you happen to see his name in the obituaries?"

"This guy at work. His name's Al. He was going to cut out the obituary of someone he knew. And there it was—Mr. Fernandez's picture."

"So you went to the funeral."

"Yeah."

"Why?"

"I'm not sure."

"Did you talk to Mrs. Fernandez?"

"No."

"Did she see you?"

"Yes."

"Did she recognize who you were?"

"Sure. I don't know. I didn't go up to her or anything. But our eyes met, and I thought that—I don't know."

"And that was all?"

"Yes."

"Our eyes met. Maybe she did know. I thought about my bike."

"You think she still has it?"

"She probably got rid of it a long time ago. I think she fell in love with us, though. With all of us. I think we hurt her."

"It wasn't you who hurt her."

"You weren't there."

Grace nodded. "Are you tired?"

"Not really."

"You want to go on?"

"Sure. But can I ask you a question?"

"Sure."

"How well do you know Dave?"

"Why is that important?"

"It probably isn't. But I think you know him pretty well."

"Why do you think that?"

"I don't know. I just think you do. When he gave me your card. It seemed like—he must know you. He seemed so—"

"So what?"

"I don't know."

"I think if you really want to know, then you should ask him."

"Maybe I'll do that."

"Good."

He liked the way she handled herself. "Good."

They crossed the Santa Fe Bridge into Juárez, the smell of exhaust all around them from the line of cars streaming from one city into the next. There were men and women and boys his age selling things, holding things up for the whole world to see, candy, curios, crucifixes, *buy this, buy this*. Maybe some of these boys had lost their parents, too. Maybe he'd wind up like them, selling things on the streets. Somehow, Andrés had sensed that their new house was going to be in Juárez, just as he knew that the Fernandezes knew nothing about any of this—just as he knew he would never see his bicycle again. He kept quiet. It was better not to say anything. And what was there to say, anyway? He was ten. He wasn't emancipated.

Mando bought two packs of cigarettes from a vendor, one for him and one for Yolie. Andrés had only been to Juárez with his father, and they'd always walked across the bridge on foot. He'd always liked it here, in Juárez. He liked the smells and the way people talked and the busy streets, with people walking, and his father had told him it was more civilized to walk to places than to drive, and his father had explained the word *civilized* that day, and he was remembering all these things as they drove into Juárez. All the smells reminded him of his father, of how things had been. He remembered how he'd gotten haircuts here and how his dad always bought vanilla for his mother and corn tortillas that melted in his mouth and tasted like Mexico. That's what his mother had told him, that Mexico tasted of maíz and the hands of the women who'd made tortillas for a thousand years. And remembering all these things made Andrés as sad as he had ever been. For a long time, he had tried not to think about his mom and dad, but now, on the Santa Fe Bridge, all he could think of was that they were dead.

Mando turned right off Avenida Benito Juárez, and down some narrow streets. The streets were crowded, and they passed a lot of bars—or it least it seemed that way to Andrés. He had been to bars with his father, and he knew the look of them. Later, he was to learn that they had been in Calle Mariscal, the district where all the prostitutes made a living. He would learn the streets of this district better than he had learned the streets of his own neighborhood. But today Andrés only had the vaguest idea of what a prostitute was.

On a small narrow street, Mando parked outside a house. It wasn't a house really, not like the houses in his neighborhood, which all had fences or rock walls or walls that were made of bricks or cinder blocks, fences and yards and flowers and grass and all that. There was none of that in this neighborhood. These houses looked like one long house with doors and windows every few yards, a cement sidewalk for a front yard, a few sad trees trying to grow here and there. Each door, he guessed, was some kind of house. Like apartments, and so he asked Mando, "Are these apartments? Are we going to live in an apartment?"

"No," he said. "These are houses. Houses aren't the same everywhere, Andy."

Mando walked up to a door that had the number 12 on it, and he took out a set of keys and opened the door. They all followed Mando inside the house. Andrés was the last to walk in. The front room was dark, but when Yolie pulled the curtains open, the room was brighter. But not beautiful. The walls were a dull gray and had water stains from a roof that leaked when it rained, and Andrés thought he smelled urine. There were holes in the wall that made the whole room look like maybe someone had fought a war in here.

The floors were covered with old linoleum, pale yellow flowers and green vines running in patterns on its worn surface. It might have been very nice when it was new, but now it was old and pale and sad, and worn down from being walked on by the parade of people who had lived here. The front room led into a kitchen, and the kitchen had a big shelf, like a bookshelf, and a table made of wood, a nice table, and six wooden chairs around the table. And there was a refrigerator and a small gas stove. "I brought the tables and chairs last night," Mando said. Proud. "The refrigerator and stove need cleaning—bought them secondhand. But they work." The kitchen led into another room, which Andrés guessed was a bedroom. And that room led to another empty room, which Andrés guessed was another bedroom. And that bedroom led into a small yard, which was as small as the two back rooms. "A courtyard," Mando called it.

"This is our house," he said. Proud. Sure. A man.

"It smells bad," Ileana offered. "I don't like it."

"I'll make it smell good," Yolie said. "I promise." She looked at Mando.

"And guess what we're gonna do, Ileana? We're gonna paint this place and make it look real nice."

Mando had been planning and planning and planning. Mando opened a closet in the first bedroom, and he took out the cans of paint and brushes and mops and a broom and all kinds of stuff to clean their house with. "We got everything," he said. "And we'll paint all the walls white. So it won't look so dark. How does that sound? And we'll paint the kitchen yellow. How does that sound?" He looked at Ileana.

"That sounds good, Mando," she said. She was happy with his answer. He was the father now.

Even Andrés liked the way Mando sounded. He didn't sound mean or angry, but nice and soft. So maybe everything was going to be all right.

But the rooms were so dark. And there weren't any windows except in the front room. "But the darkness keeps the house cool in the summer," Mando said. And so they started painting. And just as soon as they started painting, there was a knock at the door, and a girl—she was pretty—a girl and two guys, they were at the door. And the pretty girl hugged Mando and kissed him. "This is my girlfriend, Xochil," Mando said, "and these are her brothers," Enrique and Jaime. And Andrés shook their hands, and Mando's girlfriend kissed Andrés on the cheek and told him he was better looking than Mando, and that made Andrés smile.

Mando and Enrique and Jaime went out, and they unloaded four beds. Each bed was small, for one person. Twin beds, one bed for each of them. And mattresses and pillows and sheets. They weren't new, the beds, Andrés knew that. But they seemed like they were good beds, though he knew he didn't really know anything about beds. But Yolie said they didn't smell like urine and that they didn't have stains or anything like that. And so he inspected the mattresses closely and he smelled them, and they didn't smell bad. Not good. Not new. But not bad. Like old rain, maybe, almost sweet. Something like that.

So that first day in their new city, in their new neighborhood, in their new country, they all painted and cleaned and worked to make their new house into something that was good, something that was worthy of them, something that the rats wouldn't like. That's what Mando said. It was a joke. He said, "If you keep a house painted and clean, then the rats won't like it." Rats. Sure. It wasn't rats Andrés was worried about. But he didn't know exactly where the worry was coming from. He just had a feeling. Like thunder in the sky. Only the thunder was in his stomach. There would be a storm.

Yolie and Xochil cleaned the refrigerator and stove and painted the big shelf in the kitchen. Mando and Jaime and Enrique painted the living room and the kitchen, and by late afternoon, they had started to paint the front bedroom. Mando gave Yolie some money and told her to go buy some food. He gave her directions to a grocery store and told her what the exchange rate was so she would know what things would cost in pesos even though she was paying in dollars. In Juárez, you could always pay in dollars. He'd seen his father pay like that. Sometimes they gave you back change in pesos. Andrés knew that. And he kept the exchange rate in his head like he kept other things. In case he ever needed to pull the information out.

That first night, Yolie and Ileana made tacos. Andrés remembered that tacos were the last thing his mother had ever cooked for them. He was sorry he remembered. But the tacos were good, and everyone ate. But Andrés felt the thunder in his stomach. That night, when everyone was asleep, Andrés walked into the bathroom, knelt down in front of the toilet, stuck his finger down his throat, and vomited the tacos his sister had made.

It wasn't bad the first few weeks. Like they were really a family, everything new and different. But they didn't know what they were doing, not really, just a game. Mando would go out in the morning, like he was a dad and going to work. And Andrés always wondered about that, and wondered if he were working in El Paso or Juárez—but Mando never told them. When Andrés asked him where he went, Mando said, "I go to work. So we can live here." He knew Mando didn't want to talk about it. And sometimes Mando went away for a day or two. And Andrés would ask him where he was. And he would say that sometimes he had to travel. For his work. Ileana asked him where he traveled. He said he didn't like to talk about work. "Only old men who are about to die talk about work." That's what he said.

Yolie would pick up the house, like playing Mother. And she would cook. And the three of them, Yolie and Ileana and Andrés, would walk to the market and buy food. Andrés loved the market, the tomatoes and the nopales and the limes and the different kinds of chiles, jalapeños and chile de arból and anchos and pasillas, and chiles negros and chile pasado. He loved to stare at the chiles, so beautiful, all the food and the way it was displayed—like jewels and diamonds. Yolie seemed to like the market, too. She was happy when they were there, and she always knew how much to buy and always got a good price.

But she was restless. Sometimes she would go out in the afternoon, and she told Andrés and Ileana not to tell Mando. And they never did. They never knew where she went. And Andrés thought maybe it was like riding his bike around the neighborhood. Because it felt good to get out and be by yourself. And not be inside all the time.

Ileana and Andrés would stay home, and Andrés would make up stories to entertain her. Ileana and Andrés learned to keep the house pretty clean. Mando got some bricks from somewhere, and they bricked in the dirt of the courtyard, and it was like having an outside room. And he bought some pots, and Yolie planted a banana tree and other kinds of bushes and flowers in the big clay pots Mando had brought home, and it was nice. Andrés liked that courtyard. He would sleep there at night. He would count the stars. But as the days passed, he was getting as restless and bored as Yolie.

He missed school. He missed riding his bike. He missed speaking English. They had a new rule. Speak Spanish. This is Mexico. But really, they spoke both. For some reason, they hung on to their English.

". . . Mando had saved money and he'd thought of everything. The problem was, he'd only thought of the practical things. An affordable place to live, simple pieces of furniture, a couch, chairs, money for food. If we needed something, he always seemed to have the money to buy it. Nice rugs to cover the old linoleum. It wasn't bad. But it wasn't that simple. Not for Mando or Yolie. Not for any of us."

"Did you ever find out where Mando was working?"

He liked her voice. He liked the way she said *Andrés*. He looked at her. He knew he was wearing a numb look on his face. But he could make himself look numb, even if he didn't feel that way. He wondered where he'd learned that.

"Are you all right?"

"Just wondering."

"What?"

"Nothing." She wouldn't push him. He knew that. If he didn't want to answer a question, she left it alone.

"Would you like a cup of coffee?"

"Sure."

"There's a little coffee shop on this floor. I'll buy you a cup."

They didn't say anything as they walked down the hall. It was odd, to be walking next to her—as if somehow he was a part of her life. But he wasn't. He knew that. She was a counselor, a therapist, a beautiful woman. He was nothing. That's what he was.

As they stood in line at the coffee shop. Grace ordered two cups of coffee. "Small or large?" the guy asked.

"Small for me." She looked at him.

"Small. Black."

The guy nodded, and handed them their cups of coffee.

"When did you start drinking coffee?"

"My first foster home. I was sixteen."

He thought it was all right to ask her the same question. Maybe that was all right. "How about you?"

"When I got married."

He nodded. "You started late." He felt stupid.

"Yeah," she said. "My husband loved coffee. So I learned to like it, too."

He thought the seconds it took them to walk back to her office would last forever. And when he was finally sitting back down across from her, he felt better. He knew what he was supposed to do when he was in her office.

"Do you have a girlfriend?" She asked the question almost as a matter of small talk. But it wasn't. He knew that.

"I thought we were supposed to talk about my past."

"We can talk about anything we want. And you don't have to answer the question."

"I know." He tapped his finger on the table. "No."

"Are you straight?"

"Yes."

"There's nothing wrong with being gay."

"Do you think I'm gay?"

"No."

"But you think I might be, because I don't have a girlfriend."

"You sound angry. I didn't mean to make you angry. It was an honest question. I don't assume anything about anyone. I don't jump to conclusions. I ask questions because—" She stopped, then looked at him. She wanted him to understand. "I only asked you if you had a girlfriend because I wanted to know if you were close to anyone. That's all I'm getting at. Do you have any friends?"

"I don't have friends, no."

"You mentioned a guy. Al. Is Al your friend?"

"No. I wouldn't say that. I work with him. He's not really my friend. I'm not good about making friends."

"What about Dave Duncan?"

"I wouldn't call him a friend. He's my lawyer."

"You're not friends?"

"No."

"So you don't have a girlfriend. And you don't have any friends. Sounds lonely."

"Look, listening to other people's problems day after fucking day—that sounds lonely, too." He was on fire, she could almost touch the rage. He could scare people. He could make anyone afraid, if he wanted to.

He looked at his watch. "Look, I gotta go."

"Andrés, I don't want you to be angry."

He hated her calmness. So fucking easy for her to be so calm, since it wasn't her life that was under discussion. "I gotta go."

"See you on Thursday, then?"

"Can't. I got an interview for a job." He wasn't telling the truth. "Can't on Thursday."

"Next Tuesday, then?"

"Sure." He didn't look at her, didn't say good-bye. He just walked out the door.

So that's how he played it when he couldn't yell at you or hit you. He just looked away, pretended you weren't there. *So, I've touched a nerve.* She stared at the ringing telephone.

She let it ring. Let them leave a message.

# Not This Case, Judge

Dave sat at his desk, the morning newspaper unread. He'd brought it with him to the office. He stared at the headline: MAN CONFESSES TO STRANGLING EIGHT-YEAR-OLD. He tossed the newspaper in the trash, then stared at his messages. A call from a former client, a call from his ex-girlfriend, a call from someone he didn't know, a prospective client, he guessed, and a call from Judge David Caballero. A good judge. Fair, anyway. He made a mental note to write him a check for his reelection campaign. The system sucked. Writing checks for good reasons. And writing checks for bad reasons. He noticed his secretary standing at the door. She had a file in her hand. "Judge Caballero is here to see you."

"Send him in, Margie."

He stood, half surprised the judge was there in person. He'd come by before, to ask him to take a difficult case, a case nobody wanted to take. He suspected he was knocking at his door now for a similar reason. He was old-fashioned, the judge, preferred to drop in on lawyers rather than call them on the phone. A dying breed.

"Judge, good to see you."

"Dave. How are you?" His voice was friendly, controlled, formal. A voice he'd cultivated over the years. It made people feel comfortable. But never too far away from work.

Dave was already standing in front of him, shaking his hand, offering him a chair. "It's good to see you, Judge. Taking a long lunch?"

"Well, a late one anyway."

"How's Blanca?"

"Oh, she's fine. Thanks for asking. She keeps thinking of women you should marry. She keeps a list."

"That's very sweet of her, to think of me."

"Don't you believe it. You should see the list."

They both laughed—nothing forced, an easy laugh—then settled into an uncomfortable quiet.

Finally, Dave tapped his fingers on his desk and asked, "What can I help you with, Judge?"

"It's about the Gonzalez case."

"The Gonzalez case?"

"The Angela Gonzalez case."

"Oh, the little girl."

"Yes."

"Awful."

"Yes."

"I want to appoint you to represent—"

"I won't do it, Judge."

"That was fast. You didn't even let me finish."

"I don't mean to be rude, Judge. I don't need to tell you how much I respect you. You're a fine judge, and I've always tried to take my share of court-appointed cases. But this time, Judge—"

"Nobody wants this case, Dave."

"I can't do it."

"Why not? As an officer of the court, Dave, you're obliged. You have a duty."

"With all due respect to everybody's civil rights, I can't represent that man. I can't. Don't do this to me, Judge."

"You're a good lawyer."

"I can't do this. Give it to someone else. I've never turned a case down, have I, Judge? Good, bad, evil, low-profile, high-profile, murder, rape, whatever—if you handed me a case, I did my job. But not this one."

The judge nodded. "Mind if I ask why?"

"It's personal."

The judge kept nodding. "I see. Got any suggestions?"

• • •

Dave sat at his desk and looked around at his comfortable surroundings. An enviable office, neat, tasteful. Not one piece of art in sight. *You'd think a man of means would at least own a fucking painting.* He caught himself. He knew what he was doing. He beat up on himself when he was upset. The judge's visit. The things that had happened to Andrés Segovia. A little girl, dead.

He remembered a colleague talking about "sex rings." That's the phrase he used. "They use the children of Juárez, use them for their games." *Games,* a neutral euphemism. "Most of the men are from our side. We export more than freedom, baby, I'll tell you that." He hated thinking about that conversation, hated knowing what was out there. He knew most of those kids never turned out any good. Andrés Segovia was still something of a miracle.

*Hell no, Judge, I won't take that case.*

# Grace in the Afternoon

The question, Do you have a girlfriend?—he'd hated it. He objected to having been asked if he was gay, but he was just as bothered by the girlfriend question. By the friend question. Yes, bothered by those questions—enraged by them. As if she were trying to undress him. As if it were a violation. The accusation of intimacy with anyone made him so uncomfortable that he'd wanted to lash out. But even worse was the accusation of loneliness. At that one, he *had* lashed out, *loneliness is fucking listening to other people's problems day after day.*

He was angry and lost and scarred. That was obvious enough. And she had no doubt he was capable of inflicting physical or verbal pain on anyone who came along at the wrong time. She could almost touch his unpredictable, almost savage energy. But he was also articulate and controlled and had the intellect and sensibility of a poet. He saw things and people for what they were—himself included. It was strange and beautiful, the way he recounted his own history as if he were reading it in the pages of a novel. A novel where he became the elusive, romantic figure. Not quite a hero. Not quite an antihero. She'd never had a client who'd done that so artfully. She wondered if it wasn't a trick. A kind of seduction. A way of taking control.

She wrote down a few notes on her pad. Not many. Just words that would jar her memory. She put down the pen, then smiled. An ironic smile. Small world. Small enough for everyone to bump into each other's shoulders, yet big enough to get lost in if you wanted to be lost, and cruel enough to be taken from a place where you were safe, and kind enough to be loved by an older brother who thought himself a man. And kind enough to have a place to live, even if it was a humble place in a humble part of a humble city, and cruel enough to be taken away from school and an education when you were clearly born with a fine mind and a good dose of ambition. Andrés. Andrés Segovia. She didn't know exactly what about Andrés reminded her of Mister. Maybe it was because neither of them was very conscious of his physical beauty—and they were, both of them, beautiful. A woman could stare all day.

Andrés, Mister. She tried to put them together in her mind, and wondered what they would talk about if they found themselves in the same room. Such different kinds of men. She wondered how her son would've turned out if his life had been like Andrés Segovia's. Would he have turned out to be as kind and as playful? Would he have turned out as comfortable with words? What would Mister have been like if he had traveled the same road as Andrés? What made them what they were, these men? Parents? Affection? Lack of affection? Fathers? Lack of fathers? Circumstances? Environment? Poverty? Loneliness? Want? Genetics? Temperament—and where did that come from, temperament? What was it, finally, that made the difference? And as they aged, would they stay more or less the same? Would they grow harder and more bitter? Would something happen to irrevocably change the way they saw and felt about the world? Fifty years old, and what did she know? What had she learned? *Loneliness is fucking listening to other people's problems day after day.* That accusation. That echo in the room. "No, Andrés, loneliness is losing the man who owned your body and your heart." She chastised herself for that self-pitying remark. She had nothing to teach Andrés Segovia about loss or rage or loneliness. He was an expert on the subject.

"Grace, you're a disaster." She stared at the ringing phone again. She wanted simply to walk out of the office, walk out and go to a movie, then buy herself a new dress, then go to the store and buy a pack of cigarettes, then go home and put on her new dress, then walk into her backyard, barefoot, with a scotch in her hand and a pack of cigarettes, and watch the sun go down. She wanted to do all of these simple things as if she were a young schoolteacher on the first day of summer vacation. And then maybe, after she finished her drink and smoked a few cigarettes, she'd cry until she washed away all the crap and garbage in her life. And when it grew dark, she would lie down and count the stars. She thought of Andrés, a boy of ten in a small courtyard counting each star, *one two three four five.* . . . She didn't want to think of him, but there he was again, like a stalker. So many of her patients had stalked her—but it wasn't them, it was her. She'd never really learned how to let go of things. And certainly she'd never let go of Sam. That's why she'd never remarried. Of course that was why. It wasn't a complicated matter. She'd dated exactly two men in twelve years. Two men. Three dates each. Six dates in twelve years. They weren't Sam.

She wasn't even letting go of her own life. Telling herself and Mister and Richard Garza that it was okay, that she could let go, that it was time. Didn't they say that in Spanish, "Ya le tocababa"? About winning the lottery or getting married. Or dying. She was so calm about this cancer that was knocking at her door, asking her to come out. She was acting as if letting go of her own life was as easy as flicking the ashes of a cigarette. As if her life was nothing.

Maybe she was just pretending.

*Maybe I'll go buy a dress. I'll put it on my credit card. Maybe I'll be dead by the time the bill comes in.*

She was leaving her office early. Why not? The phone rang. Again. It always rang. She wasn't going to answer it. But she hadn't answered it all afternoon. Well, she wouldn't feel so bad for leaving early. If she answered it. "Hello. Grace Delgado."

"Grace." The voice sounded young and buoyant. Like a high school boy calling a girl he liked.

"Richard?"

"Are you busy?"

"I was just leaving for the day."

"Oh, well, I was wondering—" He stopped, suddenly shy. "I have an article I'd like you to read. It might help you think about some treatments."

"Treatments would only buy time in my case. Isn't that what you said?"

"No. That's not what I said, Grace. That's what you heard."

"You said it had metastasized."

"No, Grace, I didn't."

"You didn't?"

"I said it was advanced—but I said it *hadn't* metastasized."

"But it *is* advanced."

"Grace. Can I ask you a question? Do you want to die?"

"Of course not."

"There's still time."

"How sick will the treatments make me?"

"Some people hardly get sick at all—did you know that?"

"What about most people?"

"You've never been most people, Grace. Will you look at this article?"

"Yes, okay, I'll look at it."

"And—"

Grace listened to the silence on the other end of the phone.

"And will you have dinner with me? I mean, if you're not busy?"

"Tonight?"

"Why not? I was just going to make my rounds, and I should be done by seven-thirty."

"Don't you want to have dinner with your family?"

"My wife . . ." His voice trailed off, then started up again. "She left me. She hooked up with a podiatrist and moved to Seattle." He laughed, a nervous laugh.

"I'm sorry to hear that, Richard." She hadn't meant to sound so callous. Not her most empathetic voice.

"Bad day?"

"They'll get worse."

"So take advantage. Eat while you can."

"Okay, why not? How about a steak?"

Three weeks ago, she would have found eating dinner with her doctor inappropriate. She was always one for boundaries. Her professional relationships stayed professional. Friendly. Even informal. But there was always that line. She never crossed it. Never even came close. She knew some people considered her emotionally aloof. Superior. Imperious.

She'd overheard that once. She'd had a good laugh about it later. Imagine a girl from Dizzy Land being accused of that. She turned off the lights to her office as she stood at the door. She stared into the dark and empty office. Then closed the door.

On her way home, she went to her favorite dress shop. She tried on dress after dress, a blue one, a yellow one, a red one, a dress with flowers, a navy blue, floor-length dress with yellow polka dots. She bought the red one. After she left the dress shop, she stopped off at a liquor store and bought a bottle of Chivas and a pack of Marlboro Lights. Same brand she used to smoke. Same brand Andrés Segovia smoked. Three dollars. Three dollars and change for a pack of cigarettes. She always noticed the price of things, was the kind of woman who refused to buy a head of lettuce if she thought it was too expensive. That she could afford it was never the point for a woman with her disposition. *Imperious, my ass.* Almost four hard-earned dollars. Fifty cents more would buy her a lunch at Jalisco's. She shook her head, and bought the cigarettes anyway. Why fuss over the price of cigarettes when she'd just spent a bundle on a red dress?

She went home, opened the French doors that led to her backyard, took off her shoes, and poured herself a drink. She found an ashtray in the back of a drawer and took out the fresh pack of cigarettes. She opened the cellophane pack and breathed in the smell. She could almost feel Sam in the room. She could almost feel him lighting her cigarette, his hand on hers. She closed her eyes. She half expected to see him standing there. She felt a pang of disappointment when she opened her eyes. She lit the cigarette.

*Why don't you quit? Because I'll explode.* "Go away, Andrés."

She finished her cigarette and her scotch. She took a shower, put on her new dress, and stared at herself in the mirror. The light caught her diamond ring, the one Sam had given her when he'd asked her to marry him. She thought maybe it was time to take it off. So she did. She waved her naked hand in front of the mirror. She stared at the ring, sitting there on top of the dresser. She put it back on. She stared at the light—the light that was in the ring.

No, she didn't know how to let go of things.

# Order and Timing in the Universe

H i."

"Hi."

Mister stared at his mother as she guarded her front door. "You look nice. Going out?"

"Yeah."

"A date? It looks like a date, Grace."

"I wouldn't call it that. Dinner with a friend."

"What friend?"

"Richard Garza."

"Your doctor?"

"Yeah. Like I said, it's not a date. Just dinner with a friend."

"Well, maybe I should've called before—"

"No, come in. Would you like a beer?" She pushed the door open, then disappeared into the house. Mister followed her in.

He sat down on the couch, and noticed that Grace had already poured herself a drink. He picked up the drink and smelled the scotch. He hated the stuff. He set the drink back down. Grace walked back into the living room and handed Mister a beer. "I wasn't expecting you." She sat down across from him and reached for her drink. "I bought a new dress."

"Good. You deserve it."

"Nobody deserves a new dress, Mister."

"Are you in a bad mood?"

"No."

"Yes, you are. I called you at the office today. Three times. You didn't answer. I got worried. You should call me more often."

"Is this a new rule?"

"Yes."

"Okay." She nodded. She wasn't going to be stubborn. She wasn't going to start a fight over nothing. They always started a fight over nothing. "You and I—we're okay. Aren't we okay?"

He nodded. "We're okay. Maybe we've always been okay."

"Yes, maybe we always have been." She played with her wedding band. "You and Liz are very gracious hosts."

"Yes, we are, aren't we?"

They laughed. Like they used to. Mister drank his beer, and Grace drank her scotch. They talked. He told her about the coffee shop. He told her Vicente was coming for a visit. She listened. "Next time bring Liz," she heard herself say as he left.

"She does look thinner," he said to himself as he drove away. And then he thought, "Why is she having dinner with her doctor?" And then a thought crossed his mind, and he began to worry.

Grace watched herself smoke a cigarette in the mirror. She put out the cigarette and called Richard. She heard his voice on the other end. "I'm sorry, Richard, I can't."

"It's only dinner, Grace."

"I can't."

"You're a beautiful woman, Grace."

"Are you mocking me, Richard?"

"No. I've always wanted to say that to you."

"Why?"

"Because sometimes it's important to say what you think."

"This is all very strange, Richard." She thought of lighting up another cigarette. "If I wasn't dying, would you have told me that?"

"I don't know that you are dying, Grace. You have cancer. Cancer doesn't always equal death."

"Did you become a doctor because you think everything can be fixed?"

"I became a doctor because I think that living is a good idea."

"It's easier, isn't it, to tell a woman she's beautiful when she's dying?"

"Talking to people in the face of their own mortality is the most difficult thing in the world, Grace."

"Then you're in the wrong business."

"I'm not going to let you die."

"Is that right, Richard? Do I need to be present to win?"

All Andrés had wanted to do all day was sleep. But now, as he sat in his apartment, he had the sudden urge to get out, to do something. Anything. Anything except play on his computer. Not that he played. He didn't do chat lines, except to discover what they were, how they functioned. Pornography disgusted him, so that was out of the question. He didn't look for the perfect mate online, nor did he shop. He'd order an occasional book. But mostly he bought his books at secondhand bookstores. Not that he read that much. Not anymore. Mysteries mostly. Who killed who, and why. Nothing to remind him of real life. Why would he want to read about characters who were as screwed up as he was?

He stared at his computer. He didn't want to turn it on. Not tonight. It was like night school. It was like learning. It was like work. Which is all he had.

He changed into an old pair of jeans, put on a T-shirt. He would go for a walk. Maybe he would start running again. He'd done that for a while. It had helped. Pounding out rage. The problem with running was that it made him remember. So did walks. But everything made him remember. Why was it that memory was supposed to be something to be valued? Memory had been beating the crap out of him most of his life. He had the bruises to prove it.

It was still hot when he stepped outside. But a breeze was kicking up, and it looked like there was a chance for a thunderstorm. He closed his eyes, took a breath, then opened them. He walked down the street, aimlessly, without purpose. Passing time was passing time, a dull hobby for those who had too much of it—and nothing else. He tried not to think of anything, but he kept seeing that look on Dave's face. He erased it like he would delete a file in a computer. And then, without even conjuring it up, Grace Delgado's face appeared. Her eyes, severe and demanding and kind and tender at the same time. Beautiful and distant and untouchable like the western horizon. He deleted her, too. He was tired of letting himself be haunted by people who had authority over him. He was tired of remembering fragments of his life without fully understanding the entire story.

He remembered the boy who used to ride a bike around his neighborhood. That boy was the one thing he could not delete from his memory. He walked and walked until there was nothing but the walking.

Dave was leaning on his car outside Andrés' apartment house. He was talking on his cell and smoking a cigarette. He waved. Andrés didn't wave back. Dave finished his call and shut his cell phone off.

"¿Que tal, hombre?"

He resented gringos who thought they owned Spanish.

"Slumming?"

"Why are you always mad at me, Andrés?"

"I'm not mad at you, Dave."

"I've left you a couple of messages. You haven't called me back."

"I know that, too."

"I have a few questions."

"About what?"

"About that night."

"What do you want to know?"

"When was the first time you saw that guy—William Hart?"

"Who says I'd seen him before?"

"Al Mendoza does. The bartender does. Everyone. Everyone says you were yelling, 'I know you. I fucking know you.' "

"I don't remember yelling that."

"You have to help me out here, Andrés. I can't help you if—"

"Then don't."

"It's not a felony to help someone out."

"Yeah, okay."

"Will you come in this week and talk to me?"

"Yeah, okay."

"How are your sessions going?"

"Okay."

"Want to go grab a beer?"

"Don't you have a caseload or something? Don't you have to prepare for a trial or something?"

Vicente took his hand. He turned around and waved at the Rubios, as if he could see them. Someone had taught him these things. Mister thought of Vicente's mother. It occurred to him that she may have been a better mother than anybody gave her credit for. Vicente wasn't a tabula rasa. There are things he knew. "He talks," she'd said. So he would talk when he was good and ready. On his terms. Something on his own terms. That wasn't hard to understand. If you thought about it.

Mister led him by the hand. He wanted to pick him up, but didn't. He didn't seem afraid or tentative. Mr. Rubio had given him a walking stick, and he was learning to use it, though it was still something of a toy for him.

He opened the back door of the car. "This is my car," he said, "It's almost new. You can smell it." Not that he had to tell Vicente to smell it because already he was doing just that. "Here," he said, then picked him up gently and placed him in the car seat Mr. Rubio had loaned him. He buckled him in, then touched Vicente's cheek. The boy pressed his small hand against Mister's, as if to tell him he could keep his hand there for as long as he wanted. Mister kissed him on the forehead. "Aren't you something?" he said. He buckled him in, but Vicente fought him. "You don't like the belt, huh? Well, if it makes you feel any better, I have to wear one, too." Vicente clapped his hands. Mister clapped his, too. "Let's go," he said. "You like ice cream?"

Vicente nodded.

"What kind? What kind of ice cream do you like? Vanilla?"

He shook his head.

"Chocolate?"

He shook his head.

"Orange sherbet?"

He nodded.

"Good. That's my favorite."

All the way home, Mister stared at Vicente through the rearview mirror. Alert, he moved his head from side to side as if he were studying his new surroundings, almost as if he were sighted. As they neared his house, he heard Vicente's small voice. "Mom." And then, after a moment, Vicente repeated the word again. "Mom."

Mister smiled. *That's where all our stories begin, don't they? With Mom. Me and you, kid, our stories are as different as our mothers.* He pulled into the driveway. He turned off the car. He turned around and reached out his hand and touched Vicente's wandering face. "Mom. That's a good word. A holy word. Hand. That's a holy word, too. Let's go inside. I'll teach you a new word. Home. H-O-M-E. Home."

He carried him inside. He could feel Vicente's breath on his neck. He smelled of apples. His breath hadn't changed yet. There was nothing rotting inside him yet. Mom. Hand. Home.

Mom. Dad.

# Andrés, You *Are* That Boy

ndrés turned eleven that summer. That August. They'd lived in their new home for almost three months, and the days didn't seem so long, though they were hot. Everything they needed, food and beds and walls and clothes and shoes and a bathroom and even a television that mostly Yolie and Ileana watched. Andrés had no interest in television. In Spanish or in English, didn't matter, the people he saw who lived in the television weren't saying anything he understood. It was as though he had to read their lips, and when he finally succeeded in making out the words, it wasn't worth the effort. But they had everything they needed—even a fan in every room to keep the house cool, though it wasn't as cool as the air-conditioned house they'd had in El Paso.

Andrés dreamed of Mrs. Fernandez, and sometimes he got Mrs. Fernandez and his mother confused—in his dreams. School was starting. But that was in El Paso. And he no longer lived in El Paso. He lived in Juárez. And he liked a part of that. He liked the Spanish. And he liked going to the market every day. He especially grew to like watching the chickens hanging upside down and the stacks of chicharrones behind glass cases. Better than steaks, any day. Chicharrones. The woman who sold them, sometimes, she would give him one for free. He liked the vendors, the way they talked.

Yolie always bought them a burrito or tacos al carbón, or sometimes they even sat at one of the outdoor stands and ate a plate of enchiladas or carnitas—and they all ate as if they hadn't eaten for days, ravenous. And then they would buy aguas frescas. Ileana always ordered an agua de sandia because she liked the color. Yolie always ordered an agua de piña, and Andrés, he always ordered an agua de melón. He loved cantaloupe. Cantaloupe reminded him of his mother.

He'd made a few friends, and his Spanish was getting better and better, and the neighbors had stopped making fun of them because of the funny way they spoke Spanish, and they had stopped calling them "pochos."

Yolie found a bookstore because she knew Andrés liked to read, and she let him pick out some books. They were all in Spanish, but somehow Andrés found them easy to read. Well, maybe not so easy. But not so hard, either. And he had time. He wasn't in a hurry. So, if it took him a long time to read, it didn't matter. And in El Paso, school was starting. And he wouldn't be going. And he was sad. Because he liked school. But he didn't say anything to Yolie or Mando because he knew they would laugh or shake their heads or maybe even make fun of him because they'd never liked school, and had only gone because they were forced to go, and what good was school and learning when there was money to be made and a life to be lived and a world to be savored? And didn't they have everything they needed? And wasn't it because Mando was working that they had everything? But where did he work? It scared Andrés to ask that question, so he didn't. Because there was a part of him that knew.

He was turning eleven that August day. That boy who still carried the streets of his old neighborhood in his heart, that boy who still ached to ride a bike. Not any bike, but *his* bike, the one his father gave him.

"What would you like for your birthday? How about a bike?"

Andrés looked at Mando and shook his head. "No," he said, then looked away.

"You don't want a bike, carnalito?" That's what he called him now, carnalito.

Andrés shook his head. "I want a typewriter."

"A typewriter, carnalito? What the fuck are you gonna do with a pinchi typewriter?"

"Type things," Andrés answered.

"Type things?" Mando laughed and lit a cigarette. "You know what, Andy, you've always been a weird little guy, you know that?"

Andrés shrugged. "It doesn't matter. I mean, it doesn't matter what I get. A bike is okay. Or anything. It doesn't matter."

"Look, carnalito, it's your frickin' birthday," Mando said, "so let's see what we can do about that typewriter."

His girlfriend, Xochil, was standing at the door. She had a towel around her and another towel around her head. Clean and showered, and she and Mando looked at each other, and Andrés knew they wanted each other like they'd wanted each other last night when Mando had asked him to go sleep out in the courtyard—which he didn't mind because it was nice there, the way they had fixed it up, and it was cooler there at night. But he'd heard them moaning the way he'd heard his mother and father moaning a few times. And he knew that Yolie and Ileana must have heard them, too. Not that Mando and Xochil cared. They just wanted each other.

"You wanna go and find Yolie and Ileana at the market?" Mando stuck a five-dollar bill in his hand. His father had never given him five-dollar bills. He didn't want to think about where that five-dollar bill had come from. He didn't. He knew Mando didn't have a normal job, the kind his father once had.

Andrés nodded and took the money. Xochil kissed him on the forehead as he passed her. She smelled something like his mother. Something like that. At least Xochil was nice to him. And nice to Ileana, too. She and Yolie, well, they were nice to each other, too. But he knew there was something hard between them. He knew that.

He found Yolie at the market, and she was talking to some guy that had been hanging around. He didn't know where they'd met, but they'd met somewhere. Maybe they'd met when Yolie went out in the afternoon, or in the early evenings. Andrés knew that the guy was from El Paso and was even more of a pocho than they were, because his Spanish was very broken—even though he looked very Mexican. He knew he had lived in El Paso all his life. Yolie was talking to him in Spanish, and he would answer back in English, and neither of them seemed to mind and they looked at each other in the same way that Mando and Xochil looked at each other, and Andrés knew that his father would have sent Andrés away with one of his looks or one of his hard words and he would've made Yolie go inside and wash the dishes. But those rules weren't there anymore, and Mando and Yolie said it was better that way.

Yolie bought him an agua fresca and bought Ileana one, too. "Why don't you go and walk around for a while. Come back in half an hour." Andrés looked at his watch—the watch Mr. Fernandez had given him. And he nodded. He took Ileana's hand. Yolie and her guy friend wanted to talk about things, maybe each other. It didn't matter. He smiled at his little sister. "Mando gave me five dollars. I'll buy you something?"

Ileana smiled at him. "There's a rabbit in a stand over there," she said, pointing.

She was pointing toward the outdoor stands where vendors sold clothes and shoes and toys. And Andy knew she was talking about a stuffed rabbit. "Let's go see it," he said. And he kissed her. And she laughed. And Andrés thought that as long as he had Ileana, then everything would be very good.


On his birthday, Mando and Yolie had a party for him. There was Coke and a cake and Mando had gotten a table for the courtyard from somewhere and Yolie had decorated it with a party tablecloth and there were balloons and Yolie's boyfriend was there whose name was Eddie, and Eddie had brought him a present. And Xochil had brought him a present, too. And his three friends who lived on the same street, Lalo and Chilo and Oscar, they were there. They didn't bring presents, but he didn't care because he knew they were poor. Their houses didn't have all the nice things his house had. No, he didn't care about presents. He was glad they came. And Ileana's friend, Elisa, she was there, too. And they all sat out in the courtyard and it was cool that day, and the breeze smelled like rain, and Yolie and Mando were happy. He thought that it was strange that they were happier now than they had been when his mother and father were alive. And he wondered about that. And he thought that maybe his parents' death had been a kind of freedom for them. But that's not the way it had ever felt to him.

He blew out his candles, and he made a wish. He wished he could see Mr. and Mrs. Fernandez again. He wished he could go to school. That's what he wished. But he knew it was useless to wish those things.

He was embarrassed to open his presents in front of everyone, so he decided to let Ileana open them for him. And she squealed and kissed him and she looked at the presents and decided to open the one Eddie had brought for him. And when she ripped it open, Andrés smiled at what was in the box: watercolors and a pad of watercolor paper. Andrés thanked him, and he smiled at Yolie because she must've found the drawings he kept underneath his bed. And he wanted to kiss her. Because even though she could be so angry and get mad at the littlest things, she could also be very good.

When he opened Xochil's gift, he nodded. And smiled at her. A shirt. It was a very beautiful shirt. He kissed her on the cheek because he knew that Mando would like that. It wasn't bad, to kiss her on the cheek. She was nice. And then there was a bigger, heavier box. Ileana couldn't lift it from the table. Andrés had been looking at the box all evening. "I can't, Andy," Ileana said. "It's too heavy."

So Andrés reached for the box and ripped off the wrapping. And there it was. His typewriter. He hadn't meant to cry. But he did. He cried.

Mando held him tight—just like his father. "Hey, carnalito," he said, "¿que pues? Hey, hey, maybe you've had too much Coke."

That made Andrés laugh.

"And one more present," Yolie said. And she walked into the house and walked back with another present. When Andrés opened it, he saw that it had two reams of paper and typewriter ribbon and pens and pencils and two yellow pads of paper.

And he never loved Yolie and Mando more. He could never love anyone more than this.

---

"You know, I was just thinking. The typewriter. I'd forgotten. It was the first thing that got sold when we needed money. Yolie didn't even ask me. She didn't even tell me. It was just gone one day. I hated her that day. For taking it away from him."

"Him?"

"From that boy."

"That boy is you, Andrés."

"No. I don't think so. That was someone I used to be. I'm not that boy anymore."

"We don't shed our former selves that easily, do we?"

"At what point do we let go, Grace?"

"That's the question, isn't it, Andrés?"

"There's more than one question."

She nodded. "Yes." She leaned into her desk. "What did you write, when you had your typewriter?"

"I typed out a journal. Like a diary, sort of."

"Did you address it to anyone?"

"To Mrs. Fernandez."

"Why her? Why not your mother?"

"Because my mother was dead. It made me sad, to think of her. So I decided to write these, well, these letters to Mrs. Fernandez. I knew they weren't really letters. But it made it easier to write, if I pretended to be writing to someone."

"What happened to the letters?"

"I don't know. I don't remember. When the typewriter got sold, well, I just stopped writing."

"What was wrong with just writing with a pencil or a pen?"

"I was mad. I don't know. I just didn't want to write anymore."

"But you still write?"

"No. Sometimes. Not much."

"When you write, what do you write about?"

"Yolie. Mando. Ileana. And I don't want to write about them. I want to forget they ever existed."

"How will that help?"

"What's so great about remembering?"

"You think forgetting is a better alternative?"

"What's the difference between letting go and forgetting?"

"Big difference, Andrés."

"I don't get it."

He'd lied to her. He knew exactly what had happened to his writings. He remembered every detail of that day. And he hadn't told her, hadn't wanted to tell her. Why the hell did she have to know every little detail of his fucked-up life? Couldn't he keep something? He had never been allowed to keep anything—not even his gifts, not his bicycle, not his typewriter, not his mother and father, not his brothers and sisters, not his body, not his heart, not the things he kept locked up in his memory, not his fucking life. Nothing.

So he hadn't told her.

"My typewriter, Yolie, it's gone. I went to get it from under my bed—it's gone."

Yolie looked at him, then turned her attention to the meal she was cooking.

"Yolie, it's gone! My typewriter!"

"I sold it," she whispered.

"What!" Andrés screamed. "What!"

"I fucking sold it. And stop your goddamned whining."

"Why'd you sell it?" Andrés whispered.

"We needed the money, you little asshole. Where do you think I got the money to buy what we're having for dinner? Where the hell do you think I get money from?"

Andrés nodded. "I'm sorry. I didn't know."

"I should've told you."

"It doesn't matter."

"It's just a typewriter, Andy."

"Yeah."

They didn't say anything to each other over dinner. Ileana was sick that day, and Yolie gave her soup. And it was cold in the house. But at least they had blankets. That's what Yolie said. And they had food. And what did a typewriter matter?

Andrés couldn't sleep. He was thinking about Mando and how he missed him. He was thinking about his typewriter. He was thinking about his bicycle. And then he remembered his father's ring. He kept it in a box under his bed. Yolie knew he had it, knew it was gold. Maybe she'd sold it. He lit a candle and looked under his bed. He took out the box. It was there, in a pouch. She hadn't sold it. Not yet. He took it, and walked out into the courtyard. He dug up one of the bricks and buried the ring there. He placed the brick back in its place. No one would find it. No one but him. If the ring was safe, then he would be safe, too.

He went back to bed. And still, he couldn't sleep. He had a candle burning in the room and the shadows danced and they scared him. And then he decided what he should do next. He took out all of his letters into the courtyard. All of the letters he'd written to Mrs. Fernandez. Among the letters, there was a story he'd written, a story about a boy who counted stars and all the wishes he made. It wasn't a good story, anyway. What did he know about writing stories? He took all those stupid pieces of writing into the courtyard. Useless pages of typewritten words, and what good were they, anyway, all those words?

And then he began to burn the pages.

A few pages at a time. He burned them. Burned them all. And when he had finished, he smelled the ashes and he thought that maybe the ashes were the only thing he would remember.

It was cold. And then it started to rain. And he stood in that cold rain until he couldn't stand it anymore. And he thought to himself that a real man would've stood out in the rain for a lot longer than he had. And then he went inside and dried himself off and put himself to bed and he whispered to himself what Yolie had told him. "At least we have blankets." And he told himself that typewriters and letters and words didn't matter. And he told himself that he would forget all of this.

One day, he would forget everything.

Andrés hadn't forgotten that boy everyone called Andy. If he had, he wouldn't be sitting here in his apartment. At one o'clock in the morning. Chain-smoking and writing down memories of the Andrés he used to be. Andy. He hated that boy. But there was no way of getting rid of him. Why was it that the past was more real than the present? Was there a name for that sickness?

# Mother, Son, Mister, Grace

They led him from room to room. They started in the living room. Slowly, Mister placed Vicente's hands on things. *This is a plant. I give it water twice a week. On this wall, books. Books. Tonight, I'll read you one about a dog who loves tortillas.* He seemed to know what they were. Books. A couch, a chair, a table, a lamp that gives light, *we'll talk about light, me and you. Lots of discussions about light.* He placed his hand near the bulb of the lamp. *Light. Hot.* And this is a desk. He sat Vicente down at the chair, then let him feel the wood of the table he used as a desk. And this is a computer. He let him touch the keys of the keyboard. Then he took his small finger. Let's spell your name, V-I-C-E-N-T-E. He clapped.

Then the hallway, then the kitchen, a stove like Mrs. Rubio's, a table like Mrs. Rubio's. A toaster. Liz guided his hands, and together they put a slice of bread in the toaster. She let Vicente feel the heat. *Not too close. Ouch. Burn.* When the toast was done, Mister picked him up and gently sat him on the counter. *This is a counter. I slice things, onions.* He took an onion from the basket and placed it in his hands. Vicente smelled it and made a face. He took the onion from him, and all three broke out laughing. And then Mister took him in his arms and swung him around. Vicente squealed, and the house had never been this full.

*And this, this is a refrigerator. You don't get to open it.* And as he held him in his arms, Mister kissed him and kissed him. Vicente kissed him back. And he thought that love was beautiful and infinite and he remembered how Sam had held him as a boy. And as Liz watched the two of them, she wondered why she had fought him about this. She remembered the rage inside her, *Why do you want a blind and abused boy?* and she was ashamed. And she thought about her father and how his life had come to end in a loveless marriage, but today, in her house, her husband was holding the beginning of something. Oh, I love you, she wanted to whisper—not just to Mister but to Vicente. She watched as they walked to and fro, up and down the house, up and down, not a big house, and she smiled at Mister's voice, *My room, your room, bathroom. Hall, kitchen, porch.*

They made peanut butter cookies with white chocolate. Because those are the ingredients they had in the house. They washed their hands. *Always wash.* And then Liz stuck Vicente's hands in the cool, soft flour. *Flour. This is flour.* From flour, we make bread and cake and cookies. And these are eggs, Mister added, feel, yuck, and this is vanilla, smell, it smells like summer in Mexico, that's where this comes from. And this is white chocolate, taste, umm, and Vicente repeated, ummm, their hands all dirty, mixing the batter with their hands, and God, Vicente had a laugh on him, and, stay, don't move, let me put these in the oven. And, God, they were a mess, all three of them, and so, he thought, maybe a bath because Mr. Rubio said Vicente loved baths and he'd brought a change of clothes so in we go, a bath and in the middle of the bath, Vicente felt Mister's face with his wet hands and Mister kept repeating, Dad. Dad.

He dried off Vicente's little body, then Liz took him and slipped on a diaper. That was next. Peeing standing up. *Took you long enough, Mister.* That's what Grace had said. Of course, Grace had probably expected him to know everything by the time he was four. Of course, that was exactly the age he'd started calling her Grace.

Mister and Vicente sat on the rocking chair, eating from the same cookie. Vicente fell asleep and Mister counted the beats of his heart. Liz took a picture. "The first one," she whispered. And they stared at each other and listened to Vicente breathe. At first his slumber was peaceful, his breathing easy, and Mister fell asleep to the steady and regular rhythms of his breathing. He woke to the shaking and crying, to the bad dreams. *Mama, mama.* "Shhhh, Shhhh." This boy would dream her forever.

Liz took him in her arms, "Shhh. Shhhh, my baby, shhhh."

• • •

"How was your date?"

"Calling to check up on me?"

"I waited till eleven."

"You could have called me any time this evening. I changed my mind."

"You stayed home?"

"I was tired."

"Are you all right?"

"I'm fine. Are you worried about me? First you drop in to visit, and now you call to check up on me. This from a son who could go weeks without calling me."

"Are you lecturing me?"

"No. I'm done with that."

He laughed. "Sure." He paused. "You look a little thin, Grace."

"I work too many hours."

"You should slow down."

"I'm trying. I'm reading a book."

"What's it about?"

She wasn't going to tell him it was about cancer. "About a woman who works too hard."

He laughed. "Grace?"

"Yeah."

"We brought him home this evening."

She stopped for a moment. Then she realized who Mister was talking about. "And?"

"We showed him the house. We walked up and down the whole house. Not that it took very much time to do that. His room, my room, the hallway, the kitchen, the bathroom, the living room. His bed, my bed, the couch, the rocking chair—he loved the rocking chair. Over and over, we walked the house. He smelled every room, smelled some of my books. We held hands. His hands are so small, Grace, and Liz showed him how to bake cookies. . . ." She pictured them in his house. She pictured the look on Mister's face. She was almost envious of his happiness. "I bathed him, Liz changed him, I read him a book, you know, the one Sam used to read to me . . ." Some people knew how to parent by instinct. Sam had been that way, too. Like he was born knowing what to do. "He likes to laugh. He doesn't fight me, Grace. He just, well, he just sort of leans into me. He's photo tactic."

"Photo tactic? Is that a Sam word?" It had to be a Sam word. He loved *photo* words.

"Of course it is. He's like a sunflower, Grace. He leans into me as if I were the source of all light."

Photo tactic. Yes. Of course. Sam and his words. He loved to play games with them. Once, he'd left her flowers in her office with a note. *Amor, you are as photophilic as the desert.* She'd hadn't thought of the note as being particularly romantic. But that had forced her to look up the word. *Growing or thriving best in strong light.* It was true. She was photophilic. Mister, too.

"Maybe you and Liz will be all the light that matters."

When Liz and Mister had left him off at the Rubios', Vicente hadn't wanted to let go. He'd cried, reached for him. "Mama, mama." He'd given him and Liz the same name: Mama. Not that Mister cared. He didn't mind one damn bit. He'd put him to bed at the Rubios', talked to him, told him a story—one that Sam had made up for him. About a boy who had a beautiful heart, and how that boy could make plants grow and how he could make people say good things—even people who liked to say only bad things. Vicente fell asleep listening to his voice, clinging to his arms.

It was almost time to bring him home.

# Until His Heart Bursts into Flames

I want you to lose that guy. I fucking mean it, Yolie."

"Screw you, Mando, you're not my dad. And what about you, you asshole?"

"Me?"

"Yeah, every time you bring your girlfriend over, you're moaning all goddamned night long like a couple of dogs in heat. No one can sleep, and you send Andy out to count the stupid fucking stars and Ileana wants to know if you're in pain and whether or not we should check on you and she keeps whispering to me that she thinks you're really sick and shouldn't we call a doctor and what the shit am I supposed to tell her?"

"Xochil is none of your business."

"Eddie's none of your business, either. Asshole."

"He just wants to get into your pants."

"So what if he does? What if I want to get into his? Ever think of that, you pinchi macho asshole?"

They were arguing again. Since the week after his birthday. Since Mando caught Eddie and Yolie in bed. They'd had their clothes on, and they were just kissing. But Mando had gotten really mad. Mad like he used to get mad at Dad. That's how the arguments started—with Eddie. Just like when Dad was around. The fighting. It was as if they couldn't live without it. It was as if they'd called a truce, but had decided to call the truce off because the peace was too much for them—so they started again.

Andrés took Ileana out of the house. He had enough money to buy them both paletas. "You want a paleta, Ellie?"

"Piña."

"Me, too."

She took his hand.

"Why do they fight so much?"

"That's how they love each other." He winked at her.

She laughed, then leaned into him. "Will you always take care of me, Andy?" He thought of his mother.

"Siempre."

"You promise?"

"Siempre."

"Say it in English."

"Always."

"And we won't fight like Yolie and Mando."

"No. Never. We're not like that."

"And will you take me back to El Paso? When you're big enough."

"Yes. When I'm big enough."

But wasn't he big enough now? That's what Andrés asked himself that night when he lay awake in the courtyard. What was he waiting for?

The breeze was cool, and he was glad that summer was ending. It had been so hot. He tried not to think about school. He wrote on his typewriter every day. He pretended it was his job—to write something. Mando bought him two dictionaries, one in Spanish and one in English, and sometimes he wrote sentences using the new words he looked up. Sometimes, when he got tired of writing, he made some sketches on his drawing pad. They were okay. He was an okay artist, he guessed. The things he sketched looked more or less like the things they were supposed to look like. But he wished he had a teacher.

He wondered why he just didn't take himself and Ileana back to El Paso. They could find their way back to the Fernandezes' house. They could cross the bridge and ask for directions. If the Fernandezes weren't home, they'd wait. And they would beg for forgiveness for having run away. Maybe they would forgive them and take them in. Maybe they would. And he and Ileana could go to school. And Mr. and Mrs. Fernandez could take care of them and buy them the things they needed. And they could be a family, and they wouldn't have to listen to fighting all the time. Mr. and Mrs. Fernandez—they didn't fight. They were like him and Ileana. They just didn't need to fight to feel like they were alive. Couldn't they just run away, him and Ileana? Why not? And they wouldn't be in the way anymore, and Yolie could be with her boyfriend, Eddie. And Mando could be with his girlfriend, Xochil. And Mando wouldn't have to make so much money to pay for everything they needed. But he remembered that he'd promised Mando. And he'd promised Xochil, too. He promised them that they would always stay together because Mom and Dad would have wanted that. For them to be a family. That's what they would have wanted, Mom and Dad.

That night, he argued with himself. He argued with his dead mother and father. He argued with Yolie. He argued with Mando. So many arguments, and all of them in his head. He made up his mind. He and Ileana would leave. They would take nothing with them—that way they could travel fast. Just get away. He would get on his hands and knees at the Fernandezes' doorstep if he had to. And they would forgive him and Ileana when they saw he was truly sorry, and they would give them a place to live. But what if Mando and Yolie came to take them away again? And what if he never saw them again? Hadn't Mando and Yolie taken care of them? Hadn't they been good? Hadn't they been a family? Why was he doing this, breaking up their family? "You'll never be happy with anything." That's what Yolie had told him one day. When she was mad.

The next day, he walked toward the bridge. By himself. In the late afternoon. So he'd know the way. He passed some bars as he walked. There were women in some of them who sold their bodies. She had heard Mando and Yolie talking. Whores. Prostitutes. Putas. That's what they called them. He knew they worked out of those bars. And he felt bad. Because they needed the money. That's what Yolie had said. But couldn't they sell burritos or tacos instead of their bodies? And how exactly did you sell a body? He asked Mando about that, and Mando said it was more like renting a body. "You rent your body out so someone else can use it for a while. For pleasure. And you charge by the hour. You get it, carnalito?" Yeah, he got it. Sort of.

So that afternoon, he wandered through the streets and he found his way to Avenida Benito Juárez. And he saw the bridge ahead and El Paso. And he wanted just to walk across. He knew no one would stop him. He would tell the man at the booth that he was an American. "U.S. citizen," that's what he would say. He would say that and smile and give him the names of all the presidents he could think of—Washington and Lincoln, and Jackson, and Johnson, two Johnsons. And Kennedy and Roosevelt—two Roosevelts, too. And they would let him back in. And he walked toward the bridge and he wanted to go back to El Paso—run there, run until he was safe. But he couldn't because he hadn't brought Ileana with him. And he would never leave her behind. Because he loved her more than anything in the world, more than the stars he counted or his books, more than his typewriter, more than the bicycle his father had left for him, more than his dead mother and father.

He traced his steps back to his house, remembering the names of the streets and the names of restaurants so he would know he was on the right road to go home again. It was getting dark, and as he walked past a bar, a woman smiled at him. "Que lindo," she said. She said it nice. And he wondered if she was a prostitute. She was dressed up, and she smelled like she was wearing lots of perfume—all dressed up like she was going to a dance.

He thought of his mother and father, and he remembered he hadn't prayed for them for a long time. So he went to the cathedral and lit a candle and hoped they had found the right road, the one that led to the light. The one that took them into the arms of God.

When he was walking back home, a man smiled at him. It was dark, but he could see the man perfectly from the light streaming from the store window. He didn't like the man's smile. The man motioned him to come closer. But he didn't. He didn't come closer. "Ven," the man said. "¿Como te llamas?" He could tell the man wasn't Mexican. The way he spoke. And then he waved a five-dollar bill in front of him, like an offering. The man came closer. And Andrés couldn't move. He couldn't. But finally, when he felt the man's breath on him, he ran. He ran all the way home.

When he walked back inside the house, his heart was still pounding. He went into the bathroom and washed the sweat off his face and neck. He promised himself that he and Ileana would be gone before the week was over. That night, Andrés dreamed he was waving good-bye to Mrs. Fernandez. She was waving at him and Ileana. And they were walking to school. He was smiling when he woke.

• • •

Mando didn't come home that night. But that happened a lot. He was out. He liked to go to bars. He liked to go out with Xochil and have a good time. Sometimes he was gone for days. One time for a week. It was normal, him not coming home.

"He left us a lot of money," Yolie said. But the way she said it. As if, somehow, he had left them too much money. She sounded worried.

"Did you fight again?" Ileana asked.

"No. He said he had to do something. But I could tell it was something he didn't want to do." And then Yolie stopped herself from saying anything else. She nodded. "It's late," she said, "let's go to bed." But they all had a bad feeling. So they lit a candle, and listened to the wind. The first cold wind of the season. And Yolie sang a song. And Andrés and Ileana listened, and Andrés thought that maybe Yolie could be a singer. He thought that everyone should listen to her voice, because there was so much sadness and happiness in it, all at the same time. And he knew she could make the world be quiet, and he thought that maybe the world needed to be quiet. That was the problem with the world—it never stayed quiet long enough to listen.

He wanted to tell Yolie that her voice was so beautiful. But he knew that Yolie didn't like people to tell her things like that.

So he just listened until he fell asleep, listened to the first cold wind and to Yolie's singing.

In the morning, Yolie was gone. She left them a note saying she would be back in the evening. And she left some money so that they could go to the market. And Andrés thought it was the perfect day to leave. The door was open. They had a chance. All he had to do was grab Ileana's hand and walk through the open door.

But he couldn't leave Yolie alone. Not like this. Not when something was wrong. It wasn't right. Just to leave her all alone in the world. They couldn't. So they went to the market, him and Ileana. And they bought everything they needed to make dinner. A big chicken and fresh tortillas and avocados. And the house smelled nice with the chicken in the oven. He knew how to make it—he'd watched his mother and Yolie. Easy. God, the house smelled nice. With the chicken in the oven.

That night, Yolie didn't come home. And so they were alone, Andrés and Ileana. And it rained and rained. And even though rain was a miracle because this was the desert, that night it was not a miracle because the rain sounded like a thief trying to break into the house.

"I'm scared, Andy."

"Don't be scared. I'm here."

She cried, Ileana. She cried and cried. "They'll never come back," she said. "Never."

"They'll be back tomorrow, you'll see."

"No. No, they won't. It will be just like Mom and Dad. They went out and they never came back. And they left us all alone."

"No, it won't be like that."

"Everyone will leave us. And then you'll leave me, too, Andy."

"No, I won't. I'll never leave you."

He pulled her close to him, and she cried and cried until he thought she would never stop crying. And he thought the rain would never stop, either. The rain that should have been a miracle but wasn't. And finally Ileana fell asleep, too tired to cry anymore. She dug herself into Andrés' ribs, and Andrés held his sister. His tiny sister. And he didn't sleep until the rain stopped. And when he woke, it was raining again.

"If I would have just been brave enough. None of this would have happened. But I was afraid."

"You were eleven years old."

"But I knew better."

"Okay, go ahead, take all the credit. It's all your fault."

"I know that trick, Grace."

"I know the trick you're pulling, too. The trick of taking all the credit."

"I'm not taking all the credit."

"Yes, you are. That's arrogant, you know."

"I'm tired."

"That your way of getting out of this debate?"

"Maybe. But I *am* tired." He suddenly felt naked revealing something about himself that was so simple and true. He felt awkward and self-conscious, and he was glad he *was* tired—too tired to worry too much.

Grace looked at her watch. "It's late."

"You don't mind, coming in after hours?"

"I don't mind."

"I think I signed up for too many classes."

"How many?"

"Fifteen hours."

"What's your favorite class?"

"My drawing class. The human figure." He laughed. Nervous, a nervous laugh.

"That's nice."

He liked the way she said that. She sounded real and soft in all the right kind of ways.

"Are you okay, Andy?"

"Andy?"

They looked at each other for an instant.

"Andy," he whispered. "I'm okay. I think I am." He shrugged. He felt soft just then. He never knew what to do when he felt soft. "I ran into Hernandez. I hate that bastard."

"Why?"

"I don't like him because he doesn't see us."

"Us?"

"Any of us. I mean, anybody who works under him. He doesn't see Al. He doesn't see Judy. He doesn't see Octavio. He doesn't see Elvira. He doesn't see Carla. He doesn't see anybody. We're just these numbers that fit into a formula. That's all. I'd like to take his face and pound it and pound it. And pound it."

She nodded. There was nothing false about the look on his face as he spoke—almost as if he were imagining himself smashing Hernandez's face into oblivion.

"You know, Grace, Hernandez should come and see you. He needs to talk to you more than I do."

"I don't care about Hernandez." Grace paused and looked into his coal black eyes. "I care about you."

"What does that mean?"

"It means—" She paused and smiled to herself. "It means we're hoeing a long row of summer cotton." She smiled to herself and thought of Richard Garza. "You and I. Andrés Segovia and Grace Delgado. Lots of weeds, Andrés. And we're hoeing. We're hoeing as fast as we can. And if we don't get the roots, then the weeds will grow back. And all our work will be for nothing."

She could almost see his smile. A sunrise. Breaking the darkness.

He shook his head. "You should have been an English teacher."

"You should have been a writer."

He laughed. Like a dam that was bursting. "That's funny, Grace. That's very funny."

And then she saw the tears streaming down his face. And the clenched fist. There was so little difference between a fist that was trying to hold everything in and the fist that was ready to release all its frustration and rage.

She didn't stop him as he made his way toward the door. Let him have his tears. He's earned them. He's more than earned them.


It was dusk when he got home, his apartment stifling hot. He hated the late August heat. May, June, July, now August. Summers beat the hell out of him. He was ready for a cool October breeze. He turned on the air conditioner, took off his shirt, soaked with his own sweat. He wiped his face with the wet shirt and tossed it against the wall. He looked at his watch. Almost eight. He noticed the date on his watch. His birthday. Shit, it was his birthday. Twenty-seven years old. Happy Fucking Birthday. If only he hadn't looked at his watch. It would have been easier if the day had passed without him noticing. The thought occurred to him that he should do something—celebrate. He'd once heard Al tell Carla that if you pretended to be happy, then one day you'd wake up, and sure enough, you'd be happy. Maybe he'd take Al's advice and pretend to celebrate.

He thought a moment, then took off his clothes. He stared at himself in the mirror, then averted his eyes. He'd never liked looking at himself, not even his face. He tried not to think it was him he was looking at when he shaved. He pulled on a pair of running shorts and an old T-shirt. He found some old running shoes in the closet. He stepped out the door. He'd run. That's how he'd celebrate. He'd run and run until his heart burst into flames. And he would become nothing but ash. No body, no heart, no bone, no flesh—just carbon matter scattering in the wind.

He imagined himself a boy riding through his old neighborhood. He ran and ran, up Sun Bowl Drive, the lights of Juárez below and across the river. He ran and ran, stretching the limits of his body, and suddenly, he wasn't thinking about his past or thinking about what would become of him. He wasn't thinking of himself at all. He was thinking of his beating heart. He was thinking of his aching legs. He was thinking of his lungs that felt as though they were being punched by the air. And he was glad to take the punches, glad—and almost glad to have a body.

# Timing and Order in the Universe

D ave is lying awake in his bed. He is recalling his conversation with Rosemary Hart Benson. She did not seem surprised by his phone call. She was even kind. It was evident that she had no illusions about her brother. *"Do you have anything that belongs to him?"*

*"Well, yes, but I don't know exactly what you're referring to."*

*"What happened to all his things, when he was sent to prison?"*

*"I have all of his things in boxes—in my attic."*

*"How many boxes?"*

*"Quite a few. Ten or twelve boxes, I'd say. And a couple of suitcases."*

*"What's in them?"*

*"I've never looked."*

*"If I went there, could I go through his things?"*

*"Yes,"* she said quietly, *"and will you take his belongings out of my house?"*

He is recalling the conversation. He knows she never looked because she did not want to know. He does not blame her. She wants to be free of his things. She was pleading with him, will you take his belongings, she wants to be free of him, her brother. He gets up from his bed and walks into his home office. He pours himself a Grand Marnier over ice—his favorite nighttime drink. He lets the orange liqueur coat his tongue, then burn down his throat. He lights a cigarette.

Grace is at home, making a list of all her material possessions. She is taking stock of her life. But she knows that making a list of what to give to whom when you die is not the same thing as taking stock. She does not know how to measure her life. When Sam was alive, she measured it through his love. She had always measured herself through the look in his eyes. She is afraid of admitting that to herself.

Liz and Mister are lying in bed. They are talking to each other. They are talking about Vicente. They are talking about the Rubios. They are talking about the coffee shop. They are talking about Grace. They are talking and talking and talking. And finally, they fall asleep in the middle of their talk.

# The Things of This World

I'm so tired that I'm not tired at all. It happens that way, sometimes. At least to me. Maybe it's because I've never had the capacity to do nothing. *Grace, come and sit.* Sam always beckoned me like that in the evenings. *Grace, it can wait until tomorrow.* I could never wait until tomorrow. Mañana has always been a problematic word for someone with my disposition. And, anyway, tonight is not a good night for resting. I need to think, to take stock of things—to see what's on my shelves, to take inventory while I still have all my faculties.

Strange. I don't feel sick at all.

Maybe Richard Garza is right. Maybe I should go through the treatments. When he told me, I heard the word *metastasized*. I thought, I'm dead. But that's not what he said. He says that we should go ahead with treatment. I read the article he wanted me to read. Cutting off my breasts, and then chemo, and then maybe radiation. And then pills— sometimes for a lifetime. Is my life worth all of that? Most days, I'm sure. Let it go, Grace, take a dive into the darkness. But why? Why don't I want to fight when fight is all I've ever known and loved? I've fought for every inch of joy I've ever known.

Mister wants an answer.

I'm sick. Why intervene? God has sent a cancer. Should I reject the gift?

Tonight I want to sit, take stock of everything. The material things are easy. The house is paid for—courtesy of Sam's death. The most impractical man I've ever met, except when it came to insurance. The house is Mister's. He can do what he likes with it. Maybe he'll move in and raise his son in the same house where he became a man.

My clothes and my jewelry will go to all my sisters. I'll make a list. They like to fight. I need to be clear. No arguments on my account. My pearls go to Dolores. She's never spent a dime on herself. Even when she's needed something and was forced to break down and ask me for money, it was always for one of her children. Her sons can now afford to buy their mother pearls—they wouldn't dream of it. After all she's done for them. I don't forgive them their ingratitude. I'll leave her oldest son my Bible. I'll underline certain passages. He's smart enough. He'll understand my accusations.

All my *rebozos* will go to my youngest sister, Carmen. She's borrowed half of them, anyway, and never returned them. And Teresa will get my dresses. We're the same size. Her husband buys boats and expensive tools, and dresses her in rags. Whatever furniture Mister wants, he can keep—the rest he can distribute among my sisters. I'll make sure to remind Mister that he should be prepared to play referee. They'll go easy on him, though. They adore him.

Sam's two brothers have fallen on hard times. I've done my best to keep up with them. They never truly understood my Sam, never understood his intellectual bent, his love for art and books and politics. They resented him, of course they did. Not that they'd ever said anything. But Sam loved them all. Sometimes he wept. It never mattered, not to him, that they hadn't known what to do with his affection. I'll leave them money. The money Sam left so I could live. I never needed it. They can use it. Sure they can. And money's something that they understand. If Sam, who was their brother, never held a grudge, then why should I?

I've put money away for children who've grown up in abusive homes—in memory of my clients. And some money for the National Council on La Raza and the Democratic Party. Sam would like that. I'll give the Catholic Church enough to cover my wake—and not a penny more. I'm Catholic to the bone, but the church is feudal, and I refuse to feed its antiquarian habits. I'll leave a note to the rector of the cathedral and remind him that a woman gave him birth. Something for him to think about the next time he gives one of his sermons. I'm writing all this down.

I don't want anything elaborate for my funeral. A simple mass.

Someone to sing the Ave Maria. George. I'll write and ask him. His voice is as beautiful as I have ever heard. He has a steadfast heart, and doesn't suffer right-wing fools. He's been banned from singing at the church. He sleeps with men and fights for women's rights. Father Ed will come to see me when it's time. When he comes calling at my deathbed, I'll tell him, "George." He won't deny me.

This cigarette is good. As good as God.

I want mariachis at the gravesite. And I want Mister to pop some bottles of champagne. I'll order a case of Sam's favorite in the morning. That's what I want. Champagne. It's an acquired taste for a girl who's grown up in Dizzy Land. But everything in this damned and blessed world is an acquired taste. Or so Sam said. "Your mother's milk—that's the only thing we're born to drink." He was right, of course.

It's not so bad to think about these things.

What will it be like, to die? What kind of light is there in death? Perhaps there will only be darkness. Perhaps there is nothing but a long, long night.

Nothing but a long, long night.

# Everything but Sleep
# (in the Middle of the Night)

Andrés woke up in a cold sweat, his heart thumping like an angry fist pounding on a door. The man had come to him in his dream. Yolie's boyfriend. He was eleven again, and the man was beckoning, *There's someone here who wants to meet you.* His throat was dry, his heart racing, and he began pacing the room—and then he couldn't breathe, no air, God, and he knew that everything was collapsing, the walls of his apartment, his skin peeling away, his flesh exposed, and God, he couldn't fucking breathe, why couldn't he breathe? And then everything felt as if he were underwater, deep, deeper and deeper, drowning, and he had to find a way to the surface—if only he could force his way back to where there was some air. But he was so far down in the dark waters, and it was miles to the surface, where there was air and sky. He was certain that his heart was going to burst, and he was going to die, and maybe that wasn't such a bad thing. To die. And then suddenly he could breathe again. Air.

He lit a cigarette, smoked it, then lit another. He had to get out, just get out, go anywhere. He splashed water on his face, combed his hair, dressed himself—then walked out the door. He got in his car, drove around and around and around until the image of the man disappeared. And then he seemed to know what he should do next.

He parked on an empty street in Segundo Barrio and made his way to the Santa Fe Bridge. As he walked over into Juárez, he calmed himself by smoking. He didn't think about the fact that he could forfeit his bond and his freedom. The thought did not enter his mind that what he was doing was against the conditions of his bail. It wasn't his mind that was in charge tonight.

He hadn't been to Juárez since everything had happened. Not since then, though he had visited this city in his dreams, and always the dreams had disturbed him, so he had tried to shut the city out as if it had never existed, as if his life there had never happened, but if it had never happened, why did that place haunt him into his waking hours?

He knew exactly where to go—but when he got there, he felt lost again. He walked into a familiar club, dim lights, perfect. Just perfect for a place like this—a place that smelled of a century of smoke and beer and the sweat of women and men and cheap cologne and even cheaper perfume. It was just like he remembered it. Nothing ever changed, especially the things that most desperately needed to change—his life, this bar, this damned city that punished the wrong people day after day, year after fucking year, and blessed are the poor, yeah. Sure.

He sat at the bar. There'd been a magician here when he was a boy. And the magician had performed tricks, and the patrons, most of whom were waiting for a prostitute or deciding which one to go with, they'd sat there and watched the bartender magician. And he'd perform tricks for them. Make a pack of cigarettes disappear and reappear in someone else's empty pocket. Make a parrot appear on your shoulder. The magician was gone now, replaced by a younger man whose only magic was pushing drinks and girls. Presto, he placed a drink in front of Andrés, then used his chin to point at someone behind him, "Te quiere."

He didn't turn around to look. He knew it was a woman waiting to turn a trick. He shook his head, downed his drink. Then pointed at the glass. He drank another, then another. He turned around and searched the room. The tables were mostly full— couples at every table. Only they weren't really couples. He saw a woman staring at him. Smiling. He called her over. He handed her a twenty, told her to go home. He finished his fourth drink, maybe his fifth. He sat there for a moment—it was so strange to be sitting there, and he wondered if he would ever be alive. He picked himself up, then numbly walked out the door.

He wandered up and down the streets. He didn't know if he was trying to remember or trying to forget. It seemed to him that he had lived his whole life somewhere in between remembering and forgetting. He didn't know which was worse. And in any fucking case, he didn't like his choices—either way it was a limbo. As he walked down a quiet street, he found an alley and urinated, and he thought, wouldn't it be great if you could do this to all your worries and troubles, just pour them out, just piss them away? As he walked back out into the street, a man approached him. He reached into his pocket, ready to hand him the dollar he'd be asking for. But he didn't ask for a dollar. "Quieres una mujer?"

"I don't speak Spanish." It didn't matter that it was a lie. The truth was the last thing that mattered on these streets.

"I said, do you want a woman?" He had a slight accent, but his English was perfect.

He shook his head.

"What about a man?"

He shook his head.

"What about children—you like that? Do you? I got perfect little girls. Boys, too. You like that? Take your pick. You can—" Andrés didn't wait for him to finish his sentence. He had him by the collar and was dragging him toward the alley, and the man was screaming, sure, playing the victim, sure, the victim, and he let him scream, go ahead and scream, you bastard, hijo de la chingada, go ahead and scream. There wasn't anybody on the street and the alley was dark and no one could bear witness to this event, hijo de puta, go ahead and scream and Andrés floored him with one punch. He was about to grab him, pick him up, and begin pounding and pounding—but then he didn't. He just stopped. He just took a breath and stopped. It was as if he was about to take a dive into a dark pool, and something made him stop and catch himself just as he was about to jump. For once in his life, he just stood still. And saw himself. And saw his rage. And understood that rage could be quiet. Could be soft. Rage didn't have to be a killer.

He stood there in the darkness, the man at his feet. Not a man, he thought, a fucking pimp who fed off the flesh of children, not a man, a devil who dragged people into hell for a blessed dollar. He lit a cigarette. Grace's voice ran through his head, *I think a lot of men smoke a cigarette after they've killed someone. Probably smoked one right before.* He knelt down beside the man. He lit a match and stared at his face. He stared and stared. He looked for something human in his trembling face.

"Deja los niños solos, cabrón. ¿Entiendes?"

The man nodded. He looked like a scared deer.

"If I ever catch you peddling children again, te mato, cabrón—¿me explico?

He got up, walked out into the street, and walked inside the nearest bar. He walked into the bathroom and washed himself off. He felt numb and inarticulate.

He found himself walking toward his old neighborhood. It wasn't far. He still remembered. When he got to his old street, he stood outside number 12.

He sat on the sidewalk.

And then he remembered he'd left something here. His father's ring. Underneath a brick in the courtyard.

Everywhere you went, you left something behind.

Maybe someday he would come back and get it. Maybe that day would really come to pass. He picked himself up from the sidewalk and made his way back toward the bridge. He didn't think about anything. He felt as empty as the streets. But the streets at least had a design and a purpose.

His steps were slow and steady. What was the hurry? It was too late to get any sleep.

At the top of the Santa Fe Bridge, he looked back at Juárez, then looked toward El Paso. He wondered if he would ever have a country. Americans, they were always so sure of themselves—even Chicanos. So secure, as if the very country that was their home gave them a purpose. It didn't matter that it was an illusion, didn't matter at all because the word *America* created order in their minds, and for all he knew, created order in their hearts. Maybe it was a cruel word, *America,* but it was a word that kept chaos at bay. But not for him. And Mexico was as foreign as America. Mexico had its own cruelties, just as it had its own sense of timing and order. But neither place had made a space for him. Neither had claimed him as a son. And so, he thought, if he stayed right here for the rest of his life, it would be perfect. Right here. Disinherited and dispossessed. Right here—in the middle of two countries. Which was the same as nowhere.

The light of dawn brought so little comfort.

· · ·

Grace, too, woke in the middle of the night. Such a strange and wonderful dream that had come to her. A gift perhaps from her withholding God. He'd had pity on her and sent a different dream. A small reward for an insignificant worker in the fields.

At last a different dream. No soundless and swallowing night, no young Sam and no Mister spinning around in an Eden that had no room for her. So strange, this new dream, with a perfect logic that undermined the pedestrian rules of living. And such a strange and wondrous dream it was.

He'd been walking down the middle of the street, the man, and the empty street was clean, as empty of litter as it was of people, washed in rain and shining in the light of a moon that was nearly as bright as a sun, but it was clearly night, in the dream, and as the man walked, she knew who he was. Andrés Segovia. And as he moved closer and closer to where she was standing, she could see he was changing features, and then he wasn't Andrés Segovia at all, he was Mister—Mister?—and just as he was about to speak to her, she could see it wasn't Mister at all, but a complete stranger, more handsome, more beautiful than Andrés Segovia or her son or any man she'd ever met, and he held out his hand. And she knew that the hour had come and she didn't have any regrets and she knew everything was done, everything packed, no looking back. He wouldn't hurt her. All hurt was past now. She took the stranger's hand.

Arm in arm, she walked with him, down the quiet street—into the empty, expectant city. And as she turned to look at him, her heart leaped with the immaculate joy of a girl. Sam! Sam!

*God, God send me the dream again.*

# Part Three

*. . . for at evening time there shall be light.*

—ZACHARIA 14:7

# The Silent Love of Countries

For three nights, Mando and Yolie went missing. Gone. Disappeared. No one to call, no phone in the house—and who would they have called? What would they have said? And wouldn't they want to know why a boy and a girl were all alone in a house? So there was nothing for Andrés to do except do what he had always done—wait and worry. He had become very good at that. He had become an expert. He hated himself for being like that. He swore to himself that one day, when he was emancipated, he wouldn't care enough about anything to worry. About anything.

But the news was not all bad. There was enough food in the house, though the food was nothing special. That was okay. Special was not something they were used to. Andrés made simple things, beans, rice, squash with onions and tomatoes. He'd learned that by watching his mom. Easy stuff. Beans were easy—and there was bacon, so he put bacon in the pot and the house smelled good, and he made quesadillas with menonita and tortillas de maíz on the comál. He knew how to make those. They were easy, too, and Ileana loved to watch the way the farmer's cheese the Mennonites made melted in between the two tortillas and ran out onto the comál.

She had her rituals, Ileana, that girl Andrés adored. She always wanted him to burn a special tortilla just for her because she liked the way a burned tortilla tasted. She loved bean burritos with just a little bit of chile. At first, she hadn't liked beans because she said they were only for poor Mexicans, and Yolie had gotten mad at her and said, "What the hell do you think we are?" Ileana had made a face and refused to eat, but she began liking them after Andrés had made up some story about how bean burritos made the heart of a little girl burn like a fire in the cold night. That burning heart had kept the girl in the story from freezing to death.

So they ate, and they were okay, even though they weren't happy. Okay was okay. Sure. But the house was still and quiet like a breezeless day in the Chihuahuan desert. Still as death, and Andrés felt as if it were up to him to make noise so that his sister would know they were still alive. And even though Andrés didn't feel like talking, he talked. And even though Ileana didn't feel like eating, she ate. They talked and ate. And they were alive.

Sometimes Andrés sang, and he hadn't known that he could sing— but he could. He didn't know where that came from. So sometimes he sang for Ileana, and she would look at him and tell him he was an angel. And he would laugh and say that angels didn't need bodies and they didn't need to eat beans, either. He said those things to make her laugh. And she did laugh. And so, they were alive.

But there was a fear in Ileana. She would cling to Andrés, her brother, whom she loved and needed, cling to Andrés, her brother, because he was the only one left now, and Andrés could see she was afraid. And so he would kiss her and tell her everything was fine, and he would study her face and she would hope, and he could see that she was trying to believe.

It was getting cooler and cooler in the house now because the weather was beginning to change, and every evening it rained. And Andrés and Ileana would sit in the courtyard under an umbrella and watch the rain. But they were sad, Andrés and Ileana. And everything was waiting. For three nights, they were alone. And Andrés would tell stories, happy stories, stories about dogs who were lost but found their way home, and sometimes, when the dogs didn't find their way home, a good family took them in, and the dogs wound up happy and warm and wagging their tails. And Andrés made up stories about children who thought their parents were dead, but found out that they were alive. Happy stories. And everything in the world that mattered was in the happy stories Andrés was telling. And everything in the world was Ileana listening to the brother she loved. And everything in the world was waiting.

On that fourth day, they woke to the sound of the rain and the thunder. The sky was angry and shouting, and it reminded Andrés of how Mando and his father had shouted at each other and had drowned out the sound of love. They had drowned out the sound of his mother's voice. That's what Andrés thought. That's what he remembered. And he hated remembering as much as he hated worrying.

When he woke on the fourth day to the sound of thunder, that was when he decided. It was time now. To leave. Because even though they lived here, this place was never their home. And they would never belong. And they needed to find where they would fit. Even a coat needed a place where it could hang. That's what his father used to say. He understood what that meant now.

Andrés knew that this house was just a hiding place and nothing more. And he didn't want to hide anymore because it made him feel sad, made him feel as if he had done something wrong, made him feel as if he was a secret that was being kept from the world, and he didn't want to be a secret. He wanted to be a boy that everyone could see and talk to. He wanted to be a boy that rode his bike up and down on the street and laughed and yelled the stupid things that boys were supposed to yell. He was tired of being careful, because that's what Mando and Yolie were always telling him, *be careful you have to be very careful,* and they always said it in a hushed tone, the sort of hushed tone that made him feel like a secret that had to be kept out of sight, like something ugly.

He remembered one day when he'd begged Yolie, "Take us to see the Fernandezes. Just for a day. Just for an hour." Yolie had yelled at him and shaken him and there was a fire in her face and he knew he'd started that fire. "Don't you understand anything? We can't ever go back there again. Not ever?"

"But why, Yolie?"

"Because they'll take us away from each other. And they'll hurt Mando because they don't understand that Mando is helping us. They'll say that Mando is hurting us and they'll put him in jail or worse—and do you want that? Do you want them to hurt Mando?"

And so he had come to understand that *yes, they were hiding. Yes, they were a secret.* They had to be very careful.

But he was tired. He wasn't strong enough to be that careful anymore. And he knew he was betraying his sister and his brother in his heart. And he hated himself, and he knew they would hate him forever. But he had to decide between Yolie and Ileana, and so he chose Ileana. And what if Yolie never came back? What if *they* were the traitors? Maybe they had decided that they had to live their own lives. Maybe they felt like they were secrets, too, and they didn't want to be secrets anymore, either. Maybe he and Ileana were burdens. "Children are such burdens." Mrs. Gonzalez had once said that to his mother. A long time ago. And he had always remembered that. And now, he understood that better. Maybe Yolie and Mando had carried him and Ileana like sacks of potatoes—sacks of potatoes or sacks of onions that were too heavy for them to carry anymore. Maybe it was time for him and Ileana to carry themselves.

So he decided. When the rain stopped, they would leave. He told Ileana they were going out. They were going home. They were going to carry themselves to freedom. They were still little, but they were going to emancipate themselves.

"But it's raining," Ileana said.

"When it stops, we'll go out. To breathe the fresh air. Won't that be nice?"

She nodded. "Okay. Maybe we'll find Yolie. Maybe she'll be out breathing the fresh air, too."

"Yeah. Maybe. So why don't we get ready. You take a bath, and I'll find something nice for you to wear and then we'll eat breakfast, and when it stops raining, we'll go out."

So Andrés got them ready. He eyed his belongings. He knew they wouldn't be able to take anything. Just themselves and the clean clothes they were wearing. It didn't matter—what were belongings? They would take just themselves and the clean clothes Yolie and Mando had bought for them. And he felt like a traitor. And he could feel his face burning.

They ate breakfast. The last two eggs.

The rain stopped.

The house was quiet as a tomb.

Yolie walked through the front door.

• • •

"Yolie, Yolie, where were you? Where were you?" Ileana couldn't stop kissing her and hugging her. Kissing her. Hugging her. Laughing and laughing. And Andrés felt as bad as he had ever felt in his life, for wanting to take Ileana away from the sister she adored, for wanting to abandon Yolie, who had worked so hard to keep them together, to keep them and make them a family. And he was ashamed for wanting to live in El Paso just so he could go to school. What did school matter compared to a sister? He studied her, his older sister. She was older, sad and tired like his mother had looked when Mando and his father had been fighting. She looked like she needed to eat and sleep. And so Andrés offered to make a quesadilla with the last of the menonita and the last of the corn tortillas.

She said okay, but it was a weak okay, and as she ate, she said nothing as she carefully placed the food in her mouth and chewed. She ate and cried at the same time. Her sobs were quiet, but the tears were large and they ran down her cheeks and she didn't bother to wipe them away. They owned her, now, her tears. Andrés felt worse and worse. "Don't cry," he said.

"They've taken Mando," she said.

"Who?"

"The police."

"What police? The Mexican police?"

"No. He's in jail."

"Where?"

"In El Paso."

"What did he do wrong, Yolie?"

"He was caught—" She stopped. "They made him do it. He didn't want to do it. But we needed the money. And so he had to. You understand?" She looked at Andrés, and Andrés knew that she needed him to understand—so he nodded.

"He was arrested at the bridge."

Andrés *did* understand.

"He'll go to prison."

"For a long time?" Andrés asked.

"Yes. For a long time."

"Can we see him?"

"No."

"So we won't see him again."

"Not for a long time."

"Can we write to him?"

She nodded. "Okay. That will be okay."

The kitchen was quiet. "What will we do?"

Yolie looked at her younger brother. "I don't know."

"We can go back," Andrés whispered.

"No." He could hear the anger in her voice. "No fucking way. If we go back, then it was all for nothing. He's going to prison for us. *For us.* So we could be together. And you want to go back?"

Andrés lowered his head. "I'm sorry. I'll never say that again."

"I'm sorry, too," she whispered. "I won't yell at you anymore."

Ileana said nothing. And then she started to cry. "I want Mando," she said. It started to rain again. And it seemed as if the pounding rain would tear off the roof of their house. For an instant, Andrés felt as if there would never again be any light in their house. It would always be dark. And then he thought that no matter how much they'd tried to change this house into something else, it would always be that house they found the first day they moved in. A house with no light. A house with no one in it. A house that smelled of a hundred years of waste and war. A heartless, heartless house.

"Is that when Yolie sold your typewriter?"

"Yes. Around that time. I can't remember exactly. Not exactly. We didn't go to the market as much. All I know is that we had beans and rice and tortillas and fideo and potatoes. But that was okay. I still like that kind of food."

He had a strange look on his face, and for an instant Grace thought he looked like the boy he must've been when the rains were pounding his house. She nodded at him, "Well, you know, I can't go more than three days without eating beans and tortillas."

"I wouldn't have thought that about you," he said.

"Why not?"

"You don't seem that Mexican to me."

"Why?"

"I don't know. You just don't."

"Well, I don't know what you mean by Mexican. But, well, I am. And anyway, not all Mexicans grow up on that kind of food—it's peasant food, you know? It's what the poor eat—and I guess, when I was growing up, I qualified."

"Peasant food," he said, "You speak a lot of Spanish?"

"All the time. Me and my sisters." He nodded. He needed a break. From telling his story. She could tell. That was fine. A break. "You're not smoking as much."

"I'm still smoking a pack a day."

"But you're not smoking here."

He shrugged. "I smoke a lot when I leave." He wanted to tell her that he'd gone to Juárez. In the middle of night. He wanted to tell her. "Do you have family in Mexico?"

She didn't mind this small talk. "No. Not anymore. You?"

"No. Not anymore." He wouldn't tell her. That he'd gone. That he'd taken out his fists again. He wouldn't tell her—not ever. Because now it seemed to matter what she thought.

The money started to run out, and Andrés could see the look of panic on Yolie's face. She started smoking a lot more. Xochil came over to visit. She looked sad, and she and Yolie cried. And then they'd smoke. And then they'd cry some more. They sat in the living room and talked and talked and Andrés sat in the kitchen—sat still and listened. They talked about the drugs Mando had been carrying across the border. A mule—they called him that. No one cared about mules when they were caught.

Xochil said that if Mando turned in the people who'd hired him, then the Feds would cut down the time he'd have to spend in prison. She said something about a deal. But she said Mando wouldn't turn them in. "They'll kill him," Xochil said. And then she was crying again. And Andrés didn't want to hear any more, so he went into his room and typed a letter to Mrs. Fernandez.

The next day, his typewriter would be gone. They would have food on the table.

One day, Xochil came one last time. To say good-bye. She was moving to California. She begged Yolie to go with her. "Leave them with Mrs. Fernandez. Come with me. Things will go good for us there."

"No." Yolie said. Her no didn't sound strong. A weak no, and Andrés wished that Xochil would stay and stay until Yolie broke down and said yes. But Xochil stopped in the face of a weak no. When Xochil left the house, Andrés ran after her. "Stay with us," Andrés said, though he didn't know why he'd said it. Didn't even know why he'd run after her. She kissed Andrés and held his face between her hands. "Go back," she whispered. "Go back to El Paso before something else happens. Please, Andy. Please." He walked with her all the way to the bridge that led back to El Paso. "You can come with me," she said. "I'll take you to Mrs. Fernandez."

"No," he said. "I can't."

"You should at least let me take Ileana."

Andrés wanted to say yes. It would hurt to have Ileana gone. But she would be safe with Xochil in California. "Yolie won't let you take her."

"I know."

"Here," she said. She took a scrap of paper from her purse and wrote down a number. "This is my sister's number. If anything ever happens, you call her. You call her, okay?" She kissed him. Just like his mother used to kiss him. "Mando loves you. Don't ever forget that. No matter what happens."

He saw her disappear over the bridge.

When he got back home, Yolie looked as sad as she had ever looked. More sad than angry now. And he wished her anger would come back because she was strong when she was angry. And the sadness made her look old and broken. After a while, she started going out at night. She'd come back late, and Andrés could tell that she'd been out drinking. He could smell the alcohol on her breath. That's where she met this man— in a bar. That's what Andrés thought. He had money. He was older. Not old. But older. Maybe in his thirties. It was hard for Andrés to tell ages, but that's what he'd decided. Not old—but too old for Yolie. He wondered what had happened to Eddie. But he was afraid to ask her. When she got mad at somebody, she made them go away, and if you asked her about it, she would get angry. Maybe Eddie had found another girl, because guys did that. Mando—he was always leaving girls and finding new ones.

He guessed that Yolie needed a boyfriend and that maybe it didn't matter that he was older. And it was okay that he had money—maybe he would take care of Yolie and take care of him and Ileana, too. But Andrés didn't like that he was always dressed up. Like his dad when he took his mom out dancing. He dressed that way all the time. Maybe he was a businessman. Maybe that's why he was always dressed up.

Yolie had money now. And she had new dresses. And there was food in the house. And meat. He liked eating meat. So maybe Yolie would get married and they would all be the kind of family that Mando dreamed they would always be. Maybe she was doing this for Mando—and for all the dreams he'd had.

Even as he was telling her the story of his life in Juárez, he could tell she was tired. For no reason at all, he thought that she looked like a nun. The beautiful kind. The kind that gave and gave because that's what they knew how to do. And the giving made them more beautiful.

"Did you ever see Mando again?"

"No. One day, about six months after he'd been arrested, Yolie got some money. I don't know how much. Some guy came by the house and said it was from Mando. A bundle of money. Yolie hid it in the courtyard. She wanted me to know where the money was. She told me if anything ever happened, I should take the money and go back to El Paso. You know what she told me?"

Grace shook her head.

" 'You want to go back there, don't you? You want to go to school. You want to be more than what you were born to be. More than what they will ever let you be. I don't know why you love the fucking United States of America. It will never love you back.' Funny, the things you remember." He looked away from her. "You know"—he was looking away as he spoke—"I didn't understand what she was trying to say to me."

"And now?"

"She was right. America won't ever love me back. Anyway, I'm not so in love with the idea of America anymore. But maybe none of this has to do with America. But there's one thing Yolie forgot to tell me—Mexico never loved me back, either. Who the hell ever said that countries love?"

Grace wanted to shake him gently and scream, A country will never love you like a woman. "I think countries are as silent in their love as God."

Andrés broke into a laugh. "That's pretty damned silent, Grace."

She laughed with him. She felt a pain.

And Andrés, even as he laughed, he thought, God, she looks tired. He wondered what it would have been like. To be her son. To be loved by her. To be cared for by a woman like Grace Delgado.

# Order and Timing in the Universe

I t is five-thirty in the afternoon.

Andrés is in the middle of a session with Grace.

A bus, twenty minutes late, is pulling up into the downtown depot. The first passenger to get off the bus is a fifty-five-year-old white man who likes to describe himself as being half Irish, half German. He is an ordinary-looking man with a middle-aged paunch who has come to live with his sister who retired in El Paso. This man who is getting off the bus, this middle-aged man, he has been in prison for seven years. He has been released to El Paso courtesy of the Oklahoma Parole Board. He must register with the police department in the morning. His sister believes he has been in prison for armed robbery. He does not know how to tell her that he has a particular kind of addiction that happens to be against the law. He knows they call him a sexual predator. He is offended by this label. He is enraged by the lack of understanding in the world. He knows himself to be kind and gentle. Especially to children.

He sees his sister and waves. He embraces her and kisses her on the cheek. He is thinking that she is looking old.

Mister is looking for information on the Internet. He sees the time on the corner of his computer as he searches: 5:31 PM. He is hoping the information he finds on the Internet will help him with Vicente's blindness. Today he feels inadequate. He knows he and Liz will have to rely on more than knowledge and facts. He prays that his instincts are as good as he believes them to be.

Dave is looking out the window of his plane. He is flying to Baton

Rouge. From there he will rent a car and drive to Lafayette and visit with Rosemary Hart Benson. She was polite on the phone, her voice was soft and kind—but she was relieved that someone was willing to take away the boxes her brother left in her attic. She has always been afraid to see what they contain. She thinks the boxes will bring her bad luck.

Dave is wondering what he will find. So much depends upon what is in those boxes.

# Blindness and Books

Not that he liked sitting in front of his laptop computer and searching the Net. Not one of his favorite things. He preferred libraries and bookstores. But the Internet had its uses, and he couldn't argue with the speed. Even for someone as patient as he was, the speed was seductive.

He typed the word *blindness* into the space provided. In seconds, a list appeared. 623,000 entries. Too much help was no help at all. He added the word *children* to *blindness,* and his search was narrowed down to 246,000 entries. He glanced at the first few entries—most of them having to do with prevention and causes of blindness in children. That wasn't what he was looking for. It was too late for whys. What to do now, that was what he wanted to know. He added the word "education" which cut down the entries to a mere 133,000. He began combing through the list. Support groups, educational groups, state programs, federal programs, nonprofit programs. Info on braille and some online schools. How could a blind kid go to school online? He found a site entitled What's New on Blindness. Information, information. With a click, it was all yours, all that information. That was the new capital. Click, click, click, a book by a woman on braille literacy. A place called the Texas School for the Blind. Publications and more publications—for sale—click, click, he ordered a book on the fundamentals of braille, and a book about language assessment and intervention with children who had visual impairments. The book was advertised for speech and language pathologists, and there was a table of contents that included chapters on language development, assessment, and strategies for effective intervention. There was even a chapter entitled "Limited English Proficient Children." He talks. That's what she'd told him. When he wants to. But did he speak English or Spanish, or both? The thought occurred to him that someone had taught Vicente a good many things. A babysitter who spoke only Spanish—perhaps a grandmother. There were so many questions he should have asked the mother. And he hadn't. And now it was too late. Or was it? He would talk to Linda and ask her if she thought it was a good idea to get in touch with the mother again. He doubted she would consent. Why not try?

He studied the table of contents. A lot of lingo, and he wasn't an SLP, as they apparently called themselves, but he'd dive in and see what he'd learn. What could it hurt? He ordered the book. A start.

# Learning to Run

Ileana moved into Andrés' room. She slept in the bed that once belonged to Mando, the bed he'd slept in with Xochil. Andrés didn't mind. Ileana was sweet, and she liked to ask him questions at night—questions about where feelings came from. Questions about the world. "You study the stars, don't you, Andy?"

"I don't really study them," he said. "I count them."

"Why?"

"To see how many there are."

"How many are there?"

"I haven't finished counting them yet."

"How many do you think there are?"

"About one for every person who ever lived."

"One for Mom and Dad?"

"Yeah, one for them, too."

"What are they made out of, Andy, the stars?"

"Mostly hydrogen and helium. That's what makes them burn. That's what makes them light up the sky."

"Is that why Jesus' heart burns—because it's made of hydrogen and helium?"

"Yes. That's right."

"I want a heart like that, Andy, a heart like a star's."

He fell in love with the things she said. So they were roommates, now, he and Ileana. And best friends—since his other friends didn't like him that much. His other friends liked getting into trouble, stealing things, and picking on smaller kids. He didn't like that. Anyway, having friends didn't matter. Ileana mattered.

Yolie and the man whose name was Homero had their own room now. They sometimes groaned like Mando and Xochil, but Ileana never said anything about the groaning.

Yolie did everything for Homero. She washed his clothes and ironed for him. She cooked for him. Everything he asked her to do, she did.

They were like a family for a while. Everything was nice—except Andrés was bored, and he would complain, and Yolie said she might ask Homero to buy him a new typewriter, but Andrés told Yolie he didn't want one. Not anymore. He was done with writing letters to Mrs. Fernandez. He was done with words and paper. Words on paper were dead. As dead as he was.

Yolie and Homero kept buying him more books, mostly paperbacks. In English and in Spanish, and Andrés would read them, but he was getting so tired of reading and reading and reading, and he didn't care anymore. About anything.

The man told him maybe he should begin running. It would be good for him. So Homero bought him a pair of tennis shoes, special for running, and he got him a book about running and a book about stretching because stretching was important if you were going to be a runner, and Andrés read the books, and he decided it wouldn't be a bad thing if he started running. So every morning, when he got up, he would stretch just like the drawings in the book, and he began to run. At first, he hated it. But it was better than staying at home all the time, and reading was okay, it passed the time, but it was hard to do nothing but read, and after a while he liked the feeling of running, how it hurt, but how it felt good, how his legs would ache and his lungs would ache, too—but it was good and he liked it. And so he ran and ran, one mile. And after a while, more than a mile, then two miles, then three. And when he ran, he thought of Mando, of how he was in prison, and he thought of him all caged up and he thought that maybe he had to run and be free for the both of them— for himself and for Mando. And he began to talk to Mando as he ran. He would tell him everything.

*There's something about Homero that's not right. I don't like the way he looks at Yolie. And I don't like the way he looks at Ileana. And even me, he looks at me sometimes and it feels like there's a worm crawl-*

*ing around in my shirt and I shiver and feel cold. But he's nice to us, and I know he pays for everything because we don't have any money except the money you had sent to us. Homero wasn't home, and Yolie and I hid it, and I understood that she didn't want Homero to know. Which is a very smart thing.* He would talk and talk as he ran and never stopped until he couldn't catch his breath, and after a while he learned to talk to Mando with his mind. He didn't have to use his lips at all.

So he was a runner now. Running through the streets of Juárez. He found a route where there was less traffic because cars had no respect for the art he was cultivating. After a while, he knew just what streets to take and what streets to avoid. Yolie said he was running too much, that he was too young and that it wasn't such a good idea for him to be running as much as he did, but he told her it was okay, that he liked it.

She could tell he was happier, now. So she didn't fight him. Everyone needed to have something. He had his books and his running. Yolie had Homero.

*I'm a runner now. And one day I'm going to run across the bridge, and no one is going to stop me.*

"Did you stop running?"

"When I started living here again, I started. But I just—I don't know. It reminded me of everything, and I didn't want to think about it, so I just left it alone." He realized just then why he'd gone to Juárez that night—because of the running. The running and Juárez, somehow they belonged together. And so he'd needed to go there. It was so odd, how the body remembered. "I ran the other night," he confessed.

"Did you?"

"Yeah."

"Why?"

"It was my birthday. I wanted to celebrate. I thought I'd run."

"Happy birthday. How was your run?"

"Okay. It's kind of an insane thing to do."

"A lot of people spend a lot of time doing it."

"That and counting stars."

"And smoking cigarettes."

"It's insane."

"If everything was perfectly sane and ordered, what would the world look like, Andrés?"

"Like a computer."

"Better to have a heart and all the chaos that comes with it."

"Only a person with a perfectly ordered life could say something like that."

"No one's life is perfectly ordered."

"Not even yours?"

"I'm the only exception."

He laughed at her joke. She could be funny.

Everything was pretty good until after Christmas. At Christmas, they had special cookies and presents and lights—lights all over the courtyard and all over the kitchen. Yolie and Homero put them up, twinkling lights, red and blue and yellow and green. Yolie learned how to make mole—not the kind that came in a jar but the real kind that took all day with all different kinds of chiles, chipotle and chile pasilla and unskinned almonds and cloves and tomatillos and peanuts and sesame seeds and garlic and Mexican cinnamon and a special kind of chocolate, and the house smelled as beautiful as it had ever smelled, and then they all made tamales because Yolie said it was what Mom would've wanted, and he thought of the time when Yolie had yelled at him and told him *never, ever* to tell her again about what their mother would've wanted. And he thought that people changed their minds about things all the time—but it was something they had to do on their own. When you tried to make someone change their mind, they wouldn't. They just wouldn't.

So they made tamales and Ileana mostly made a mess, but she laughed all day and she was so happy and beautiful and Andrés thought that whatever her heart was made of, it burned, and it was the only light in the house that mattered.

It was a good Christmas, and the house was warm, and they burned lots of candles so the whole house looked like the inside of a church, and Andrés thought that maybe there wouldn't be any more sadness. There had been enough of troubles and enough crying, and maybe now all of that was over. But he knew that Yolie wasn't happy. It was as if she was acting. Or maybe it was just him. Maybe he just couldn't believe that everything was going to be okay. He was like a dog guarding a house, ready to leap at any intruder. A good guard dog never slept all night. And that's what he was now, a good guard dog. And he hated himself. Because he couldn't believe that they were at peace now. And maybe he was just making things up about what he saw on Yolie's face because he didn't like Homero. Deep down, he didn't like him. But maybe that only meant that his heart was getting hard. Mando had said that every man's heart had to get a little bit hard—because if it didn't get hard, he would just stay a boy. So maybe he was becoming a man. Being a man, that was a good thing.

But right after Christmas, everything began to change. Homero began to stay out late. On New Year's Eve, Yolie waited for him to come home. She was all dressed up. They were going to a dance, and she looked beautiful. And she was a woman now. And he thought that maybe Yolie could find a better man than Homero, someone younger, someone who would make her more alive. Homero made her into someone old. Yolie waited and waited, but finally she said she wasn't going to spend the New Year waiting for a man who was never going to come, so she went out by herself.

Andrés told her he would go with her.

"No," she said, "you stay here with Ileana."

She gave them some firecrackers and told them they could go out at midnight and light them. And she left. She had this look. He knew that look. She was going out because she was determined to live.

At midnight he took Ileana outside, and they lit firecrackers. And there were lots of people out on the streets. Some were banging pots and other kids were lighting firecrackers and everyone was yelling and hugging each other and repeating over and over, "¡Feliz Año Nuevo!" And the streets were so full, and suddenly Andrés realized Ileana wasn't next to him and he felt something inside and he started searching the crowded street, *Ileana, Ileana,* and then he saw her and he grabbed her and hugged her and they went inside.

Ileana fell asleep on his shoulder. But it didn't matter, because he wasn't sleepy. He just lay there, listening to his little sister breathe, and waiting for Yolie to come home. Like the guard dog he'd become.

It was very late when he heard Yolie come in. He could hear she was with someone. Homero, he thought. Yolie must have found him. He could hear them laughing and talking softly and he knew they were having sex and he didn't want to hear. And when they were quiet, he fell asleep.

When he woke up, there was a man sleeping in Yolie's bed. And the man wasn't Homero. He hated that he had to walk through her room to get to the kitchen. He hated the thought of Ileana waking up and seeing their older sister in bed with a stranger.

He walked into the kitchen and sat there. He waited until Yolie and the man stirred. They said something to each other, then the man got dressed and left. He didn't say anything to Andrés when he walked past him. Like he wasn't even there. Andrés shook his head, then walked toward the doorway between Yolie's room and the kitchen. He noticed that the man had left some money on the bed. He looked at Yolie and didn't say anything.

She didn't say anything either.

Homero came back a few days later. It went that way for a while. Homero would come and go. On the nights he didn't come home, Ileana would say, "It's not right, that he doesn't come home."

"It doesn't matter." Yolie didn't seem concerned or worried. Almost like she didn't care. "He helps us," she said. "That's all that matters."

After that, Yolie started going out. She would get dressed up and go out and she wouldn't say anything to them, just that she would be out late. And then it became every night. Every, every night. And Homero never spent the night anymore, though sometimes he would come over during the day and he and Yolie would talk, but they would talk in whispers and send Andrés and Ileana out to the market or on some errand so they could talk. And sometimes Homero would come by in the evenings when Yolie was getting ready to go out, and they would go out together, but it wasn't like they were boyfriend and girlfriend, not like that. It was more like they were working together. More like that. And Andrés thought there was something very wrong—but he didn't quite know what. But he was starting to make up stories in his head about what was happening.

One day, when Yolie was taking a shower, he found lots of money in her purse. Dollars—lots of ten-dollar bills. And he wondered where she was getting the money. So he decided to ask her what she did when she went out every night.

She smiled at him. "I got a job waiting tables at a bar. Homero found the job for me. I make good money on tips." That's what she said. "You know what tips are?"

Andrés nodded.

Maybe she was telling the truth.

It was hard to say, because he had become very suspicious. He was beginning to understand that no one ever told the truth.

One day in February, it snowed. It snowed and snowed. That was the day a man showed up at the door. A man he'd never seen before. He wasn't old. Maybe a little older than Mando. Andrés answered the door. He wanted to talk to Yolie. Andrés let him in.

The man talked to Yolie, explained who he was. An old friend of Mando's. He seemed nervous or scared or sad or confused or something. Something wasn't right. And finally he just said, "Mando's dead."

"What?" Yolie had this look on her face. "What?"

"He was killed. In prison. He got in a fight with the wrong guy. He's dead, Yolie."

Yolie began wailing and wailing. He didn't know anyone could cry like that. A wind was coming from inside her. Andrés didn't know what to do, so he just held her, and rocked and rocked her as if she was a baby, but nothing could stop her from crying. For hours and hours, she wailed and wailed like a strong spring wind, and finally Andrés got scared, and he didn't know what to do because Yolie couldn't stop crying, so he went next door to ask the women who lived there to come over. Well, they weren't really women, Andrés knew that, they were really men, and Yolie had told him they were called transvestites, and she said they were nice and they shouldn't be afraid of them. She had told him and Ileana to go to them if anything ever happened, because they would help them. And he thought Yolie was right about them, the transvestites, because even though it was strange that they dressed and acted like women, they were very nice. So he went to their door and knocked. One of them who called herself Silvia answered the door.

"Yolie won't stop crying," Andrés explained. "My brother, Mando, he was killed in a fight in prison, and now Yolie won't stop crying."

So Silvia went with him to his house, and she held Yolie in her arms, and she took a pill from her purse and gave one to Yolie and made her drink it. And Yolie calmed down and fell asleep. So Silvia went next door and got her friend, Amanda, who looked more like a real woman than Silvia because he was smaller—not like Silvia, who had big hands and big feet and big shoulders. They both came over and decided to make a caldo de rez. Because it was freezing outside—and so they made soup, and the soup was delicious, and Silvia and Amanda told Ileana and Andrés that they should always go to them if they needed anything. And when Yolie woke up, Silvia made her take a shower, and they combed her hair real nice, and they made her eat soup.

Andrés was glad they were there. They knew exactly what to do. And he didn't care if they were men pretending to be women. He liked them. And Ileana liked them, too.

That night, Yolie didn't go out. It was too cold, and she was too sad. And she cried all night. But not like before. Not like howls. Just sobs. Ordinary sobs.

The next morning, she looked harder, like she was made of stone.

Ileana and Andrés didn't say anything to her. They knew she didn't want them to.

"Yolie was never the same."

"What changed?"

"She was hollow after that. Empty. She just didn't care. Not about us. Not about herself. Well, she still cared some for Ileana. I don't know what she felt about me. Sometimes I thought she must have loved me very much. Other times, I think she hated me. Anyway, she didn't give a damn about herself after that. She'd loved Mando so much. I understood that. Because that's the way I felt about Ileana."

"Did you ever mourn your brother?"

"Yes."

"How?"

"What do you mean?"

"Everyone mourns in different ways. Yolie cried all day. All night. Then she locked him away in a part of herself no one would ever touch."

"I didn't say that."

"I know you didn't."

He nodded. "When the snow melted, I ran. I ran and cried and cursed. That's how I mourned him." *I've been mourning him all of my fucking life.* He didn't have to tell her that. She already knew.

# Timing and Order in the Universe

G race is reading an article in the newspaper. The article states that a human rights group is protesting the fact that so many child molesters are being released to the border area: "One activist angrily stated, 'There is nothing to keep these men from venturing into Mexico. There is no protocol in place. These men are released to the border and perpetrating their crimes against the children of Juárez with impunity. It is like setting loose a big game hunter in the middle of a game preserve.' Such views are overstated, says an official with the federal prison system. 'Alarmist viewpoints do nothing to help develop a public policy that is in the best interests of the general public.' " Grace puts down the newspaper and thinks of Andrés Segovia. She thinks of Mister. She thinks to herself that she might have killed any man who would have ever touched her son. She looks at the crucifix hanging on her wall. For a moment, she understands that Christianity is an impossible religion. What does it mean to forgive?

Dave is sitting in a musty attic in Louisiana. The space is dark and damp, and having lived in the desert all his life, he is uncomfortable with the unfamiliar smells. He has already decided that the South is too gothic for his tastes. He has decided that Rosemary Hart Benson is a tortured soul. She hates no one comfortably—a curse she no doubt acquired from her devout Catholic mother. That is what he has decided. "Take what you want, and will you please throw the rest away." He is looking through the third box—and it is here that he finds what he is looking for (though he did really know exactly what he might find). In this box, he finds photographs of boys. He does not know how many photographs there are—perhaps a hundred. Perhaps less than a hundred. In each photograph, a boy is sitting and looking at the camera. Some of them smile. Some of them look sad. Some of them have no expression at all. He looks at each photograph. The boys seem to range in age from seven or eight to fourteen. It's difficult to tell. All the boys are clothed. And then he understands. He has taken a photograph of each boy before he touched him. They are, in the photographs of this sick and twisted soul, images of untouched boys. As he goes through each photograph, he wants to throw up. He wants to scream. He wants to curse. He takes a deep breath. *This.* This is what he came for. He knows there is a sad story behind each picture. He looks away, then continues to go through the photographs. He cannot turn back. He is here. He must finish. He keeps looking at the faces of the boys, and that is when he finds himself staring at a photograph of Andrés Segovia. At twelve, he was very much still a child. Some boys were already on their way to becoming men at twelve. But not this boy, perhaps the most beautiful boy he has ever seen. He is as sad as he is beautiful. He wants to hold Andrés in his arms and tell him no harm will come to him. But he knows that harm has already come. He hopes it has not come to stay.

# The Quiet Before the Storm

It was odd, how already the house seemed empty without him. Mister pictured him growing into the bed he and Liz had bought for him. He pictured the house full of his photographs. One picture for every year—five, six, seven, eight . . . What would he look like as a man?

He looked in the mirror. He wondered if a man's body changed when he became a father. Sam had once told him that the shape of the human heart changed every time it loved someone. So the shape of the heart was always changing. If his heart had changed shape because of Vicente, then wasn't it also true that his entire body had changed?

But what did Sam know, anyway? He was no scientist. Just a romantic guy from the barrio who spent his entire life trying to figure out the meaning of things. Especially love. Sam was always trying to get at the root of the human heart. It was a thing with him. He was convinced that love wasn't metaphysical. Well, perhaps metaphysical in part. But its roots were in the physical body, the mind or the heart or the flesh, which was more intelligent than most people believed. *The body is intelligent.* That's what he had on a note that he tacked above his desk. Well, Sam was no dualist. *Sex feels good. Why do you suppose that is, mi'jito?* Sam always told him things like that—but he'd been too young to ask the right questions.

Maybe the heart did change shape. And not just when it loved. When it was hurt. When it was angry. When it hated. When it remembered. When it yearned. When it mourned.

Liz.

Vicente.

Grace.

Sam.

Heart.


"You can take him home next week."

"It's just Wednesday, Linda."

"Another week—that's—"

"An eternity."

"Relax."

"The Rubios need a little more time. It's not too much to ask, Mister."

"No, it's only right."

"They want to know if they can visit him."

"Of course."

"I think they've really fallen for this kid. Especially Mr. Rubio."

"They can visit any time they want."

"I think it would be a good idea if you called and told them that. I think it would be easier on them if you called."

"I can do that."

"You're a good egg, Mister."

"Sure I am." He laughed. *A week. Not such a long time. Liz will be disappointed.* He practiced saying, It's only a week, Liz. Not so long.

# Andrés Segovia.
# That's a Beautiful Name

ndrés learned how to connect all the dots. It was like finding the Big and Little Dippers. Once you saw the constellations—once you found them—everything was perfectly clear. He knew now that Yolie worked for Homero. He would find men who would pay to sleep with his sister. He understood that, and he hated Homero for doing that to his sister, and he hated Yolie for letting it happen.

One night, Homero came by. He said both he and Ileana should get dressed, make themselves look nice. So Yolie helped Ileana get dressed, and she looked so beautiful, and Andrés wore a nice shirt and Homero took them out to dinner, and it was nice to be taken out to dinner. They hadn't been out to dinner for a long time. Not since their mother and father had died. Not since then. And Andrés and Ileana ate and ate. Like they'd never eaten before. And afterward, Homero took them to a place. He said it was a private club. But Andrés thought it was just a bar. He'd seen them from the outside, but he had never been in one. The club was quiet, and Homero told him and Ileana to sit at the bar, and he ordered a Coke for both of them—with cherries.

Yolie was angry with him. "Why did you bring them in here?"

"They have to begin learning. How many times have I told you that?"

"They're too young. Leave them alone."

Yolie told them to go home. "Go on," she said. "Just go home."

Homero didn't like it, that Yolie was sending them home.

"Finish your Cokes," he said. He didn't say it in a nice way.

"Take them home, Homero. Now!" Yolie was angry.

"Callate, Puta," that's what he said. And he raised his arm like he was going to slap her. But he stopped himself. Yolie looked at him, and Andrés swore her eyes were knives and she was cutting him up like he was a piece of paper. And right then, at that moment, he loved Yolie, loved her with all his heart.

Yolie nodded at them. "Go home," she whispered.

Andrés took Ileana's hand. "C'mon, let's go." He wanted to hug Yolie and to kiss her and tell her that they should all go back. But he knew he would never go back to El Paso without her. So they were all stuck together now. No matter what happened.

Stuck. Together.

On their way home, off Calle Mariscal, he saw them. On a quiet street, Silvia and Amanda. They were standing at a doorway to a bar with a blinking neon light that read, "La Brisa." They were laughing and smoking cigarettes and wearing high heels and red dresses. He waved at them. And they made a big fuss over him and kissed him and kissed Ileana and told them they were beautiful, and they wanted to know why they were out. "It's not safe," Silvia said. "Where's Yolie?"

"She's with Homero," Andrés said,

"*Ese hijo de la chingada,*" Amanda said. "Your sister should keep away from that man."

"Shhh," Silvia said. "Anyway, it's too late for that. C'mon, let's take you home. It's not safe."

They walked Andrés and Ileana home, Silvia and Amanda, and Amanda whispered to him that he should keep away from Homero. Silvia gave Amanda a look, but she said if they ever needed them for anything, they could always go to La Brisa, and someone would know where to find them.

"You trusted them?"

"Sure I did. It's funny, isn't it? Two fake women were the most real things I encountered on those streets." *I might have even loved them.*

• • •

One night, when Yolie was out, Homero came by the house. Andrés was reading a book to Ileana. "That's nice," Homero said. But Andrés could see that Homero was a fake. Nothing real about his smile or his words. "Yolie won't come home until very late," Andrés said. He wanted Homero to leave.

"I know. I just wanted to come by and visit you. Just to make sure the both of you were all right."

"We're fine," Andrés said. But he said it through his teeth.

"Oh, so you bark like a dog?"

"I bite like one, too," Andrés said.

"You have your sister's fight."

"I don't want you to come here anymore," Andrés said.

"You'd have starved without me. Ask your sister, she'll tell you. I own her. I own you, too."

"Get out," Andrés said.

Homero smiled, then nodded. He wasn't angry, not really. Andrés knew Homero wasn't afraid of him. Who could be afraid of a boy like him? He got up to leave. He put a ten-dollar bill on the table. "This is your first paycheck," he said.

"Take your money," Andrés said.

Homero smiled and walked out of the house.

"I should've left. Right then and there, I should've left."

"But you couldn't leave Yolie, could you?"

"No, I couldn't."

"So you hate yourself. For loving her."

"I'm not that virtuous. I was just afraid."

"Maybe you are virtuous. There's a thought."

"Yeah. Sure."

"I don't know many men who aren't threatened by transvestites."

"It's not a virtue to trust good people. Transvestites don't hurt anybody. Men who look normal, who dress normal, who talk normal, they hurt people. Homero was a well-dressed, more or less educated man. He looked like a man is supposed to look like. Big fucking deal. We should all be afraid of normal-looking men. Transvestites? They're nothing to be afraid of."

"Knowing who to trust is a virtue, Andrés."

"You're bound and determined to make me out to be a decent guy."

"That's my job."

"You'd be better off selling shoes."

A few minutes after Homero left, there was another knock at the door. Andrés thought it was Homero again, but when he went to the door, his heart beating, he relaxed. It was Silvia. "I saw him come in here," she said. "I don't like it that he comes here when your sister's not here. What did he want?" She was angry. She knew all about him. Andrés showed her the ten-dollar bill he'd left on the kitchen table. "He said it was our first paycheck."

"Your sister has to get you out of here. Where is she?"

Andrés shrugged. "She's out."

"Never mind. I know where to find her." She shook her head. "Lock the door. And don't ever open it for anyone."

The next morning, Andrés told Yolie what had happened. After she was awake and drinking coffee and smoking. "I know," she said. "Silvia told me everything."

Andrés looked at her. "What if he hurts Ileana?"

"He won't. You worry too much."

But she was as worried as he was. Andrés could see that. But he could also see she didn't want to talk about it.

Things went normal for a little while. Normal for them, anyway. Yolie worked almost every night. Sometimes she had a night off, and she would cook a meal and go to bed early. Silvia and Amanda checked in on them every night before they went out. One night, Andrés heard Silvia arguing with a man right outside their door, on the sidewalk.

The man called her a puta, an hija de la chingada and everything else that was bad in the world, and he told her he was going to kill her. Andrés didn't like it, that the man was calling her those names. He opened the door and watched them yell at each other. "Te voy a matar!" he yelled.

"Si puedes," she yelled back, "Yo soy mas hombre que tú."

That's when he slapped her. She fell against the wall, then slipped on the sidewalk, her heels coming out from under her. Andrés jumped in between them when he saw the man was going to kick her. "Dejala," Andrés said.

The man clenched his fists and jaw, deciding whether he should hit Andrés or not. He shook his head in disgust and walked away. He helped Silvia up.

"Don't ever let a man touch you like that," she said. Then she laughed. "Hombrecito," she said. "Eres mi hombrecito."

He didn't mind, that she called him her little man.

That night Andrés understood that everyone had troubles. Silvia and Amanda—troubles. People looked at them, hated them. He knew they were transvestites and prostitutes, and he knew that meant trouble. And Yolie, she was a prostitute, too. And that meant trouble—especially because she worked for Homero. He was supposed to protect her. That's what Silvia said, but no one needed that kind of protection. She called Homero a cabrón and a pinchi and an hijo de la chingada. She hated him. Everyone had troubles. But his mother and father and Mando, they didn't have troubles anymore. He hadn't prayed for Mando. He'd prayed for his mom and dad, but he'd forgotten to pray for Mando. Maybe he took the right road. Maybe he found his mom and dad. Maybe they were living in the light now. Maybe people didn't fight anymore when they spent their days in that perfect light. Maybe Mando and his dad would be happy and talk like men were meant to talk.

He hoped the dead couldn't see the living. He hoped his mother couldn't see what was happening to them. She didn't deserve to see this.

A few days later, Homero came to visit again. He talked to Yolie, who was getting ready to go out. They talked on the sidewalk. They argued. But they argued in whispers, so he and Ileana couldn't hear. When Yolie came back inside, she looked numb and afraid. She was shaking when she lit her cigarette.

"What's wrong?" Andrés asked.

"You ask too many questions." She kept smoking and smoking. "Ileana's going with me tonight," she said.

"What?"

"Nothing's going to happen to her."

"She's just a little girl," Andrés yelled.

"Nothing's going to happen to her."

"I won't let you take her. I won't let you—" He felt the slap of her hard hand against his face. The force of it made Andrés fly across the room. He didn't say anything when he looked up at her. He picked himself up and walked into the courtyard. He sat there trying not to think about anything. Before she and Ileana left, Yolie walked into the courtyard. "A man will be coming. Do you understand? Do what he tells you to do. If you don't, Homero will hurt Ileana. Do you understand?"

Andrés nodded.

"I'm sorry," she whispered.

Andrés looked away.

The man came. He wasn't old. He was a gringo. He was thin and well dressed and handsome and had a nice voice, and he wasn't too old—it was hard for Andrés to know how old he was. Older than Mando had been—but not so very old. "Did someone tell you I would be coming?"

Andrés nodded.

The man lit a cigarette.

"I won't hurt you. I like you. Don't you know how much I like you? Can't you see? Come here. Sit by me."

He thought of Ileana. He thought of what Homero might to do her. If he didn't do what the man said. So Andrés sat next to the man.

"What's your name?"

"Andrés Segovia."

"Really?"

Andrés nodded.

"Andrés Segovia. That's a beautiful name. You're named after an artist." The man placed his hands on him as he talked, "A guitarist from Spain. Did you know that? That doesn't hurt, now does it?"

# Grace and Morning Mass

Today, she stared at the light streaming through the stained-glass windows. Saint Monica was wiping her tears as the light of heaven fell on her face. She remembered the story. She had never ceased to pray for the conversion of her son, Augustine. God had come to her in a vision and said, "Do not worry, woman. Your tears have saved your son." All the light in the window entered through Monica's radiant face. Her mother had told her that it was because of Monica's tears, that God made her son a great man. And she remembered one more thing about Monica. When she was dying and she was far from home, she was asked if she was afraid to be buried in a foreign place, a place where she was a stranger. "Nothing is far from God," she said. "Neither am I afraid that God will not find my body to raise me from my slumber." It was Sam who had given her that detail about the life of Saint Monica. And so she had decided to name her first child Monica. Because Monica had not been afraid to die. A woman who was not afraid to die was not afraid of anything. But Monica, her first child, was stillborn. Sam had wanted a tribe. The second one, a girl. Another Monica, she'd died a few days after her birth. And Mister, too. Mister had almost died. But Sam swore to God that he'd go to mass every day of his life if God let this boy live. And Mister had lived. Their Mister. And he was all the tribe Sam had needed.

Sam had been as good as his word. Every day of his life, he went to daily mass. And when he'd died, Grace had picked up the ritual. Because she felt the world would be poorer and sadder without his prayers. So perhaps she would do her part to carry the load. She knew, of course, that he'd prayed for unorthodox causes—socialists, the demise of capitalism, Leonard Peltier. She'd never had Sam's penchant for iconoclasm, nor had she shared his commitment for changing the social order. Hers was a more common calling. And, anyway, it was Mister who'd inherited his politics—though he hadn't inherited his devout Catholicism.

She smiled. Here she was, in the middle of mass, recounting the history of her family—Mister and Sam. She chastised herself for not making enough room in her heart for Liz. Was it too late for family? For Mister and Liz and Vicente. She stared at the stained-glass window of Saint Monica. She spoke to her. *You weren't afraid to die. Teach me.* Today, that was her only prayer.

# All the Hovering Angels

"his is for you. We won't tell Homero, will we? It will be our secret, eh?" He placed the twenty-dollar bill on the table. He
turned around and stared at Andrés, who was sitting on the
couch with his head bowed.

"Now don't be sad." He walked over to Andrés and kissed him
on the forehead. "You're a good boy. You're a very good boy. Now, look
at me."

Andrés made himself look at the man. Maybe then he would leave.

The man kissed him again on the forehead. He walked over to the
table and kissed the twenty-dollar bill the same way he'd kissed him.

"I think I could fall in love with you."

*I won't ever fall in love—not with you, not with anything. Not ever.
Not ever again.*

Andrés stared at the money on the table. He wanted to burn it like he'd
burned all the letters he'd written to Mrs. Fernandez. He felt dizzy. He
got into a fight once, when he was eight. A boy had hit him in the side of
his head and he'd felt numb and dizzy and he'd had to sit down on the
ground, and the whole world was spinning—and he'd felt ashamed that
everyone had seen that he hadn't been able to hit the other boy back. Because he hadn't known how to fight. He felt that way now, like the
world was spinning, like he didn't know how to fight. And somehow, he
felt like the whole world knew what he had done. For twenty dollars.

He stumbled toward the bathroom and vomited. He lay there on the floor for a while. Finally, he took a shower. He couldn't keep himself from shaking, could barely dry himself, he was shaking so much. Maybe a cigarette would help. He knew where Yolie kept them. He walked to the drawer and opened it, then found a pack. "They're mine," he said. "They're mine now." He took the pack to the courtyard and lit a cigarette. He inhaled, held the smoke in his lungs, then slowly let it out. He was dizzy again, but he didn't care. He smoked the whole cigarette. He felt sick. He stumbled to the bathroom again and vomited. He vomited and vomited until there was nothing left, but his stomach was still trying to turn itself inside out.

He was cold. He put on a coat. It was too small for him now, his coat, but it was okay, he was warmer. He felt the hot tears on his cheeks, and he wondered why he was crying. Why was he crying? That wouldn't help. Crying never helped. When his mother and father had died, what good were his tears? When Mando died, what good had it done him or Yolie, that they'd cried? He wouldn't cry anymore after this, that's what he told himself.

But he couldn't stop himself. So he cried.

And then he stopped. He smoked another cigarette. He didn't get so dizzy this time. He fell asleep in the courtyard and dreamed his mother was hovering over him. And then his mother became Mrs. Fernandez. And then Mrs. Fernandez became Silvia. And they were all angels.

Andrés woke in the middle of the night. He was cold. All the hovering angels were gone. He thought maybe there had been a funeral. Someone had died. Everything was black—the sky, the clothes he was wearing, his heart. He made himself get up. He smoked another cigarette. He didn't want to look up at the stars. He didn't want to. He finished his cigarette and went to bed.

Ileana was asleep. She was home. She was safe. He kissed her, then fell into his own bed. Maybe, when he woke, he would discover that it was all a bad dream. But in the morning, he understood that it had all been real. He felt sick and ashamed and he didn't want to get up, so he didn't. He fell back asleep. The next time he woke, Yolie was sitting at the foot of his bed. She was just sitting there, watching him. He wanted to tell her he hated her. For everything that had happened—he hated her and Mando, even though Mando was dead, because all of this was his fault, too. But hating them didn't change anything.

He turned toward the wall, and stared at it.

"If we don't do what he says, he'll hurt Ileana."

Andrés said nothing.

"Do you understand?"

*The man hurt me. Does it matter? Do you care?* "I understand," he whispered.

"I'm sorry."

"No, you're not. If you were sorry, you'd get us out of here."

"If you leave, he'll hurt Ileana. Do you understand?"

"Yes."

"Don't hate me."

"I told her I'd hate her till I died."

"Why shouldn't you have hated her?"

"She was caught."

"It's not your job to defend what she did, Andrés."

"What is my job?"

"Your job is to live."

"They didn't get to live. Why should I?"

"That's not your fault."

"What's it like to wake up in the morning and be glad?"

She thought of Sam, how she'd wake next to him, or if he had already risen, how she'd find him in the garden.

"Do you know what gardenias smell like?"

"Yes."

"That's what it's like to be glad. You wake searching for the smell of gardenias. Or the smell of oranges. Or the smell of agaves. Or the smell of rosemary. And you think, God, I can smell. And you walk out and you see the light falling on everything—on the delicate leaves of a mesquite or the brilliant white of an oleander in bloom that almost blinds you or the bougainvillea that explodes pink like a firecracker. And you think, God, I can see."

"You sound like a poet."

"I was married to one. He died."

"I'm sorry."

"He taught me how to look at things. How to smell things. How to understand the miracle of having a body."

"I don't think having a body is such a miracle."

"That's all you'll ever have in this world, Andrés."

"Maybe that's why I hate everything."

"Andrés, what your sister and brother did. We both know they didn't mean for you and Ileana to get hurt. But they were wrong. And that man, that bastard, Homero, who used you to make money—"

"He turned me into a prostitute. You can say it."

"Twelve-year-olds aren't prostitutes."

"What was I, then?"

"A boy. A boy who was sexually abused."

"And got paid for it. For three years. I worked for three years. I think that qualifies as prostitution."

"I think that qualifies as sexual abuse in the extreme. In the fucking extreme—if you don't mind my language."

"No, I don't mind." He smiled. Just the same, it was a sad smile. He lit a cigarette.

"It makes me angry that you hate yourself for something that somebody else made you do. Don't let them take any more. Don't you do that, Andrés."

"None of this does any good, Grace. All these visits, all this talking, all this strolling down fucking memory lane. It doesn't help. And you know why it doesn't help? Because everything that's happened—it lives so deep inside me that the only way I can ever get rid of it is to die."

"That's not true, Andrés."

"It is true. Happiness isn't in the cards for everyone, Grace."

"You know what I'd do? I'd reshuffle the deck. I'd redeal the cards."

"You can't win every hand."

"You can't lose every hand, either, Andrés."

"I have, Grace. I fucking have."

His sadness was unbearable to watch. Far worse than his rage. He looked so defeated in that sorrow—like he was surrendering, like the battle was too much. But when he was angry, he was at least alive and fighting—even if he wasn't clear who the hell he was fighting. Or why. His rage was at least a kind of understanding that if he didn't keep fighting, he just might perish. His life had taught him at least that one lesson.

God, she wanted him to be angry again. His rage had helped him to survive—and it was possible that his rage was the only intelligent response to what had happened to him. The emotions the body conjured had their own logic. Perhaps the body was vaster, larger, much more complex and mysterious, than psychologists or physicians ever dreamed. Who knew? Who really knew the secrets of the human body? Maybe that was the only reason she had clung to her Catholic God all these years—because a God-made man was the most beautiful thing imaginable. It was the most beautiful thing in the world.

*Be angry, Andrés. Who are we to rob you of your rage?*

# Becoming Light

Grace arrived back home, tired. Every day, a little more tired. She had some medication. Richard had brought it over himself. Paid for it, too.

"You're going to go broke doing that for your patients."

"What a lovely way to go bankrupt," he said.

She'd almost wanted to kiss him for saying such a thing.

Maybe she'd take her medicine. He said it would help. And if it didn't, then she didn't have to take it.

She stepped out of the car and stared at the palo verde that had grown tall and graceful in the front yard. It needed so little care. So little water—and there it was, blooming in a drought. Why couldn't people be that way? Why couldn't they just take what little there was and grow?

She turned the key to her front door and pushed it open. She saw her dog lying in the middle of the room. "Oh," she whispered, "so you've left us."

"She'd stopped begging for food. I knew it was just a matter of time."

Mister looked up at Grace as he knelt beside the dog. "I was twelve when you got her. She slept on my bed until I moved out."

"To marry Liz."

"That dog never liked Liz."

"Well, dogs are like people. They're not always right."

Mister smiled at his mother, then kissed the dead dog and took her in his arms.

"Where do you want me to bury her?"

He followed his mother into the backyard. "There," she said. Mister looked at the bare spot in the corner.

"What happened to the Spanish broom?"

"Aphids. I couldn't save it."

He nodded and laid the dog down. Dead now, with no hope of heaven. Dogs were lucky—they didn't need to live forever. They weren't as greedy as people.

He hadn't noticed Grace wasn't standing next to him anymore.

"Grace?"

He saw her walking back into the yard with a shovel. She handed it to him. She wondered if now wasn't as good a time as any to mention the word *cancer.*

They let themselves fall into silence. They'd always done that, let each other go their separate ways—even when they were together. Mister thought of the day Grace had brought the dog home. A present for Sam. He loved dogs. And that dog had loved him back. Howled for days after he died, looked for him, mourned for him. But after a while, she was fine, and she turned to the survivors in the house for all her needs— her walks, her food, her daily doses of affection. And Grace, she remembered the day she found the dog—in a box someone had tossed in the trash bin behind her office building. Not that she ever went in that alley. But that afternoon, she'd shredded some of her old files and decided to throw them out herself. And there was the puppy, filthy and whining, thrown away like a piece of trash. She'd reached for the dog and took her inside and bathed her in the sink of the women's bathroom. The puppy couldn't have been more than a few days old. She'd brought the dog home at lunch and placed her in a box in the backyard. Sam and Mister went crazy, crazy when they found her. They spent the whole evening trying to pick the right name. But it was she who had named her. "Mississippi," she said as they argued. They'd both looked at her and laughed. "Perfect!"

• • •

"You think this is deep enough?" Grace thought he looked like a piece of gold against the evening sun, sweat pouring down his face and neck. Her grandmother had always said sweat was sweet and holy. She'd always thought her grandmother was a little crazy. She didn't think that anymore. Children were so hard on adults. They expected so much and understood so little.

"Grace?"

"I'm sorry?"

"Are you condemning yourself for something that happened in the past again?"

"Of course not?"

"You're not a good liar, Grace."

She looked down at the hole Mister had dug for Mississippi. "I think that's deep enough." She watched Mister pick up the dog and place her gently in the grave he'd dug.

He began shoveling the dirt over the dog.

"Let me," she said.

He didn't argue with her.

He watched her shovel the dirt over the body of the dead dog. She was getting a little thinner. It was as if she was becoming the light.

"Grace, do you think it's true what the curanderos say about animals?"

"That they carry us across the river into paradise?"

"Yeah."

"It's a nice thought, isn't it, Mister?"

"Maybe Mississippi will be there, to take us across the river. To take us to Sam."

# Grace and Morning Mass

He was standing there in front of the doors to the cathedral, almost as if he were a sentry on watch. He smiled as he saw Grace walking up the steps. A soft smile. He knew she'd come. She rarely missed. "Morning," he whispered.

"Morning," she whispered back.

"Grace, I want to talk to you about a treatment."

"I'm feeling a little ambushed."

"You won't return my phone calls."

"It's too late, Richard."

"You don't know that, Grace. I'm the doctor."

"And I'm the patient."

"It's my job to make sure you make an informed decision."

She looked at him. She opened her mouth to speak, but then thought better of saying anything at all. She didn't want to argue with this man. This good man. And outside the cathedral. Before morning mass.

"I thought you were a fighter, Grace."

"When I fight, I have to believe I can win."

"You can."

"Don't do this, Richard. Please don't do this."


Today, she was angry. She wasn't in the mood for begging. She ordered Saint Francis to raise her dog Mississippi from the dead. "She was as good a servant as any. When that man tried to hurt Mister when he was walking to the store, do you remember? She leaped on him like a wild animal. She was protector and companion, and it isn't right that heaven prefers humans to animals." On listening to her own prayer, she asked forgiveness for eating meat. It was a sin, after all, to eat animals. She was heartily sorry.

And then she prayed to Mary Magdalene, protector of prostitutes, transvestites, and addicts. Why not? God, in his ironic sense of humor, had chosen her to be the first to see Jesus risen from the dead. Today, she prayed for Silvia. *If she isn't in heaven, see to it. And guide the girls on both sides of the border. You know what I mean. You know exactly what I mean.*

*And tell the good doctor to leave me the hell alone.*

# No One Can Run from a Fire

"Get up, hijito de mi vida. It's time to leave." Silvia's voice was soft, like a silk scarf moving over his body. He didn't want to wake, just lie there and listen to her voice. "Corazón, tenemos que irnos de aqui inmediatamente. La situación es muy grave, amor. Hay mucho peligro."

He rose from the bed reluctantly. He let her dress him. Her fingers were so soft.

When she finished dressing him they left the house.

There was no one left to say good-bye to.

The streets of Juárez were empty, and he was glad that everyone was sleeping. The prostitutes and the tranvestites and the boys and the girls who had to do what Homero and the other men told them to do—they were all resting.

They walked hand in hand, him and Silvia. She led him to the bridge, and as they reached the arch of the bridge, they looked down at the river.

"They've made it so poor," she said. "It wasn't always like this. The waters once flowed wild, and they weren't hemmed in by cement, and they roared with the fierceness of America. Before they came. But when they came, they came with armor and rage. They came with their Jesus and their crosses and we have never been wild again—neither us nor the river."

"Not you, Silvia," Andrés said, "no one can tame you."

"Oh, amor, if you were a man, I would take you in my arms and never let you go." She clutched him, then let him go. "Run," she said, "go back to where you came."

He ran toward El Paso. He ran and ran and ran, the lights of the city sparkling like summer stars. He disappeared into the light.

Andrés woke to the cramps in his calves. His heart racing, he threw the covers off the bed and walked to the window. He didn't like thinking about Silvia. It was all too sad. But here he was at one-thirty in the morning, thinking about her. He'd always thought of her as a real woman. Not like a man at all. He hated men. All of them. Every single fucking one of them. Himself included.

"What did he do to you, Andrés?"

"Nothing."

"You don't have to lie to me."

"He does what men do." Andrés looked away from her.

"What?"

"You know what I'm saying, Silvia. Don't make me talk about this. I don't want to talk about it."

"Your sister's letting that pimp turn you into—" Andrés could see the fire in her eyes. "I need to talk to your sister."

"What for? She knows. Homero's in charge of us, now."

"Homero's not in charge of anything, that pinchi. Ese cabrón es un hijo de la chingada y uno de estos dias me lo voy a chingar."

"He'll hurt Ileana. If we don't—you know. If Yolie and I don't. He'll hurt her."

"Where is she?"

"She lives with a woman Homero knows. Yolie says she'll be safe with her. That they won't make her do what—you know, what we do. They won't make her. If we just do our jobs."

"You're just a boy."

"It doesn't matter, Silvia." He lit a cigarette.

"You shouldn't be smoking. You're too young."

"I'm a lot older, now."

"I'd like to kill Homero."

"Don't argue with him anymore. He'll kill you."

"Fuck him."

"He'll kill you, Silvia. He showed us. He showed me and Yolie. He took us to a place, and there was a woman dead on the ground. And he said, 'She got what she deserved.' Just leave it alone, Silvia."

"You and Yolie have to get out of here."

"He has Ileana."

"He won't hurt her."

"Yes, he will. You know he will."

He lit a cigarette, then turned on his computer. He remembered all the letters he'd written to Mrs. Fernandez. He didn't remember anymore, the things he'd told her in all those useless letters. He thought that maybe in one of them he'd told her that he loved her. Sure, he had. He was eleven and had wanted a mother. Sure, he'd told her that. I love you. He hadn't loved anyone for a long time. He'd loved Yolie. He'd loved Mando. He'd loved his mom and dad. He'd loved Ileana. God, he'd loved her more than he'd ever loved anyone. And he'd loved Silvia. And they'd left him alone in the world. And he hated that.

And now, he just couldn't love anymore. Maybe it wasn't such a big problem. Loving had never done him a damn bit of good.

He stared at his computer screen, then started writing. Writing and writing, though he didn't know what good it did.

He'd had so many sad days, Andrés. But today was the saddest. Homero was taking Ileana to live with a woman who would take care of her. "You can visit her every day, if you want." Andrés said nothing. He'd loved her from the first day his mother had brought her home. He'd taken care of her. She was his. It wasn't fair. Why was he doing this to him?

"Yolie, you have to stop him! You have to stop him. She's ours. She belongs to us, not to him."

"It's too late to stop him." It was like Yolie had died. Like her heart had stopped beating. There wasn't anything in her eyes anymore. "It's too late," she whispered.

So Ileana was going away. To live with an old woman. "She's just an old whore," Silvia said, "an old whore who's too old to attract any takers. But Homero still owns her."

Yolie packed all her things. "Tomorrow you have to go. But we'll visit every day. We promise." She didn't say anything else. When Ileana tried to cling to her, she pushed her away. "Shut up! Just shut up!"

Ileana refused to stop crying. "Don't let them take me!"

"Shhh," Andrés whispered, then held her. "When Yolie's asleep," he said softly, "then we're going. I'm taking you back to Mrs. Fernandez."

"Will you stay with me?"

"Yes. We'll both stay."

Andrés thought of Yolie. But she was dead. That's what he thought. Yolie was dead now. If she was alive, she would be helping them to get away. But something had happened to her. She was broken. She couldn't be fixed.

He had to save Ileana—that was all that mattered.

When Yolie was asleep, they slipped out the door. Andrés knew the way. He'd taken this trip a thousand times in his head. He felt his heart pounding. Ileana didn't say anything. Not a word. When they reached Avenida Juárez, Andrés took a deep breath. He could see the bridge to El Paso in the distance.

That was when he felt the hand on his shoulder.

He turned around and saw Homero. "Are you lost?"

Andrés shook his head. His heart was pounding. Nothing could make it stop.

Homero took Ileana by the hand. "Let's go home."

No one said anything as they headed back home.

When Homero took them inside, he slapped Yolie, for letting them get out. He stayed the night on the couch. In the morning, he took Ileana.

Andrés refused to talk. He didn't say a word for three weeks. Sometimes men would come. He knew what they wanted. He didn't talk to them. Anyway, they hadn't come to talk. He didn't care. Not about anything. Not anymore.

The first thing he said when he spoke again was, "I want to see Ileana."

Yolie took him to her. Ileana hugged him, and he spent most of the day with her. "I'll always love you, Andy." That's what she told him.

He went to see her three times a week. And she always said the same thing. "I love you, Andy."

But he felt dirty now. And her love was pure. And he knew he didn't deserve to be loved by her. So it hurt to go to see her. But always he would ask her. "Does anyone touch you?"

"No," she said. And he knew she was telling him the truth because he could tell that she was the same. The world he and Yolie were living in hadn't touched her.

The old whore used to watch them when he visited. She would cook a meal for them and let them talk. Mostly, Ileana would tell him stories she made up in her mind. He'd stopped writing stories—now it was she who was the storyteller. And the stories were all for him.

A year passed, and then another. And they lived that way. Andrés visited Ileana, and the visits were the only thing in his life that mattered. He and Yolie never said anything to each other anymore. He would buy the food with the money Homero gave them. The money they earned. He bought the food and cooked. Yolie didn't do any of that anymore. She hardly ate. He knew she was taking drugs. Her eyes were always glazed over, as if a film of frozen ice were covering them. She laughed sometimes, but her laugh was hollow.

Andrés asked her once to stop taking drugs. "It's all that matters, now," she said.

Silvia and Amanda didn't live together anymore. Silvia kicked Amanda out. "She does more drugs than your sister." Amanda didn't live another year. They found her dead on the street one December night. On the Feast of Our Lady of Guadalupe Silvia cried. They were like best friends, now, Andrés and Silvia. Some nights, Andrés would go to La Brisa and talk to Silvia and her friends. They all told him he was beautiful. But he didn't feel beautiful, and inside he knew he was nothing but dirt.

Three years, they lived like that. Yolie on drugs and sleeping with the men Homero sent her way. Him, too. He would do what the men told him to do. That's how they lived. But it didn't matter because Ileana was still pure.

On his fifteenth birthday, he noticed that he was becoming a man. He was sprouting hair everywhere—under his arms, on his legs, between his legs, especially—and on his face. It was strange, to see himself with hair. Everywhere. Maybe, because he was a man, now, the men wouldn't want him. He hoped the men wouldn't want him.

He went to see Ileana on his birthday. He hadn't seen her in a week. He bought some mangos for Carmen. He didn't call her the old whore anymore. She wasn't so bad. That old woman, she loved Ileana and took care of her. Even Silvia, who sometimes visited Ileana, didn't call her the old whore anymore. "Carmen's had a bad life." That's what Silvia told him. "Her husband died when she was young. A bad life. Sometimes, she still calls herself Mrs. Fuentes. As if that makes her more respectable. I told her to fuck respectability. Fuck all that." Silvia. She told him things. She made him laugh.

He took the mangos and went to see Ileana. But when he arrived at Carmen's house, he found Carmen lying on the floor, bruised and bleeding. She was sobbing and sobbing. "Where's Ileana?" he yelled. "Where is she?" But all Carmen could do was moan. He ran to get Silvia, but she wasn't home. He ran to La Brisa and found her there, sitting at the bar, putting on her makeup. "It's Carmen," he said. "And Ileana's gone. She's gone!" He tried to keep the tears away, but they were there. She took off her heels and ran back with him. They helped put Carmen to bed, and Silvia washed the blood off her lip and inspected her bruises. She stopped crying and moaning, and Silvia gave her a cigarette. She looked at Andrés.

"I sent your sister away. She's safe."

"Where did you send her?"

"With a friend. She's safe, I promise you. Homero said it was time for her to go to work. So I sent her away. I wasn't going to let anybody touch her. She's a little girl. What kind of animals sleep with little girls? What kind of man makes money on that? He almost killed me. I thought the slaps would never stop. But I didn't tell him. I didn't tell him anything. He would've killed me—but his new woman stopped him. He'll do anything for his new women. For a while, anyway. He's not going to pay for this house anymore. He said I could live in the street for all he cared."

"You can live with me." Silvia always said generous things.

"You're sure Ileana's safe?" Andrés was numb.

"She doesn't live in this town, anymore, mi'jito."

"Where did they take her?"

"They took her across."

"To El Paso?"

"Yes."

"And from there?"

"I don't know. My friend knows a woman who wants a little girl."

"What if the woman doesn't want her?"

"That child is an angel."

"What's the woman's name?"

"I don't know."

"How can you not know?"

"I didn't want to know. In case Homero beat it out of me. What if I told him? What would he do to her? I can't tell him what I don't know. He's brutal. He's an animal."

"But what about your friend?"

"I told her never to come back here. She worked for Homero. If she ever comes back, he'd kill her. For defying him. She'll never come back."

Andrés said nothing for a long time. "I'll never see her again."

"But she's safe, hijo de mi vida."

He nodded. "Yes."

"She'll send word. When Ileana is safe. She promised me."

Andrés kept nodding. Andrés, who was almost a man now. At fifteen.

"You should go—both of you. If Homero knows you've helped me, he'll get even with you."

"I'll cut his balls off if he comes near me." Andrés thought Silvia just might do it. "You don't have to work for him anymore."

Andrés nodded.

Andrés watched Silvia make soup for Carmen. She fed her. "I used to call you the old whore," Silvia confessed. "I'm sorry."

Carmen laughed. "But that's what I am. Just an old whore."

That was the first time he ever got drunk. Yolie kept a bottle of Kentucky bourbon on the shelf in the kitchen. Sometimes her clients wanted something to drink. She always made sure to have a bottle. When he got home, it was there. And it was almost full. He took the bottle and went into the courtyard. He took a drink, then lit a cigarette. He drank straight from the bottle. He hated it. But he didn't care. He hated a lot of things—this was easy, drinking bourbon. Easy as pie. He thought of

Ileana, how she was free now. It didn't matter that he'd never see her again because she was safe, and she didn't have to live this kind of life. Her life would be good. She was safe.

It was good to be drunk. To be numb. To not care. He understood now why Yolie liked drugs. It must be something like this, he thought. Sometimes heaven was feeling nothing. Maybe being drunk was a little like dying and going to heaven. Like living in the light. He kept thinking of Ileana. She was eight now. Eight years old and smart and beautiful, and she had all her teeth now. He was glad that she was the one who had been saved. He laughed and laughed and laughed, and then he thought that maybe he wasn't laughing at all. Maybe he was crying.

He didn't know how long he'd been sleeping out in the courtyard. It was early afternoon when he'd started drinking. It was night, now, and the banging on the door woke him. He stumbled to the door, and stared at a man. He knew that man. It was one of the men who had come to him before. Half gringo, half Mexican. "You've grown," the man said.

Andrés smiled at him. "I'm not working tonight."

"I have money. I have lots of money."

Andrés shook his head. "I'm done with all of this."

The man came closer. That's when Andrés reached for his collar and flung him to the ground. The man looked up at him. "Homero will make you pay."

"Fuck you, and fuck Homero." Andrés walked away, his head pounding and pounding as if it were a door someone was trying to knock down. Maybe that was the day when the fire inside him got started. The fire that kept everyone at bay. The fire that scorched anyone who got close.

The fire that was burning him up alive.

# Timing and Order in the Universe

I t is early in the evening. Tonight, Grace is looking at an article regarding women who have cancer—why some survive, why others
don't. It isn't strictly a medical essay, though it is written by a doctor.
Richard Garza had left it in her mailbox with a note: "There's hope and
there's still time." She wonders at herself. She is frustrated and charmed
by her doctor's tenacity. She has already decided not to seek treatment,
but tonight she will read the article. He went to so much trouble.

Andrés Segovia is having a conversation with himself as he looks in
the mirror. Every time he looks at himself, he looks unfamiliar. Sometimes he thinks he is looking at himself for the first time. He is never satisfied with the stranger he sees in the mirror. Today, he thinks the man he
is staring at is old. He sees an aging face.

Dave is talking to the DA at a small bar down the street from the
courthouse. They are old friends—just as, at times, they are old enemies.
They are discussing the charges against Andrés Segovia. Dave is trying
to get him to drop the charges. The DA listens patiently to all his arguments. He is trying to be sympathetic. But the answer is no. "Sorry—but
in my opinion, your client took a life. In the state of Texas, that's murder. Look, it's not capital murder, no premeditation, so look, maybe you
can talk me down to manslaughter. Your client was reckless, and there
isn't any doubt about that. No doubt at all." Dave is equally patient as
he listens. "Involuntary manslaughter." They nod at each other. The DA
shakes his head. "Look, he could get a pretty light sentence. Five to fifteen—with parole."

"He doesn't deserve this, Bobby. You know I'm going to put the victim on trial. You know that, don't you?"

"If you can."

"Just watch. He's not going to spend one second in jail. Not one worthless second."

"We all fight to win, don't we?"

The DA raises his bottle of beer.

Dave is thinking this is a waste of time.

Liz and Mister are looking over an empty building on the East Side. Dolce Vita East. They have decided to open up a second coffee shop. Liz looks over the abandoned building. "It needs work."

Mister looks at her and asks, "Are we afraid of work?"

They laugh. They decide they will make an offer on the building. As they walk back to the car, Liz says maybe they should name the new coffee shop after Vicente.

# Touch

"D o you ever let anyone touch you?" She'd asked him that. She knew the answer before she asked. "Define touch." And there it was again, that rage that owned him. There it was, knocking down his door.

Just as he was about to leave, she'd taken out a dictionary. "Let's see," she said. "Touch. Yes, here it is. I like the first definition. 'To cause or permit the body to come in contact with so as to feel.' "

"That's an old dictionary, Grace."

"It's about as old as you are—which isn't old at all."

"Dictionaries are outdated the minute after they're published."

"Okay," she'd answered. "So you think a newer dictionary has changed the meaning of the word—substantially, I mean? Here," she said, then pushed the dictionary in his direction.

It smelled of book mold. Like the old part of a library. He'd stared at the entry. *Touch.* "Here," he said, "I like this definition better. 'To disturb or move by handling.' "

He'd shoved the dictionary back across the desk. She'd reread the entries. "Mine is the first definition. Yours is the seventh." She'd nodded. "But here, let's not quibble about rankings. Let's take number fifteen. 'To affect the emotions of; move to tender response.' " She'd smiled at him.

That's where they'd left the discussion. With Grace having the last word.

"I don't like dictionaries much," he'd told her as he walked out the door.

He hadn't liked the discussion. He didn't like thinking about touch. He didn't know anything about that word. Dictionaries didn't know crap.

He showered, shaved, looked at himself in the mirror. Well, he looked fine. He'd always looked fine. The way he looked, that had never been the problem. Or maybe it had been the problem. *You're a beautiful boy,* and why were the voices there, but he knew why and he knew they would always be there, the voices, knocking at his door, taking over his house.

He slipped on some jeans. He looked in his closet and realized that all of his shirts were the same—all of them were white cotton shirts. All of them. It was like having only one shirt. He'd never even realized that, God, was he screwed up or what? Twenty-six years old, and never been on a date, and all his shirts were white? What was that? And who cared, anyway, about clothes? Some of his T-shirts were black, so that wasn't white. A few pairs of khakis and jeans, that's what he wore. And who cared? They covered his body. That's what mattered. He lit a cigarette, his hands trembling. He ran a finger up his arm. Touch.

# Emancipation—There's a Word

Maybe he would go for a run. Maybe that would help. But how would running help anything? He walked to the window and opened it. He looked at his watch. It wasn't that late. Just before midnight. He wasn't sleepy. He turned away from the window as he heard the phone ring. It could only be Dave. Nobody else had his number. He walked up to the phone and stared at it. On the fourth ring, he answered it. "You asleep?"

"No. You always call people this late, Dave?"

"Sometimes. Yes. You wanna grab a beer?"

Andrés walked to the window and lit a cigarette. "What are we, pals?"

"Let's grab a beer."

Andrés blew out a smoke ring and watched it. "Sure," he whispered. "Why the hell not?"


"I've been wanting to tell you something. For a long time, now."

"So what's been stopping you?"

"Not everything's so easy to say."

"I thought everything was easy for a guy like you."

"Why? Because I'm a gringo?"

"A rich gringo. A rich gringo lawyer."

"Oh, the whole fucking world belongs to me? Is that it? The world doesn't belong to anyone."

"Oh, that's a pretty lie you tell yourself."

They stood there for a minute. On the street. Talking in the dim light. Just like they'd talked that night when he'd bailed him out of jail.

"So you got a place where you like to go have a beer? You know, wind down?"

"I don't think I know anything about winding down. I don't think you do, either."

"Common ground. At last."

He lit a cigarette. "I know a place. It's called El Ven Y Verme."

Dave laughed. "That's funny. I like that. Do they allow rich gringo lawyers?"

"Only if they're with people like me."

His foster mother was stable. That's about all Andrés had to say for her. She was strict and decent in a dull kind of way. He called her Mrs. H. For Mrs. Herrera. Mrs. Herrera sounded too formal. And she wasn't his mom. And didn't want her to be. And Mr. H—well he was even duller than his wife.

He wasn't allowed to smoke. He wasn't even allowed to have cigarettes. So he started taking a toothbrush in his backpack, so he could find a place to brush his teeth before he came home. He called it home even though it wasn't. It was just going to be a place where he waited until he was emancipated.

That would take three years.

In his house in Juárez, he thought, sometimes, that he would die from worrying. Here, in the house of Mr. and Mrs. H, he thought he would die of boredom. But they bought him a computer, and he was learning things, and he was back in school, and even though he'd missed more than three years, they put him in the same grade he would've been. Only he had to catch up on his math. And so he did that. He studied and studied, and fell in love with the computer. Because it saved him from his boredom.

At school, he didn't have any friends. He didn't care. He kept to himself. Once an older guy stopped him as he was walking back home after school. He asked him if he wanted to go for a ride. He knew about older guys. He said no. The guy offered to buy him beer or cigarettes or

anything he wanted. So he just looked at the guy and said, "Fuck you."
And the guy got mad, but he didn't care. He could go to hell. Everyone
could.

And one day, he got in a fight. Some guy was telling another guy in
the bathroom that if he didn't get him some money, he was going to kick
his ass. And Andrés got mad, and told the guy to leave the other guy
alone, "Just leave him the hell alone."

"Fuck you. I'm gonna stick a knife up your ass."

And so they got in a fight. The other guy got in some good jabs, but
Andrés was faster and angrier, and soon Andrés had the other guy on the
ground. And the school cop came into the bathroom, and before he
blinked, he was in the principal's office. They called his foster mother,
Mrs. H, and she cried and said she didn't know what was wrong with
Andrés. "Never says anything. Never does anything, either," she said.
And Andrés knew she didn't care for him. He was just a project. She'd
wanted someone who would love her. And he wasn't doing his job.

And Andrés got mad and said he didn't have anything to say—not
to her. Not to anyone.

That's when they sent him to his first counselor. He didn't remember
her name anymore. She told him that he needed to work on his anger.
And she wanted to know where his anger came from. And Andrés didn't
care, and so he looked at her and said, "From God."

And he and that counselor never got along. Because she was a Christian, and she didn't like jokes about God.

That first day, she kept asking him what had happened at the
school, and Andrés wondered why it was wrong to help someone, why
wasn't that other guy in counseling? Why didn't they do anything to
him? So he would talk to the counselor, but not much. She asked what
had happened to him in Juárez. She said she knew about that from the
social worker—but he never told her what really happened. Maybe a little piece. But just a piece of it. But what had really happened to him, he
never told her. Fuck her. He wasn't going to tell her.

But everything was okay, because every week, he would go to meet
Silvia. Sometimes on Saturday mornings, and sometimes on Saturday
afternoons. He would call her and leave a message at her sister's house.
And then she got a cell phone, because it was easier to get a cell phone
when you lived in Juárez than to get a regular phone. And he would

leave messages, and they always managed to get together. They ate something together. They talked. And she was like having a home, Silvia. She was the only person in the world who knew him.

He never told anyone about Silvia—not the H's and not his counselor and not his social worker. No one knew about Silvia. She was a secret. Because Andrés knew they would never let him see her, if they knew. Not the H's and not his social worker and not his counselor, who was a Christian. They would tell him that Silvia was an abomination, which was Mrs. H's favorite word. A word she found in the Bible, she said. He'd read parts of the Bible, but he didn't remember that word.

School was okay. And the H's let him keep his computer, and he learned so many things, and he thought that all he needed in the world was a computer and Silvia. So everything was okay. Sometimes girls would talk to him. And he knew they were flirting with him. And he was nice to them, but when they wanted to go out and do something, he said no.

He joined the running team, and he listened to the guys talk about girls, about what they wanted to do with them, and he thought he didn't like guys much. He thought guys were all pieces of shit—and he was a guy, so he knew he was a piece of shit, too. He wasn't any better than they were. And so he ran with them. He was the best runner. So they left him alone. If you were the best at something, people let you be.

So everything was okay. Except that one day Mrs. H wanted to know what he did on all those Saturdays when he took the bus downtown. "I just like to walk around," he said.

"And do what?"

"Just walk around. I watch the people. They shop, they do things. I just like to watch all the people."

She didn't believe him. Not that he cared. "You can't go anymore," she said. "And it's time you started going to church."

He didn't like her church. "I'm Catholic," he said, though really he wasn't anything. He would never be anything.

"You live with us. You don't know. You're only a boy. You'll go to church with us. And you won't be going downtown anymore. There are things boys shouldn't see."

He didn't say anything. He'd been there almost two years, and he was sixteen now, and he only had two years to go. Less than two years.

But he wasn't going to stay. So that night, he called Silvia on her cell phone. She didn't answer. It was night, and he knew she was working. At La Brisa. So that night, he put a few things in his backpack, and he left. He had to leave his computer. He thought of his typewriter. That made him sad. But one day he'd buy his own computer.

He walked across the bridge to Juárez, though it scared him. He knew he shouldn't be going back. He shouldn't. He knew that. He was trembling, and he smoked all the way to La Brisa, one cigarette after another. And when he got there, he ordered a beer. And the bartender recognized him and told him he shouldn't be drinking, but he poured him a beer, anyway. "You looking for Silvia?"

"Yeah," he said.

"She's working. But she'll be back."

So he waited for a long time. He smoked and sat at the bar, and a few of the girls said hello to him, girls he knew. They were really boys, but they called themselves girls, and so he called them girls, too. And they told him he looked like a man now. And they were nice to him. Nicer to him than the social worker or Mrs. H or his first counselor. He'd started seeing a new one, and she was nicer, but not as nice as the girls. Not as nice as Silvia.

And that's when everything happened. As he was sitting there at that bar, thinking about things and smoking too many cigarettes, Silvia ran into the bar, and he could tell something was wrong. "He's after me," she screamed. "Homero, he's after me. Me va matar. Me va matar!" She kept screaming that.

She didn't even notice Andrés sitting there. Not until Andrés said, "It's okay, Silvia. It's okay."

Silvia embraced Andrés, calmer now, though she was still upset. "You shouldn't be here," she said. "You crazy boy. You should be home playing with your computer."

"I left," he said. "She was going to make me stop going downtown. I was never going to see you again."

"You crazy boy," she said. She lit a cigarette, then downed a shot of tequila to calm her nerves. "I have to get you out of here. If Homero finds you here, he'll kill both of us. He's still mad about what you did. And I helped out one of his girls, and he came after me tonight. He beat up the guy I was with. He said he'd kill anyone who was with me from now on."

"You have to come back to El Paso, Silvia. You'll be safe there." Andrés begged and begged her, until she agreed.

She knew Andrés wouldn't leave without her.


"I don't remember exactly everything that happened that night. Only that we came back across. And that somehow someone told Homero they saw us. He was one mean sonofabitch. We didn't know it, but he followed us into El Paso. He must've been right behind us."

"You never told me that you'd been to Juárez that night."

"No. I guess I didn't. It wouldn't have made me look very good in front of the jury."

"The jury wouldn't have known. The jury knows what we tell them."

"Maybe I didn't trust you."

"Maybe you still don't."

"I'm here having a beer with you. That's as close as I get to trust." Andrés downed his beer. "I didn't mean to kill him. We stopped to get a cup of coffee at the Hollywood Café, Silvia and I. And she said I was going to have to go back to the H's. And I told her no way in hell. I told her I'd have to get new foster parents. I told her I didn't care. And I made her promise that she wouldn't go back to live in Juárez, and she said yes, but I knew she was only telling me that so I'd shut up. And as we walked out of that place, and turned the corner, that's when it happened. He had a knife. He grabbed me and put the knife to my throat, and I thought I was dead. And for a second I didn't care if I died. I didn't. And he made us go into the alley. And then he lunged at Silvia with the knife and kept digging it into her. Again and again, and it happened so fast. And I don't even remember what I did. I think I was screaming. I don't know. I don't remember. I just remember cop cars—and me standing over Homero. And I knew what I'd done to him. And I didn't even care. I didn't mean to kill him. But it's—I mean, well, look, it's fucking hard to be sorry."

"You never told me that she was your friend."

"I loved her." Dave could see his hands trembling. He hated to see him like that—wounded and hurt. He hated that more than anything.

"You could have told me."

"I don't want to talk about her. I don't."

"You didn't kill Homero."

"Sure, I did."

"He died of a heart attack."

"As I was beating the crap out of him."

"His bruises were minor."

"So why did they charge me?"

"It's complicated. What do you remember about your hearing?"

"Not much. You made some kind of deal. Look, you want to know the truth? I wasn't paying attention. You cared more than I did. You got me off. That's all I know. I guess I never cared to know the details."

"Those details are your life, Andrés. You can't just check out like that."

"Why not?"

*"It's your life."*

"And what a life it's been, Dave." He pointed at the bartender and then at his empty glass. "Look, Silvia was gone. Everyone was gone. Even Ileana. But at least she wasn't dead. She was out there somewhere in the world. But she didn't belong to me anymore. So Silvia was the end of all that. So I didn't care. And then you decided that it wasn't the end for me, so you rode into town on your goddamned BMW and rescued me."

"And you've never forgiven me for it."

"I told you then I didn't give a shit. What you did, you did for yourself. You did it for Dave, not for Andrés Segovia."

# He Was Happy

I'm bringing him home this afternoon, Grace."

She was sitting in her backyard, drinking coffee as she talked on the phone. Staring at the morning light. She pictured his smile.

"Grace?"

"I'm here."

"You're not saying anything."

"I'm listening to you be happy."

"Really?"

"Yes. Really, amor."

"You haven't called me amor in a long time." He paused, then whispered, "I love you, Grace. I always have."

"I know, amor."

"Liz and I are doing the right thing."

"Yes, you are."

"Grace?"

"Yes?"

"Is there something wrong?"

"Mister, have you been talking to Richard Garza?" She stopped herself from saying anything else. Already she'd said too much.

Mister listened to her silence. There was something wrong.

"You're bringing a son home today, Mister. We shouldn't be talking about me."

"Grace—"

"When you and Liz get settled in with Vicente, we'll talk."

"You mean it?"

"Yes."

"You promise?"

All that hope in his voice. "I promise." She could picture his smile. She shook her head.

"Coming over tonight? Liz and I want you to come."

"To see my new grandson? Of course, amor."

# Apocalypse:
# Everything Happens in an Instant
# (Timing and Order in the Universe)

This is the story of the world: A man gets into a car. He takes a drive. It is not an unusual thing—to get into a car and drive it down the street. For an instant, the man is distracted as he drives. This, too, is not unusual—the world has many distractions. Too late, he sees a car has run a red light. He tries to react—the reflex of his foot on the brake—and though his reflexes are good, there is no reflex quick or agile enough to avoid the impact. There is a screeching—a look of panic on the faces of the two drivers who realize, *God, God, all the angels and saints*—and then a crash. Metal on metal. Metal on bone. Blood. Perhaps a scream, perhaps a final prayer *I am heartily sorry for having offended thee, and I detest all my sins* and a man or a woman or a child who was alive a second ago is dead now. The man, who was in the middle of his life, has suddenly reached an early end. There is a randomness to this ballet of death. This is the order of things. This is the secret to understanding the universe.

Everything happens in an instant.

Normalcy. And then apocalypse.

Mister and Liz took the day off. To prepare. They cleaned the house. They dusted all their books, cleaned the already clean wood floors, mopped the bathroom, scrubbed the tile, put a new bedspread on Vicente's bed, fussed with it out of nervous energy. They sang as they worked, lost and happy in the pleasure of their pedestrian tasks. Mister hung up a Diego Rivera print that Liz had found in a vintage store. Children breaking a piñata. He would tell Vicente stories of the painting, would give a name to each child, would tell him about the artist one day, and about the murals he painted in Mexico City, largest city in the world. And Vicente would come to know it, to see it, to understand everything about this image that he had chosen to hang on his wall.

They did not stop until everything was spotless—the kitchen, the bathroom, the hallway, the two bedrooms. The back porch was swept, and reswept. Everything was rearranged, for a blind boy to find his way around. Everything was ready. In this house, nothing would ever hurt him.

When they were done, they showered.

They made love to each other in Vicente's new room.

Grace closed the file, made sure it was labeled properly, then placed it back in its rightful place. She nodded approvingly as she thumbed through a cabinet full of her files. It was a good system, her records beyond reproach. She was proud of that—a symbol of her professionalism. She hated people who were careless with other people's lives. Perhaps her files were as much a tribute to her care as they were to her pride. *Not a virtue, your pride, Grace.* Sam's accusations had been too gentle. And he had always been too quick to forgive her.

She looked over her files one more time. So many of them. So many cases. So many lives. Well, this had been her life's work. Maybe she was an archivist after all. Maybe her sense of order would survive her, if only in the files she left behind. But maybe they could still be of use. Too many of her clients were recidivists, addicted to their broken lives, always returning to their crippled ways. Her files could still be of use.

She was confused now about seeking treatment. Maybe she'd just been angry over the news. Maybe she'd lost hope. Or maybe she was just afraid. That made her normal. The dream had come to her again. Sam and Mister were clinging to each other, spinning each other around. Around and around until they became the light itself. She woke, their names in her throat.

But God had sent another day. She'd almost wept at the sight of the morning sun.

And then Mister had called.

In the lateness of the afternoon, Mister called the Rubios. "I'm on my way."

If Mr. Rubio was sad to let Vicente go, there was no trace of that sadness in his voice. "He's waiting for you. He spoke today, for the first time. He patted his heart and said, 'Mister.' "

Mister hung up the phone. And patted his own heart.

He stared at Grace's picture on the shelf as he was walking out the door. He picked it up and kissed it. "I'm not afraid, Grace." He put the picture back down and walked into the kitchen. Liz was grating cheese for the tacos. "Are you sure you don't want me to go with you?"

"No. I want you to be the first thing he senses when he walks into this house."

Andrés didn't come back to his house that night. He thought of Ileana, and then remembered it was his fifteenth birthday, and maybe this was the best gift anyone could have given him—his little sister wasn't dead, and she didn't have to live like them, like him and Yolie.

But he wasn't going to do this anymore. Not anymore. He would wait and hide and lurk in the streets and get Silvia to help him. He would stay until Carmen got word that Ileana was safe. Then he would leave. Not that there was any going back to Mrs. Fernandez. It was too late for all that. But he knew there were people who took in children, and though he didn't feel like a child anymore, he was still only fourteen. He knew that you couldn't do anything when you were his age—except maybe what he was doing now. And he would never do this again. No one would ever touch him again. Not ever. For any reason. He'd kill them first.

He didn't care about Yolie anymore. And Yolie didn't care about him. She was lost. She was in a worse hell than him. She wouldn't last long. He knew that. The drugs were in her and owned her, and she spent all her money on getting them. Silvia had tried to get her to stop. Even Silvia, who thought everyone could be saved, even Silvia thought Yolie was lost.

He didn't know what time it was, but it was late. He decided to go to La Brisa to see if he could find Silvia. The bar was dim. He sat at the bar, the bartender poured him a Coke, and he lit a cigarette, and as he lit it, he saw her. He waved at her, and she came up to him and kissed him. "Mi hombrecito."

She was the only one who could touch him now. He told her everything, what had happened, what he'd done. "You did the right thing," she said. "I know a place you can stay—until we hear word about Ileana. Then I'll take you to El Paso."

She took him to a house that was not very different from the house where he lived. A lot of people lived there, a group of transvestites. She told them Andrés needed a place to stay. They were nice to him, and told him he could stay for as long he needed to. He was tired, and they made a space on an old couch and told him that was his new bed. He fell asleep, even though there was a lot of noise in the house. He had already learned to sleep through every kind of noise.

When he woke, he found a suitcase at the foot of the couch with all his things in it. And a note from Silvia. "Never tell Yolie where you are. She'll sell you to Homero for another fix."

He stayed there for a few weeks. He didn't know how long, maybe a month. Silvia told him not to go out. "Homero has people everywhere," she said. "He owns half the whores on the street, and if they see you, God knows what that bastard will do to you."

So he didn't go out. And every day, Silvia would go and visit Carmen and ask about Ileana. Andrés felt like he was a prisoner, like he would be a secret forever. That was his punishment for agreeing to leave Mr. and Mrs. Fernandez with a broken heart. You have to pay for everything you've done. His mother had told him that. And so now he would have to pay, for everything he'd done for the past three years. He knew that God had stopped believing in a boy like him.

One day, Silvia came by early in the morning. She seemed sad, and he knew something was wrong. "Ileana?" he said. He felt his heart throbbing faster and faster.

"No, it's not Ileana. Carmen has heard nothing."

"What, then?"

"It's your sister, Yolie."

"What?"

"Carmen found her lying in an alley, most of her clothes torn off. She's dead, Andrés. She's gone." Andrés didn't know why Silvia was crying. Yolie hadn't been nice to her—not ever. But there she was, sobbing for Yolie, and he wondered why some people stayed soft no matter what happened to them. Not him. He was hard, now. Maybe harder than Mando or Yolie had ever been. He'd been a soft little boy. But that boy had been killed, and this hard boy was the only thing that was left—a boy so hard that he didn't even cry when he heard his older sister was dead. He didn't even ask where she was going to be buried. He didn't care about anything.

He lit a cigarette, and told Silvia not to cry. "No llores. Ya basta de laigrimas."

"Silvia made sure Yolie had a church funeral. She made all the arrangements. Though I don't remember how she did it. I do remember that she changed back into a man when she went to see the priest at the cathedral. It was strange to see him dressed as a man. He was a woman to me. I never even asked him his real name. You know, I didn't go to the funeral."

Grace nodded.

"You don't disapprove?"

"Why would I disapprove?"

"She was my sister."

"You have every right to hate her."

"I do hate her."

"And so you're a bad man—because when you were fifteen, you were so angry and so numb that you refused to go to her funeral?"

"I don't forgive myself."

"One of these days you're going to stop beating the crap out of yourself."

"You don't know about some of the things I've done."

"And if I knew, I'd hate you, is that it?"

"Yes, you might."

There was a softness in his voice that she had never heard before. "I don't think so." She smiled and nodded at him. "You wouldn't mind, would you, if I had one of your cigarettes?"

"I thought you quit."

"I've picked it up again. You see, Andrés, the thing about life is that we're always backtracking. We think we'll never pass a certain street again—not ever. We think we're done with it. And years later, we're on that street again. Retracing our steps. Looking for something we left behind."

"Cigarettes. We're looking for cigarettes."

He was smart and could say such charming things. If life had been different for him, he would have been like Sam—educated and sophisticated and intellectual. And she wondered if maybe that's what she saw in this young man—a stunted beauty of a man who might still grow. Even in his damaged state, he could light up a room. He could fill it with a presence that was large and rare. Like Sam. And wasn't it funny, that this young man should come into her life even as she was dying? She could feel it, that death. It was beginning to have a presence, too. Yes, wasn't it funny, that she should feel such affection for this young man. That she should care so much. They were friends, that's how it felt. She, who never let things like this happen with her clients. But it didn't matter anymore. Because he was the last. And she was free of her professionalism. But she wasn't free to be careless. And anyway, she didn't have to worry about carelessness. She didn't have it in her.

She let him light her cigarette. "Tell me. I want to know how you came back."

"To El Paso?"

"Yes."

Mister didn't notice. Not at first. Mister didn't notice that there was a man and a woman at the Rubios' front door. He was in his head, having a conversation with Vicente, *What should we name your bear?* When he stepped out of the car, he did notice. The man was holding a gun to the woman's head. He could see the whole scene clearly. Everything became perfectly clear to him in that instant. It was Vicente's mother—he recognized her. Mr. Rubio tried to wave him away, but it was too late.

The man turned to Mister and pointed the gun at Mr. Rubio. "I'll kill him, you fuck. If you say a word, I'll kill him. Then fuckin' kill you, too."

Mister nodded. Grace had taught him to stay calm when things went wrong. So he tried his best to be her son, *stay calm, steady, calm.* But his beating heart wasn't cooperating. He told himself everything was going to be okay. Everything was going to be fine. He and Vicente and Grace would be having dinner in an hour.

The woman wore a look of panic and disbelief. She looked at Mister, and he knew she was saying, *I'm sorry, I'm sorry,* and he wanted to tell her that it was okay, that everything would be okay and that it wasn't her fault and he hoped she knew that with the way he looked at her—but it was so hard to tell what she saw in his face. Maybe he was wearing a look of panic, too. He didn't know.

For an instant, he thought of running. He could save himself. But he emptied himself of the urge. Everything would be okay. None of this was happening. It was a joke or a bad dream, and he would wake soon, and he and Vicente would get in his car and go home. Go home to Liz, who was waiting for them. And Grace would be coming, too.

"You'll regret one day that you didn't say good-bye to Yolie."

Andrés nodded. "I'll regret everything one day."

"You don't talk like a boy."

"What do I talk like?"

"Like an old man."

He shrugged.

"Amor, it's time for you to go back."

"I won't. Not until I hear word about Ileana."

"She's everything, isn't she?"

"Somebody has to make it out alive."

"What about you?"

"I'm already dead."

"Don't talk like that. You're just a boy."

"I thought you just said I talked like a very old man."

"You're still a boy."

That's what they said to each other, Silvia and Andrés, the evening of Yolie's burial. They talked and smoked, and then walked to Carmen's house, even though Silvia said he shouldn't be out on the streets. Carmen was packing her things when they arrived. "I'm leaving in the morning. I'm going back to Jalisco. Homero gave me a day to leave." She smiled, such a sad smile. "I should have left a long time ago." Then she laughed. She handed Andrés a handwritten note. Andrés unfolded the note. "Ileana's living in California. She's safe." He found himself running down the street, running and running and running and running, and he found himself in that bar where Homero had taken him and Ileana one night, and when he rushed into the bar, he saw him, Homero, and he jumped on him like a tiger pouncing on his prey, and he was pounding on him, pounding and knocking him to the ground, and he heard himself yelling, "I hate you! I hate you! You sonofabitch! Rot in hell, you sonofabitch!" Andrés didn't remember anything after that—except that Silvia and another man carried him out of the bar before Homero could get up from the floor where he was lying. And he remembered Silvia whispering, "I'm taking you back tonight."

"We won't take anything," Silvia said. He watched her change and become a man again. He didn't like it, that she changed back into a man. He hated men. He hated them because of the things they did. "I was born in El Paso, did I ever tell you? My name is Guillermo."

"I like Silvia better."

"Me, too. But not tonight."

"Where are we going?"

"My sister's house. She lives in El Paso. You'll be safe, now, like Ileana."

He nodded. When they were both dressed, they went out into the streets. They made their way to the bridge. At the top, over the river, in between the two flags of the two countries, Andrés looked back.

"Don't," Guillermo said, "Never look back. Nunca, nunca, nunca." As they walked toward the American side of the bridge, Guillermo whispered, "When they ask you to declare your citizenship, just say American."

"I can't prove it."

"You can prove it with your English."

"What about you?"

"I have my papers. If they ask, tell them I'm your uncle."

Andrés felt his heart beating as he waited in the long line. When it was his turn, he smiled and said, "American citizen."

The man in the uniform looked at him. "Are you alone?"

He thought his heart would burst. "I'm with my uncle." He turned around and pointed at Guillermo, who was waiting right behind him.

The man nodded and motioned him to keep moving.

Andrés smiled and walked on. When he left the building, he waited for Guillermo. When Guillermo caught up with him, Andrés broke into tears. Guillermo held him and told him he was safe now. "It's over," Guillermo kept repeating the words. Andrés repeated the words, too. He wanted to believe. *It's over.*


"It's still not over, Grace."

"No, I suppose not."

"I never even bothered to look for Ileana."

"It's not too late." She opened her drawer, then took out the sheets of paper. "I think these belong to you." She placed the pages on her desk.

"Where did you get those?"

There was a fire in his eyes. She was glad for the fire. She picked up the pages and handed them to him. "Take them. I'd read them if I were you. You might find something that's at least worth the paper it's written on."

Andrés took the sheets of paper and stared at them. He folded them carefully and placed them back in his shirt pocket.

"That's why you got mad—because they took what you wrote away from you."

"What do you suggest would've been the appropriate response?"

"Did you at least give one of them a decent punch?"

"One of them had to go to the dentist."

She laughed, then shook her head. "I don't approve of violence." She looked at him and searched his face. "You should look for her."

"And if she's dead?"

"And if she's alive?"

"Alive. There's a word."


The man waved him inside with the gun. Mister watched the man, the look of rage and confusion on his face. He stared at the waving gun. It's like a movie, he thought to himself, one of those movies with a familiar plot, the part of the crazed man played by a mediocre method actor.

The first thing he saw when he entered the living room was Vicente clinging to Mrs. Rubio. She looked at him, but said nothing.

"Sit down. Everybody, sit the fuck down!" The man, the crazed man, kept Vicente's mother by his side.

He sat down next to Mr. Rubio on the couch. Mr. Rubio squeezed Mister's hand.

"What are you doing?"

Mr. Rubio shook his head and shrugged.

"Don't fucking move unless I tell you to." He looked at Mister, then looked at the woman. "Puta. You're nothing but a puta, Alicia." Spanish wasn't his first language. "That the guy you gave our son to? That the guy?"

Alicia shook her head. Mister knew her name now.

He slapped her hard, and she stumbled to the floor. He pointed the gun at her. "I asked if he was the one."

"Yes," Mister said. "I'm the one."


Andrés remembered waking up in Guillermo's arms. He looked around the room and saw the picture of the Sacred Heart of Jesus. The flames were calm, calmer than the flames in his own heart. He slipped out from under Guillermo's arms and went to the window. He looked out into the backyard. There was a hummingbird sucking on a blossom on the pomegranate tree. He didn't know anything about hummingbirds except that his father had told him that they liked to fight. So maybe you could like to fight and still be beautiful, like the hummingbirds.

On that first day, Guillermo took him everywhere. They walked through downtown, and Guillermo bought him clothes—shirts and pants and shoes and tennis shoes and underwear and T-shirts and socks and everything. "For a new life," he said. Guillermo borrowed his sister's car, and he took him out to eat at a place called the State Line, and they ate ribs and potato salad and bread and barbeque beans, and they ate and ate until Andrés thought he would burst.

And afterward, they went back to his sister's house, and they sat on chairs in the backyard and smoked and talked. "Tomorrow, you have to go see a caseworker."

"I don't want to."

"You have to live somewhere. They'll give you a nice family—unless you want to go see if Mrs. Fernandez will take you in."

"No. Let her alone."

"Then we have to get you into the system."

"The system?"

"You know, there are people who care for kids—"

"I'm not a kid."

"Okay. But you're a minor."

"I don't want to live with anybody but you."

"I live in Juárez."

"Move back here."

"That's my home. I won't come back here. And besides, you need a decent family."

"You're decent."

Guillermo kissed him.

Andrés looked at him. "I want you to be Silvia again."

"I am Silvia. Only when I come to El Paso, I have to be Guillermo—and that's not who I want to be. You understand, Andrés?"

Andrés nodded.

"My sister thinks I'm taking advantage of you. She gave me a lecture."

"Then your sister doesn't know you."

"Well, a man with a boy—what is she supposed to think?"

"I'll tell her."

"Don't tell her anything."

"She just wants us to leave, doesn't she?"

"Yes."

"Will I see you?"

"Every week. We'll make a date. Saturdays at noon at San Jacinto Plaza. We'll smoke and talk and have lunch."

"You promise?"

"And did he keep his promise?"

*"She."*

Grace nodded. *"She.* Did she keep her promise?"

"Yes."

"Almost every week for two years, Silvia and I saw each other."

"And then what happened?"

"It's a long story."

"I have time."

"When she died. No, that's not right. When he killed her—that's when I decided it was over. First my mother and father. And then Mando and Yolie. And then Ileana—"

"But Ileana may be alive."

"I lost her just the same." He lit a cigarette. "Mom and Dad and Yolie and Mando and Ileana. And then Silvia. And then I just said, Screw it all to hell. It's over."

"And here you are."

"Yeah. Here I am."

"Maybe you're just in love with being an outsider. You can join the human race any time you want to."

"What makes you think I want to join? I live in the kind of world that looks at me like I'm some kind of freak. You know, when I told Dave I hadn't gone to college, he flinched. Just for a second. He was so surprised. I don't think he could believe a guy like me could be smart or articulate about anything—because I hadn't gone to college. Maybe it's better if people think you're stupid or slow. They don't expect anything. I live in a world that doesn't expect anything of me because it's already decided I don't matter."

"What the world expects? What does that matter?"

"I wasn't born a gringo, in case you hadn't noticed."

"I wasn't either, Andrés. *In case you hadn't noticed.* And I wasn't even born a man."

"Big fucking deal, Grace. I was born a man and used like a woman. You don't have a goddamned thing on me."

"This isn't a contest, Andrés. You win the one that says you've been screwed over more than anybody else in the universe. You win that one. But that doesn't mean that I don't know anything. I know a few things about what the world does and doesn't expect of you. I never worried that much about it. I went to the University of Texas. Already that made me more successful than most people who grew up in my neighborhood. And every time I did spectacularly well in my classes, and I'm here to tell you that I did spectacularly well, I could always see the look of surprise on my professors' faces. You don't think I noticed? What you saw on Dave's face, I saw every damned day of my academic career. So what, Andrés? I wanted to do something, *to be something*—and I did it. I don't think I deserve a medal, and I don't think I'm particularly special. I wanted to do something, and I figured out a way to do it. But I'll say this, too, Andrés, I was lucky. I was a very lucky girl. I had someone who kissed away all my bruises." She smiled. "Me and my Sam, when we were young, we had a lot of fight."

"I'm glad for you."

"Are you?"

He looked at her. He wanted her to understand this one truth. "Whatever you have, I'm sure you've more than earned." He clenched his teeth. "The war I'm fighting—it's not against you, Grace."

"At least you're fighting."

"And you, Grace? Are you still fighting?"

She was surprised. By his question.


All he saw was the man's eyes, dark as a sky about to let loose a flood on the land. He looked back and pleaded—but only with his eyes.

The man looked down at Alicia. "So you thought he'd make a better father? You think he looks like me? Do you? Do you, goddamnit!" He pointed the gun away from the woman and pointed it in Mister's direction. He'd never dreamed an end like this. He looked at Vicente. That's how he wanted to leave—looking at Vicente.

When the bullet struck his heart, he had enough breath in him to utter Liz's name—and then Grace's. Their names echoed in the room for an instant. And then everything was quiet. And the light was gone.

He was at least spared the carnage that followed. His turned out to be the kindest death.

Andrés arrived at Grace's office at 4:00. Exactly on time for his appointment. Mister left his house at 4:30. He arrived at the Rubio's at 4:54—exactly six minutes after Robert Lawson arrived with Alicia Esparza at his side. At 5:07, as Andrés was leaving Grace's office, Mister was dead, warm blood still flowing out of his chest. At 5:25, when Grace was getting into her car to go home, everyone else in the Rubio house was dead—the gunman included.

Robert Lawson left a note and put it on the kitchen table before he pointed the gun at himself: "This is what happens in a world where fathers don't count."

He left the boy Vicente alive. Unable to wake anyone up from their sleep, Vicente decided to lie down next to Mister.

# Grace, Liz, Light, and
# the Sadness of Dreams

The emergency room at Thomason Hospital resembled a morgue. Grace Delgado and her three sisters sat in the waiting room. They said little, but when they managed to utter a word or two, they spoke in whispers. Grace was stoic, just as she had been after Sam had died. She retreated to her own desert, prayed and fought with God there. Her sisters would touch her, squeeze her hand, kiss her. She let them. A fleeting thought ran though her head—that her sisters had always loved her more than she had ever loved them. She was wrong, of course, but typically, she was overly harsh on herself, even in her fleeting thoughts.

Liz paced the room, away from Grace and her sisters. Grace knew enough to leave her alone.

"Would you like some water?"

Grace looked up at the familiar voice and took the cup of water Dolores was holding out toward her. She drank. She hadn't realized how thirsty she was. She pictured Mister's face, unscarred and youthful and perfect, his dimples making him seem even younger than he was. He'd loved to smile and laugh and speak his mind. Such a lovely and tender young man. She thought of the expression on his face when he'd dug a grave for Mississippi. He was perfect in that light.

She looked up and found herself staring into the grave face of a young, but tired doctor. "I'm looking for a Mrs. Delgado."

Grace nodded. "That would be me. But I think you're looking for her." She pointed her chin toward Liz. She rose from her chair and made her way to where Liz was pacing the floor. "Liz," she whispered. The doctor was standing beside them.

"Mrs. Delgado?"

Liz looked at the doctor numbly. "Yes?" The question hung in the air.

"I'm very sorry—"

She stopped him in mid-sentence. "I want to see him."

"He's not, I mean, I have to warn you, he's—"

This time it was Grace who interrupted him. "Would you be so kind as to let my daughter-in-law have a few moments—" Her voice dropped, almost cracking.

The doctor nodded.

Grace took Liz by the shoulders. "Go on," she whispered. "I'll be in when you've had your time."

Liz and Grace searched each other's faces for a moment.

"It's okay," Grace whispered.

Liz nodded, then followed the doctor through the swinging doors that read: NO ENTRANCE WITHOUT THE PERMISSION OF HOSPITAL STAFF. She turned back and looked at Grace, her lips trembling.

She didn't know how long Liz had been in the room with Mister. She was beyond caring about time. She sat in a chair that faced the swinging doors. She did not take her eyes off the door. She sat almost motionless until Liz appeared, her eyes red, her hair disheveled. Their eyes met. She rose from the chair where she'd kept vigil. Liz was standing in front of her. "I think he'd like it if you spent a few moments," she said quietly.

"Yes," Grace said.

"Even now he's beautiful," she said, her voice breaking down.

He seemed not dead at all. His hair, still wild as a flame, his face as calm as a breezeless dawn. Not dead at all—except he'd lost his color. She touched his forehead, then ran her fingers through his hair. She gasped, then felt the hot tears and the convulsions, the pain in her heart, the same pain she'd felt when Sam had gone. She'd told herself that nothing would ever hurt like that again. But she'd been wrong. This was worse, this awful, relentless, merciless gnawing at her heart that made her wince in pain, that made her fall to the ground on her knees and clutch at herself as if she were trying to claw away the pain. She did not hear herself screaming *my son, my son.* She did not hear her words breaking down into wails. *Nooooooooo myyyyyyyyyyyyeeeee soooooooonnnnn,* her cries becoming an astonishing howl. This was loss, this was pain in its cruelest, purest form, and it seemed she would break and she didn't care if she did, didn't care about anything because there wasn't anything left but this hurt that was eating away at her body with a hunger that was even more ravenous than the cancer.

She became a stream, and the only waters that flowed through her were of him, Mister, being held out to her the second he was born, his eyes alert, his nest of thick black hair begging to be combed, Mister trying to convince her not to make him go to school, *Sam can teach me everything Grace,* Mister standing in front of an empty building, *Grace, this is my new coffee shop, La Dolce Vita,* that grin impervious to cynics, Mister wailing at Sam's grave. She wanted it to stop, to stop, and yet she wanted the images to run through her forever, and God, she was, she was breaking, and then—right there—in the midst of all these wordless articulations, the dream came to her. The dream, her friend of many years, it came to her. And now she understood it as she never had. There they were—Sam and Mister, spinning each other round and round and round, until they were one with the blinding light.

She opened her eyes and found herself kneeling on the floor.

She picked herself up.

She kissed him one last time. "Amor," she whispered. That was the last word she had spoken to him. It was a beautiful and worthy word, as beautiful and worthy as her son.

She pulled her hand away. And left the room.

# What Are We—Asleep?

Andrés hadn't been studying long. He'd come back from his session with Grace. He'd put on some coffee and lit a cigarette. He thought about Ileana. Maybe she was still alive. He'd put aside his thoughts, then opened the book he was reading for his history class. Then the phone rang. He picked it up. "How's it going, Dave?"

"How'd you know it was me, caller ID?"

"No one else calls me but you."

"You should get out more."

"My lawyer told me I should study. So I study."

"Glad to hear it."

Andrés listened to the long pause.

"Listen. Bad news."

"I'm listening."

"Grace Delgado's son."

"What about him?"

"He's been killed."

"What?"

For a second after he'd hung up the phone, he'd wanted to get in touch with Grace. Isn't that what people did, get in touch with each other when something bad happened? Isn't that what people did? He shook his head, changed into his running clothes, and ran. He found himself at the Santa Fe Bridge. He wondered what her son had been like. He wondered if Grace would have time for him now. He clenched his fists for being so selfish.


Mister's story was front-page news. Everywhere he went that morning on campus, all he heard was outrage. By noon, outrage was beginning to get on his nerves. He didn't know if the response was good or bad. Appropriate and decent perhaps. But shallow, too. People were outraged by drug dealers and prostitutes and gangs. People were outraged by high property taxes and bad schools. People were outraged by trash on the sidewalks of the city and crooked or stupid or do-nothing politicians. People were outraged by men who killed innocent people. Not that anybody did anything about anything. It was always easier to be disgusted after the fact. It was easier to shake your head and be outraged, as if the outrage was proof of civility—a sign that the world hadn't died, that it could still scream out in horror, proof that its heart was still beating.

And who the fuck was he to put a bucket of water on those flames of after-the-fact outrage? Except that he was too cynical and too hard to cry about the whole sad affair. In his world, wasn't that sort of thing normal? What was public outrage to him? Public outrage was as capricious as it was respectable. He'd read too many vacuous editorials in tossed-out newspapers to feel any sympathy for the tender and myopic sensibilities of its virtuous readership. He didn't even know what virtue was anymore. Was virtue the enraged man who killed transvestites because their very presence perverted the natural order of things?

Hadn't virtue come to him in the form of an old whore who'd saved his sister's life? Hadn't it come in the form of a transvestite whose friendship had pulled him out of hell? This, finally, is what he knew. He knew this man whose name was Robert Lawson. He'd known men like him all his cursed and sorrowful life. Their names were carved on his heart like graffiti. That man, Robert Lawson, that selfish, crazy bastard, had something in common with Mando and Yolie, and with his father. They trampled the world with their sick and twisted and crooked kind of love. The bastard didn't think that anyone else's love mattered at all. As if a father's love knew everything, could see everything, could cure everything. And what would have happened if that man, Robert Lawson, had been allowed to keep his son? What would have fucking happened then? Men like him and Mando, they didn't understand anything but their own imperfect hearts. That was their sickness—that they believed themselves to be the center of all light. That kind of light was a darkness of the land. A plague that was killing them all.

He spit on the ground. Spit on men like Robert Lawson and Mando Segovia. *Screw you all the way to hell.*

He dropped the morning newspaper. He tried not to think of Grace. If he thought too much, his heart would soften. And what would he do with a soft heart in a world that killed men like her son? All he was trying to do was adopt a boy.

No. He didn't want to think about Grace.

# No Morning Mass Today

Mister was gone now. She felt the weight of that permanence, the pedestrian deadness of the meaning of "gone," all through the night. And such a long night. There was so little drama in the kind of dull numbness that set in after a loss. The dullness was omnipresent as a watchful god, even after she'd fallen asleep, exhausted from her grieving and the attendant details that came with a death. The living were always left with attendant details.

When she woke, she thought of Liz, of how she'd said, "I have to go home." Grace had let her go. But she had sent two of her sisters to drive her home. And later she'd called her, but there was nothing but sobbing on the other end of the telephone. "It's good to cry," she'd whispered. When she hung up, she took her own advice.

The last time she'd cried herself to sleep was the night she buried Sam.

She was numb and groggy as she pulled herself out of bed. The light in the room made her head throb even more. She slipped on a robe and stared at herself in the bathroom mirror. She brushed her teeth and thought it was strange to be doing such a normal thing. What right did she have to be doing normal things? She took two aspirin. She chewed them, winced at the taste, then cupped some water in her hands from the faucet and washed the taste away. But the taste remained.

She could smell the coffee. Dolores had stayed the night. Grace had been too tired to fight with her. The smell of the freshly brewed coffee reminded her of Mister. Everything would remind her. Everything would make her feel the guilt, the misspoken words, the impossible demands. That's how it was in the beginning. That's how it had been with Sam. She'd recalled every disagreement until she almost broke under the weight of her own punishment. *Don't, Grace, please.*

She made her way into the kitchen. She glanced at the headlines in the morning paper. She didn't have the stomach to read it. She pushed the paper away, then watched Dolores walk in from the backyard. "When did the dog die?"

"I forgot to tell you. Mister and I buried her."

Dolores handed her a cup of coffee, then kissed her. She wondered why everyone around her was so demonstrative, and wondered why temperaments were so permanent. She had the urge to go and exchange hers at her nearest department store.

"What are you beating yourself over this time?"

"I wasn't."

"Ya te conozco, Graciela."

"No es nada."

"You've always been so hard on yourself, Gracie."

"Maybe I'm just plain hard."

"Don't, amor."

Grace stared at her older sister, her fine features, softening with age. Her voice, too. Beautiful.

"I wonder what will become of the boy?"

"What?"

"The boy. Vicente. Do you think Liz will still want him?"

Grace looked into her sister's serious face. "He's alive?"

Today, no morning mass for Grace. Instead, she made up her mind to go see Liz. When she arrived, she stood outside the house. Mister had landscaped the house with desert shrubs and trees and cacti. It was so peaceful and calm. No signs of chaos or bullets or the violent intrusions of the outside world. Here, everything was just as Mister had left it—perfect for a man and a wife and a son.

On the night she had come to dinner, Mister and Liz had showed her the house, everything they'd done to it, and it was so apparent that this house was full of the abundant gifts her son had possessed—full of books and art and wood floors perfectly sanded, perfectly stained, perfectly varnished with Mister's steady, patient hands. She rang the doorbell, her hands almost trembling.

It didn't take long for Liz to answer the door.

They studied each other's eyes, saying nothing. Finally, Liz smiled weakly. "Would you like some coffee?"

Grace nodded.

"I'll put a fresh pot on."

As Liz ground the coffee, Grace wandered through the living room, not knowing what exactly she was searching for. She touched his books, sat on his couch, and thumbed through the art books on his coffee table. He had a bookmark in one of them—then she found that the bookmark was a photograph. It was a picture of Mister between her and Sam. He was four, and they were both kissing him. He had a look of fullness on his face.

She thought of Andrés. Even today, he haunted her. She wondered if he had ever worn that look of fullness. So much hunger written on his face—so much want and rage and confusion. And yet it was her Mister who was dead, and Andrés who was alive. It wasn't fair, to compare them, as if somehow some men deserved to live more than others. It wasn't fair, and yet her mind had compared them because the mind had its own capricious triggers. She bowed her head. Andrés deserved to live. And so had Mister. And all these random thoughts were useless, anyway, as if the business of living and dying was a question of "deserve."

She closed the book. Liz was standing over her, a cup of coffee in her hand. "You take it black?"

Grace nodded.

"Like Mister."

"Yes."

Liz saw the picture Grace was holding in her hand. "It was his favorite picture."

Grace put the picture back in the book and shut it. "It was all so much easier when Sam was alive. For both of us."

"Mister loved you, Grace."

She didn't bother to wipe the tears from her face. "Not that I made things easy for him."

"I never made things easy for him, either, Grace."

"He must have been addicted to loving difficult women." Grace took a sip of coffee through her tears. "It's good coffee."

"What's going to happen to us?"

Grace shrugged. "Are you going to take Vicente?"

"He was Mister's idea. I'm sure you've guessed that, by now."

"You wanted him, too. I could see that."

"Not anymore."

"But Liz—"

"I don't want him, Grace. He'll just—"

"He'll just what?"

"It doesn't make any sense without Mister."

"Why not?"

"Did you come over here to play counselor?"

"I'm sorry if I sound like one," she whispered. She got up from where she was sitting and walked to the window. She pushed aside the curtain and looked out into the morning sun. "This is a wonderful house. Shame on me for waiting so long to come here."

"We didn't exactly invite you over."

"I could've invited myself over. And you wouldn't have thrown me out, either. I've always known that. I didn't do anything to help things along." She looked at Liz. "I have a client. His name's Andrés. He's been coming to me. A troubled young man, but I've grown to care about him. He's beautiful. In a different way than Mister—but beautiful. You know, it's sometimes easier to care about strangers than to care about your own flesh and blood. He has a sister, her name's Ileana. It's a complicated story. He lost track of her when he was a boy. Now he's afraid to go find her."

"Why?"

"Because he's afraid. What if she's dead? What if something happened to her?"

"What if she's alive?"

"Exactly, Liz. Don't you see, Liz? Did you know that when I looked at Mister, sometimes all I saw was Sam? I was seeing Sam when I should've been seeing my son. Andrés is afraid to look for a sister, because he's afraid he just might find more despair. Well, he just might. And he might find that he's stronger than he thinks. But what if he finds his sister? What if he does, Liz? I stayed away. It was easier that way. Maybe for both of us. We never quite got over Sam's death—neither one of us. You don't want that boy anymore because he'll just make you think of Mister. But, damnit, Liz, who does that boy have now?"

Liz sat on the couch, head bowed, tears running down her face. "It's too hard. It's too goddamned hard."

Grace slowly walked toward Liz, then knelt on the floor. She placed her hand under Liz's chin and lifted it. "There comes a time we have to send the dead away."

"I can't."

"I think you can."

# Whatever Gets You
# Through the Day

*You should tell him, Dave.* Grace was good at giving advice. And she wasn't wrong. But he'd backed down so many times that it seemed normal now, to live with this not telling him. It was like forgetting someone's name when you first met him. And the next time, for whatever reason, you were too embarrassed to ask the man's name, because he remembered yours and he was so friendly—and you had your pride, and you didn't want to appear to be egotistical because he remembered your name, after all, and how was it that you didn't have the decency to pay attention to other people's names when they were introduced to you. And you kept running into this man, and each time you smiled and finessed *How are you? Lots of work?* and hoped the man didn't notice you never called him by his name. And every time you saw him, you wanted simply to look him in the eye and ask. "I'm sorry. I don't remember your name." It would be so easy and simple to confess that. But what would he think, after all these years of speaking to each other on the street? The problem could be so easily resolved. But you never 'fessed up, because your pride didn't let you, and so you've learned to live with this stupid and insane fear that you'll run into that man again—and of course you will. It was like that, this not telling him. Only worse. Much worse.

Grace was right. About everything.

He wondered how she was doing. God, they killed her boy. He'd taken flowers to her house. She'd offered him coffee, and they'd talked. She looked sad and sleepless. But something else. She was in mourning,

yet she seemed so calm. She showed him a picture of her son. There was
something about him, even in the picture. What a world this is. You'd
think they'd all be used to this by now. When was the last day the fucking world had lived without a killing? This was normal, after all. Apocalypse was normalcy. What a world this was. How was it that he was so
in love with living? How could that be? Maybe he wasn't in love. Maybe
it was like smoking. Living was just another addiction. Isn't that what
addicts always told themselves? That it was love. Isn't that what he always said? "God, I love to smoke." Whatever gets you through the day.

He shook his head and laughed. And lit a cigarette.

*I'll take Andrés to the funeral. And afterward, I'll find the words.*

# Timing and Order in the Universe

The city is obsessed with the story of Vicente Jesús, the only survivor of what the media has dubbed "the Adoption Massacre." They have turned Mister into martyr and saint. There are reporters from as far away as Lyon, France, and Sydney, Australia. They are descending on the city. They are coming to see firsthand. They want the world to know. They are inviting themselves to attend Mister Delgado's funeral.

A few reporters camp themselves in front of Liz and Mister's house. Liz calls Grace in tears. Grace drives to the house, helps Liz pack her things, and brings her home. On the way out the door, she grabs a reporter by the collar and shames him for the way he practices his profession.

Offers to adopt Vicente Jesús are pouring in from around the country. It is like buying a lottery ticket. Someone has started a home page with Vicente's picture on it. Mister's picture also appears on the site.

On the day of the funeral, there is standing room only at St. Patrick's Cathedral. As Grace walks Liz down the aisle, she is surrounded by a sea of mourners. She knows there are gawkers in attendance, but she also knows her son was greatly loved. She stops and greets an old friend, then another, then another. She sees faces of many former clients. She has never seen many of these people outside her office. She is moved by their presence. She is perfectly composed and gracious. When she sees a face she recognizes, she thanks them for coming. As she embraces a woman she has known since childhood, she is distracted by the flash of a camera. When she looks up, she sees Dave escorting a young man out the door. She pats his arm in gratitude as he walks by. And then, she sees Andrés. He smiles awkwardly. She knows he does not know what to do or say. She looks at him and takes his hand, then squeezes it gently. She looks into his beautiful face. She is looking for her son. She thinks to herself that she will be looking for Mister in the face of every young man she sees.

Liz has made her way to the open casket in front of the church. She kneels and stares into the face of her husband. She wants to be strong. She is thinking of how he was in the habit of kissing her every time he walked into the room. She remembers telling him, "You don't have to kiss me every time you see me." She remembers his answer, "Yes, I do." She does not hear herself wailing.

Grace turns to her daughter-in-law, and leads her away from the casket.

# Prayer

I buried a son today.

Mister was a good man. You, the giver and taker of life, the source of darkness and light, you know I speak the truth. He *was* a good man.

Last night I woke to the sound of thunder. I loved the anger of the skies and the blessings that it brings. The light was wonderful and strange. I opened the window, and let the rain pour in, so cool against my skin. I wrapped myself around the curtains. I danced a waltz and cried for all my losses.

My men are gone. My Sam. My son.

Your cruelty is greater than I ever thought. I'm told your love is greater. I'll soon find out.

I stood there in the rain, and when it stopped, I wandered through my house. So big, this house. Too big for only me. I found a poem I never finished. I'd placed it in a book Sam loved to read. Two lines, was all I ever wrote:

> *For years I've dreamed your eyes as black as night*
> *I long to see your face in perfect light.*

Not a poem at all, a couplet. I finally understand. I've been in love with being my Sam's widow. *Endiosada.* You know that word.

I won't play the widow anymore.

I loved my Sam.

And loved my son.

You know that boy, Vicente? If Liz won't bring him home, *I will.* I intend to bring him home. I intend to raise him. I intend to finish what my son has started.

You know what's in my heart.

And now you know that I intend to live.

And one more thing. Forgive me. For Liz—for the way that I misjudged her.

# The Story of Dave

Andrés looked at him. Waited. He'd started to say something. He looked at him—to let him know he had to finish saying what he'd started.

"I need to tell you a story."

"A story?"

Dave had a look on his face.

Andrés nodded. "A story? Okay." He didn't know why he was whispering—except that Mister Delgado's funeral had made him feel soft, and Dave was sober as a morning cup of coffee.

"I don't know if you'll like this one." He hadn't touched his food. He pushed the plate away. "I could use a beer."

"Me, too."

"Why don't we move out to the patio? We can smoke there."

"It was my birthday. Twenty-one-year-old hotshot about to go to law school. Yale. I owned the goddamned world. Well, me and my old man, we weren't close. He worked. Not because he had to, but because he liked to think he made all that money he inherited. People like to think they work for what they have. The fucking lies we tell ourselves. Well, never mind all that. Anyway, it was golden boy's birthday. Only that evening, golden boy got into a fight with his old man.

*You're not taking that girl out—not in that car I gave you.*

"*That girl.* I knew what he was accusing me of. He was telling me I was only going out with her to displease him. He was right, of course, well, mostly right. Nothing original at all about our fucking little drama. Son needs to get back at father for the sin of being absent. So he does things to make his father mad, predictable things, stuff that took no imagination, things like staying out and drinking, things like picking girls he knows his father wouldn't approve of. Boring fucking story. So, anyway, golden boy goes out for a spin in his car. Nice evening. Picks up his girlfriend, drives around in his beautiful new car. It's his birthday. He's twenty-one and going to law school and has a beautiful girl hanging on his arm who's even more beautiful because his father doesn't like her. So he drives and drives, not caring where he drives because everything is beautiful for him, the day, the girl, the car."

And then Andrés knows. He knows exactly what he is going to say. And so he watches Dave's lips as he keeps talking. And Dave, he knows that Andrés knows exactly where the story is going and why the story is being told.

"And then, in one instant, everything in the world changes. I can still see the car running the red light. I can still see the panic on Marina's face. I can still see me trying to stop, but I was going so fast, and if I hadn't been going so fast, it might not have mattered that the car had run a red light. But I was going so fucking fast. And I knew I couldn't stop—and it was all over in an instant." He stopped, his hands shaking as he brought the cigarette to his lips.

"And then they were all dead. Marina. She was only twenty. And Santiago and Lilia Segovia. They were forty-eight. And golden boy. Not a scratch—not a fuck—"

It was strange to watch tears run down his face, to see him feel. A part of Andrés didn't care, didn't care at all. He'd cried his own rivers, but those rivers were dry now, and he was glad about that. What were Dave's rivers to him?

"Shut up," he said. "Why don't you just shut the fuck up?"

As Andrés walked home, he kept thinking of the stunned look on Dave's face. What had he expected him to say? It's okay, it's fucking okay. *They were forty-eight years old, Dave. You could have at least spared my mom.* He could feel his jaw clamping down, his teeth grinding, his fists tightening. He didn't care the sun was beating down as if it were taking a belt to him.

When he got home, he changed into running clothes. He didn't care what the sun would do to his skin or his heart, let it beat the crap out of him—what did it matter, anyway. He was just a dumb thing, a piece of dust with memory, less useful than a computer and less valuable. As he ran, he thought of Silvia, he thought of Ileana and how she was probably a woman now, and he kept saying to himself, *be all right, be all right,* because even now she mattered when nothing else mattered at all. And for no reason or maybe a reason he did not understand, he pictured the look on Grace's face, her son dead, dead for no good reason, another angry man imposing his will on the world, but there she was, Grace, and he wondered how she could look so beautiful—even in grief, a woman who had become her name. Some people got uglier, some people became more beautiful, and he wished he knew why. He ran and ran, as if all of the faces that were appearing inside of him would dissipate if he could just run fast enough, as if all the faces might ascend, flinging themselves toward the God who made them and had abandoned them to the hell of his body. He felt an aching in his legs, in his lungs, he ran, his sweat stinging his eyes, he ran and ran, until finally, when the pain was too much, he stopped.

Maybe they had all gone away. All of them.


He felt odd, almost nervous, a rumbling in his stomach. He couldn't quite get at what it was he was feeling. He pictured Dave telling him a story and then pictured himself saying, "Shut the fuck up." He pictured his father, probably angry about something, such an impatient man, impatient with his wife, with his children, with his life. He pictured the whole damn scene, his father smoking a cigarette and saying something mean to his mother, something rash, his mother turning away, the wedding gift on her lap. And then his father, speeding up because he was careless and in a hurry, and then just gunning the engine in his new, secondhand car through the red light. *Shut the fuck up.* And then he understood what he was feeling. He should've recognized the shame sooner than this, he who had such an intimate relationship with that word.

He lit a cigarette and stood in front of the window. He wasn't looking for anything, just looking out. He was suddenly moved by Dave's tears. He *was* sorry, sorry that Dave had carried this thing in him for years, sorry because no one should carry such things, and certainly not carry them for so many, many years. And he felt them, those tears, and it made him sad, the pained look on Dave's face, and he knew he'd worn that helpless look himself—a hundred times, a thousand times, and he remembered Grace's voice and her definition: *To affect the emotions of; move to tender response.* And it seemed that the anger had left him—if only for a moment. And it was heaven, not to be angry. And he was glad that he was carrying Grace's voice inside him, because the voice he usually carried around with him was burning and filled with self-hatred and he was tired of hating himself, tired of hating Dave, tired of hating everything in the world. He realized that the minute he'd met Dave, he'd known that he suffered from something, but he had never cared to know what that something was. And now, as he stood there, looking out his window, it was so strange to discover that he cared for this man, that he liked him—because he was a good man. Not perfect, but who needed perfect? To know a good man, that was enough.

He smiled to himself because it was a beautiful thing to know that he had more than just hate and loathing in his heart. Maybe there was something good in him, too. Maybe Grace was right.

He walked toward the phone. He found Dave's card in his wallet— then called his cell. He heard Dave's voice.

"So this is your apartment?"

"Yup. You wanna beer?"

"Sure."

Andrés walked to the refrigerator, opened two beers, and found Dave sitting on his beat-up couch. He didn't even seem out of place. Andrés handed him a beer. He wanted to tell Dave he was sorry—for walking out on him at the restaurant, for telling him to shut the fuck up. "Sorry I haven't had you over before," he said. He laughed.

"Sure you are." Dave laughed, too.

"It was an accident," he whispered.

Dave nodded.

"*It was, Dave.* It was an accident." Even he, Andrés Segovia, who could be as hard as cured cement, even he was surprised by the softness in his own voice.

"I wanted to tell you, Andrés—and then I didn't. And then I thought I should leave it alone."

"So that's why you've spent your life stalking me."

Dave smiled, then laughed. "That's an interesting way to put it."

"You always managed to find me. No matter where I'd go, or where I'd move. I never even knew how the hell you always managed to find me."

"You find people you want to find."

"You sent me to Grace, didn't you?"

"I thought she could help you."

"Did she help you, too?"

"After the accident, I refused to talk. I mean, I didn't say a word. Not to anyone. I refused to go to law school. I refused to do anything. I would sit and stare and say nothing. And I don't know how my mother learned about Grace—but she did. And she took me to her. And I would go every day, but only because my mother would take me. And I would sit there for an hour, every day, and say nothing. Grace would ask me questions. I liked her voice, but I still didn't talk. And so even she stopped asking me questions. But she told my mother to keep bringing me. And this happened for weeks and weeks. And one day, when I came in, Grace handed me a book. And I began reading it. And I took it home and read it. And when I came back the next day, she asked me what I thought of the book, and I shrugged and I didn't say anything. And then she gave me another book, and I started reading that book, too—and I stayed up all night reading that damned book. When I went in to see her, I sat there and I cried. For the whole hour. And when my mother came, Grace sent her away, and I kept crying and crying and crying and Grace held me and said, and said, 'Sshhhhhhh.' I don't know how long I cried, I don't, but it was hours and hours. And when I stopped, her blouse was soaked with my tears. And she smiled at me and said, 'My name is Grace. And your name would be.'

"And then I laughed. And she laughed. And I said, 'My name is Dave.' And for the first time in my fucking life, I heard my own name."

Andrés nodded. He wanted to thank him. For sending him to Grace. But he didn't say anything.

As they sat there, they settled into a quiet. They seemed to have no words left in them. "Well, I guess, that's my story." Dave shrugged. "I should go."

Andrés nodded. He walked Dave down the hall, then just kept following him as he went down the stairs and out the door of his apartment house. It was a warm night, as still as a summer night could get, all the winds gone.

"Dave, you asked me once where I learned to be so fucking ungrateful. Maybe I'm not as ungrateful as I seem."

That made Dave smile.

Andrés stood there as Dave drove away. He thought of the funeral and Grace. He thought of Ileana, and suddenly he felt that she might really be alive. And maybe, he thought, he would ask Dave for one more favor. *Help me find my sister.*

He walked into his apartment, opened a window, and looked out into the night. He remembered the boy who used to count stars. He sat there, on the windowsill, trying to picture Ileana.

He had never been this tired.

He threw himself on the bed, and slept.

He didn't dream.

When he woke, he thought of Mrs. Fernandez. He was certain she still lived in the same house.

# Who Was She Now?

Grace spent the night organizing all of her photographs. There were hundreds of them. Perhaps thousands. Pictures of her and Sam before they were married, a picture of the two of them dancing at a club in Juárez, a picture of her and Sam at Venice Beach. And hundreds of pictures of Sam and Mister, of her and Mister, of her and Sam and Mister. The photographs outlasted them.

The thought occurred to her that she'd always thought of herself in terms of her men—Sam's wife, then Sam's widow. And of course, she was Mister's mother. Who was she now? She wasn't the woman in the pictures. Whatever she had been, she was something else now. *Someone* else. A childless widow with breast cancer—she laughed to herself. To wind up like this, she who had spent her life telling other people that their job was to live.

She walked past Dr. Richard Garza's receptionist without signing in. "Excuse me, but do you have an appointment?" Grace didn't bother to turn around and address her. She just continued walking toward Richard's office. She ran into him, face to face, in the hallway. "Grace?"

She could see condolences written all over his face—but she wasn't in the mood this morning. She glared at him so he'd know she wasn't here to be pitied or condescended to. It was as if she was grabbing him by the collar with that one look. She looked him straight in the eye. "You said it wasn't too late. You said you had a plan."

He looked at the stubborn woman standing in front of him, her hair uncombed and wild, her eyes red with tears, her face wounded. In that moment, he thought, she was as beautiful as she had ever been.

# Timing and Order in the Universe

A man of forty-eight is boarding a plane. He is going back to Portland, Oregon. His brother has agreed to take him in—under certain conditions. The man is hopeful he will be able to meet his brother's demands. Perhaps it is his last chance. In the last two weeks, twelve men have left El Paso, all of them having arrived here seeking children and asylum.

An underpaid lawyer who works for Legal Aid has worked tirelessly toward sending these men back to where they came from. She read, by accident, a magazine article on sexual predators who were being dumped on the border. She swore she wouldn't rest until she made the practice stop. By chance or by design or by coincidence, she ran into an attorney at a cocktail party. His name was Dave. Nice looking. He wanted to have dinner. She had something else in mind. He was more decent than she'd expected—and ripe for what she had to say. He lent a paralegal, a secretary, his office, his phones, his faxes, everything he had. *Let's embarrass the shit out of those assholes who think it's fine to dump their trash in our front yard.*

Three months ago, today, Grace buried Mister next to Sam. She is looking at herself in the mirror. She no longer has breasts. She's shaved her head. She is standing before a mirror as Liz hands her a red scarf to wrap around her head. Grace wraps it expertly. "Red suits you, Grace. You sure you won't let me get a wig for you?"

Grace turns to her and laughs. "Sure. Make me a blond."

Today, another chemo treatment. She thinks she hears Mister laughing at a joke.

Vicente is asleep in Mister's old room. He is a sleeper, like Mister used to be. He wakes and cries, *Mama Mama.* His voice is deep for a child. Liz and Grace rush into the room. Liz sits on the bed and takes him in her arms. She breathes in his smell.

Grace watches them. She thinks that life is crueler and more beautiful than she had ever imagined.

Andrés is studying for a history exam. He is lost in his books. He is the best of students, a good and hungry mind. He still feels explosions in his gut—but Grace reminds him that anger's not so bad. *Just don't go around hitting people.* He smiles at Grace's voice in his head. Cancer has made her softer.

He looks at the photograph he keeps on his desk—a gift from Dave. "This is you, Andy, before anyone ever touched you." He looks at the photograph every day. It is like a book he is learning to read.

He looks at his watch. He works in Mister's coffee shop—Liz's, now. He promised her he'd work the morning shift, so she could take Vicente to the doctor.

# Good Man, Take Me Home

A ll that's left is for me to deliver my closing arguments. I sense this jury will refuse to punish Andrés Segovia another minute. I see the faces of the women on the jury. They reach out to him. I saw their look of horror as I showed them William Hart's trophies. Sad little boys looking up at the camera.

The DA called. He said, "He does a year. We'll call it a day."

I hung up the phone. Quietly. I'll invite him to lunch. And invite Andrés to tag along. Afterward, I'll give the bastard the check.

When I put Andrés on the stand, he appeared stoic, almost arrogant. He was trying too hard to hold himself together. I could see the trembling in his hands, the slight quiver in his voice. All this time. All this waiting—it's worn him down. He's changed in these ten months. He smiles more. At times, he almost seems like he's become a boy.

He knew all the questions I would ask. We practiced. Practiced and practiced and practiced. And yet, for all our practicing, even I was not prepared to hear the rawness of his words. It was as if I was hearing him for the first time. I heard in his voice a man who had decided that he was going to live. He had learned how to spell out the word *enough*. And so he told us everything. Of how it was he came to live in Juárez. Of how he fell into the hands of a man named Homero. Of how he was forced to become food for hungry men like William Hart to feed off. I saw the anguish on the faces of the men and women sitting on that jury. They were brought to tears at what they heard. They won't convict.

How many times have I closed in front of a jury? At least a hundred times. Twice that, for all I know. And yet tonight, I feel as if I've never done this. All night, I'll pace and think. I'll prepare my words. I'll organize my thoughts. I'll write them down. I'll practice, practice, practice. This matters more than I can bear.

Grace says she'll pray tonight. *Grace, pray that God will send his light into my heart. Pray your Catholic God will give me words.*

I was thinking of Silvia today. She was born with a compass. I wonder how you get to be that way. I've always felt so lost. I hated Dave last week. We were going over my testimony. Going over it and over it and over it. And I was so fucking sick of it all, sick of recalling and recalling and recalling. When do I get to forget? But I didn't hate Dave for making me remember. I hated him for giving me this hope. He's so convinced I'll walk. And if I don't? Five or ten or fifteen years in jail? *But I killed a man. I killed a human being.* Dave shakes his head. *Andrés, I don't believe that. He wanted to die—can't you see that? That man committed suicide. He could've saved himself. At worst, you hit a man. At worst, it was an accident.* He gives me hope.

Grace, too, gives me hope. She is still so beautiful. She shaved her head, and I can see the sun there.

When I was on the stand, I felt alive. It was strange and sad and wonderful, and I was talking. I remembered that I had always felt like I was someone's secret. And I knew that I had never stopped feeling like that. But I wasn't Mando's secret anymore. I wasn't Yolie's secret. I wasn't Homero's or William Hart's secret.

I was Andrés Segovia. I was a boy who wanted to go to school and ride a bike. *I wasn't anybody's goddamned secret.*

# Timing and Order in the Universe

This is the way the story ends. With a man named Dave Duncan who is stretching out on his patio, his shirt off. He is thinking of what happened yesterday afternoon in the courtroom. He is playing the whole scene over in his head. Ten months, he had lived for that verdict. He is still savoring the moment. He will lock that moment away in his memory and remember it in times of darkness. He smiles, then laughs. It is a perfect day. He does not want to be alone. He picks up the phone. He is calling the only woman he has ever loved. "Your heart is too busy and restless. It has no room for me." That is what she said when she walked away. He knew the truth of her words. But he has decided to make himself worthy of all she has to give. This is what he is telling himself as he hears the phone ring. When she answers the phone, he will say, "Do you want to know what is in my heart?"

Andrés Segovia is whispering the word *emancipated* over and over again. He is in love with that word. He is walking toward Mrs. Fernandez's front door. He trembles slightly, but pays no attention to the trembling. He has paid too much homage to his internal fears. He vows to stop worshiping at that altar.

He rings the bell and waits. No one comes to the door. He rings the bell again, then waits. The seconds are cruel and interminable. Finally, Mrs. Fernandez answers the door. She looks into his face as if she is looking into a deep well. He had expected her to look older, but she is not nearly as old as he thought she would be. He watches her as she scrutinizes everything about him.

He cannot stand all this silence, so he decides to speak. "You don't know who I am." He shrugs, and thinks to himself that this is just another one of his missteps. What did he think he would accomplish with this visit?

"I knew you would come," she whispers.

"I'm sorry," he says, "for what we did to you." For the first time in his life, he is not ashamed of the tears. He is free now, to ask forgiveness. That is why he has come. "Forgive me."

He feels her hands wiping away his tears.

He does not flinch at her touch.

"Hijito de mi vida, you were a boy." She takes him in her arms. He does not think he will ever stop sobbing. "Shhhhh," she says, "No more. No more, hijito." She smiles into his face.

He does not know what to say next. "I've begun looking for Ileana."

"You'll find her. I know you will."

He nods.

She leads him to the garage and shows him what she has been keeping all these many years. "I pay the boys in the neighborhood to keep it in shape."

"My bike! My bike!" He laughs. And what a laugh. He is hopping on a bike in the same neighborhood where he grew up, in the same neighborhood where Sam Delgado once told a girl named Grace that she was beauty itself.

This is the way the story ends: with Andrés Segovia riding a bike, a man becoming a boy again.


Grace is in Richard Garza's waiting room. She is teaching Liz an old nursery rhyme in Spanish. Vicente repeats everything she says. He talks now, talks and talks. He laughs and tries to escape their reach. Liz places him on her lap. He reaches for her face, his small hands searching. *Phototactic*—Grace smiles at the memory—and then she hears her name on the receptionist's lips.

She feels a rush of blood run through her heart. Liz nods, her eyes as hopeful as anything she has ever seen. She thinks of Mister and Sam.

She respects the floor as she walks down the hall toward Richard Garza's inner sanctum. She is remembering her dream, how she always stood apart from the love Sam and Mister shared—as if they had never loved her. She is trying to forgive herself for her blindness. And then she remembers telling Liz that the time comes when they have to send away the dead.

She sees Richard Garza at the end of the hall. He is holding the door open for her. He is holding her charts. Grace is looking into his eyes, and he is smiling. And then she knows the answer to the question she has been holding in her heart.

The story ends with Grace.

# Acknowledgments

There are times when the endeavor of writing a novel is overwhelmingly solitary. But no one writes a novel alone, *certainly not me*.

I would like to thank my students, who give me new words every day—and who continually teach me that hope is more than just a mere abstraction. I see that word written on their faces week after week, semester after semester.

Jaime Esparza explained some necessary details in the criminal justice system. He also provided me with an invaluable tour of the El Paso County Jail. I thank him for his friendship and generosity.

Always, when I needed to remind myself that the world I lived in was far larger than my imagination, I turned to Ray Caballero and to Enrique Moreno. My life and my work are all the better for their decency, their true friendship, and their intellectual honesty.

I am grateful to Richard Green, who has been my agent for more than ten years. He read and reread several versions of this manuscript. I treasure his mind, his heart, and his loyalty.

I am eternally grateful to Patty Moosbrugger, who stepped in as my literary agent with unflinching faith, and equally unflinching professionalism.

Rene Alegria at Rayo/HarperCollins is everything a writer could want in an editor—he is self-possessed, intelligent, and articulate. He also happens to be a tireless advocate. No writer could ask for more.

My wife, Patricia, knows better than anyone the cost of living with a writer. She willingly pays that price with uncommon and extraordinary grace. Love is never truly earned—but that is no reason to be ungrateful for the beauty of the gift.

I am surrounded by good and admirable people. I am the luckiest of men.